# Praise for Miklós Bánffy

'Bánffy is a born storyteller'  Patrick Leigh Fermor, from the Foreword

'A Tolstoyan portrait of the end days of the Austro-Hungarian empire, this compulsively readable novel follows the divergent fortunes of two cousins, the politician Abady and gambler/drunkard Gyeroffy, detailing the intrigues at the decadent Budapest court, the doomed love affairs, opulent balls, duels and general head-in-the sand idiocies of a privileged elite whose world is on the verge of disappearing for ever.'
Adam Newey, '1000 Novels You Must Read', *Guardian*

'Just about as good as any fiction I have ever read, like *Anna Karenina* and *War and Peace* rolled into one. Love, sex, town, country, money, power, beauty, and the pathos of a society which cannot prevent its own destruction – all are here'  Charles Moore, *Daily Telegraph*

'Fascinating. He writes about his quirky border lairds and squires and the high misty forest ridges and valleys of Transylvania with something of the ache that Czesław Miłosz brings to the contemplation of this lost Eden'  W. L. Webb, *Guardian*

'Pleasure of a different scale and kind. It is a sort of Galsworthian panorama of life in the dying years of the Habsburg empire – perfect late night reading for nostalgic romantics like me'
Jan Morris, *Observer* Books of the Year

'Totally absorbing'  Martha Kearney, *Harper's Bazaar*

'Charts this glittering spiral of decline with the frustrated regret of a politician who had tried to alert Hungary's ruling classes to the pressing need for change and accommodation. Patrician, romantic and in the context of the times a radical, Bánffy combined his politics – he negotiated Hungary's admission to the League of Nations – with running the state theatres and promoting the work of his contemporary, the composer Béla Bartók'  *Guardian* Editorial

'Like Joseph Roth and Robert Musil, Miklós Bánffy is one of those novelists Austria-Hungary specialised in. Intimate and sparkling chroniclers of a wider ruin, ironic and elegiac, they understood that in the 1900s the fate of classes and nations was beginning to turn almost on a change in the weather. None of them, oddly, was given his due till long after his death, probably because in 1918 very much was lost in central Europe – an empire overnight for one thing – and the aftermath was like a great ship sinking, a massive downdraught that took a generation of ideas and continuity with it. Bánffy, a prime witness of his times, shows in these memoirs exactly what an extraordinary period it must have been to live through'
Julian Evans, *Daily Telegraph*

'Full of arresting descriptions, beautiful evocations of scenery and wise political and moral insights'
Francis King, *Spectator*

'Plunge instead into the cleansing waters of a rediscovered masterpiece, because *The Writing on the Wall* is certainly a masterpiece, in any language'
Michael Henderson, *Daily Telegraph*

'So enjoyable, so irresistible, it is the author's keen political intelligence and refusal to indulge in self-deception which give it an unusual distinction. It's a novel that, read at the gallop for sheer enjoyment, is likely to carry you along. But many will want to return to it for a second, slower reading, to savour its subtleties and relish the author's intelligence'
Allan Massie, *Scotsman*

'So evocative'
Simon Jenkins, *Guardian*

'Bánffy's loving portrayal of a way of life that was already much diminished by the time he was writing, and set to vanish before he died, is too clear-eyed to be simply nostalgic, yet the ache of loss is certainly here. László has been brought up a homeless orphan, Bálint's father died when he was young and the whole country is suffering from loss of pride. Although comparisons with Lampedusa's novel *The Leopard* are inevitable, Bánffy's work is perhaps nearer in feel to that of Joseph Roth, in *The Radetzky March*. They were, after all, mourning the fall of the same empire'
Ruth Pavey, *New Statesman*

# THEY WERE DIVIDED

Count Miklós Bánffy (1873–1950)

MIKLÓS BÁNFFY

# THEY WERE DIVIDED

VOLUME THREE, THE TRANSYLVANIAN TRILOGY

*Translated from the Hungarian by*
PATRICK THURSFIELD *and* KATALIN BÁNFFY-JELEN

*Foreword by*
PATRICK LEIGH FERMOR

MACLEHOSE PRESS
QUERCUS · LONDON

First published in the Hungarian language in 1940
First published in Great Britain by Arcadia Books in 2001
This paperback edition first published in Great Britain in 2024 by MacLehose Press

An imprint of
Quercus Editions Limited
Carmelite House
50 Victoria Embankment
London EC4Y 0DZ

An Hachette UK company

The authorised representative in the EEA is Hachette Ireland, 8 Castlecourt
Centre, Castleknock Road, Castleknock, Dublin 15, D15 YF6A, Ireland

Original text © Miklós Bánffy 1937
Translation © The Estate of Patrick Thursfield and Katalin Bánffy-Jelen 2001
Foreword © Patrick Leigh Fermor 1999
Introduction © The Estate of Patrick Thursfield 1999

A CIP catalogue record for this book is available from the British Library

PB ISBN 978 1 52943 468 2
EBOOK ISBN 978 1 90812 904 8

Typeset in Minion by MacGuru Ltd
Printed and bound in Great Britain by Clays Ltd, Elcograf S.p.A.

Papers used by MacLehose Press are from well-managed
forests and other responsible sources.

# THEY WERE DIVIDED

MIKLÓS BÁNFFY

**Central Europe: 1913**

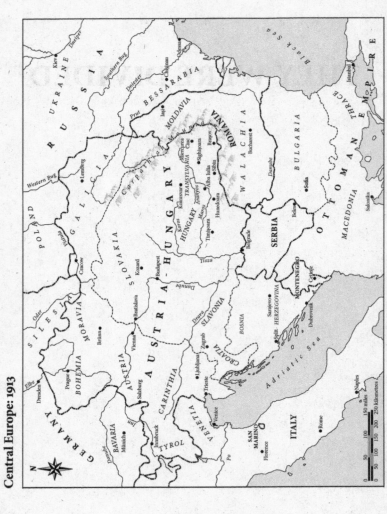

# Central Europe: Present Day

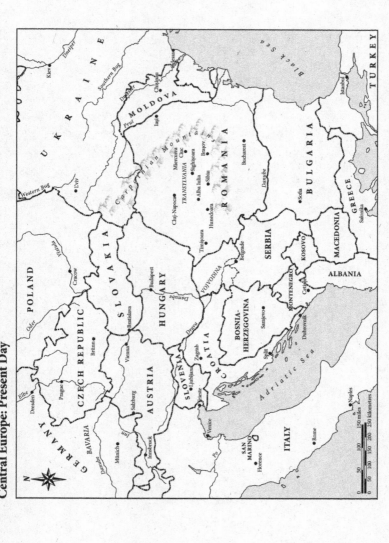

# Cast of Characters

*(In order of appearance in the three volumes of The Transylvanian Trilogy)*

**COUNT BALINT ABADY**
Main character of trilogy. Son of Countess Roza Abady and the late Count Denes Abady. Heir to castle and estate of Denestornya. Member of Parliament. Nickname 'AB'.

**COUNT LASZLO GYEROFFY**
Orphan. Cousin of Balint Abady. Brought up by his Kollonich grandfather and aunt. Nickname 'Laci'.

**COUNTESS ADRIENNE UZDY**
Oldest daughter of Count Akos Miloth. Married to Count Pal Uzdy. Mother of daughter Clemmie. Nickname 'Addy'.

**COUNT PAL UZDY**
Husband of Adrienne, owner of castle of Almasko, and also a house in Kolozsvar. Father dead, son of Countess Clémence Uzdy.

**COUNTESS CLÉMENCE UZDY**
Lives with her son Pal at Almasko. Mother-in-law of Adrienne Uzdy.

**COUNTESS JUDITH MILOTH**
Second daughter of Count Akos Miloth.

**COUNTESS MARGIT MILOTH**
Third daughter of Count Akos Miloth.

**COUNT ZOLTAN MILOTH**
Only son of Count Akos Miloth.

**COUNT AKOS MILOTH**
Father of Adrienne, Judith, Margit and Zoltan. Nickname 'Rattle'.

**COUNTESS MILOTH**
Wife of Akos Miloth. Sister of Countess Ida Laczok.

**COUNTESS ROZA ABADY**
Mother of Balint, widow of Count Tamas Abady, her first cousin. Owner of Denestornya castle and estate.

**COUNT JENO LACZOK**
Owner of Var-Siklod castle. Father of Anna, Ida and Liszka Laczok.

**COUNTESS IDA LACZOK**
Wife of Jeno Laczok, sister of Countess Miloth.

**COUNTESS ANNA LACZOK**
**COUNTESS IDA LACZOK**
**COUNTESS LISZKA LACZOK**
Daughters of Count Jeno Laczok.

**COUNTESS LIZINKA SARMASAGHY**
Known to everyone as 'Aunt Lizinka'. Malicious gossip. Cousin of Balint's grandfather.

**COUNTESS ADELMA GYALAKUTHY**
Widow. Mother of Dodo Gyalakuthy.

**COUNTESS DODO GYALAKUTHY**
Daughter of above. Very rich heiress.

**COUNT TIHAMER ABONYI**
Married to Countess Dinora.

**COUNTESS DINORA ABONYI**
Formerly Malhuysen. Former mistress of Balint Abady. Married to Count Tihamer Abonyi.

**COUNT ADAM ALVINCZY**
Father of four sons.

**COUNT FARKAS ALVINCZY**
Oldest son of Adam Alvinczy

**ADAM, ZOLTAN, AKOS ALVINCZY**
Three younger sons of Adam Alvinczy.

**COUNT ISTVAN KENDY**
Cousin of the Abadys. Nickname 'Pityu'.

**COUNT SANDOR KENDY**
Cousin of the Abadys. Nickname 'Crookface'.

**COUNT AMBRUS KENDY**
Distant cousin of Crookface. Known as Uncle
Ambrus.

**COUNT JOSKA KENDY**
Another cousin. In love with Adrienne Uzdy.

**COUNT DANIEL KENDY**
Old, poor and drunkard. Cousin of Crookface
and Ambrus Kendy.

**COUNT EGON WICKWITZ**
Austrian army lieutenant. Nickname 'Nitwit'.

**MIHALY GAL**
Old actor, friend of Balint Abady's grandfather
Count Peter Abady.

**ANDRAS JOPAL**
Nephew of Mihaly Gal, inventor, tutor to
Laczok boys at Var-Siklod castle

**PRINCE LOUIS KOLLONICH**
Owner of Simonvasar castle. Co-guardian
of Laszlo Gyeroffy. Father of Klara, Niki and
Peter.

**PRINCESS AGNES KOLLONICH**
Born Gyeroffy. Aunt of Laszlo Gyeroffy and
his guardian. Second wife of Prince Louis
Kollonich. Stepmother of Klara. Mother of
Niki and Peter.

**DUCHESS KLARA KOLLONICH**
Daughter of Prince Louis Kollonich. In love
with Laszlo Gyeroffy, who is also in love with
her.

**DUKE NIKI KOLLONICH**
Brother of Klara Kollonich.

**DUKE PETER KOLLONICH**
Brother of Klara Kollonich.

**COUNT ANTAL SZENT-GYORGYI**
Owner of Jablanka castle. Married to Princess
Kollonich's sister, Elise.

**COUNTESS ELISE SZENT-GYORGYI**
Married to Antal Szent-Gyorgyi, sister of
Princess Agnes Kollonich, born Gyeroffy.

**COUNTESS MAGDA SZENT-GYORGYI**
Daughter of Antal and Elise Szent-Gyorgyi.

**COUNT STEFI SZENT-GYORGYI**
Brother of Magda.

**COUNTESS FANNY BEREDY**
Wife of Count Beredy. A beautiful singer.

**SZABO**
Prince Kollonich's butler.

**COUNT JAN SLAWATA**
Councillor to the Foreign Office.

**COUNT FREDI WUELFFENSTEIN**
Foolish Anglophile.

**ISTI KAMUTHY**
Young M.P. Foolish Anglophile who speaks
with a lisp.

**PRINCE MONTORIO-VISCONTI**
Suitor to Klara Kollonich.

**ILUS VARGA**
Klara Kollonich's maid.

**KRISTOF AZBEJ**
Unscrupulous lawyer to Countess Roza Abady.
Manages Laszlo Gyeroffy's estate.

**MRS TOTHY AND MRS BACZO**
Housekeepers to Countess Roza Abady.

**ANDRAS ZUTOR**
Balint Abady's forest ranger. Nickname
'Honey'.

**KALMAN NYIRESY**
Balint Abady's forest supervisor.

**GEZA WINCKLER**
Balint Abady's head forester.

**GASZTON SIMO**
Dishonest notary in Balint Abady's
constituency.

**DR AUREL TIMISAN**
Romanian lawyer.

**DANIEL KOVACS**
Notary in Lelbanya – Balint Abady's
constituency.

**COUNT IMRE WARDAY**
Guest at Fanny Beredy's dinners.

**MADAME SARA BOGDAN LAZAR**
Farmer. Befriends Laszlo Gyeroffy.

**COUNT TAMAS LACZOK**
Brother of Count Jeno Laczok. Railway
engineer.

**BARON GAZSI KADACSAY**
Unconventional soldier. Owner of fine horses.

**NESZTI SZENT-GYORGYI**
Rich cousin of Antal Szent-Gyorgyi.

**ZSIGMOND BOROS**
Transylvanian lawyer. M.P. A shady rogue.

**MAIER**
Butler to Uzdy family. Formerly worked in
lunatic asylum.

**COUNT TISZA**
Minister-President of Budapest Parliament.
Admired by Balint Abady.

**PALI LUBIANSZKY**
Politician. Opposed to Tisza.

**TIVADAR MIHALYI**
Leader of opposition in Budapest Parliament.

**FERENC KOSSUTH**
Important politician.

**MINISTER-PRESIDENT JUSTH**
Important politician.

**ANDRASSY**
Important politician.

**GEZA FEJERVARY**
Politician, elected Prime Minister.

**JANKO CSERESZNYES**
Unscrupulous demagogue, ally of lawyer Azbej.

**KRISTOFFY**
Minister of Interior in 'Bodyguard'
government.

**SAMUEL BARRA**
Politician: opposed to Ferenc Kossuth.

**MIKLOS ABSOLON**
Political leader of Upper Maros region. Uncle
of Pali Uzdy. Brother of Countess Clémence
Uzdy. Traveller.

**COUNTESS LILI ILLESVARY**
Daughter of Countess Illesvary, niece of
Countess Elise Szent-Gyorgyi.

**CONTESSA JULIE LADOSSA**
Laszlo Gyeroffy's mother.

**REGINA BISCHITZ**
Daughter of shopkeeper. Sympathetic to Laszlo
Gyeroffy.

**MARTON BALOGH**
Former butler and servant to Laszlo Gyeroffy.

For my dear children, for whom I first started on this translation of their grandfather's greatest work so that they should learn to know him better, he who would have loved them so much.
K. Bánffy-Jelen

In loving memory of Patrick Thursfield, 1923–2003

# Foreword

## by PATRICK LEIGH FERMOR

I first drifted into the geographical background of this remarkable book in the spring and summer of 1934, when I was nineteen, halfway through an enormous trudge from Holland to Turkey. Like many travellers, I fell in love with Budapest and the Hungarians, and by the time I got to the old principality of Transylvania, mostly on a borrowed horse, I was even deeper in.

With one interregnum, Hungary and Transylvania – three times the size of Wales – had been ruled by the Magyars for a thousand years. After the Great War, in which Hungary was a loser, the peace treaty took Transylvania away from the Hungarian crown and allotted it to the Romanians, who formed most of the population. The whole question was one of hot controversy, which I have tried to sort out and explain in a book called *Between the Woods and the Water** largely to get things clear in my own mind; and, thank heavens, there is no need to go over it again in a short foreword like this. The old Hungarian landowners felt stranded and ill-used by history; nobody likes having a new nationality forced on them, still less, losing estates by expropriation. This, of course, is what happened to the descendants of the old feudal landowners of Transylvania.

By a fluke, and through friends I had made in Budapest and on the Great Hungarian Plain, I found myself wandering from castle to castle in what had been left of these age-old fiefs.

Hardly a trace of this distress was detectable to a stranger. In my case, the chief thing to survive is the memory of unlimited kindness. Though enormously reduced, remnants of these old estates did still exist, and, at moments it almost seemed as though nothing had changed. Charm

---

* John Murray, 1980.

and *douceur de vivre* was still afloat among the faded decor and the still undiminished libraries, and, out of doors, everything conspired to delight. Islanded in the rustic Romanian multitude, different in race and religious practice – the Hungarians were Catholics or Calvinists, the Romanians Orthodox or Uniat – and, with the phantoms of their lost ascendancy still about them, the prevailing atmosphere conjured up the tumbling demesnes of the Anglo-Irish in Waterford or Galway with all their sadness and their magic. Homesick for the past, seeing nothing but their own congeners on the neighbouring estates and the few peasants who worked there, they lived in a backward-looking, a genealogical, almost a Confucian dream, and many sentences ended in a sigh.

It was in the heart of Transylvania – in the old princely capital then called Kolozsvar (now Cluj-Napoca) that I first came across the name of Bánffy. It was impossible not to. Their palace was the most splendid in the city, just as Bonczhida was the pride of the country and both of them triumphs of the baroque style. Ever since the arrival of the Magyars ten centuries ago, the family had been foremost among the magnates who conducted Hungarian and Transylvanian affairs, and their portraits – with their slung dolmans, brocade tunics, jewelled scimitars and fur kalpaks with plumes like escapes of steam – hung on many walls.

For five years of the 1890s, before any of the disasters had smitten, a cousin of Count Miklós Bánffy had led the government of the Austro-Hungarian empire. The period immediately after, from 1905, is the book's setting. The grand world he describes was Edwardian *Mitteleuropa*. The men, however myopic, threw away their spectacles and fixed-in monocles. They were the fashionable swells of Spy and late Du Maurier cartoons, and their wives and favourites must have sat for Boldini and Helleu. Life in the capital was a sequence of parties, balls and race meetings, and, in the country, of *grandes battues* where the guns were all Purdeys. Gossip, cigar smoke and Anglophilia floated in the air: there were cliques where Monet, d'Annunzio and Rilke were appraised; hundreds of acres of forest were nightly lost at *chemin de fer*; at daybreak lovers stole away from tousled four-posters through secret doors, and duels were fought, as they still were when I was there. The part played by politics suggests Trollope or Disraeli. The plains beyond flicker with mirages and wild horses, ragged processions of storks migrate across the sky; and even if the woods are full of bears, wolves, caverns, waterfalls, buffalos and wild lilac, the country scenes in Transylvania, oddly enough, remind me of Hardy.

Bánffy is a born storyteller. There are plots, intrigues, a murder, political imbroglios and passionate love affairs, and though this particular counterpoint of town and country may sound like the stock-in-trade of melodrama, with a fleeting dash of Anthony Hope, it is nothing of the kind. But it is, beyond question, dramatic. Patrick Thursfield and Kathy Bánffy-Jelen have dealt brilliantly with the enormous text; and the author's life and thoughtful cast of mind emerges with growing clarity. The prejudices and the follies of his characters are arranged in proper perspective and only half-censoriously, for humour and a sense of the absurd come to the rescue. His patriotic feelings are totally free of chauvinism, just as his instinctive promptings of tribal responsibility have not a trace of vanity. They urge him towards what he thought was right, and always with effect. (He was Minister of Foreign Affairs at a critical period in the 1920s.) If a hint of melancholy touches the pages here and there, perhaps this was inevitable in a time full of omens, recounted by such a deeply civilized man.

*Chatsworth, Boxing Day, 1998*

'And the fingers went on writing in letters of fire upon the plaster of the Wall of the King's palace. And the third word was UPHARSIN – thy kingdom shall be divided.

'But none could read the writing so drunk were they with much drinking of wine, and they wasted the Lord's vessels of gold and silver which their ancestors had laid up in the house of the Lord, and they argued with each other praising their false gods made of gold and of silver, of brass, of iron, of wood and of clay until there was no strength left in them.

'And the armies of the Medes and Persians stood ready before the walls of the city and in the same night everyone within it was slain.'

*PART ONE*

# Chapter One

Balint Abady stepped quietly into the family box at the theatre at Kolozsvar. Even though he knew it well, for the Abadys like all the other old families in the district rented the same box every year, he still had to grope his way in the darkness to hang up his coat. Still somewhat blinded by the light from the stage he sat down in the best seat facing the stage, for his mother had stayed at home at Denestornya. Balint himself had driven up from the country, just for one night, because he wanted to see the gala performance of *Madam Butterfly* that was being given that evening, and especially the Butterfly herself, the famous Yvonne de Treville, who often came from the Opéra Comique to sing in Kolozsvar.

He was late and the great love duet that closes the first act was just beginning. The music throbbed with passion, with love and desire; the sweet tones of the violins carried Puccini's soaring melodies and above it all was the pure smooth voice of the French diva.

Balint was on the point of surrendering to the music when he felt himself overcome by a strange feeling of agitation, as if he were in the presence of an overpowering force, a force even more potent than the storm of emotion that was being enacted before him on the stage. It was like an electric shock to his nervous system and something, he knew not what, made him turn around.

Adrienne Miloth was sitting in the next box, almost directly behind him.

He was startled to see her there because he had heard that she had gone to Switzerland with her daughter and he had not thought she would have returned so soon. This evening he saw that she and her sister Margit were guests in the kindly old Countess Gyalakuthy's box. There she sat; and though she was so close she seemed as insubstantial as a phantom.

Her face was lit only by the moonlight from the stage which cast the faintest glow on her delicately aquiline nose, her cheeks and her

3

generous mouth. Balint could just see the pale sheen of her skin where the neck and shoulders merged into the deep décolleté of her silver dress. Everything else was hidden in the darkness of the theatre.

She was looking straight ahead, quite motionless, as still as a marble statue. In the reflection of the cunningly contrived moonlight on the stage Adrienne's eyes shone emerald green; and she sat there rigidly, without moving a muscle, though he could hardly believe that she had not seen him come in because he had sat down just in front of her. They were so close that with only the slightest movement their arms would have touched.

Balint felt that he could not stay there another moment. It would be impossible for him, for them both, to sit next to each other and behave as if they were strangers. How could they listen together to that passionate music which spoke so eloquently of desire and love and desperate yearning? No! No! No! He must not stay! He could not stay!

The memories of their love so overwhelmed him that he found himself trembling. He got up silently and slipped out of the box, reeling slightly like a man who has been struck a heavy blow.

Though he could not sit next to her he still could not leave the theatre in which she sat; so he descended the great stair, crossed to the other side of the auditorium and, with his coat on, stepped through one of the doors and stood at the side of the stalls in the shadow of the balcony. No-one would be able to see him there, he thought, so he would remain until the act came to an end and then slip out before the lights went up. From there, too, he could gaze at Adrienne whom he had not seen for more than a year: and even then it had been a mere glance from afar.

She did not seem changed. Maybe her face was a little thinner, perhaps there was a trace of bitterness about the lines of her mouth, but she was still supremely beautiful, every aspect of her as lovely as when she had been his love, his friend, his companion in body and spirit, in those days when they had planned to become husband and wife. But an implacable fate had separated them.

In his imagination he saw her stripped of that shining metallic gown, bright as a suit of armour, standing naked before him as she first had five long years before in Venice, then so often afterwards in their little hut in the forest, or at the Uzdy villa, or at her father's house at Mezo-Varjas, or in Budapest, indeed anywhere their homeless love could find refuge. Balint's heart contracted with bitterness when he thought once again of

4

how he had been forced to abandon her and how she had ordered him to marry Lili Illesvary whom she herself had picked out for him.

Adrienne had then made her conditions: their affair must cease, and she would not even meet him socially unless he got married and so erected a barrier between them. He had found he could not comply and so they had not seen each other again.

The love duet continued, growing ever more intense, more impassioned. For a moment its message of love and desire was overshadowed by two brief echoes deep in the orchestral texture of the music with which the Shinto priest had cursed the lovers' happiness; and when he heard it Balint felt most poignantly that it symbolized the story of their own doomed love. However, this sad reflection did not last long, for that song of yearning flowed out from the stage, stronger than ever, irresistible and triumphant. It was as if the whole wide world was composed of spring and moonlight, blossom and sublime melody. As the music mounted to its stormy climax Balint felt as moved and shattered as by the climax of love. It was the music of their past, now forever denied them.

The curtain fell to a tornado of applause, and Balint slipped quietly out.

The October night air was already cold. The sky was clear and the pavements glistened from the light rain that had fallen that afternoon. Without thinking where he was going Balint started to walk towards the centre of the town. He walked at random, with no object except to be alone, alone with the torment of all those thoughts by which he had been assailed that evening. Glancing at his watch he saw that it was just a quarter past nine. This gave him nearly three hours of freedom, for at midnight he was expected to go to supper at the house of the prefect, who, as general director of the Kolozsvar theatres, was giving a party after the performance in honour of the French diva. For three hours, then, he could try to walk off his chagrin, to master that surge of bitterness that had been stirred up by the sight of Adrienne sitting so close to him.

As he wandered aimlessly along the dark streets he was assailed so fiercely by a torrent of haphazard memories that he felt like a man pursued by the Fates from whom it was impossible to hide. And yet hide he must! It had been the same the previous summer, on the only other occasion that he had seen Adrienne since their parting.

*

Then he had just been leaving the hospital, after bringing in one of the stable lads from Denestornya, when he caught sight of Adrienne through the bars of a tall iron fence. He had shrunk back into the shade of the doorway so that he shouldn't be seen: but from there he followed her with his eyes as, with head held high and looking straight ahead of her without a glance to left or right, she strode determinedly up the path which led to the lunatic asylum or, as most people euphemistically called it, the House with the Green Roof.

Off to see that mad husband, Balint had thought bitterly, he whom she had never loved and who had never loved her.

His heart had swelled, like that of an exile who catches a glimpse of his forbidden home from far away.

As he had hidden then, so he felt impelled to run now, to escape from the theatre and wander anonymously through the town. Without realizing where he had been heading Balint found himself in the main square, and here he was almost overcome by a strange lassitude. It was as if that impulse which had hurled him out of the theatre had sapped all his reserves of energy.

He walked on, without taking note of where he was going, until, at the corner of the marketplace, he almost knocked over the charcoal grill of an old woman roasting chestnuts. Ashamed of himself, he stopped and in an attempt to pull himself together, and to make amends for his clumsiness, he bought a paper cone of nuts that the woman held out to him. As he started absent-mindedly to peel them he remembered that he had been invited out to supper and had better not arrive with stained fingers. Abruptly he shoved the warm paper cone deep into one of his coat pockets, deciding to give it to the first child he might meet: but although he passed several hanging about near the iron bridge or in front of the cinema, by then the chestnuts had been forgotten.

Of course, he reflected, he ought to have married Lili Illesvary. Everything would then have been different. He could have met Adrienne and, with no constraint between them, talked of their by now shadowy past in a way that could provoke no comment if overheard. They could have met as old friends, if nothing more. At least it would have meant that he would have seen her from time to time and touched her hand as he kissed her fingers. Also he would have had a home of his own, and a family to return to, instead of wandering aimlessly with nowhere

6

he wanted to go. That was what he ought to have done, yet he had carelessly thrown away even the half-happiness such a marriage would have brought him. Now he had nothing; no love, no family, nothing! It had been entirely his own fault. The opportunity had been there, at Jablanka in the middle of December, and if he had failed to take the opportunity offered he had no-one but himself to blame. But he had done nothing.

His host, Antal Szent-Gyorgyi, and his sons had welcomed him as warmly as ever, without being over-demonstrative which in that house was thought to be not very good form. His cousin Magda's greeting was a shade more enthusiastic, for she gave him a teasing smile and pressed his hand a little harder than was usual. His aunt Elise, Countess Szent-Gyorgyi, received him with maternal warmth and tenderness and somehow, though without ever alluding to the matter, contrived to let him know how much she approved of, and would encourage, his marrying Lili. It was clear to Balint that they all knew that that was why he had come to Jablanka, and that everyone was in favour. Canon Czibulka, or Pfaffulus as he was nicknamed in that house, an old and intimate friend of the Szent-Gyorgyis, also discreetly showed that he approved the match by giving a special antenna-like movement of his bushy eyebrows when he first shook Balint by the hand. Pfaffulus had already been at Jablanka for several days as the shoot had been held unusually late and, as Advent had already begun, he came over daily from Nagy-Szombat to say Mass in the castle chapel. The priest's tacit approval warmed Balint's heart for it made him feel that in that house everyone knew about and looked kindly on his plans to ask Lili to marry him.

All the same he did not see her until all the guests assembled in the lofty stucco-decorated drawing room which had been the monks' refectory before the former monastery became the Szent-Gyorgyis' country home. She came in from the library, which was at the opposite end of the room from where Balint was standing, seeming almost to glide weightlessly across the highly polished wooden floor. She was dressed in a flowing white tulle gown and she moved with that quiet assurance natural to girls brought up in the highest society. As she crossed the room she nodded to those other guests she had already seen and went up to greet two new arrivals, the guests of honour who had just come from Vienna. Once again Abady smiled as he admired the impeccable way in which she moved, reflecting how perfectly she fitted into those grand surroundings and what a perfect background was formed for her by the great white hall-like room, the crimson and gold furniture and the huge family portraits in their elaborate frames. For all the apparent frailty of the girl, as she moved slowly around that luxurious room in her diaphanous creamy white dress, her step as light as that of any butterfly, one could still sense that inner core of steel that was the mark of her race.

So this, thought Balint, is the girl who is going to be my wife! Infinitely well-bred, the scion of countless generations whose sons and daughters, being always rich and independent, had never needed to marry some ugly duckling for her dowry or accept anyone second-rate for his money. Now she had nearly come up to where he stood. She did not increase her speed nor for a moment change her demeanour; and yet there was something special in the movement she made in putting out her hand to him, in the yielding softness with which she took his, and in the joyful flash of her cornflower-blue eyes.

Balint sensed it all at once and knew exactly what it meant.

During the three days of shooting Lili was often to be found beside him and remained with him for the whole of the most important beat on the third day when once again Balint found himself allotted the place of honour at the extreme right-hand end of the line of guns. They somehow seemed to spend hours together, and even on those long afternoon walks on which, of course, they were never alone but always accompanied by several other young people, the two of them often seemed to be left to walk some twenty or thirty paces behind the others. And then Lili, who otherwise was lively and talkative, would remain silent, leaving it to him to decide what they would talk about. She was hoping he would propose: and that is when he ought to have done so, either in the long hornbeam avenue or else when coming back from visiting the thoroughbred mares.

Recalling that moment Balint conjured up in his mind the thin layer of powdery snow that covered the frozen ground and which had crackled under their feet. The others had lingered by the fences of the paddocks and that is when he should have spoken. It was there that he ought to have uttered those few banal words that were the classic form of suggesting marriage. And yet for some reason he had held back and said nothing. Stupidly he had said nothing. Had he felt that in that wintry landscape his voice would sound too matter-of-fact, too cold and businesslike, too unspontaneous? But of course he knew then, just as he knew now, that it would not have mattered how he had said it, for the girl had only been waiting for him to speak.

Balint stopped at the bridge over the millstream. For a moment he thought of going on into the park, which at that hour would be completely deserted, and he walked on a few steps before reflecting how silly it would be to get his patent leather evening shoes all muddied just before he went to the prefect's evening party. Far better to go where he could stay on the sidewalk, where the slight humidity from that afternoon's rain would have left few traces. So he continued along the road which led to the railway station.

As he wandered so aimlessly in the night Balint thought back to that time a year before when he had spent so many autumn evenings just wandering about the streets as aimlessly as he was now doing. Anything, he had thought, to keep on the move and quiet his growing anxiety as he waited for Adrienne's letter, that letter which would at long last announce that she had started the business of her divorce. Until then every little note she had sent him had just been one more excuse for delay: '... it is impossible now', or 'Not yet, we have to wait, wait, wait!' That was what she had written, and then he had not understood the dreadful dilemma in which she had been placed, fearing to make any move that might push her sick husband into insanity, that insanity that had come all the same and forever destroyed their hopes.

He wondered if Adrienne was still sitting in Countess Gyalakuthy's box at the opera or whether she too had left the theatre devastated, as he had been, by the cruel chance that had brought them physically so close after so long apart. Had she too been shattered by that cruel game the Fates seemed to be playing with them?

Somehow, he thought, he must arrange that this should never happen again. He would leave Kolozsvar the next day, indeed if it had not been for that stupid supper party, he would have gone that very night.

In the morning he would go back to Denestornya, to his mother and to that old home which was the only place in the world where he could find peace. My home, he thought, with its age-old beauty and magic, where, though always enveloped in a veil of sadness, there were only the two of them to wander in that enormous house: he and his old mother. And now there always would only be the two of them. There was

9

no-one else, there never would be anyone else. There was no future and no young life to follow.

Had he proposed to Lili at Jablanka then at least he might have had that hope. What madness had prevented him?

It had been quite clear that the Szent-Gyorgyis, in their typically unobtrusive way, had made sure that there would have been no obstacles in the path of such a marriage. They had even thought about the difference of religion and, with a tactfulness that amounted almost to an art, had taken pains to let him know that his being a Protestant would create no difficulties.

The memory came back to him with sudden clarity, perhaps because it had all been so surprising.

On the afternoon of the second day of the shooting party Balint had just changed and was on his way to join the others in the drawing room when he met Pfaffulus in the passage. He had the impression that the priest had been waiting for him.

'I was just on my way to the chapel,' said Canon Czibulka in his slight Slovakian accent. 'If you've never seen it perhaps you'd like to come with me? It's really very fine, well worth seeing.'

They walked together to that part of the former monastery that formed the rear part of the cloister court and faced the main entrance over which was the refectory now transformed into the main drawing room. In the centre of the first-floor gallery which encircled the court was a massive stone doorway, whose carved and ornamented architraves framed the doorposts which bordered a pair of huge doors inlaid with many different kinds of precious woods in the full opulence of ecclesiastical baroque.

Pfaffulus pushed open the doors which swung back noiselessly. They went in.

The chapel was the size of a church and the semi-circle of windows behind the altar must, Balint had realized, have projected out towards the mountainside. Although darkness had nearly fallen there was enough evening light to cast a soft mystical radiance in front of which the lines of the baldaquin over the altar stood out as if etched in black on grey. Then Pfaffulus had switched on the electric chandeliers and the chapel blazed with light. It was indeed beautiful.

Along each side wall stood the carved wooden stalls where the monks had sat for worship, the panelling divided by columns which supported a carved rococo veil that seemed to swirl with an almost musical rhythm towards the altar. All along its border were placed winged angels' heads and surmounting all this splendour was the monastic order's symbolic bird, a raven carrying bread in its beak, huge and gilded, like an emphatic exclamation mark floating above the mellow brown woodwork of the canopy itself. Over the tabernacle the baldaquin, fringed with golden tassels and supported by twisted columns, supported a picture of the Virgin surrounded by a golden sunburst. On each side angels dressed identically in blue and gold, with gilded wings, knelt in the exaggerated attitudes so beloved in the baroque era.

A thick floral carpet covered the stone flags on the floor. 'It is beautiful, isn't it?' Pfaffulus had said; and he took Balint round showing him the carvings on the stalls and explaining the reliefs, all of which commemorated some miracle or incident in the life of the holy Saint Paul the Hermit, founder of the order.

Then he crossed in front of the altar, genuflecting swiftly as he did so, to show Balint the Abbot's stall and a series of holy pictures by well-known artists. They had almost returned to the chapel doors when the priest stopped and sat down, a thoughtful look on his fine expressive face. It was as if he had just remembered something.

After nodding appreciation at Balint's words of thanks he looked up at the younger man and, seemingly unable to keep to himself what had come so strongly to his mind, grasped Balint's arm and pulled him down to sit beside him. As he did so he said:

'Do you know what this chapel means to me? I love it as if it were a living human being, not only because of its beauty but also because of so many things that have happened to me within its walls.'

He explained that it was at Jablanka that he had started his professional career, as tutor to Count Antal Szent-Gyorgyi. Later, after several years spent in Rome, he had returned as the castle's resident priest; though he had never accepted any parish of his own even though the count was patron of several rich livings and pressed him to take the best of them. He told Balint that he had preferred to remain quietly where he was and continue his studies in canon law.

Then he gave an especially sweet smile and went on: 'I have another very dear memory. It was in this church that I officiated at the wedding of Count Antal's other sister, the Countess Charlotte who married a Swede, Count Olaf Loewenstierna.' As he said these words Pfaffulus's thin pointed nose seemed to grow even longer and he raised his eyebrows expressively. 'It was very bold on my part, as the bridegroom, of course, was a Protestant and I should not really have performed the ceremony without the promise that the children should be brought up as Catholics. But what could I do? The old count gave his orders and said that one could not ask such a thing of a Loewenstierna, who was descended from one of Gustavus Adolphus's generals; and anyway he would despise the young man if he abandoned his family traditions. If he, as a good Catholic father, did not demand it, then I should not either. Naturally I did as he wished.'

Here the round little priest had leaned forward and spoken confidentially into Balint's ear.

'Of course I had committed a fault; even perhaps a sin, yes, a sin. And yet it was my sin, and mine alone, because in such circumstances only the priest can be at fault. I went straight afterwards to see the Prince-Cardinal. It was then Monsignor Simor. To him I confessed my fault, my crime. I knelt before him and he gave me a thorough scolding and some pretty harsh penances with which to atone for my lapse. Then he invited me to eat with him. Afterwards he had said: "You were wise, my son, not to ask for guidance because no permission would ever have been given. Yes, you did the wise, the clever thing. The family of Szent-Gyorgyi have done much for our church for several centuries and so they fall into a very special category. I am sure that this is how the Roman Curia would regard the matter too."'

Czibulka had then fallen silent, gazing ahead as if conscious only of his own memories. Then he had got up and looked at Abady as if excusing himself for having burdened the young man with such personal reminiscences.

'You must forgive my idle chatter,' he said. 'I seem to have gone on at length about things which only concern myself. But this chapel, you see, means so much to me.'

Then he had made another quick genuflection towards the altar, switched out the lights, and escorted Balint out of the chapel. They walked back together to the drawing room where everyone was gathering for tea.

*

12

They had thought of every way to encourage and reassure him, and so everything had depended on him and on him alone. And then he had let the moment pass and so thrown away his chances, if not of love then at least of a kind and loving wife, of a family, and of a nest to come home to.

It had been on the last evening of his stay that he had let the final opportunity escape him. He had dressed for dinner early and when he had entered the drawing room he had found it deserted. Then, through the open doors to the library, he had seen Lili, who for some reason of her own had also dressed before the others. She had been kneeling on a chair drawn up to a long table in the centre of the room, leaning forward with her bare elbows reflected on the polished wooden tabletop as she turned the pages of a large album of engravings. She had seemed totally engrossed in the pictures before her.

At that moment he had instinctively known that she had come down early to the library with a single purpose, and that that had been, if possible, to give him one final occasion on which to make his proposal, final because it had been the last night of that gathering at Jablanka to which he had been invited just for that purpose.

'Do you know this collection?' Lili had asked when Balint had come up to her and leaned beside her on the table. 'It is very rare. It's the record of a journey to Egypt by a Hungarian, a Count Forray. Aren't these coloured engravings lovely? Do look! Look at this one! Isn't it beautiful?' and as she had looked up at him the question in her wide open violet-blue eyes had had nothing to do with the pictures on the table.

Together they had turned the pages slowly; and as they did so sometimes their arms or their fingers had touched and sometimes they had exchanged a word or two: 'This must be Malta!', 'Do look at the camel driver!', 'The Khedive's palace ...', words without any real meaning whose purpose had only been to break the silence.

Several times Balint had thought that the moment had come to speak the words for which she was waiting. He had only to take her hand and murmur a few short sentences and with that simple action he would have wiped out the past and started a new era in his life. Adrienne had wanted it that way and had expected it of him; but somehow the right words had never come, only those banal phrases about the engravings in the album on the table before them. And yet, as he was saying something obvious about the temple at Karnak and how large its stones were, he had been wondering if he ought then to have said 'I love you', which would have been a lie, or whether all that would have been needed was 'Will you be my wife?' until the moment had passed and they had been obliged to get up and go into the drawing room where the other guests had started to gather.

Lili had then got down from the chair on which she had been kneeling and slowly straightened up. Balint remembered that he had wondered then if she thought he might have been embarrassed to speak under the bright glare of the electric chandelier above them, especially as she had walked straight over to one of the deep window embrasures, where the thickness of the old walls would have made them invisible to the guests in the other room. She had gone right up to the window and then, with her face close to the glass, and clearly to find another reason for the move, she had murmured, 'Do look at the frost. It is like flowers made of ice!' and then she had turned and glanced back at him.

But Balint, who had followed her only as far as the beginning of the deep window embrasure, had just stood there still looking at the vast library.

The walls were lined with wooden bookcases almost to the ceiling, all curved and convoluted with elaborate carved and gilded decorations and divided by twisted columns of different precious woods. Above the elaborate cornice were metal conch shells and gilded *putti* brandishing highly coloured heraldic shields, all in the most sophisticated manner of the Viennese baroque. The atmosphere of abounding opulence was overwhelming, and when Balint had watched the slim girlish figure of Lili stepping so elegantly across the inlaid parquet floor he had suddenly felt that all this was her proper background, where she truly belonged. This somewhat foreign luxury, itself so truly Austrian, was her birthright; and yet it was alien and strange to anyone with his downright Transylvanian background. How could he uproot her and carry her off to his own so different home? Even if she were in love with him, he had thought, would she not feel herself transplanted into an alien, possibly hostile, soil. For all its size and grandeur, Denestornya in its simple Hungarian way could not compare with this sophisticated splendour, just as the way of life in Transylvania could hardly be compared with what Lili was used to. All this had flashed through Balint's mind as he had stood there looking at her, and it was like a sudden draught of cold air in his face. More, it had been just one more inhibition to be added to the others.

'It must be icy outside.'

'It was six below zero at dusk.'

'How bright the moonlight is!'

'That's why it's so cold. The sky is quite clear now.'

With these and other meaningless, inane phrases they had filled in the gaps between pauses that seemed endless to them both. At length Lili had turned away from the window. For an instant she had looked straight into Balint's face and then, seeming to glide across the floor, she had returned to the drawing room without saying another word.

Knowing now that he had finally lost her, Balint had followed her slowly, his heart filled with sadness: and yet it had been a mild sadness and on his face had been the slight ironic smile of someone who had had to forgo a pleasure he had never really expected to be his.

What madness it had been to throw all that away!

Thinking back to the past Balint stamped his feet in momentary anger and quickened his pace. In a few moments he found himself in the square in front of the station, which was full of bustle and noise for the express from Budapest had just arrived. Several luggage-laden motors passed him on their way to the city centre and this sudden rush of activity brought Balint to a halt. For a moment he hesitated, trying to choose between continuing on the muddy pavement in front of some warehouses, or crossing the road which was even muddier. Neither seemed sensible.

As he stood there motionless for a moment newsboys ran forward offering the capital's midday papers. Thinking that anything might be a distraction from his self-torment, Balint stopped one, took a paper at random, pressed a coin into the lad's hand, stuffed the paper into one of his greatcoat pockets and, without waiting for the change, turned away and started to walk back to the city centre. I'll go to a café and pass the rest of the time reading, he said to himself; but he had only gone a few steps before he had already forgotten what he had just decided.

At dinner on the last night of his stay at Jablanka they had discussed the problem of Croatia. The Friedjung trial had been brought before the Viennese courts at the beginning of the month, December, and the

Austrian newspapers had arrived at the castle that afternoon. They had all written about the case, and almost everything that had been printed had been disagreeable and critical.

It had all started when Professor Friedjung had written a most controversial article, which had been published in the *Neue Freie Presse* at the end of March 1909. The subject had been the annexation of Bosnia-Herzegovina, and in it the professor had named some fifty Croatian politicians whom he had accused of belonging to an irredentist organization supported by the government of Serbia. It had been fairly obvious from the start that Friedjung's revelations had been inspired by the Austrian Foreign Office, for the material for the article could only have been provided by the Ballplatz. That these accusations should have been broadcast to the world's press in this way had shown the whole affair to have been part of a plot by which the Dual Monarchy was to be forced into sending an ultimatum, with impossible terms, to Belgrade and then, when Serbia inevitably refused to comply, declaring war.

Some trouble had been gone to in order to prepare the world diplomatically for these developments. Germany had already confirmed her solidarity with Vienna; Russia, though reluctantly and with a bad grace, would not intervene, and various other European powers had made it clear to Belgrade that Serbia would receive no support from abroad.

The article in the *Neue Freie Presse* had appeared on March 25th, which had also been the date planned for the ultimatum, though this had never materialized because on the same day the Crown Prince of Serbia, George Karageorgevitch, had resigned his post as head of the pro-war party. A few days later Serbia showed herself willing to accept any terms offered her. Nevertheless the incendiary article had appeared and events later showed that, no matter what had transpired in Belgrade, the Friedjung article was part of a far-reaching plan hatched in Vienna and would have been published anyhow. A month later the monarchy's Prosecutor-General arraigned another group of fifty-four Croatians, all accused of treason. This had been brought about by Baron Rauch, the Coalition-nominated Ban of Croatia, who was as anxious to see irredentism wiped out in Zagreb as were the Austrian politicians to stop Serbian irredentist activities in Vienna. The Zagreb trial had lasted five months and had ended that October with thirty-one of the defendants found guilty. Appeals had been launched, and it had been fairly obvious that they were likely to succeed since the whole prosecution had been based on the weakest of cases. The Zagreb trial had provoked a most dis-agreeable anti-Austrian feeling abroad and the French press had written about the 'Death of Justice' in Vienna. The strong reaction abroad and the indecisive results of the Zagreb trial now gave new heart to those who had been pilloried by the Friedjung article and so they had accused him of slander. This trial had opened at the beginning of December and Professor Friedjung had at once declared that he could prove the truth of everything that he had alleged; and he presented documents to support his accusations. These, of course, had been provided by the Ballplatz and sent secretly to the famous and respectable historian. Then, as the trial entered its second week, things began to go wrong; some of the documents had been shown to be forgeries.

It was this that had been the principal subject of conversation that last night at Jablanka. It had been the considered opinion that the professor had been right in principle and that those he had accused, especially Supino, the author of the Fiume Resolution, had certainly been Serbian agents, but that the Austrian Foreign Ministry had care-lessly failed to verify all the material produced by their own spies. It had been clear that, unfortunately, there had been more than mere muddle or justifiable human error. What had emerged was no less than intentional falsification. It had been generally accepted that this was always to be expected when recourse had to be made to common or garden spies, who were often paid by both sides, and especially in this case where some of the secret agents had been Serbs who, no doubt, had received the false documents from Belgrade with the full knowledge of the Serbian government!

Naturally this had been discussed frequently during the three days' shooting at Jablanka and whenever the scandal had been mentioned it had always been in that bland, well-informed, unexaggerated, half-spoken, half-insinuated manner which was the well-bred style adopted by the Szent-Gyorgyi circle. On the last evening it had seemed to Balint that they could talk about nothing else and though, the year before, he had been fascinated by the political discussions in his cousins' house, now his own inner turmoil prevented him from taking any interest in what they were saying. On that last evening he felt he could no longer stay talking politics with the group around the drawing-room fire; and so, as soon as everyone had drunk their coffee, he left the room and went to see his aunt. It was, of course, right that he should do so as he would be leaving at dawn to catch the Budapest express and would have no other opportunity of taking his leave. But his hurried flight to Elise Szent-Gyorgyi's own sitting room was really because he could not bear to remain in the same room as little Lili whom he had just hurt so much. To reach his aunt's rooms he had to pass once again through the library, and there, on the table, still lay the album of Forray's travels, slightly askew, just as it had been left when Lili had pushed it aside and gone to the window. The big red and gold leatherbound volume glittered under the savage glare of the chandelier overhead and had seemed to him the *corpus delicti* – the proof of the crime he had just committed against both himself and her. His heart had constricted when he saw the book lying there in front of him.

His aunt Elise had been sitting in her usual chair which was protected from any draught by a glass screen. In front of her were two women guests from Vienna. Before he had come in they had talked only of unimportant Viennese society gossip but this had stopped when Balint entered the room. Then she had grabbed his hand in her own and forced him to sit down on a sofa beside her chair. For a moment neither aunt nor nephew had spoken. The two Austrian visitors had grasped at once that their hostess wanted a few words alone with Count Abady and so, after a few desultory sentences, uttered only so as not to make it look as if it were his arrival that had caused their departure, which would not have been polite, they took their leave saying that they hoped the countess would forgive them but that they were expected at the bridge tables and had then disappeared from the room.

'It is nice of you to come to me so early,' said Balint's aunt, who had been born a Gyeroffy in far-off Transylvania, and she looked closely up at him with her large brown eyes. 'I love to talk to you. When you're here I don't feel quite so far from home!'

She had smiled and put her hand on Balint's arm. He lifted it at once and put it to his lips. For a few moments neither had spoken and then Elise Szent-Gyorgyi had started enquiring after all her old friends and relations, starting with Balint's mother. She asked after people she had not seen for more than twenty years and told her nephew little anecdotes about them, things that had happened during her girlhood, tales of country balls and May Day festivals and picnic outings to the forests of Radna. She asked after the father of the four Alvinczy boys because he had once been her favourite dancing partner – very handsome he had been, she said, and admitted having something of a crush on him while she was still in the schoolroom; and also after old Uncle Daniel Kendy, even then too fond of the brandy, who had been so much admired by all the young girls because he had been so good-looking and elegant and they had heard that he had cut a dash at the court of the Empress Eugénie and so was the first *homme du monde* any of them had ever met. And so she had gone on reminiscing about her youth and her own home and letting Balint tell her everything he could recall that had happened to her old acquaintances. From time to time she had paused for a moment and imperceptibly the little pauses had grown longer. Balint had had the impression that behind her very real interest in everything he could tell her had lain something else, something that she had been turning over in her mind, uncertain, perhaps, how she could bring up the subject.

Balint had thought that she would probably ask about her other nephew, Laszlo Gyeroffy; but this time her mind had been on something else ...

After a little time Countess Elise had fallen silent and had then seemed lost in her own thoughts. Then suddenly she had said, 'You can have no idea how good it is to hear all this!' and turning again to her nephew she took his hand and kept it in hers. She seemed to be looking into the far distance.

'Do you know,' she had gone on softly as if confiding in him some carefully guarded secret. 'Do you know that after all these years I still feel that Transylvania is my real home, not here in Northern Hungary. I feel at home there; not here! The people there are my own kind, but here they are somehow like foreigners, like Austrians, like Viennese. Don't misunderstand me, I am very happy here and my life with Antal beside me has always been a happy one. But that is because I have always loved him so much. We married for love, and I would have married him, and no-one else, no matter how poor he might have been or what sort of life he led.' Then she had paused for a moment before going on: '... but all this ...' and she made a wide circular gesture with her hand which somehow embraced, as clearly as if she had spelled it all out, the castle at Jablanka, the vast estates, their assured position in society, 'all this ... this is still not really me. It has always been strange. This world is not my world and has never really become so. Now that I look back on my life I can see that it has been our great love, and only that, which has made

19

our marriage so happy. Not only my love, but his also. It is that which has made everything right and harmonious for both of us. It's true. It is love, true love, which is the only thing which makes it possible to endure everything and which absolves everything. If we had not had it ours would have been a life of disagreements and bitterness for both of us.'

Then, as abruptly as she had begun, she fell silent again. After a moment or two she had given a light laugh and said, 'Oh dear, how I do run on! Prattling away like anything ... and such nonsense too. All that chatting about the past has made your old aunt think of ... well ... so many things.'

So this was what she had wanted to tell him, and for which she had had to prepare herself. She had spoken only so as to be of some help and consolation to him, so as to reassure him that although she had seen at once that he had failed to ask Lili to marry him and that he felt guilty about it, she at least sympathized and did not blame him. Somehow she had made it clear to him that she had understood his reasons perhaps even more clearly than he himself, and that somehow she knew not only that he was still in love with someone else but also that he instinctively thought of the charming Lili as an alien creature from another world. Balint had been deeply touched by his aunt's delicacy and finesse and even more by the obvious love and goodness that had made her speak of such things. It had been a bitter hour for him and he had needed help and affection: he had been all the more grateful because he had sensed that for him, and him alone, Countess Szent-Gyorgyi had revealed something so intimate of her life and feelings that she would never had admitted to anyone else; and she had done it only because she knew that he had needed help.

Aunt and nephew stayed together for a long time in the cosy intimate little sitting room, all cushions and soft upholstery, that Countess Elise had made for herself. The carpets were deep and soft, and the furniture comfortable and unpretentious. The walls were covered in some dark material. It was in complete contrast to the grandeur of the rest of the castle where the huge white and gold rooms were filled with elaborate baroque furniture much of which had been gilded. Everything at Jablanka was perfect of its kind, as well as being very grand ... but it was also, perhaps, a trifle cold. In the little private sitting room where the mistress of the house had made her nest, everything, whether large or small, was a souvenir of her Transylvanian girlhood. Most of the

20

quantity of pictures came from her old home at Szamos-Kozard and she even had two little oils of the old manor house before her brother had rebuilt it. There were watercolour portraits of her Gyeroffy parents, grandparents, aunts and uncles; and innumerable little pictures of children, mostly relations, were scattered all around the room, on tables, window sills, and on hanging shelves, along with countless small objects, photographs and miniatures, all of which held for her some memory of times long past and cousins long since departed. All of this had spoken unequivocally to Balint of his aunt's deep and ineradicable love for her homeland … and also of the spiritual barrier she had never really vanquished that stood between her real self and this grandiose westernized world in which she had lived so many years. That evening, for the first time, Balint had understood the little room's almost symbolic meaning.

A year had gone by since that last evening at Jablanka and yet, as he wandered along the dark streets in the drizzling rain, he could now see it all in his mind and relive everything that had then happened to him. Once again he saw the two of them sitting in that slightly over-heated room which was so different from everything else in the house. It was like a tiny island, he thought suddenly, which Fate had one day wrenched away from its parent Transylvania and deposited there so far from home.

Reliving those bitter memories during those hours of aimless wandering did nothing to alleviate Balint's deep-rooted bitterness, so much so that he now felt he could not face a happy social gathering in his present mood. For a moment he wondered if he could make some excuse so as to get out of going altogether, perhaps sending word that he had developed a bad headache, or some such lie, but then, he thought, how could he do it? He could hardly go up to the prefect's front door and say that he wasn't well enough to come, for the doorman would be certain to tell his master that it was Count Abady himself who had delivered the message! And if he sent a waiter from one of the cafés that were still open it would soon be known that he had been seen there. Better, perhaps, to go home and send round his valet with a visiting card and a little note? He looked at his watch and saw that it was already half-past eleven and all the servants at the Abady house would be in bed asleep. He would have to wake someone, who would then have to dress, and it would all take far too long. He was already late for the party, and the other guests, and the famous French singer, were no doubt at that very moment waiting for him. No doubt, as he spoke good French, he was expected to be the diva's supper partner, and if he waited any longer it was more than likely that everyone would have gone in to eat and that his place, beside the guest of honour, would remain empty. It would be a gross lack of politeness to stay away a minute longer than it would take him to reach the house.

All this was going through his mind as he walked, now more swiftly than before, towards his host's house. He knew that the opera had ended some time before because a number of carriages bringing other guests from the theatre had already passed him in the street, which was now again silent and deserted. Everyone must have already arrived at the house. Balint quickened his pace almost breaking into a run, because he realized that whether he wanted to or not he would have to go to the party.

The prefect's house blazed with light, but the street outside was deserted except for a one-horse carriage which was waiting to one side of the front door.

Abady was just stepping hurriedly past it when the tall figure of Adam Alvinczy, Margit's husband, jumped out and grabbed his arm.

'I've been waiting for you,' he said excitedly. 'Margit sent me to catch you here!'

Somehow Balint was not surprised, as he had sensed that the chance encounter with Adrienne was bound to provoke something no-one could foresee.

'Well?' he said. 'What is it?'

'We knew you'd be here. Margit says you're to come at once ... there's some trouble at home; that's why she sent me. Come on then! Quickly!'

As they got into the carriage Adam called out to the coachman to drive at once back to the Uzdy villa.

Balint felt his throat constrict so that he could hardly speak. Somehow he managed to ask what had happened.

'I don't know,' said Adam. 'All I can tell you is that when we got home from the opera Adrienne rushed straight to her room and locked herself in. Margit has stayed near her, in the bathroom next door, as she doesn't dare to leave her entirely alone. She is very worried.'

They did not speak again. As they drove out of town towards the Uzdy villa on the Monostor road all that could be heard was the clatter

22

of the horses' hooves on the paving stones; and to both men the five minutes' journey seemed far longer. As they drove along Balint could think only of one thing, the small Browning revolver, that deadly little weapon which Adrienne had once asked him to buy for her, though she had carefully concealed from him that even then she had thought of killing herself with it. Since that day, and especially when a little later they had parted, perhaps forever, after the month they had spent together in Venice, the thought of that revolver had haunted him, for he knew how uncompromising she was and also how haunted she was by the spectre of that ultimate solution to her troubles.

And now the spectre walked again, and perhaps what he had always feared had finally been accomplished. He was in agony lest they should arrive too late to prevent what he knew instinctively to be uppermost in her mind ...

The carriage stopped in front of the wrought-iron screen which divided the villa's garden from the road. Adam opened the little-used side gate with his own key and called to the coachman to wait where he was. Then he and Balint hurried in, past the long dark single-storeyed wing of the house which reached almost to the banks of the Szamos and which contained Adrienne's own apartments, and entered the building through the glazed veranda that ran along one side of the main entrance court. Adam at once turned not to the right, to the door to Adrienne's sitting room, but to another door at the left which led to her bathroom.

They went in as quietly as possible. Inside they found Margit crouched at the end of a narrow bench with her ear pressed to the keyhole of the door which opened into the bedroom. Hunched up like that she might have been taken for a young girl if her advanced state of pregnancy had not shown her to be a grown woman. As soon as they entered the room she turned towards them and got up. Then she drew Balint to her side and, speaking very softly but with great determination, said:

'Thank goodness you've come! Now you must stay right here. It's alright, I know you're expected at that supper party but Adam will go in your place and will explain that you're not feeling at all well. It won't look at all strange as everyone will have noticed that you left the theatre early, and they'll think it most considerate to have sent someone in your place. No-one will be at all put out.' She turned to her husband, saying: 'You did keep the carriage, didn't you? You'd better hurry now. I'm sure you'll carry it all off excellently ... Oh, and you'd better send back the carriage as we may need it. Tell the man to wait and give him the key to the small gate.'

Margit had obviously worked everything out in advance and, being cool-headed no matter how anxious she might be, gave her orders clearly and simply.

As soon as Adam had gone she turned to Balint and, in a whisper that could not have been heard from the next room, told him exactly what had happened that day. In the morning Adrienne had got back from Lausanne where she had gone to place her daughter in a boarding school. Countess Gyalakuthy had heard of her return and asked her to join the others in her box that evening. She said that somehow she didn't much like the idea, that opera was not really for her, '... but as we thought you were at Denestornya ...'

'I only came up for this evening.'

'Yes, but we didn't know that then. Anyhow it's beside the point. I was sitting beside her in the box and I could see her face. It was terrible, because I know her so well ... but nobody else noticed anything. I was very scared for her, but there was nothing I could do. It was impossible to leave, and anyway I don't think she wanted to move. At last the opera came to an end and we could go. We brought her home in our carriage and she never uttered a word. We came in with her, though she clearly didn't want us to; in fact she did all she could to make us go away at once. Adam waited outside but I refused to leave her. She looked terrible, terrible. I've only seen her look like that twice before ... but never so intensely, so determined. I was really afraid for her; her eyes were without expression, glassy ... and her hands were shaking. I managed to stay with her until she had undressed, but then she suddenly pushed me out of the room and locked the door. That's when I sent Adam to find you because there wasn't, there isn't, any more that I can do. I don't know what she's up to in there. Once or twice I heard her groping about and then it seemed as if some small objects fell onto the floor. Since then I've heard nothing ... for quite a long time. I've knocked repeatedly, but she doesn't answer though I know she's awake ... she's certainly awake. Only you can help now!' She stopped, and then, after a pause, went on:

'If it isn't too late: I know she's got some veronal.'

Balint got up and stepped towards Adrienne's bedroom. Then with tightly clenched fist he knocked twice on her door and in a loud voice said, 'It's me, AB. Please let me in!'

24

They waited. It was only about twenty seconds, but to those in the bathroom it seemed like an eternity. They heard nothing, no words, no footsteps, nothing. Then the key turned twice in the lock. Abady at once grasped the handle: the door opened before him. He stepped quickly into the room and closed the door behind him. Inside, the room was in complete darkness, but Balint knew it too well to need any light. He knew everything in it, even the warm scent which might have been that of carnations or other flower petals but which came from no manufacturer's bottle and was like no perfume from a shop but which rather was the slightest, yet intoxicating aroma, as of a subtle secret poison ... it was the intimate scent of his love. Only two steps and he was at the side of her bed. He sat down quietly.

'Is it really you?' asked a muffled voice from deep among the pillows. 'Yes.'

His hands sought her shoulder and started to caress the hair that curled loosely about her. Then he spoke again, thickly as if he could hardly get the words out:

'This has no sense, no sense at all.'

For a few moments there was no reply. Then she clutched at him with both arms holding him in an embrace so tight she might have been a drowning swimmer clinging to her saviour. Their lips met in a long, hungry kiss.

Between them the stiffly starched shirt of his evening dress crackled softly.

Balint wanted to switch on the light but Adrienne was still too upset to let him do so.

'Margit is waiting outside. I must tell her you're alright,' said Balint. 'Besides, I must see my hair isn't ruffled ... and put my tie straight ... I'll need the light to do that.'

'No, no! Not yet! You don't need the light just for that ... and anyway it doesn't matter!'

'But Margit may want to come in. It'll be better with the light on.'

'No, she mustn't come! Not now! Tell her she can go home and come back later ... but I'm not having any light, not now!'

There was nothing he could do to persuade her, so he smoothed his hair with his hands and did what he could to straighten his collar and tie. Then he went back into the bathroom.

Margit was lying at full length on the narrow bench beside the wall. She was fast asleep, with her head cushioned on her soft arm, like a faithful guardian at rest as soon as danger was past. She seemed to be sleeping so deeply that Balint felt it was cruel to wake her.

'Is it alright ...?' she muttered before she was fully awake.

There was no need for Balint to say anything because Margit saw from his face that all was well and at once said, 'I'll be going home now,' and her little mouth stretched wide as she yawned deeply. Then she slipped into her evening fur coat and with hardly another word bade Abady farewell and disappeared. How Abady was to leave the house if she locked the gate behind her and took away the key, she didn't say, though whether this was because she was still so sleepy or whether she may have other reasons no-one could have told, for little Margit never explained and never said anything that was not strictly necessary.

Balint turned off the bathroom light and returned to the dark bedroom.

The clock in the neighbouring monastery struck three. Its sound reverberated in the darkness almost as if it chimed in the room itself.

The sound woke them. They had fallen asleep entwined in each other's arms, the curves of their bodies fitting closely together with the ease of long-standing habit, just as a pair of great cats such as pumas or panthers sleep coiled together in luxurious repose. Adrienne had found her accustomed place with her head tucked into Balint's shoulder and her strong richly curling hair partly covering his lips and nose; but he slept all the deeper for, far from disturbing him, these wild locks of hers were like links in a magic chain that had bound them together for so many years. These lovers needed no-one else, for both found everything that was needed in the other, every gesture and movement of their love-making, whether new or familiar, was accepted with trust and serenity, even their unity in the climax of love; and on this day it was just as it had always been whenever they had been able to come together to lose their own selves in each other.

'It's already three, I ought to get dressed,' he murmured into the thick tangle of her curls.

'Are you cold?' she asked, but she did not move.

'No! But I can't stay for ever ... and I really must put on the light.'

'If you must; but promise me not to look around! Promise!'

'I promise.'

Balint switched on one of the little bedside lamps and Adrienne picked out one of her wraps for him.

Although Balint had meant to keep his promise, as soon as he started to put on Adrienne's silken kimono he could not help seeing that the little Browning revolver was lying on the table beside the bed and that on the floor nearby were a number of tiny unused cartridges, little copper bullets and the yellow cardboard box from which they had come. He realized that she must have tried to load the revolver but that she had dropped the box in her agitation and that it must have been only this chance that had saved her life. Adrienne noticed that his face had clouded over and took his head in her hands, turned it back towards her and started kissing his eyes with her wide generous mouth. She did not let go but pulled him down again as if he were her prisoner among the soft pillows and cushions on the bed. Later, when they could again look each other straight in the eyes, her expression was gently apologetic and there was something shamefaced in the little smile with which she looked up at him. They did not speak about what they both knew he had seen there.

They talked about all sorts of things and then, prosaically enough, about the fact that they were both hungry.

'And there's nothing in the house because we were all going to eat at Margit's. This is awful,' Adrienne wailed in mock dismay.

Then Balint remembered the chestnuts which, though he had hardly known what he was doing, he had bought on that long lonely bitter walk the evening before. Finding his coat among the clothes he had strewn on the floor by Adrienne's bed, he searched in the pockets and found them and also the paper he had bought a little later.

'I've got this bag of chestnuts, but they're stone cold. Perhaps we could warm them up?'

'That'd take far too long, the fire's been out for ages,' said Adrienne, laughing. 'I'm so hungry! Let's have them as they are! They'll taste every bit as good.'

So as not to soil Adrienne's sheets with the chestnut peelings they used the newspaper as a tablecloth in the centre of the bed and leaning over from each side they tackled the long-cold nuts with gusto. As they did so Balint told how he had nearly knocked over the old woman who was roasting the chestnuts and how, automatically, he had bought the paper from the news vendor in the station square; and he related both tales as if they were unreal amusing anecdotes from a remote past which now hardly concerned them, indeed as if they had never really happened.

It was the same with all the suffering they had both endured during the past year and a half. The pain and bitterness and the torment they had both gone through all those months when Uzdy's incipient madness was slowly growing to its climax; the ultimate catastrophe of his complete breakdown; Adrienne's renunciation of their love and her decree that they must not see each other; and the seemingly endless days and nights of sorrow and self-recrimination that they had both suffered; all these things now vanished from their minds like the mists of early morning. Not only did they not think about it but they barely even wondered if there had ever really been any reason for the torture they had endured. They did not remember it because it no longer existed, because they were together again and at home in each other's arms, because they belonged to each other, a real couple, male and female of the same species, and because anything which did not concern them now was as unreal as a mere phantom.

So, together on the wide bed, he in her silken wrap and she with her nightdress slightly torn and slipping down over one shoulder, they fell on the sooty chestnuts with hungry delight.

'Wasn't it lucky you bought them!' said Addy.

## Chapter Two

When Karoly Khuen-Hedervary formed a new government in January, 1910, few people, and especially those who had been immersed in the fantasy world of Coalition politics, believed it would achieve any more than had its predecessors. Everywhere it was said that the new government would soon suffer the same fate as that of General Fejervary five years before for it was still believed that a government made up of people not in Parliament had no solid base and therefore would not stand the pace. Indeed so frosty was the lack of welcome with which it was received that when Khuen-Hedervary announced that Parliament was to be adjourned he was met with an immediate motion of 'No Confidence'.

But things had changed and the political climate in 1910 was not at all what it had been five years before. The public had become disillusioned and now there were not many who bothered themselves with anything so trivial as a change of government.

In 1905 such had been the general optimism that people had really believed that Hungary stood on the threshold of a new golden age. The resounding promises of reform and improvement which had been brandished as the election slogans of the parties forming the Coalition – as, for example, the separation of the army commands and the establishment of an independent Customs service – had everywhere been taken as if these goals had already been achieved or, if not exactly achieved, at the very least only temporarily delayed by the unpatriotic plots of their political opponents, that wicked *camarilla* whose sinister influence would be swept away as soon as the Coalition came to power. Few people had then paused to reflect that the trade unionists would never really co-operate with any other group and had only joined in the call to overthrow the existing government because they themselves had never expected to be called upon to face the realities of political power; nor that there were forces in the running of a great nation far greater and more complicated than were admitted in the seductive paragraphs of the radical press. It never occurred to the majority that the real national interest lay in the sound administration of agriculture, industry and commerce, in the defence of the realm and the maintenance of law and order; and in fair treatment of the ethnic minorities and the underprivileged. It was on how such matters were handled that the prestige of the Dual Monarchy and its position as a great power rested; and it was on Austria-Hungary's position as a great power that the continued prosperity of the individual depended. And yet, simple and logical as this proposition might have appeared, it still seemed beyond the grasp of the general public.

During the period of Fejervary's government the leaders of the Coalition began to grasp that their fight was hopeless because they had argued themselves into a totally false position. It was this that led to the famous *Pactum* between the radical coalitionists and the emperor.

And now they made their first great irremediable mistake: they declared publicly that the compromise was a triumph. This barefaced lie, like the principle of original sin, bedevilled the five years of their reign until, totally divided, quarrelling over every issue, accusing each other of ineptitude and incapacity, the Coalition ended in total fiasco. The general public, for once, grasped what had happened and withdrew its support, turning away with bored contempt. Khuen-Hedervary quickly grasped what was happening and cleverly turned the situation to his own advantage.

The new government's initial programme was intentionally, and wisely, colourless and confined itself to generalities. The only exception was a declaration of support for the idea of introducing universal suffrage, expressed only in the vaguest terms. Indeed the whole document was so imprecise that everyone, conservative or radical, could read into it support for anything they themselves desired.

The first real action taken was to correct some of the most glaring of the Coalition's mistakes. Rauch, the Ban of Croatia, whose rule had been so disastrous, was dismissed and the judgements in the Zagreb treason trial set aside. All prosecutions for sedition that were pending against representatives of the ethnic minorities were immediately abandoned.

The country started to breathe more easily as the consequences of the rash measures of the recent past were gently swept aside. It was all somewhat grey and colourless, but it was obvious that matters were being handled with simple common sense and so everyone began eagerly to prepare themselves for the inevitable general election. Such was the mood when Parliament was adjourned.

Everyone was content except for some members of the Independence Party who had brought forward a bizarre theory that as they had been elected to office and as the budget had not yet been voted, there could be no new elections. When Khuen-Hedervary rose to move the adjournment they made such a noise that no-one could hear a word he said.

Khuen remained standing at his desk and waited until the uproar died down, but as soon as he opened his mouth again the commotion raged once more. At last seeing no other solution, as this was likely to go on indefinitely, he decided to move closer to the stenographers so that they at least would be able to hear and take down a record of his words. Hardly had he stepped down from his place when some rebellious members sitting on the extreme left jumped up and started bombarding him with anything they could lay their hands on such as books, inkpots and paperknives. A heavy inkpot struck him on the forehead and blood poured down his face. Despite it all, and throughout this unexpected tempest, Khuen-Hedervary maintained his usual good-humoured calm.

This appalling scene scandalized the public, and even the party leaders of those who had behaved so badly condemned what had happened. The unruly members' excuse, which was published on the following day – namely that they had thought the Minister-President was moving from his rostrum to insult them personally – was believed by no-one. It was indeed absurd to imagine that one frail elderly man was about to tackle physically a group of several hundred able-bodied members sitting together on the benches at the extreme left-hand side of the Chamber. When, on December 13th, 1904, the same group, more or less, had attacked the security guards in the Chamber, the public had believed their tale not knowing, though the members had, that the guards had been expressly ordered not to retaliate if provoked. Now no-one credited this kind of fantasy. Everyone thought that, rather than try to excuse themselves, it would have been better and more dignified if they had admitted the fault and merely explained that they had been carried away in the passion of the moment. That at least would have been honest, or could have been taken as such, and might have suggested extenuating circumstances. As it was, all that happened was that the riotous members and their parties lost all respect; and the incident was not forgotten when the time came for the elections and the voters started to weigh up the Coalition's record.

The result was soon seen: barely a hundred candidates from the three main parties of the Coalition were elected to the new Parliament. On the other hand Khuen-Hedervary's supporters got a huge majority, and it was generally thought that now some constructive work could be begun.

Begun? Yes; but whether he would be able to achieve anything was another matter.

Obstruction, that cancer at the heart of all attempts to put through progressive measures in the Hungarian Parliament, which had paralysed successive administrations for the previous ten years and which had now become the habitual weapon used by the insubordinate left wing even against its own leadership, might well be used again to frustrate the new government. It could rise at any time, brandishing no matter what popular slogan, and it would always find support in that section of the press whose only allegiance seemed to be to the troublemakers. There were also other sources of possible weakness, less obvious, less familiar, but these lay hidden for the present from both the government's supporters and their political opponents.

The government announced that its first aim would be electoral reform. As this was only mentioned in outline everyone could declare their support, whether they wanted only minor changes or radical reform of the suffrage qualifications. Thus a substantial majority declared its support for the cabinet without anyone knowing which standpoint was the stronger even inside the government party. The Independence Party, as it had been for some time, was split in two. Kossuth and his followers took up a moderate stance while Justh led his splinter group so far to the left that a few months later they joined up with the socialists. It was this later move which led to that surprising situation when Tisza and Kossuth stood together on the same platform while the other wing of the government party, led by Laszlo Lukacs, made approaches to Justh and the left-wingers.

All this proved the old adage that where elections were concerned it was best to leave such important issues in as much uncertainty as possible.

It was also clear to some observers that one reason for Khuen not making any more precise declaration of his policy was that he had no wish to antagonize Tisza, for without him and his liberal party followers' support he would be bound to fail to obtain any reform at all. Khuen's over-riding purpose was to re-establish harmony between the King and the Parliament, the twin pillars of the Constitution, and to this end he subordinated any other consideration and welcomed to his side anyone who would serve his purpose, even if he was not otherwise an ally or supporter. And so was formed the 1910 Parliament which was the first one in many years not to be composed entirely of blinkered politicians blinded by their own unthinking allegiance either to the 1867 Compromise or to the independence principles of the Men of 1848; and which consequently was also the first Parliament to take notice of what was going on outside the Kingdom.

As the traditional party slogans had become anathema to many people a surprisingly large number of districts – thirty-one in all – voted for candidates free of any party commitments. This had never happened before. Another side effect was that many of the new members, though they belonged officially to one party or another, by no means always followed slavishly that party's official line. This was clear for all to see when it came to dealing with the project for electoral reform. It began at a conference of conservatives held in the Vigado building where Istvan Tisza and the extreme Independent Mihaly Karolyi were shown to hold the same opinions. On the same day the former Minister-President and Protestant leader, Dezso Banffy, met at the town hall with two pillars of the conservative party, Pal Sandor and Gyula Lanczy, and also with the Christian Democrat Giesswein and the democrats Vazsonyi and Jaszi, to agree their joint programme for a radical revision of the right to vote.

There was at this time another issue which transcended traditional party lines: this was the Transylvanian Movement. This had come into being as a result of a widespread feeling in Transylvania that its indi- vidual traditions and history, as well as its own very special spirit, had become less and less recognized, let alone respected, by the central gov- ernment in Budapest, who were all too apt to think of Transylvania as just one of a string of otherwise insignificant provinces. Nothing of its riches, either of historical achievement or individual culture, nor of its real problems, was accorded any real importance in the capital. The Transylvanian spirit was slowly being drained away in the maw of Hun- garian self-sufficiency and at best was ignored. So delicate, so subtle were Transylvania's real problems that it needed much knowledge and experience to know how to handle them. When the central government did interfere it did so with brutal indifference, usually doing more harm than good.

Balint Abady had seen this with growing concern and so was one of the founders of the movement whose aim was to encourage a better understanding and a more just treatment of his beloved homeland. He first drafted a programme and then in March started canvassing his ideas and whipping up support from his fellow Transylvanians, starting with Tisza himself in Budapest. Through the lawyer Timisan he tried to interest the Romanian minorities. In all this he deluded himself that he was only doing his duty, but the reality was, of course, that this plunging into work on behalf of Transylvania and immersing himself once more in the development of the Co-operative movements, was really for him little more than a narcotic taken to relieve the pain of his sorrow and self-torment.

Tisza, though sympathetic to Balint's ideas, still ordered his followers to hold aloof from the movement because it smacked too much of particularism. Tisza listened politely with his habitual quiet, somewhat derisive smile. He told Balint it was all very interesting ... but he didn't offer any support.

Balint, bitterly disappointed, had gone on with his self-chosen task, but without joy or hope, despite the fact that the first public meeting was not inauspicious.

The banner of the Transylvanian Movement was unfurled on March 12th at one of the principal hotels in Vasarhely.

Also present with Balint were the other original founders of the movement, Istvan Bethlen, Miklos Banffy, Zoltan Desy and Gyozo Issekutz as well as many others who attended without knowing in advance anything of what they were about to hear. Among them were many who were not native Transylvanians but who had come to represent districts in the province as a result of the peculiarly feverish atmosphere of the elections at the time of the Coalition.

Abady brought with him his detailed proposals for the movement's programme and in his speech he concentrated on three points: the forthcoming electoral reform, Transylvania's special commercial interests, and the many problems posed by the existence of the minorities.

The first two subjects met with little comment or opposition, but the third at once aroused all sorts of conflicting reactions. Balint wished to obtain support for a new law governing the rights of the minorities. At this point the representatives of the Szekler people started to demur, mostly those who were not of indigenous Szekler origin but who had come into Transylvanian politics from Budapest or the Great Plain, and who had been invited only because of their official positions. At once an acrimonious discussion started which threatened to get worse as Abady stood firmly by his proposition. Then Istvan Bethlen, who was presiding, decided to adjourn the meeting for a short while so as to give himself a chance to talk it over with Abady in private. Bethlen well understood the implications of what Balint had proposed and agreed with everything he had said. Nevertheless, seeing the mood of those who disagreed, he advised Balint to drop any specific details concerning the actual proposed law lest further discussion should bring about the disruption of the meeting and thus bring the movement to a halt before it had even got under way. He proposed that Abady's text should be allowed to stand as it was, in general terms, but that discussion of the details of the proposed minority law should be left until later, it being understood that when the movement was firmly established the matter could then be brought up again and the introduction of the law openly demanded.

Abady was reluctant to agree, but could see no alternative. As a result his amended speech was read at the general session of the conference which was held at the county headquarters the following day. His proposals were accepted unanimously by the thirty-odd delegates, who included Under-Secretaries of State, prefects, MPs and other elected officials in the presence of an exceptionally large audience. Everything of real importance was contained in the section of the speech entitled 'To all the Peoples of Transylvania'.

After a short introduction, during which he referred to the forthcoming elections, he said: 'Now is the time when we should all stand together, regardless of party, in all matters which affect our native land and which affect our peaceful existence now and in the future. It is time to put an end to that harmful situation where decisions affecting us are taken without our being consulted. That is all wrong. We no longer ask, we demand, that our special conditions should be taken into account in all lawmaking that concerns us. Finally we must have our say in all affairs that concern the well-being of our own homeland.

'This demand is justified historically. When Transylvania was made an integral part of the kingdom we surrendered unselfishly the autonomy we had known for centuries and refrained from imposing any conditions in return. We did not stop to worry about the possible loss of material or personal advantages which had been part and parcel of our inherited independence. But ... but this patriotic selflessness merits the *quid pro quo* that the central government should show as much special understanding, love and consideration for intrinsically Transylvanian matters as we would have shown ourselves. This is their moral obligation, but today there is no sign of it ... unfortunately.

'It is unfortunate, too, that with very few exceptions we have found ourselves treated as unwanted stepchildren so often are, disregarded, ignored, not worth bothering about! And if they do for once take a casual glance at the many complicated issues of which our society is composed, and the problems these entail, no-one tries to understand what it is all about.

'We suffer deeply from this indifference and ignorance. In particular we are forced to witness the degradation of our ethnic minorities, the destruction of our middle class and the continual recession in our industry and commerce.

'A national policy that is as uncaring as it is ignorant as regards our minority problems is now increasingly provoking dangerously irredentist and seditious tendencies, tendencies which can be justified as provoked by unfair treatment. We must say outright that for centuries in Transylvania people have lived happily together regardless of race or creed or language and that to do this we need more than manufactured opinions and slogans borrowed from other lands and other peoples. These merely inject poison into our system.

'With full knowledge of our own national circumstances, and in the interests of all Hungary, it is clear that we must eliminate those walls of mistrust which otherwise divide us. We must tear down those artificial barriers which separate our peoples; we must disregard all difference of language and religion, and above all we must strive to ensure that there is trust, mutual trust, between the ruler and the ruled. Everybody who is or wishes to be at home in this country must be welcomed and made to feel at home with confidence that nowhere will he find any form of discrimination, for that will never bring peace and ease and prosperity to our land. No administration can achieve anything without consultation and mutual trust.

'In making these considerations the basis for our demands we offer a friendly hand to anyone who, regardless of race or language or religion, desires to work for the peaceful evolution of our land.'

This ended what Balint had to say about the question of the minorities. Then he tackled the subject of economics.

'We demand that the central government fulfils its moral obligations towards us and that firstly this is shown by a just investment in Transylvania's cultural and material welfare. At present everything goes to Budapest and nothing comes back.

'Almost nothing is initiated nationally to encourage our commerce, though in the last ten years commissions dealing with Szekler and forestry matters have been notable exceptions. However, the artificial separation of our economy from that of the rest of the country has resulted in stagnation and idleness. All the profit of our rich mineral deposits, our mines, forests, power stations – as well as the accumulated receipts from high taxation – in no way returns home to benefit our own land or its inhabitants.

'It is time, therefore, to call an end to fruitless begging and dreary complaint. We must make it clear that only by acceding to our demands can the country safeguard the future of the average landowner and ensure that a prosperous middle class can be firmly established. For the prosperity of all we must encourage the building-up of small and medium-sized agricultural estates, regardless of the creed and nationality of the landowner. It is on this that the advancement of our social and cultural order depends and, above all, it is upon this that the life and dignity of our agricultural population depends. Our peoples must have the liberty and the right not only to work and earn their daily bread but also to own land and gain respect and prosperity as equal citizens of the same country.

'We must have our fair share of the implements of commerce and industry, and so we demand from the national railways, which until now have only served our country in a derisively feeble fashion, that services are introduced that are worthy of the real importance of our land. And we insist that central authority should back fully the development of our industrial potential.

'It is our duty to point out to all Transylvanians that it is in their interest, again regardless of race, language, creed or party, to join this movement. It is their duty, too, to do this now when we stand on the threshold of elections that can influence our entire future.'

Finally he spoke about electoral reform.

'At the forefront of all political activity stands the question of introducing a just system of voting rights for everyone.

'Admitting the rightness in principle of a system of universal suffrage and in no way wishing, even if we could, to hold up the process of emancipation, we must be careful to do nothing that could hinder the introduction of a law designed to broaden the basis on which we elect those whose function is to make our laws. At the same time we must raise our voices in protest if the chosen route seems to us to be wrong. To the whole nation we must then say that there is no progress if it is not done right, and if we disregard those dangers which would be inherent in any ill-considered legislation. Remember that once this reform has become a reality, it will be here to stay and will not easily be changed or modified. We must be on our guard to make no false steps.

'We cannot accept as a qualification for the right to vote any such simplistic formula as being able to read or write or speak Hungarian properly. This would be no valid criterion of either patriotism or the capacity to vote intelligently. Our conviction is that the coming law must first of all avoid any withdrawal of existing rights, which would only foster resentment and encourage old hatreds, and that secondly it must be based on a realistic approach to the rights of the individual, allowing him in all cases to be able to select those whose integrity, decency and patriotic spirit, and their political maturity, qualify them for a seat among the lawmakers.

'We must raise our voices in the cause of sanity and balance, and if we do object to any proposals we think ill-thought-out or immature, it must be that we do so only because our aim is peace and harmony in everything that affects the well-being of all and that we set our face against any legislation which appears to favour only a limited section of our society. In defending Hungarian sovereignty we are also defending the security of property and culture.'

Before coming to a close he listed the movement's aims and demands and then ended with a few resounding phrases.

'As individuals, scattered over the land, we will achieve nothing. Let us therefore unite, regardless of party loyalties and political conviction, to serve our country as best we may. Let the voters shake hands and stand together to serve those whom we elect to make our laws. And never forget, no matter under what banner you fight, that we are all successors to those worthy forebears whose role, whether eminent or obscure, played such a vital part, century after century, in keeping alive the honour and prestige of Transylvania!'*

---

* Translators' Note: The body of this speech encapsulates much of Miklós Bánffy's own first speech to Parliament made after the summer election of 1910 when he presented himself to the electorate as a candidate independent of all party ties. All his life, whether as a Member of Parliament, Minister for Foreign Affairs, or as a private citizen, Bánffy fought hard for the principles of honesty, decency, tolerance and co-operation between people of all creeds and classes, and above all justice and fair treatment for his beloved Transylvania. P.T. & K.B.-J.

# Chapter Three

These were the things that Balint was thinking about when, early in the afternoon, he started on his way back to Denestornya.

He was encouraged by the fact that so many had rallied behind his call for support for his proposed Transylvanian Movement. Of course it had only been a beginning, but it had been full of promise, and if every motion in Parliament that concerned Transylvania sparked off another meeting, another discussion, and another agreement, it would not be long before the movement became a force that no-one would be able to ignore. And this itself would have further and more widespread effects. Sitting upright behind the steering wheel Balint felt himself once more young and strong and full of hope. The car, as if catching some of its owner's happy mood, seemed to purr with joy and power as it started up the slope of the Felek.

As he drove Balint thought back to that time, more than a year before, when in the same car he had driven away from Denestornya after breaking off all relations with his mother because she would not accept his decision to marry Adrienne as soon as she could become free. Although he had been back several times since – for Countess Roza had forgiven her son as soon as she learned that Adrienne's divorce had become impossible since her husband had gone mad – almost immediately after Balint's visit to his cousins at Jablanka, then again in spring and in summer, and lastly a few days before when he had come from there to attend *Madam Butterfly* at the Kolozsvar Opera, this was the first time that he had felt he was really returning home. Previously there had been no joy in his visits and they had left no mark on him. He had gone back merely out of duty and habit, and he had never been able to throw off the leaden depression that stemmed from those agonized hours of sorrow and self-reproach.

Until this day everything he had done he had done automatically, but now he felt alive again, thinking with pleasure and eagerness of all the work that lay ahead for him. Now he made plans, fantastic plans, involving ever more work and more responsibility. Such was the effect of his rediscovery and repossession of Adrienne.

Work, more work! He felt he could tackle anything.

The previous spring he had been asked to accept the chairmanship of the Consumers' Council. Then he had hesitated and the question had been left in suspense. Now he decided to accept, but only for Transylvania, and his mind was soon busy thinking out the innovations he would propose and how he would try to improve the range and quality of the goods offered at country markets. He remembered seeing wide-bladed scythes in Holland, similar, he thought, to those in use in Tyrol. Perhaps these could be imported through the Co-operatives? He would introduce new and improved seeds, such as peas ... and maybe soya beans. This would all have to be discussed with the agricultural experts so as to be sure of suggesting what would be most likely to succeed and which would prove the most beneficial: he would have to ask Aron Kozma who understood so well the needs and tricky moods of the village folk.

Where, he wondered, would he find Kozma now? And then he remembered the hunting at Zsuk which had just started and decided he would go himself, which he had not been able to do for the last year because if he had gone to Kolozsvar there had always been the risk of meeting Adrienne. Of course he could then have stayed at the Hunt Club residence at Zsuk, but he had not been in the mood even though his mother had offered him the best horses in the Denestornya stables. While he had been in that black depression nothing had seemed worth doing, but now everything was changed. He could go where he liked. Everything was wonderful and full of beauty and the promise of joy and pleasure. Life was once again full of delights. Why, he would ride every day and every evening he would go back to town ... and every night ...

Already he started to choose which horses he would take with him – Handsome, of course, and Ivy – and which other? Menyet was promising enough, but at only four she was still rather young. Perhaps Csalma, who was sound and rather slow-moving, but all the same reliable. He would have to think it all out and discuss it later.

So ideas tumbled over themselves in his brain and he was filled with hope and new ideas and expectations. By now he was almost over the last pass of the Felek, which the carters had nicknamed the Horse-killer, and started descending a slope bordered by a few scattered houses.

Then, unexpectedly, he had to brake and bring the car to a stop.

A huge flock of sheep blocked the entire road. There were so many that Balint thought there must be between five hundred and a thousand, and this meant that he would have to wait for some time before he could go on. He knew well that sheep would never get out of the way but would just crowd together behind the leading ram, and that the leading ram would not move unless the shepherd was walking ahead. Also there was nowhere else for them to go, for the road through the village was bordered by solid fences, in addition to which it was a steep downhill slope, and the shepherd boys, knowing that anything that frightened the flock would probably make them panic and that some might get trampled to death if there was a stampede, called hurriedly to Balint, 'Stey, Domnule! Stey! – Stop, Master, stop!'

Balint did as he was asked and switched off the engine because he realized at once that it would take some time before the sheep could be got through the village and out into some meadow. It was not unknown for it to take nearly a day for a really large flock to cover only a mile or so, which, reflected Balint, just showed that they were not altogether stupid if instinct prevented them from damaging their hooves. And yet it was not always so for those mountain-bred animals were tough and resilient and could be made to move more swiftly when they were on their way to market. Now that they were being taken from one grazing ground to another the leading ram swayed gently from one foot to another almost as if he were performing some slow dance movement while the rest of the flock munched unhurriedly as they went. Some owners used to take advantage of this by renting summer and winter grazing grounds some two or three hundred kilometres apart and for the two or three weeks that it took to go from one to the other the flock fed gratis at the side of the road.

And so Balint was forced to wait; and on this occasion he did not even feel mildly put out or impatient but called back at once: 'Don't hurry! Take it slowly! Slowly!', for his heart was filled with love for everyone including the dirt-covered shepherds who never changed their clothing for weeks on end, the evil-smelling, greasy sheep flowing like a slow river before him, the dogs filling in the rear and the old donkey, heavily laden with the milking cans and the shepherds' few belongings. All this is part of our birthright, he said to himself, it belongs to us and to us alone, for strange though it may be, it is one of the peculiarities of our land and is different from any other.

When the road was finally clear Balint stepped on the pedal and went on his way past woods and forests bright with the golden, copper and saffron colours of autumn and water meadows still vividly green.

41

Everything seemed beautiful to him, even the occasional bare clay hillside which shone brightly in the late afternoon sunlight. Deeply he inhaled the air that blew so strongly in his face as the car raced homewards.

Just before he reached the village of Also-Bukkos he noticed a man on a horse just turning onto the main road from a track that led from a nearby valley. It was Gazsi Kadacsay whose own property was not far away. Balint was astonished to see him for Gazsi had never been known to miss a day's hunting and the season at Zsuk had already begun. He braked and called out:

'Servus, Gazsi – greetings! What are you doing at home at this time? Surely the hunt can't do without you?'

Gazsi cantered up to the car, and when he spoke it was with unusual seriousness, quite different from his habitual joking manner.

'That's just a lot of nonsense, my fr-r-riend. They can do very well without me.'

Then he went on hurriedly as if wanting to change the subject.

'Are you on your way to Denestornya? If you are going to be there a little while I'll r-r-ride over to see you. There's something I'd like to talk over with you.'

'Come whenever you like, my mother is always pleased to see you … and me too, I want your advice on which horses to take to Zsuk this year.'

'Hor-r-rses! Of course, always hor-r-rses!' Gazsi spoke bitterly, and smiled in a strange manner, bending his head sideways so that his long nose once more resembled the beak of some disconsolate bird of prey. 'But I can't come right away as I must go to my sister's at Szilagy for some family business. Can I come in four or five days? It won't be too far ahead?'

'Of course not, I'll expect you.'

They exchanged a few more words and then Kadacsay, calling out 'Servus!', turned his old saddle horse away and moved slowly off.

Balint drove on wondering at the change in his old friend and fancying that maybe he had some money troubles which would explain why he had seemed so gloomy. A few moments later he had forgotten all about it for he himself was so filled with joy and happiness that the possible troubles of other people could not touch him.

*

Roza Abady sat on a little bench in the great horseshoe-shaped court in front of the stables at Denestornya. Five colts had been selected as the best of that year's products and it was now, in autumn, that she always decided which should be paired off to go into harness and which would be reserved for riding. All the horses would soon go into winter quarters but whereas the saddle horses would wait until the spring before their training began, Countess Abady believed in starting to teach the future carriage horses as early as possible when they would be at their most responsive. She knew that no harm would come to them if their first lessons were sufficiently light and steady and no weight was put on their backs. On the other hand it was important to build up the tendons and leg muscles by carefully controlled road work. At her right stood Simon Jager, the chief stable lad. He was a short man of about fifty who stood very straight as if he were sitting on a horse, his bowed legs slightly apart. He had served in the Hussars some thirty years before and he still wore a short pointed waxed moustache. His cheeks were smooth and red and, though he came of peasant stock, his feet were unusually small. He was the owner of his own land, an estate of some twenty acres, but he still took pride in working for Countess Roza at Denestornya – 'at Court' as the local people would say among themselves – not only because it gave him much prestige in the village but also because he loved doing it. His father and grandfather had done the same before him, and his great-grandfather had been head keeper to that Abady who had been governor of Transylvania. And that is how he had acquired his name, as *Jäger* was the German word for a sporting estate's professional keeper. And so it had been passed from father to son at a time when many peasant families did not use surnames.

On the left of the countess was Gergely Szakacs (whose name meant 'cook') who had been chief stable lad before Simon, who was twenty years his junior. He too came from the same district and though he was now pensioned off Countess Roza always liked to have him at her side on these occasions for she much appreciated his knowledge and judgement. He came willingly (even though his pension had been paid somewhat haphazardly when the lawyer Azbej had managed the Abady estate office) for he loved his old mistress whom he knew to be good-hearted, and had been too proud to complain. Also he did not really need the pension money because in the course of a lifetime's hard work he too had put some capital aside and owned a good house of his own.

43

All the Szakacs had been tall and good-looking and this one had been no exception. Now he was somewhat bent and walked with a stick, but he was still a distinguished figure, with short-cut hair and well-trimmed beard, and had an air of authority which suited his position as one of the pillars of the Protestant church.

Despite the fact that she herself was as expert as any of them, Countess Roza always liked to have these two with her when these important decisions had to be made. Jager and Szakacs could voice opinions without being asked, but Feri Rigo, the head coachman who was also always present, could only speak up when appealed to. At present he was standing some ten paces away and passing on his employer's instructions to the other lads who were walking and trotting the young horses.

The selection took a long time and finally there were just three colts from which the pair had to be chosen. Countess Roza asked for two of them to be walked up until they were side by side facing where she was sitting, as that was how they would appear when in harness as a pair.

Roza Abady looked at them for a few moments in silence. Then she rose and walked all round them with her two companions close behind. The young horses stood quite still, not moving until she got close to their heads when both stretched out their necks expecting to be given lumps of sugar; but as today was one of decision and not of cosseting, none was forthcoming. Back went their ears in disappointment. At last she spoke:

'They are very much alike, but I fancy this one is just a trifle shorter. Young Simon, please bring me the measuring stick!' She still called him 'Young Simon' – though as chief lad he was addressed as 'sir' by everyone else – just as she had thirty-five years ago when he had been a little stable boy and she had been almost grown up. Apart from this she had never used the familiar form of address after he had been promoted.

'I have measured him already, my lady … when he was brought in. He is two centimetres shorter, but he comes from a line that has always developed slowly and I'm sure that in a year or two's time he will have caught up and then they'll be just the same.'

'We should still try him beside the Merges filly,' suggested old Szakacs, waving to the lads to bring up the third choice whose name was 'Mandula'. Taking the halter he said, *'Komelo'* – a strange word that for most people held no meaning.

Many years before Szakacs had gone to England with Countess Roza's father who had wanted to find a thoroughbred stallion to improve the breed in Transylvania. There he had learned many things including the English way of strapping the horses with only one hand – though putting the whole body's weight behind it – the use of flannel bandages, how to make a bran mash and what was meant by 'blistering'. He also learned a few stable commands in English, though they became somewhat tangled when he tried to use them himself. But the stable lads, and the horses, soon understood what was expected of them; and now Mandula stepped smartly forward as if she already knew that *Komelo* meant 'Come along!'

Again they looked for a long time at the three possible choices and, as in all long-established studs where the breeding followed a set pattern, there was really very little to choose between them, and any one would have been a splendid match with either of the others. Finally Countess Roza turned to the coachman, Feri, and asked what he thought.

'If your ladyship pleases, I would be happy with any of them; still I rather think that Csujtar's trot is the longer and that he would therefore be better for carriage work.'

Simon Jager's eyes shone: 'Mandula would look well with our other hunters', he said. And in so speaking of the horses as 'ours' he was doing what everyone employed at Denestornya always had. Everything about the great castle and the estate was known, even to the youngest and humblest stable lads, as 'ours', in the first person plural, in *pluralis majesteticus* – the royal 'we'.

They would say: this is 'our' lucerne, 'our' oats, 'our' meadows, mares and stallions, 'our' cattle, oxen and donkeys. Everyone used this majestic 'we' and 'our', from the great heights of the butler and the chief stud groom, through the footmen, barn and storekeepers, huntsmen, gardeners, cooks, estate mechanics and smiths, down to the humblest scullery maid or stable boy. 'Our' carriages, 'our' farm carts, 'our' pots and 'our' pans. It was even used of the Denestornya wildlife – 'our' deer, 'our' hares, 'our' pheasants – exactly as if it belonged to them, which in a very real sense it did, for they were intensely proud of Denestornya and everything about it as if they were in reality the owners of an estate which had no rival in the entire world.

This spirit had crystallized through many, many generations, for there was hardly a single family in the village some of whose members had not, at one time or another, done their stint 'at Court'; and none who had not been the better for it, not only because everything was 'found' for those who were in the Abady employ and so those who had any money of their own could save it. Likewise if any of them thought to build, for example, a house on their own land (for nearly all the peasant families owned some land) they were freely given all the wood or quarried stone they needed. If a pig died it was replaced from the estate farms, and no-one worried about sickness or old age, either for themselves or their families, because the 'masters' would take care to see that everything was provided. Not that anyone had, or needed, a contract, for all these things were taken for granted. A man had only to ask, and he was given as soon as he had spoken to the 'master' and explained his problem. The deep feeling of unity in the little village near the castle, the community spirit and the general feeling of goodwill and fellowship, sprang directly from these ancient traditions. As a result hardly any so-called 'foreigner' – which meant anyone from any other district, however close it might be – ever stayed long in the castle service. The only exceptions at that time were Countess Roza's two housekeepers, who had come to her in her lonely widowhood, and who had then so ingratiated themselves with their mistress. As it was, both Mrs Baczo and Mrs Tothy were loathed and feared by the other servants, who resented the fact that the two women would always tell her whatever they might wish her to believe.

The decision had almost been taken to return Mandula to the stud to be trained later as a saddle horse, while the other two would be paired off for carriage work, when Countess Roza decided to take one more close look at them all. She rose and started to walk round them again when a loud blast from a car horn was heard from outside the horseshoe court and, almost before the countess had time to look up, her son's car came rushing through the great gates.

At the sight of the little group and the three young horses Balint slammed on the brakes, stopped the car and jumped out so quickly that it almost seemed as if he was rushing towards her before the car had stopped.

At once Countess Roza understood that something extraordinary had happened to her son, for it was a long time since he had seemed so young and happy and active. Here was a complete contrast to the sad and listless figure he had been for so long and, though she could not know what it was, she was sure that there was something and was determined to find out the reason. She peered at him with slightly screwed-up eyes, as she did when carefully examining her young horses, though by the time he reached her side she gave no sign that she had noticed any change in him. At once she started to tell him what she had just been doing and to ask his opinion, not that she really needed anything but his approval of the decisions she had already made. Nevertheless she went through the motions of asking a number of unnecessary questions and appearing to weigh up, once more, the arguments and reasoning which had led to her deciding to make a saddle horse of the Merges filly and send the other two for carriage-training. Then mother and son walked back together to the castle door ... and all the while she was keeping the talk going as long as she could so as to give her more time to look into his eyes and study his expression. There certainly was a difference, but what had caused the change she could only wonder.

Tea had been laid on the covered veranda outside the big first-floor drawing room in the west wing.

For the countess only coffee and buffalo milk was served, but as Balint had just arrived the housekeepers quickly put out a full spread of cold meats, hot bread, sweet and savoury cakes, freshly churned butter so rich that it was practically melting on its silver dish, honey in the comb, quince jelly and three different sorts of jam. As if this were not more than enough Mrs Tothy and Mrs Baczo reappeared every few minutes carrying in more covered dishes of hot cakes and doughnuts straight from the oven, fritters, muffins and scones; and then they stood silently to one side with huge smiles on their fat little faces as the son of the house fell on the unexpected repast with the appetite of a wolf.

Countess Roza watched it all with a secret smile that could hardly have been detected by anyone else, casting covert glances at her son's expression as he devoured dish after dish. Not that she asked anything about what she most wanted to know, for she knew better than that. Instead she kept up a flow of small talk, recounting what had happened at home during the five days since her son had gone to the opera in Kolozsvar. Holes had been dug in the orchard where they had planned to put in some seedling fruit trees; that morning there had been some early frost, but only on the lower meadows near the river; the young footman Sandor had announced that he would soon be getting married; and that very same morning they had heard a fallow buck calling from some way off in the park. And with every little tale that she told Countess Roza was wondering: what has happened? What could have happened to put him in such a good humour all of a sudden? And what could she do to find out?

By now the sun was beginning to set. The peaks of the Jara mountains turned slowly to purple and the sky above was streaked with orange and deep carmine. Here and there thin vaporous clouds were to be seen, and through them the rays from the sinking sun soared high above etching great lines of fire on the brilliant green and pale blue of the darkening heavens. The edges of the few clouds were ringed with a rosy fire and it seemed as if the whole world were bathed in a golden light that reached all around them, penetrating even the dark entrance to the Torda gorge, casting a soft glow over the distant grasslands of the Keresztes plain and on the nearby riverbanks, and even into the deepest recesses of the wide glazed veranda.

Blinking slightly at all this brightness Countess Roza at last tried a more direct approach. Brightly, but still carefully, she said:

'But you haven't told me about the opera! How was the *Madam Butterfly*? Was it well done? Was it as beautiful as everyone expected?'

Balint gave a few banal replies saying that, oh yes, it had been lovely, very grand, very beautiful. 'And the French singer?'

'Excellent. Really beautiful! Superb!'

All these answers, despite their superlatives, he gave somewhat hurriedly without offering a single phrase to explain what he meant or justify his praise. It seemed that for some reason of his own he did not want to be forced into giving details and, as this was so unlike her son, who never had any difficulty in expressing himself with ease and fluency and whose descriptions of what he had heard or seen were usually vivid and to the point, Countess Roza realized at once that she was on the right track and that if something had happened at the opera she would have to feel her way with caution if she were to find out what it was.

'They tell me it's a most dramatic piece. What part did you find the most exciting, the most touching? How was the entr'acte before the last act?' Having read the newspaper articles – which Balint had missed – it was soon obvious to her that she knew more about the tragic love of Cio-Cio-San for Lieutenant Pinkerton than did her son, who did not seem at all familiar with anything except the long first-act love duet, for it was to that that he always returned whatever she might ask him about the rest of the work. And then he started to peel an apple and seemed so absorbed in so doing that it seemed to her better to let the subject drop.

Knowing her son so well Countess Roza thought it would be better not to insist any more. One more question, however, she did ask. She wanted to know if he had seen any of their friends at the theatre, and so learned that Margit Miloth and her husband had been in the Gyala-kuthy box next to the Abadys; and, though Balint said nothing about Adrienne, his manner was suddenly so awkward and constrained that his mother quickly decided to change the subject, not bringing the matter up again, and then only with great circumspection, until they were seated at dinner that evening.

She reached the subject in the most roundabout manner, as was her way. First of all she talked about the hunting at Zsuk. Then she asked which families had brought out debutante girls that season, and asked if the autumn social life in Kolozsvar was as lively and amusing as it usually was when the hunt season began. She wanted to know who had opened their town houses and who was going to give balls and dinners; and in this way she eventually arrived at her destination, which was to ask about the prefect's supper party. Now she discovered her first important fact: Balint had had a headache and had not attended. He had been sorry to miss the occasion for he would have liked to have met the diva and seen so many of their friends, but it had been a rotten sort of migraine and he hadn't felt up to it, admitting for the first time that he hadn't even stayed until the end of the performance. Perhaps, he said, thinking no doubt that it was quite an adequate excuse, he had been rather vague about it when they had discussed his doings over tea that afternoon.

In fact the inadequacy of the excuse was just what Countess Roza wanted to hear, for it immediately gave her a clue as to what had really happened. It was clear to her now that her son had met someone at the theatre, and it was for this person's sake that he had left early and for whom he had failed to go to the party. It could only have been Adrienne; and Countess Roza knew it as surely as if he had spelled it out.

For a moment her old anger flared up once again. That woman! That accursed woman! But then her wrath dissolved again almost as quickly as it had appeared.

For twelve long, miserable months after she had forbidden Balint to come home to Denestornya, Countess Abady had sat alone in her great house; and even after her son had been allowed back he had been so gloomy, so distracted, so totally uninterested in everything in which he had formerly taken such pleasure and so listless, that it had been like living with a ghost. Every time that she had looked at her son's weary face her heart had constricted and, though she never for a moment thought that she had acted in anything but his best interests – and, of course, to preserve the family's prestige and honour – it had been a daily sorrow to see him so heartbroken. Only now, this very day, had he been his old self again, young and cheerful and filled with hope and the joy of being alive. She hadn't seen him like that for so long, oh, so long; and her joy and thankfulness for his being restored to his old self prevented her from analysing the reasons too carefully lest they should be too difficult to accept. Nor for a moment did she question the rightness of her royal decree – however arrogant and tyrannical it might have been – but she now realized that since he could never marry that woman, since he could never bring her to enjoy the Abady house and inheritance, what did it matter if by seeing her he could be made happy once more? Of course it would mean that a proper acceptable marriage for him would now be put off for a few more years, but she could accept that as the price for once more seeing peace and happiness in his face. It only took her a moment to think this out and accept the situation for what it was and so she quickly stopped asking any more awkward questions. Without appearing to have noticed her son's hesitation and embarrassment she switched smoothly to less controversial subjects.

'Tell me about those two daughters of Laszlo Gyeroffy's old guardian, Stanislo. Do they have red-blonde hair like their father's famous wig? And the second Kamuthy girl – I suppose those are the new ones this year – is she as roly-poly as her brother or is she like her elder sister?' Balint, now alive and unconstrained again, did his best to imitate those moonfaced, simple-minded girls and was so successful that Countess Roza roared with laughter and even called upon the two fat housekeepers who sat in silence at the end of the table to do the same and agree with her delighted applause.

'Yes, indeed!' said one, and the other echoed, 'Indeed, yes!'

Recently these two had tried their best to ingratiate themselves with Balint. Their old ally and supporter, the rascally lawyer Azbej who for so long had managed Countess Abady's affairs, was no longer there since he had not long before resigned from acting as her agent. The little

50

lawyer was no fool and, as soon as Countess Roza had made peace with her son, he realized that if he were not very careful the young master would soon find out many things Azbej would rather remained hidden; and that he would then be called to account without mercy. It was better, he thought, to go before this could happen and so, during the previous winter, he had made the journey to Abbazia where the mistress was spending the cold season and told her that family matters of his own obliged him to leave her service. The explanation he gave was that, with the principal motive of doing a service to the countess's noble family, he had bought Laszlo Gyeroffy's estate of Szamos-Kozard (which, of course, no-one else would have bought) and to do so he had used his wife's money. Now he would have to give up everything else in order to be free to run the place. Of course it had all been done only to serve the interests of the gracious countess's most illustrious family. He took with him a sheaf of impressive-looking accounts and a carefully worded dispensation which only required the gracious countess's signature. This obtained he went on his way and the gracious countess herself had said how sorry she was to see him go.

With Azbej's departure Mrs Baczo and Mrs Tothy at once lost that precious ally with whose protection they had been enabled to lord it over Countess Roza's household. They knew that the other servants detested them both, knowing what advantages they had gained from their privileged position and how much they had been able to profit by it. Now they needed a new protector, and both thought they could do no better than to get the young master on their side. Only he would be able to protect them if their mistress, or even he himself, somehow got wind of what they had been up to for so long; and so they worked it out that, if they paid their court well and pleased him and somehow earned his approval, then he would be less inclined to start looking into how they had run the kitchens and stillrooms and asking why the bills for butcher's meat, sugar, coffee and cooking fat had been so high.

It was true that since his return the young master had shown no sign of being interested in anything, let alone such awkward matters as household expenses. When Azbej had first left and Balint had come home nearly everyone employed at Denestornya had one great fear. The estate foremen, the farming tenants and many others had all been guilty of persistent falsification of their accounts which Azbej had overlooked because, if he protected them, they in turn would say nothing about his own even more profitable thieving: now they were all scared to death that Count Balint would at once put his nose into everything. But it hadn't happened: Count Balint did nothing. It was the same with the administration of the forest holdings in which he had formerly taken such a deep personal interest. He came, he went. He had looked around and dealt without joy with whatever was put in front of him. He had made a few enquiries, but had initiated nothing new and indeed treated everything with the same listless indifference.

While at home at Denestornya Balint, as he never had before, went to bed late and got up late. For days on end he would hardly leave the house, not even to go out riding, but would sit for hours reading some book or other.

But from the day he returned to find his mother with her beloved horses in the horseshoe court, all was different. At dawn the next morning he rode out with Simon Jager and jumped all the fences in the paddock. At midday it was with happiness in his voice that he told his mother that for the first time that year he himself had heard the fallow deer calling in that thicket in the park they called Magyaros; and then he told her that he wanted to go to Zsuk for the hunting and wondered if she would let him have three of their good hunters.

'But of course I will,' she cried, delighted. 'You don't have to ask! Do whatever you like! Take whichever you like! They're all yours, you know!'

This was no more than Balint had expected. He had known exactly what his mother would say, almost word for word, yet he knew she would have been offended if he had omitted to ask. To play the fairy godmother, to give presents, hand over precious possessions, particularly to her son, was for the Countess Roza one of the great pleasures in life. It was a part she liked to play, and yet it was not really a part as in the theatre but a genuine side of her character. That is how she felt; and the fact of being asked was as important to her as the giving. Had she not been asked, it would have been taken as an affront to her natural goodness and as an unjustified liberty; for no-one must ever forget that everything was hers and that everything depended on her wishes.

Balint went on to mention that Baron Gazsi would shortly be paying them a visit and also that he would like to invite over the young Aron Kozma as he wanted to discuss Co-operative matters with him.

Countess Roza looked up at her son with interest.

'Which Kozma is that?' she asked. 'Does he come from the prairie lands?' and, when Balint confirmed that that was so, she went on: 'What sort of age is he? What was his father's name?'

'He is the eldest son of Boldizsar, and he has his own land near Teke,' said Balint, who went on to explain what advanced and successful landowners the Kozmas had become and how both generations, the father's and sons', had all turned out to be serious and hard-working and progressive.

The old lady appeared to be paying attention to everything Balint told her, but when she spoke it was obvious that she was really only interested in the first thing he had said.

'So this one is Boldizsar's eldest boy, is he? Boldizsar was the middle one of five brothers and they all grew up here, at Denestornya. Their father was our agent when I was a child, and I knew them all well and used to play with the younger ones. Well! Well! Well! Invite him, do!' She paused for a moment and then went on, with a little smile at her own private memories, saying, 'Invite him, but tell him to wire and say when he is coming. I'll need to have the heating put on in the guest rooms in plenty of time.'

'It isn't cold yet, Mama.'

'It doesn't signify. The weather might change any day and ... it is better to know in advance.'

It did not occur to Balint that his mother had had no such qualms when told of Gazsi's visit.

## Chapter Four

Five days later Gazsi arrived, riding his thoroughbred mare Honeydew, who was now so changed that it was hard to believe that it was the same animal who a couple of years before, had been the terror of all the jockeys on the track. Now she seemed as quiet as the old spotted farm donkey, though it was true that she allowed no-one but Gazsi on her back.

'I had to r-r-ride over,' said Gazsi apologetically, 'because Honeydew needed the work. Actually I would far rather have dr-r-riven and then I could have brought a suitcase with me. But no-one else can even walk this beast and only the other day, when I went to my sister's, she kicked the young stable boy in the belly. It's r-r-real slavery, looking after this one,' he said as he dismounted in the horseshoe court, and he bent his head sideways and looked plaintively at Balint as he always did when making a tragi-comedy of whatever he was doing. This time, however, Balint sensed that he was not joking for he seemed unusually serious and went on to say something quite out of the usual for him: he spoke of his clothes.

'I know I oughtn't to pr-r-resent myself to Aunt Roza looking like this,' he said, 'so scr-r-ruffy and unkempt, but I have brought something to change into in my saddle bag. But you can't get much in, I'm afraid.'

'Really, Gazsi,' said Balint, 'that doesn't matter for you! Why, my mother's quite used to receiving you booted and spurred.'

'Of course, of course! Who would expect anything else from a peasant like me?' and he sounded so bitter that Balint instantly regretted speaking as he had.

As it happened the saddle bag produced a sort of dinner jacket which had been made by a tailor in Torda. Though his shirt was wrinkled and his collar worn, when he presented himself at the dinner table, Gazsi looked tolerably presentable, indeed almost European. He had obviously made an effort to look civilized, hopeless though his case might be, and he wore an unusually serious air.

Later that evening, when the two young men had drunk tea and eaten some stewed apples with Countess Roza in her little first-floor drawing room, Balint escorted his guest back through the huge empty dining hall and down the stairs to the ground floor. They did not speak, for Balint had already noticed how unusually silent and preoccupied his guest had been, both at dinner and afterwards. It is true that he had told a number of amusing tales, in his usual wry, self-mocking humorous way; how he fell into the water while chasing an otter and how the beast just sat on the shore laughing at him; about the guard dog at a vineyard who was tethered by a long wire and how he had stood still while the dog ran circles around him until it was he who was tethered – and then the dog had bitten him; and several others of the same sort, all clownishly acted out for the amusement of his hosts. Even so Abady sensed that he was going through the motions of being his normal self while his heart was not really in it. He had noticed that each time Gazsi paused for a moment a slight frown appeared on his forehead, suggesting that the same dark thought had once more taken possession of him. Balint wondered what on earth could be the matter and became increasingly worried, waiting for his guest to tell him what it was. At last he did. When they reached the foot of the stairs, Gazsi turned aside and said, 'I'd like to talk something over with you. Can we ...?' and stopped.

'Better come to me,' said Balint. 'The servants will soon be round to take away the lamps as my mother doesn't like to keep them up late. I'll give you a candle to get back to your room.' They turned and crossed the entrance hall, and as they did so they could see the lights on the floor above going out, one after the other, until finally one solitary glimmer could be seen moving slowly along until it too disappeared behind an arch and was seen no more.

Soon the two young men were seated facing each other at the table in Balint's circular ground-floor room in the castle's north-west tower. A small reading lamp cast a glow between them, but the rest of the room was in darkness.

Kadacsay hesitated for a moment before starting to speak. Looking now more than ever like a raven with his beak tilted slightly to one side, he seemed to be looking hard at the armrest of his chair as if he would get inspiration from it. Then, speaking slowly with long pauses between each phrase as if to underline that he was choosing his words with extra care, he said, 'I have just made my will ... Yes, my will. It seemed the r-r-right thing to do ... now ... and that is why I came to see you, to ask ... to ask you to agr-r-ree to be my executor-r-r ...'

Balint found this sinister and upsetting. The fate of his own father flashed through his mind, for Count Tamas Abady had developed cancer when he was hardly older than Gazsi was today, and had died within a few months. Had this happened to his friend? Was this why he had seemed so sad and preoccupied? So, trying to hide his concern, he interrupted Gazsi, saying, 'You're not ill, Gazsi? If anything is worrying you I hope you've seen a doctor?'

'No, no! I'm all r-r-right ... as good as ever-r-r, I just thought it seemed sensible to ... to be pr-r-repared, to be r-r-ready ... just in case ... in plenty of time ...'

Then he went on to tell Balint exactly how all his affairs stood and that he had settled everything with his sister when he had been over to see her a few days before. He explained all about what his property brought in, with detailed facts and figures, and told Balint that he had settled all those small debts he had incurred when still in the Hussars so that all that now remained was the disposal of his family inheritance.

'For Heaven's sake, what makes you think of death when you're still so young and healthy?' broke in Balint again, now somewhat irritated by such gloomy thoughts when he himself felt so happy.

'Does everything have to have a reason?' asked the other, and smiled quizzically. 'Perhaps one day my darling Honeydew will go a little cr-r-razy again, throw me and then r-r-roll all over me? Who knows, she killed a jockey like that once! R-r-rather a suitable death for me, don't you think? After all, everyone knows I only know about horses. Anyhow, why be frightened of death? Didn't Schopenhauer say something about it being only our will to live which makes us scared of death and that it was a purely animal reaction? Or perhaps I've got it wr-r-rong …?' and he waved his hand in a gesture of mock dejection before laughing briefly. Then, far more seriously, he went on to tell Balint that he had decided to leave everything he could to his sister's two sons on one condition. That was that each of them, before he came into his inheritance, must spend at least two years at some university abroad, in England or in France, and that it would be Balint's responsibility to choose where. If they didn't agree they were to get nothing. 'I'm determined,' he said, 'that they shan't turn out to be useless fools like me!'

Touched by what he was hearing, Balint listened hard to everything that Gazsi had to say; and all the time he was thinking how tormented his old friend must have been, and how for years he must have lived with this inner turmoil and so now was doing the only thing he could to provide for his nephews what he had yearned for in vain for himself. Later he would remember one or two especially poignant things that Gazsi had said about himself, about his unfulfilled hunger for knowledge and self-understanding, and how this hunger had led him to grab eagerly at any book he could lay his hands on, especially those on history and the modern school of German philosophy. In this way, it seemed, he had tried hard to compensate for years spent only in the saddle and in playing the fool.

'Of course I'll do what you ask,' said Balint. 'I'm flattered that you should have that sort of faith in me. All the same it's not very likely that

I'll have to put my oar in. You'll probably live for years and send the boys to England yourself ... and any others who are not yet born!'

Gazsi got up, laughing as he said, 'Even Habakkuk got a r-r-rude answer when he asked the Lord about the future!' and, so as to cover his deep emotion at Balint's ready acceptance, he laughed loudly at his own irreverence. Then he took Balint's hand, wrung it warmly, holding it in his for a little longer than usual, in the way that one does when saying goodbye.

At eight o'clock the following morning they went out riding; not before, because at that time of year the dawn was invariably followed by a thick fog on the flat land beside the Aranyos which was where Balint wanted to go to try out the young horses. Since Gazsi had brought Honeydew, who had been ridden in several first-class flat races, they were only going to try short distances so that the novices from the Denestornya stable could keep up with the experienced thoroughbred mare.

Five horses had been saddled and were waiting for them in the horse-shoe court. Apart from Honeydew, there were Csinos and Ivy with Balint's own saddles, and Menyet and Csalma with the stable lads. All four were very much alike, tall bay mares, about sixteen hands, with long elegant necks, wide shoulders and 'a lot of ground under them'. The only difference between them was that one was a shade darker and one a shade lighter than the others, and if Honeydew with her fine bones and pulled-up belly like a greyhound had not been in sight – she was being held slightly apart from the others in case she should take it into her head to start kicking out – they too might have been taken for English thoroughbreds with those unmistakable lines of the true racehorse.

The little band of riders walked slowly out through the great gates of the courtyard, Balint and Gazsi side by side in the lead – though Gazsi prudently held Honeydew a pace or two behind because the mare was already beginning to put her ears back and he needed to be careful to control her uncertain temper – while Simon Jager and two stable lads followed a couple of lengths behind them. The hoofbeats echoed loudly as they rode under the wide arch.

After crossing the bridge that spanned the former moat they turned left towards the river. Below them most of the wide valley was still covered in wave after wave of thin mist, so diaphanous that it might have been made from the torn remnants of some giant shawl of soft cotton. It spread over the whole plain far beyond the junction with the Maros and, wherever the sun's rays had been strongest, glimpses could be caught of the trees and meadows beneath. In some places, where the plantations were thickest, the park could clearly be seen, but in others thin wisps of early mist still clung to the tips of the tallest poplars until the tiny patches of autumn leaves looked like golden coins suspended in the air. The little band rode down through the bright contrasting colours of the separate groups of birch, pine and maple until, after describing a wide arc, they found themselves where the lingering morning mist reduced all colours to pastel. Although by now one could see some distance ahead it was like looking through milky glass, as in a dream landscape where everything appeared to be at an infinite distance.

They rode over a little bridge, beneath which the river seemed to be giving off wisps of steamy vapour. A kingfisher darted past them with a startled cry, its sapphire-blue plumage drawing a sharp line just above the surface of the water for an instant before it vanished into the deep vegetation beside the river.

'It'll soon be winter if that one has arrived,' remarked Kadacsay in a whisper: and then again they did not speak.

The horses' hooves made hardly a sound on the soft turf. The landscape before them seemed more and more unreal with tall groups of Austrian pines looking like black islands in a white sea. When they were quite close to the woods in which they would soon be engulfed those orange-coloured rays of the sun that had succeeded in penetrating the mist above cast a pale dove-grey haze over the silver foliage of the poplars and gave a rosy tint to the dense leaves of the undergrowth. It was as if Nature were blushing as she was undressed by the sun.

From the depths of the mysterious woods suddenly came a deep rumbling roar not unlike the roll of some giant drum, or empty wooden barrel, though it clearly came from some living source and not from any dead piece of wood. It was an angry sound, filled with demand and desire, a mating call or a battle cry.

They all stopped and the horses pricked up their ears. 'It must be a fallow stag,' whispered Balint. 'He can't be far away!' and he turned his horse and trotted swiftly along a narrow grassy path which led through the wild tangle of willow trees and elders, beneath arches of giant topolya, until they reached the ford. The reeds by the riverbank were tall now and stood like a wall in front of them. A narrow path had been cut through that led down to the flat pebbles below the bank. At that season there was not much water in the sluggish little stream, indeed it barely came up to the horses' hocks because most of it had been diverted a mile further upstream to drive the mill. The Aranyos was always like this in autumn and it was hard to believe that the mighty torrent to be seen in spring was the same river. Of course the proof was there to see on the further bank, which was a small perpendicular cliff two or three metres high, cut clean like some geological illustration with clear-cut layers of pebbles, dark humus, alternating strands of clay and stones, until finally reaching down to a base level of bluish-coloured slate which had once been the bed of some prehistoric sea.

They followed the path through the reeds and crossed the ford, and now, for the first time, they could look out over the Keresztes plain, the largest in Transylvania, towards the bald slopes of the Mezoseg, broken only by canyons of yellowish clay, with here and there little square patches of vineyard; over to the right to the hills of the Maros and to the left, far, far away, to the vertical line of the Torda cleft. Still further in the distance, almost melting into the clouds, were the soft grey outlines of the Jara range. The plain was bathed in sunshine and in front of them were the great fields of now harvested oats at the sides of which enough ground had been left unploughed for three horses to gallop side by side. These were the autumn training grounds, for here the going was not so hard as it became inside the park itself. Along one side posts marked a six-hundred-metre stretch.

They rode the horses twice round the perimeter of the field, as a preliminary workout, and then tried out the speed of the five-year-old Csalma and the novice Menyet against that of the experienced Honeydew.

Balint, Simon Jager and one of the stable lads watched from the side. The first try-out went smoothly enough and Csalma kept up with Honeydew without difficulty, even though the mare went full out.

'She'll do us proud, my lord,' said Simon, and then, almost under his breath. 'I wouldn't give any of our horses for that spindly goat! At five thousand metres she'd be well behind!'

Gazsi now trotted over to Balint, said a few words of praise for the Denestornya mare and then, signalling to the lad to bring up the young colt that was to be tried out next, cantered back to the starting post. Then something quite unexpected happened.

Young Pisti, the lad, said *'Komelo'* sharply and dug his heels into the colt's sides to bring him up in line with Gazsi's thoroughbred and the latter, perhaps believing that the command was for her, or because she was suddenly reminded of those days on the racecourse at Alag which she had so hated, and resented being shouted at once more, put her head between her forelegs, arched her back in a crescent and, turning a full circle, bolted in every direction in the wide open field. Gazsi was taken by surprise and thrown almost at once; but being the horseman he was he landed on his feet without further mishap.

Not so young Pisti! The colt snorted, flung up his tail in a trumpet shape – just like Honeydew – and leapt into the air so that the lad was thrown up like a shooting star and fell to the ground head first.

Both these things happened so quickly that it was like a volcano erupting and the others roared with uncontrollable laughter. Though his mount too tried some tricks of her own Balint managed to canter fairly calmly over towards Gazsi. At the same time Simon Jager galloped at full speed after the colt, who was heading for home in a panic. It was one of Simon's great passions to catch bolting horses at full gallop. The last time he had done it had been two years before when Balint had been hunting at Zsuk and Simon had brought up his reserve mount. Whenever he was out riding he always kept a sharp eye out for a fall and then he was off, racing after the riderless mount uphill and downhill, standing upright in his stirrups, not bent forward like jockeys in a race but with his ramrod back as straight as the Hungarian Hussars of old. In a second the riderless colt and his pursuer had crossed the river and vanished into the trees beyond.

'What a bitch!' cried Gazsi when he had caught Honeydew and remounted. 'Didn't she just thr-r-row me again, the horr-r-rible mare!' But he wasn't angry; it was all a joke to him, and Balint, looking at the mare with her flattened ears, her mouth drawn back and, in her eyes a wicked-looking twinkle, fancied that it was the same for Honeydew.

The second trial never took place as one of the chief participants had bolted, and so Gazsi and Balint started for home. They turned into the park towards the island of trees called Nagyberek – the Big Wood, and Balint said, 'Let's follow the trail through the woods and maybe we'll get close to the deer. Those fallow stags are completely reckless when in rut, far more so than the red deer. They're restless as anything and stay out of covert for far longer.' Then they sent the remaining lad home and the two of them turned into the thick undergrowth.

Now there was hardly a trace left of the morning mists. The sun shone brightly through the tangled mesh of hops and other wild vines, picking up the autumn yellow of the summer's hemlock stalks and making the dark web of the bishop's cap creepers look as if it were a grille that protected passers-by from the flames that seemed to shine from the dry grass behind. Here the filtered sunlight picked up the strange contorted bark of a centuries-old tree and the red glow of another, and everywhere there were bright patches interspersed by dark blue strips of shadow. Where there was light it was blinding, and nothing seemed solid and three-dimensional, for the crowns of the giant trees around them cast their shadow at random until even the outlines of the bushes that formed the undergrowth were blurred and insubstantial.

It was still a dream forest, though quite different from what it had been in the thick mist of early morning. Here and there berries gleamed bright red against orange-coloured leaves, the lemon yellow of the maples was mingled with the bronze of the native oaks and everywhere were clutches of tiny berries that shone like black diamonds. There were so many that they might have been floating freely in the air. Sometimes the two riders found themselves crossing small clearings, now vividly green, before plunging once more into the lush jungle-like thickets.

From time to time they reined in the horses and stopped to listen. All around them they could sense an unrest that seemed almost to vibrate. It was a feeling rather than anything they could hear. Sometimes there was a faint sound as of a dry twig being snapped underfoot, though they might have imagined it. And sometimes they heard again that deep rumbling call, though they could not tell from which direction it came. Was it in front of them – or behind – or was that too only in their imagination?

The horses too were fully alert, their nostrils flaring wide and their ears pointing now in one direction and now in another, as if they were also aware that they were close to something wonderful and mysterious.

After a little while they found themselves on the bank of a former riverbed. Kadacsay was a little behind and stopped while Balint went slowly ahead. The riverbed itself was filled with reeds and tall grass and sharp smacking noises seemed to come from its muddy bed. Hardly had Gazsi turned his mare's head towards the noise and started to lean forward in the saddle to peer at whatever was there than a full-grown fallow buck jumped out of the thick reeds and for an instant stood there without moving, only some ten paces away from horse and rider. His widespread shovel-shaped antlers sprung proudly from between the eye-horns on his forehead and his red-brown coat had a line of clear white spots. He was not a big animal – only the size of a yearling colt – but his defiant stance made him formidable enough. Honeydew gave a start and backed a pace or two and the two animals gazed at each other, each as surprised and impressed as the other. No doubt the stag was as startled by the sight of this strange golden-yellow animal as the mare was by him. He pushed forward his muzzle that shone like patent leather and hesitantly made one or two steps forward. Then, no doubt catching the scent of a human somewhere near, he quickly recoiled and vanished back among the reeds.

Gazsi trotted forward until he had caught up with Balint.

'My dear-r-r fellow! Something mar-r-rvellous! A stag comes out in fr-r-ront of us, and Honeydew is fr-r-rightened. Honeydew! For the fir-r-rst time in her life the beast has had a shock! I could feel it thr-r-rough my leg muscles. Her hear-r-rt was r-r-racing! I never thought I'd live to see something impr-r-ress her!'

Later they saw some does and their young, but only from a distance, and a few minutes later they heard some loud clashing sounds which were almost certainly caused by two stags fighting. Then Balint and Gazsi turned their horses and rode slowly home.

Throughout the morning's ride Gazsi had seemed his usual cheerful self but Balint soon realized that this had probably only been because he had been cheered up by their adventures. When he asked when Gazsi would be going to Zsuk all the answer he got was, 'Oh, I don't know. I don't think I'll go … it's too bor-r-ring. Nothing but hor-r-rses, hor-r-rses, hor-r-rses! Always hor-r-rses! What for, I ask you? I've had quite enough. They bor-r-re me …' and that tight little frown had appeared again on his forehead.

'But the hunt is unthinkable without you!'

'Then they'll have to get used to it, won't they?' replied Gazsi gloomily.

They returned to find Countess Roza cutting flowers in front of the house. She wore thick buckskin gloves and had already cut a large quantity from the beds that lined the inner court and were thus protected from the early frosts. She walked gaily towards the two young men, giving the impression that she was preparing for some very special occasion. As well as this exceptionally festive manner they noticed that she wore the smart bonnet she normally put on only when she went to church. The wide satin bow was tied coquettishly under her chin and she had put on some new clothes that were noticeably smarter than those she usually wore, even to the extent of sporting a new white lace collar and frills at her wrists. She seemed years younger than when they had last seen her.

'Take these flowers,' she said to one of the footmen who was just passing, 'and tell them to put them in the guest rooms.' With a spring in her step she came towards her son and Gazsi.

'Now tell me all about it,' she said. 'What did you see on your ride? Let's sit here in front of the house; I love it here when the autumn sun is out.'

She led them to a stone bench from where one could see into the horseshoe court and listened with glee to Gazsi's story – which he made the most of – about how idiotic he'd been allowing the mare to throw him, and about the meeting with the stag and how he had felt Honeydew's racing heartbeats when it was her turn to be frightened. And of course he praised the young horses raised at Denestornya until Countess Roza's eyes gleamed with pleasure. And all the time she was listening she kept on turning her eyes towards the great entrance gates beyond the outer court.

At one moment she said, apropos of nothing, that Aron Kozma was arriving that morning on the eleven-thirty train, and then turned back to listen to Gazsi once more.

Later on, when they went in to lunch, she made the visitor sit at the place of honour on her right, for even though he was not of their class he was a visitor and a stranger while Gazsi, as a distant cousin, was treated as family. She talked mainly to Kozma, asking after all his family, his father and uncles, but especially after his father, of whom she spoke with great warmth and much sympathy.

No-one could have told from her manner to the son how angry she had been, year after year, with the father. It had only been once a year and why this was no-one knew but she. The truth was that, starting on her fiftieth birthday, Aron Kozma's father, Boldizsar, had sent her birthday greetings on a postcard and that every year he had mentioned her age for all to see. Before her fiftieth birthday he had never even written a letter of congratulation – nothing until the open postcards when she was fifty – and even she had no idea why he did it. She supposed that it must be revenge for some – by her – forgotten childhood slight but remembered by him for forty-odd years. She had only been thirteen years old when Aron's grandfather had stopped being the Abadys' estate superintendent and had moved away from Denestornya. Since then she had never again met Boldizsar or any of his brothers, all her former childhood playmates, and however hard she tried she could not recall any possible occasion when she might have offended one of them. On the contrary she had loved them all, particularly Boldizsar, who was the same age as she and who was her very special friend. It was very annoying not to know the reason why he should so obviously set out to provoke her and yet he did, year after year, and each time it happened it spoiled her day and made her angry. But now there was no sign of all this: today Countess Roza was all smiles.

It was her form of revenge. If the father was malicious she was determined to charm the son so that when he returned home he would recount how charming and gracious she had been, how affectionately she had spoken of his father, and how gay and happy she seemed to be. She had carefully planned her reception of the son so as to show the father how ineffectual his malice had been. When Boldizsar got to hear of how sprightly and youthful she was, despite her age which he never failed to mention so gratuitously, she would have had her revenge; for she was sure it would be a real punishment for him to believe that she hadn't even noticed his impertinence.

For Countess Roza the game was an easy one, for she was kindly by nature and now she had many happy childhood memories to recall and relate. And while she did so she often looked covertly at the young man's face, as if searching in his dark-featured Tartar looks for a resemblance to her old playmate.

When they had finished their coffee after lunch the hostess suggested that they should all go down to the lower part of the park to look at the horses which, after the hay had been gathered in the meadows in the mountains, were always brought back to graze at Denestornya.

'We should start at once,' she said, and asked Balint to order the horses to be put to an open carriage so that they could do the rounds before it got dark.

'My dear Mama, it's only five minutes' walk. They're all quite close to the house, just the other side of the millstream.'

'Never mind that, I'd rather drive. Will you come with me?' she said to Aron. 'They could drive us round the park so as to give you some idea of the place as it's your first visit.'

This offer was also intended as an honour for the visitor, an honour which Countess Roza always enjoyed bestowing because she, like her father and grandfather before her, had spent much of her life in planning and beautifying the castle's surroundings. She loved it all and she was proud that she had been able to carry on the family tradition of planning not only what she herself would enjoy but also for the future, for her successors. She and her forebears had always known and understood that this sort of landscape, whose noblest feature was the plantations of trees, was only achieved through the devotion of several generations. To see the effect that was then planned one had to wait at least half a century, and so Countess Roza's pride in what had been so unselfishly achieved was only natural.

While his mother and their guest strolled down to the horseshoe court where the carriage was waiting for them Balint took Gazsi straight to the rose gardens which had been laid out on the terrace in front of the north side of the castle. From there they only had to descend a double flight of stone steps to find themselves on a wide path leading through the park which was bordered on each side by plantations of native oak trees whose tall straight trunks and pointed crowns always reminded visitors of cypresses. Here they waited for a minute or two while the carriage was driven in a wide semi-circle to cross the first bridge over the river. A few hundred paces in front of them was the millstream, and in the meadows beyond they could see mares and their offspring through the mostly bare branches of the intervening trees.

For a few moments they walked on slowly without speaking. Finally Balint said: 'I've been thinking a lot about everything you told me yesterday. I'm sure that your trouble is that you're too much alone at Bukkos. You think too much, and then you start brooding! You ought to get married ...'

'The devil I should!' exclaimed Gazsi with an angry wave of his hand.

'I mean it!' said Balint. 'If you got married you'd see everything in quite a different light ... and you'd have little Kadacsays you could bring up in whatever way you wanted.'

'Devil take it,' repeated Gazsi and paused. Then, a little later, he said, 'I could never cope with a girl of our class, you know, I'm ... well ... I'm,

I'm too much of a peasant myself. Some little maidservant, perhaps, from time to time, that's my style, if you like ... but some over-r-r-refined young *comtesse*; no thank you! Anyhow I'm such a clod that there's no-one of that sort who'd ever want to marry *me*!'

'Oh yes, there is; plenty of them. What about Ida Laczok? She's been pining for you for years. She'd marry you tomorrow if you asked her,' said Balint and then went on to say what a nice, clever and simple girl she was and, just as an added bait, how everyone knew she had always been in love with him.

'The devil she is!' said Gazsi once more, but with less disbelief than before.

'It's true! Ever since the ball at Var-Siklod – don't you remember? She'd be just right for you. Pretty, healthy, very competent in the house too. You know her mother relies on her, not on the others. She's the right age and what's more she's no-one's fool.'

This time Gazsi made no answer at once but looked unusually thoughtful. Then he said, 'Perhaps you're right ... but ... Bah! Who knows?'

Then they talked of other things.

Countess Roza's visit to the brood mares lasted for some time because she took the opportunity to tell her guest everything there was to know about each and every one of the twenty-four mares and their pedigrees and offspring. Her discourse was long and detailed, and, to anyone interested in breeding horses, extremely informative, because she knew what she was talking about and had had many years' experience.

One of her most interesting theories was about the transmission, not only of build but also of character and temperament, and how to ensure its continuity in a breeding programme. After a while she drove off with Kozma to show him more of the estate while Balint and Gazsi walked up to the pine woods that covered the highest part of the parkland.

By the time they got to the top of the hill the afternoon light was already beginning to fade to a uniform greyness. They had arrived just where one of Balint's ancestors had had built a little classical pavilion or summer house which consisted of little more than a domed roof supported by stone columns. It was surrounded by some of the oldest pine trees in the park and before it stretched a wide clearing bordered by plantations of different specimens of rare trees. At the bottom of the hill there wound the path they had ridden along that morning and beyond it could be seen the castle's walls with, above them, the conical roofs which capped the corner towers. The old stonework was etched in deep violet against the pale evening sky and the patina on the copper casing on the roofs no longer shone green but seemed black against the saffron-yellow of the sunset.

They sat down, even though it was starting to get cold.

'What a wonderful place this is,' said Gazsi. 'I've never been here before.'

They sat in silence for a little while. Then, though without knowing what train of thought led him to the subject, unless it was the contrast between the beauty and richness of Denestornya and the squalor and unhappiness he had recently witnessed, he said suddenly, 'I saw Laci the other day, poor fellow!'

'Really? Where? When?' asked Balint eagerly.

'Just the other day … when I was coming back from Szilagy.'

For a moment Gazsi said no more. Then he related how he had been passing through Kozard and that, in front of a largish peasant's house on the right-hand side of the road, he had seen Laszlo Gyeroffy sitting on a broken-down garden chair. It was only just as he was driving past that he had realized who it was and, as it had taken a moment or two to make the coachman understand what he wanted, he had already been driven well past the house before he had been able to stop and get out. Then he had had to walk back, past some empty land, to reach the place where he had seen Laszlo. As he had nearly got close enough to call out a greeting Laszlo had got up, turned away from him and slipped quickly into the house.

'I didn't know what to do. Should I go in after him … or just go away again? I'm such an ass in this sort of thing. Well, I just tur-r-rned on my heel and left. What else was there to do? He saw me coming, so I r-r-reckoned that if he went in it must be because he didn't want to see me.'

'How did he look? How was he?'

'I think he looked thinner, but I can't be sure. There was a fence between us, and a little fr-r-ront gar-r-rden … you know what those houses are like. I just looked up the path, but all I could see was a bottle and a glass beside the chair. He must have been sitting there dr-r-rinking. When he went in I saw him clutching the door-r-rpost and thought that per-r-rhaps he was ashamed for me to see him dr-r-runk. That's why I didn't go in … per-r-rhaps it was stupid of me. I'm sor-r-ry now I didn't follow him.'

'I haven't had any news for ages,' said Balint. 'I wrote a couple of times last summer, but I never got any reply.'

Then he told Gazsi all that he did know, which was simply that he had heard that Laszlo had sold his property, but that he still lived there in an old servant's house he had kept. On his mother's behalf Balint had written to Laszlo offering him a home at Denestornya, either in a separate suite on the first floor or else in his grandfather's old manor house close by; but they had never had any answer. No doubt this was the way Laszlo wanted it for perhaps he had thought that he wouldn't be free to drink as he pleased.

'You remember Azbej, my mother's old estate manager? It was he that bought Kozard from Laszlo. He says he gives Laci some sort of annuity, but I don't know how much. I am not in touch with Azbej anymore,' he added drily.

For a few more moments they sat there together, not speaking but both of them thinking about Laszlo's sad life. Then Abady got up.

'Come along,' he said. 'My mother will be waiting for us for tea.'

Together they walked silently down the hill. When they had almost reached the castle Kadacsay looked at Balint and said, 'You know I really do feel sorry for poor Laci … but at least he's lucky to have something to care for, even if it is only the dr-r-rink!'

Before dinner Balint carried Aron Kozma off to discuss with him various matters to do with the Co-operatives. Aron himself had some ideas for which he wanted Balint's approval; and there were certain proposals that Balint put forward which he did not think were feasible. Aron had a logical mind and was full of commonsense, and from that short discussion there emerged some straightforward practical measures from all the somewhat nebulous ideas that had been spinning around in Balint's head since his reunion with Adrienne.

As both guests were going to leave Denestornya early the next morning goodbyes were said that night.

'Please,' said Countess Roza as she offered her hand to be kissed, 'greet your father from me, tell him everything that you've seen here and tell him too that although the years go by I am still quite sprightly and do not at all feel my great age!'

She had prepared this parting sentence early that morning and intended it as a poisoned arrow for her childhood playmate. She was determined to let him know that his uncalled-for mockery had had no effect upon her, and that his efforts to vex her with his peculiar form of birthday greetings had had no effect whatever.

As she spoke she was sure that it would now be Boldizsar's turn to be annoyed and this pleased her so much that she smiled with renewed benevolence at his son.

# PART TWO

# Chapter One

Laszlo Gyeroffy lived in the house in the village that he had kept when he had sold his Kozard estate a year and a half before. He had kept it for the sake of his old servant, Marton Balogh, principally because he wanted to be sure that the old man had somewhere to live and would not be thrown out on the street, which he was sure Azbej would have no qualms about doing when he took possession of the manor house. He had originally thought of giving the place to Balogh outright, because it had never occurred to him that he might need it himself.

Not long after Laszlo had been flung out of Sarah Bogdan's house in a snowstorm and fallen dead drunk into a ditch near Apahida, a small one-horse cart had been driven along the main road. In it had been Bischitz, the Jewish storekeeper from Kozard who was driving home after a day in Kolozsvar. With him had been his daughter, Regina, who was the eldest of his children and the only one bright enough to feed the horse and look after the cart while Bischitz went about his business.

The storm had caught them when they were halfway home and their worn-out nag of a horse could hardly make any headway against the driving snow. By the time they had reached the iron bridge near Apahida they were hardly moving and it was because of this that they had seen Laszlo by the feeble light of the cart's paraffin storm lamp.

He had been lying face downwards at the edge of the ditch and he had been almost completely covered by snow. It was Regina who had first seen that there was someone there, and they had known who it was because of the familiar check of the coat he was wearing.

At once they had stopped the cart, pulled him out of the snow, and found that although he was by now almost sober again, he could hardly move but, though frozen stiff, was at least still alive. Together they had lifted him into the back of the cart, laid him down gently and driven him back to Kozard. Bischitz had thought he would leave him at the manor house, but it had been so late when they arrived, and the horse had been far too tired to manage the climb up to the house, so the shop-keeper's wife had made up a bed for him in the only good room in their little house.

Laszlo spent one night there.

In the morning he woke with a high fever. The doctor was sent for, as was Azbej, and when the doctor pronounced that Laszlo would cer-tainly develop pneumonia and would have to stay in bed for weeks, Azbej flatly refused to take him in at the manor house declaring that it was quite unthinkable to look after him there because he was about to start repairing the house and had that very day brought out the masons to start work. There could be no question, he declared, of having Laszlo looked after in his old home. And so it came about that the solution was found of carrying him to the house he still owned on the outskirts of the village and moving in Marton Balogh to look after him. The old servant nursed him and Regina came in often to help, which she did eagerly and efficiently. He was ill for several months, and though by the end of the summer he had got over the pneumonia, he was left with a nasty persis-tent cough; but his life had been saved.

At first Azbej paid whatever was necessary, largely because he thought this would be a good mark in his favour if ever the Abady family started to look into his dealings with their cousin Gyeroffy. This only came to an end when months had passed and Laszlo was still not fully recovered. One day Azbej told the shopkeeper that he would pay no more, and for a few days no-one knew what to do or what would become of the invalid. Then a Dr Simay, an elderly lawyer from Szamos-Ujvar, arrived unher-alded at the store. Bischitz had met him some twenty years before and indeed it was to him that the shopkeeper had sold the portrait of Laszlo's errant mother, Julie Ladossa, after the distraught Mihaly Gyeroffy had slashed it almost in half and thrown it out of the window. Dr Simay had arrived just as unexpectedly then as he did now. This time he asked to speak to Bischitz alone. From that day on it was Bischitz who had pro-vided whatever money was needed for Laszlo's illness, and afterwards, though by no means lavishly, who had supplied whatever Laszlo needed to live on. For this he was given just forty crowns a week, no more, no less, and on that meagre allowance he managed to keep Laszlo alive. He was forbidden to lend him any money and was not allowed to give him credit at the store. He had also had to swear not to reveal where the money came from.

As it happened Laszlo never even asked. Sometimes he would get angry with Bischitz if he wanted better or more brandy, for only this seemed to hold any interest for him. He never complained about the food – and anyhow never seemed to want very much. Old Balogh dug the garden behind the house and grew what potatoes and other vegetables they needed and, as he and Laszlo ate very little else, most of the allowance was spent on drink. The accounts were sent, by order, not to Laszlo but to the old lawyer, Dr Simay.

In this way a year had passed, during which Laszlo had really been too weak to go further than the chair outside the front door. Sometimes he did not get as far even as that but sat indoors doing nothing. Occasionally he would get hold of a newspaper – always several days old – and then he would glance over it without much interest. He never read anything else. Every now and again he would find his way into the store and exchange a few words with whoever came in. Usually, however, he talked only to Bischitz and his wife or, if they were busy elsewhere, to young Regina, for even though the child was still not quite thirteen, she was intelligent, knew where everything was kept and what its price was, and so was often entrusted with keeping the shop.

A strange relationship started to grow between the sick man and the child. It had always been one of Laszlo's oddest characteristics that as soon as he had a certain amount of drink under his belt he shed his usual silent and morose air and became instead talkative and boastful. When this happened he would suddenly show himself immensely proud of his once grand position in Budapest society, when as *elotancos* – the official organizer of all the great balls and social occasions – he had been one of the most popular young men in the capital. Later, when he had come back to Transylvania disgraced and ruined because of his inability to pay his gambling debts, his old friends would tease him relentlessly whenever he began to talk about his grand past. Now, though he only had little Regina to listen to him, the same thing would happen whenever he was full of brandy, of which he now needed far less than before to make him drunk and loquacious. After only a tot or two he would begin to tell the girl all about the luxuries and grandeurs he had once known. He only had to get started and words poured from him, tales about the reception for the King of Spain and grand balls at the palace or other great houses, banquets and dinners and dances and scintillating evening *soirées*. Bischitz and his wife were no good as an audience for Laszlo since they believed it was all untrue and it bored them. But not little Regina.

She never gave a thought as to whether it was true or not. She did not care. For her it was all as magical and as real as fairyland: the great golden rooms, the velvet-covered furniture, the mountains of flowers, the lovely elegant women in silk and satin who floated in the arms of slim-waisted men in traditional Hungarian costume or officers in full dress uniform, kings, queens, princesses and princes. It was all far more beautiful than any other tales she had read or been told. And for her, Laszlo, sitting before her, thin and wan, often unshaved and unkempt, his once elegant clothes and expensive shoes now worn and mended, was a prince of legend, doomed by some horrid spell to a life of squalor and misery, but nevertheless still the true ruler of all that splendour of which he had formerly been the central figure.

Whenever he came into the store she would lean on the counter drinking in every word he uttered. Her Titian-red hair surrounded her beautiful but still girlish face like an aureole of flame. Her doe-like brown eyes, fringed by long curving lashes, opened ever more widely as she listened and her mouth, with lips startlingly red against her pale skin, was slightly open as she feasted on all he had to tell. For Regina it all had the effect of some wondrous magic potion, and when Laszlo stopped, as he occasionally did, she would at once refill his glass with brandy and push it towards him, for she knew that he could only go on as long as he was properly supplied with his own brand of magic potion.

From time to time she would ask him some question, as if she hadn't understood something he had said; and then he would tell her even more fabulous details of footmen in gold-braided liveries, carriages lined with silk, tables covered in gleaming plate and porcelain all laden with extraordinary food, and finally of the jewels, giant pearls and rubies, diadems and tiaras sparkling with diamonds of the finest water.

She never wanted to hear tell of anything else and, as Gyeroffy never wanted to talk of anything else, for Regina the great world consisted only of this fabulous luxury and pomp.

Several years before, when she had still been quite a small child, some inborn curiosity had drawn her to 'The Count', as he was called by everyone in the village. It had been enough simply to catch a glimpse of him from where she stood half-hidden inside the shop doorway, or from across the street or over the fence of the manor house demesne. More recently it had been a great joy for her to be able to help nurse him when he was sick, but none of this had counted for anything compared with the ecstasy of being alone in the shop, with The Count sitting before her and telling his tales only to her. This was a joy so magical and so mysteriously exciting that her young spirit was completely conquered. All the grandeur and glitter of which he spoke was to her little more than the natural background to the fairy prince who sat there with her. For her the only reality was the young man himself, and everything that she heard from him was like some metaphysical halo with which he was crowned but of whose existence only she, Regina, was privileged to know, and which only she could see. It seemed to her, too, that this dream prince sought her out, waiting to come to the shop when he would be sure of finding her alone. He would keep watch until her father left the shop on some lengthy errand such as going into Szamos-Ujvar or visiting his little parcel of thirty acres of land which was farmed for him by some luckless debtor, and then in no time at all he would come in. It only happened occasionally, perhaps once every two or three weeks; but when it did it was certain that Laszlo would appear, and because the shopkeeper's wife also had several smaller children to mind and the household chores to attend to, it was equally certain that the young man and the girl would be left alone together.

Regina believed that he came only to see her and whenever she thought of this her heart seemed to throb high in her throat.

And, of course, in one sense she was right: Laszlo did look for the moments when he would be sure of finding her alone, but it was not her young beauty that drew him to seek her out, indeed he had never even noticed it. He had not even seen that the child was swiftly turning into a desirable young woman. For Laszlo there were two reasons why he chose those moments to go into the shop, and these two reasons were quite enough for him. The first was simply that Regina, unlike her father, poured generous measures of brandy and often of the best without Laszlo having to ask for it; and the second, which for the young man was probably the most important, was that it meant he could talk about himself and about that magical past when he had had the world at his feet and which had been so cruelly snatched from him. He could talk about the Casino Club, and the Park Club, about dinners and dances in great private houses where he, as *elotancos*, would lead the dance. He could talk about the perfections of Countess Beredy and of her exquisite little palace overlooking the ramparts of old Buda, and of the great white country castle of the Szent-Gyorgyis. He could describe the grandeurs of princely parties at the Kollonich palace near Lake Balaton, recounting over and over again how the state rooms were decorated and how they all led out of one another, how the sunlight gleamed on the myriad gilt bindings of the books in the library, how the park was laid out like an English garden and how the shooting parties were organized with precision and stately attention to precedence. Above all he could talk to his heart's content about everything that related to his love for Klara. He could describe her little room where once, and only once, they had kissed; he could tell of the dresses she wore and of those little bouquets of saffron-yellow carnations that she always carried as a symbol of their love. He could tell Regina everything, even if that everything was now long lost to him, and through no-one's fault but his own. In fact he did not tell everything to Regina. He never told her Klara's name or anything about her except those things by which she was surrounded, her dresses, scents, flowers, the rooms through which she moved and the little capes she would put round her shoulders when going out of doors. Her name and her person were too sacred to be mentioned or described, in much the same way as certain primitive peoples hold it taboo to say the name of their god. For Laszlo the brandy washed away any hint of self-recrimination and left him only with the euphoria evoked by his memories of gaiety and beauty and grandeur.

During the previous winter old Marton had occasionally fed his master on roast hare. He never spoke about how he had obtained it, indeed he never spoke about it at all but merely put it on the table. Laszlo was too listless and filled with his own sad thoughts to notice and at that time merely ate automatically whatever was put before him. But when the first snows of Laszlo's second autumn in the cottage began to fall and old Marton served up roast hare again, his master looked up and said, 'Hare? Where did you get that?'

He was not particularly interested, and had asked the question only for the sake of something to say.

'It came.'

'What do you mean, it came? Did somebody send it?'

Marton did not reply but gathered up the dishes and, with much clattering of plates and knives and forks, put everything on a tray and carried it out of the room. Laszlo had often been irritated by the old man's taciturn manner and called after him angrily, 'Will you answer me! Where did that hare come from?'

Marton paused on the threshold of the kitchen and looked back at his master. For an instant a light seemed to glitter in the old man's eyes. Then he muttered, 'It came!' and went out slamming the door behind him.

For years Marton had been a persistent and adroit poacher, and it had been the passion of his life. He had been a widower for many years and he had no friends. Throughout Laszlo's long minority he had lived alone in the unfinished manor house and there had been little change when Laszlo came of age, for he was hardly ever there. The old man was a tied servant who received a living wage from the estate manager and who was able to fatten a couple of yearling pigs annually for himself. He did not need to poach for his dinner but he was drawn to it by some inner yearning for adventure and so that he could feel himself superior to the other folk in the village; for he knew only too well that many of them despised him and thought him mentally deficient. He did not mind, but whenever he trapped a hare he would skin it at once and roast it – and as he ate it he would smile to himself not only because he was enjoying a good meal but also because he felt that somehow he had scored over all those who despised him, the villagers, the gamekeepers, and even the estate manager himself.

Old Marton never tired of telling himself that one had to be a pretty clever fellow to be a good poacher. One had to know what wire or thread was right for each kind of trap or snare and he even knew that the best, though hard to come by, were violin strings. While he still lived in the manor house he had found a packet in one of the drawers and, as Laszlo had long before sold his violin, old Marton quickly slipped it into his own pocket. Of course one had to know, too, exactly how to set the snare so that no passer-by should see it and steal it before the game had been caught. Neither was it an easy matter to go round checking the snares, either at dawn or any other time, without being seen by some curious eye. Furthermore one had to have the devil's own cunning, and a lot of knowledge and experience, before one could succeed in getting one's prey home undetected.

He had been at it for years, but he had only occasionally been able to bring something home for the pot as in those years small game was scarce in that part of Transylvania, especially on such a run-down estate as Kozard. While he had been lodged in the servants' quarters of the manor house he would set his snares near the boundary of the park. This had been comparatively easy and it had not been necessary to take many precautions against being seen for no-one lived nearby; but since he had moved down into the house in the village things had become more complicated. Azbej had the park fences repaired and so old Marton had no excuse if he were discovered wandering about inside. The only hunting ground left was the forest, down by the riverbed and up the hillside beyond. It was more difficult, but also more exciting.

The old poacher laid his plans carefully and, so as not to make himself conspicuous, went out only occasionally, and when it seemed most likely he would catch something, for example when it looked as if it would snow the following day. He knew that hares were particularly sensitive to the weather and at such times always made for the thickest parts of the woods. At such times old Marton would go off to gather kindling: at least that was what he would tell one of the estate gamekeepers if they happened to meet and if, and only if, the other man was bold enough to ask what he was doing. This hardly ever occurred for he was known to be surly, a man of few words who usually gave a rude answer if spoken to. The following day at dawn he would visit his traps and snares, and if anything had been caught in the night he would bring it home concealed under his jacket, while he carried a heavy bunch of dry twigs so that anyone could see why he had been in the forest. At such times he would walk with his back bent as if tired out from his heavy labours and heaving great sighs as he staggered past the outlying cottages. And all the time he would exult inwardly, his soul pouring out a paean of triumph and joy, for he knew that he was cleverer than them all, for was he not carrying home the fruits of his illegal poaching under their very noses while they knew nothing, nothing at all?

Of course the whole village knew and had always known, but they would never have told it either to Azbej, whom they hated as a quarrelsome martinet – and a stranger to boot – or to old Marton himself, for if they had let the old man know that everyone knew what he was up to, there would have been no more fun to be got out of it. As it was they watched everything he did. They saw when he sauntered out to the forest pretending to search for kindling, and how he staggered back under huge loads in the morning before stealing off to the next village to sell the skins. They watched the whole comedy and laughed their heads off when he was out of earshot. Even the children would enter into the spirit of the game, sometimes calling out: 'What are you carrying, Uncle Marton?' and when the old man merely growled back 'Can't you see? Wood, of course!' or 'Mind your own business, you little bugger!' they would pull faces behind his back and laugh about it all the following week.

Laszlo knew nothing of all this.

But on that one day it happened that he was stone cold sober and in a foul mood because his weekly allowance had all been spent and at the shop they wouldn't give him any more to drink. Little Regina would have given him something, but it was Friday afternoon and because of the Sabbath Bischitz would not be leaving the shop and so Laszlo would have no opportunity of getting the girl on her own. He got more and more desperate. Money had to be found somehow or he felt he would go mad. At that moment he happened to glance at the worn chest of drawers – a worthless piece of furniture from one of the old servants' rooms that Azbej had generously allowed him to take from the manor house. On its top lay a long smooth leather case with triangular little canvas covers on the corners to prevent it from scuffing and a tiny elegant snap-lock. It was an English-made case for a pair of guns, though now it held only one. It had been sent after him from Desmer when Sara Bogdan Lazar had sent back everything that had belonged to him. The feeble lamp cast only a faint glow and yet the smooth hard leather and the brass of the lock and clasps on its leather straps still shone brightly. Laszlo gazed at the case as if hypnotized.

Laszlo had entirely forgotten that he still had it. He got up and looked at it more closely. There, stamped in the leather top, was his name, engraved with a slight spelling mistake – Count Ladislas Gieroffy – just as it had always been from the time, so long ago, when the pair of guns had been a Christmas present from his two aunts in Western Hungary. He stroked the letters lightly, thinking back to that Christmas in the Kollonichs' great country house when he had been just eighteen. Christmas at Simonvasar! In the library there had been a Christmas tree that reached to the ceiling. The room had been lit by thousands and thousands of candles. Everything had been so bright and Klara had been there ... in a white dress ... still very slim and girlish ... and he could remember her eyes, ocean-grey, and wide open with joy and happiness ...

For an instant he stood still, lost in his memories. Then he shook himself and pressed back the catch almost with loathing and lifted the lid of the case until it rested against the wall. There lay the gun, its stock and barrel in separate compartments, and there lay too the place for its pair which had been sold long before. He wondered why he had kept this one, he who had no money for brandy, let alone for cartridges.

Of course he must sell it at once, and he wondered why it had not previously occurred to him to do so.

He took out the gun and put it together. It was so perfectly made, as neat as any chronometer, that it opened noiselessly and the stock and barrel fitted together with a barely perceptible click. Slight though this was the sound made Laszlo shudder, for it reminded him of the count-less times he had heard the same sound, without then even noticing it, at the great annual shoots at the Szent-Gyorgyis' or the Kollonichs' and now it was like a great chime of bells from some infinite distance, from a past which was no more. Quickly Laszlo took the gun apart again and put it hurriedly back in its case. He knew he had to get rid of it as quickly as possible.

Grabbing his hat and jacket he ran out of the house like a man pursued.

For a little while Laszlo followed the road through the village, and then he turned off down a track that led to the old fuller's mill on the banks of the Szamos where there lived a man called Fabian. He was known only by his first name for being of Czech or Moravian origin his family name was Szprnad and no-one at Kozard could pronounce it properly. He was obviously rich and so had been known as 'The Mil-lionaire' ever since he had arrived in the village a year before. As well as the mill he had bought up a wool-combing business and had also built himself an oil press. He seemed to be half peasant and half townsman and had come from Borgo where, people said, his father had kept an inn. It was soon obvious that he was an astute businessman: he was also a great drinker and sometimes would carouse so long with his friends that the entire supply of beer in the village was consumed and more had to be sent for in a hurry.

Laszlo had first met him in Bischitz's shop and the newcomer had at once bought him so many tots of brandy that Laszlo had passed out and had to be carried home. Fabian had knocked back just as much, but it had not seemed to have any effect on him and indeed he hardly blinked even after more than a dozen gills of the strongest brand. Since that day the two men had formed a sort of drinking friendship – it had no other basis – and from time to time Fabian would carry Laszlo off to Szamos-Ujvar for an orgy of drink and gypsy music and sex with the town whores which would last well into the next day. The local tarts were what one might expect in such a small provincial backwater and as for the gypsies they came mostly from the poorest of their kind whose families scratched a living digging clay. This is what Fabian enjoyed for he could only relax in the sort of company where the music was unbelievably noisy, where he could tear off all his clothes and where the women were fat.

Laszlo went down the little path that had been trodden in the snow until he could see a faint glimmer of light from the fuller's window. The throb of the oil press was like a giant's heartbeat, and Laszlo, knowing that Fabian was often away travelling, prayed that this time he would find him at home.

He was just in time, for round the corner came Fabian driving his sturdy little cart. The fuller was of medium height and broad of shoulder. A white sheepskin hat covered his shaven head and he wore a beard that was trimmed round the corners of his mouth as far back as the ears so as to show off his wide black moustaches of which he was very proud. His thick fleshy exceptionally red lips were full of life and vigour and all the hair on his face seemed to be brushed horizontally sideways. He stopped the cart and greeted Laszlo boisterously.

'What's this, Count? Coming to pay a visit? That's wonderful!' he shouted in a voice of thunder and, although he spoke Hungarian fluently, one could tell from the long drawn-out vowels that it was not his mother tongue. 'I'll drive you home,' he went on, 'but I can't stop as I've been asked to supper at Iklod.' And he shoved out a giant fist and pulled Gyeroffy up beside him as if he had weighed no more than a feather. They drove on slowly for the road was all soft snow and mud.

Laszlo said he wanted to sell his gun, a valuable one, made in England. 'How much?'

'Whatever you say,' answered Laszlo.

'Count, you're mad!' said the fuller laughing, and he gave the young man a playful push with his massive shoulder. Then he added, 'I can give you some money if you're short.'

'Certainly not! If you want the gun then buy it … but no handouts. That I won't accept!'

'Let's have a look at it then.' They got down at Laszlo's little house and went in. Fabian bought the weapon at once but refused to take the case even though Laszlo pressed it on him. What did he need with the case, said Fabian. It would only get in the way and anyhow it had Laszlo's name on it. He went out, threw the gun under the seat in the cart and paid for it at once, two hundred crowns in cash, which was an absurdly low price for such a splendid double-barrelled Purdey. Of course Fabian had no idea what a treasure he was getting and even fancied he was being overgenerous. Then he drove off.

Laszlo remained alone in the darkening room. Two banknotes lay upon the table before him and so he had enough money to drink himself into oblivion. With money he could drink, and with drink he could forget … and now especially he needed something to wash away that sentimental heartache he had momentarily felt when Fabian had seized the Purdey with his great coarse hands and practically run out of the door with it. Why, he wondered, had that action given him such a sudden stab of pain? Why now, suddenly, when so long ago he had decided that anything that reminded him of his lost past was hateful. Oh, well, it was good that he had seen the last of it!

Laszlo was still barefooted since he had taken off his sodden boots and socks on coming into the room. He decided he would have to send old Marton out for brandy so he picked up one of the notes and stepped out into the hallway that separated the part of the house where he lived from Marton's own lodging. This was a widish room with a fireplace, behind which was the kitchen that had been used by all the inhabitants of the house when it had lodged two tenant families. He opened the door opposite and there was the old servant crouching down on the floor with a candle beside him: he was stretching the hare-skin on a plank of wood. Caught in the act he stared up at his master too dumbfounded to speak. Laszlo burst out laughing.

'You old rogue! Now I've caught you! Out with it, where did that hare come from?'

'I caught it.'

'How? Not while it was on the run, I'll be bound.'

'With a snare.'

'Bravo indeed! I like that. Very clever. Where, may I ask?'

Balogh did not want to answer that. Still, he said, 'In the forest.'

'I see! In the forest! Well, if Azbej can steal my forest I suppose I can steal his hares! Why not? Now go over to Bischitz's and bring me half a litre of brandy, the best he has. We'll talk about all this later ...'

And so Laszlo became a poacher, and his life was changed. In a few days he had learned the essentials from old Marton, how the snares were prepared and where were the most likely places to set them. After a while they would go in turns to the forest, Laszlo in the evening to set eight or ten snares in places they had already planned together, and Marton at dawn to collect the game. They caught two good hares in the first week.

This was the first thing in many years to give Laszlo any pleasure. His fingers, trained to the intricacies of the violin and keyboard, soon adapted to tying the most delicate of snares; and these he hung with such skill and art where his prey had trodden a path at the foot of a thornbush thicket, or along a branch, that neither man nor beast could have said they were there.

There was only one snag: he soon found that hares rarely went deep into the forests when the weather was fine nor even when the sky was merely overcast. Then they stayed out in the meadows and ploughed fields. They went to the woods only when it was exceptionally windy or when there was snow in the air. Then, and only then, was it worth the effort of setting the traps and snares.

This was not enough for Laszlo, for he had become so fond of this new game that he wanted to play it every day.

Between the house where Laszlo lived and the road was some wooden-plank fencing but only on each side, running from the road to the little stream that ran at the bottom of the slope behind the house. On the left there was only a hedge between, a piece of vacant land between Laszlo's little house and the Bischitz's shop; while on the right, between it and the grounds of Laszlo's old manor house, Azbej had added a fence of dry sticks near the bank of the stream. There, as the place was sandy and close to water, he had also placed his new hen-run. Azbej had started to raise Orpingtons whose brown eggs were so popular that he hoped to export them even to England. A long henhouse had been built with a flat sandy yard between it and the stream. At the far end, just under the slope of the hill on the top of which had been built the manor house itself, the new owner had built a house for the farm overseer. It was all neat and clean and new – a model chicken farm – and the yard was filled with big golden hens who scratched disconsolately at its sterile surface where no insects, or worms, or other favourite morsels were to be found. Their eyes darted from left to right as they searched in vain. Their only excitement came, twice a day, when their feed would be brought in ... and that was all. They were bored. Every so often one would approach the dry-wood fence and peck its way along searching for some way of escape to the Paradise Garden beyond.

Late one afternoon Laszlo strolled down to the bank of the stream near to where old Marton was cutting up a fallen alder tree. The first snows had come and gone and it had been dry freezing weather ever since. That day it had clouded over and Laszlo went down to ask the old man if the snow was coming again, because if so it would be a good moment to set the traps in the woods and he would have time to do it before it got dark.

Marton stopped his work, leaned on his axe and threw back his head. He wiped the sweat from his face and from his long moustaches, and sniffed the air.

'No snow today!' he said laconically.

Laszlo stood there for some time watching the old man as he worked. He felt thoroughly out of temper because he had set his mind on going to the woods that evening. Finally he turned and started slowly to walk back to the house.

The branches of the fallen tree had blocked the garden path so Laszlo was forced to make a detour along the hedge beyond which Azbej had erected his fence. Until that moment Laszlo had been thinking of nothing but his annoyance that the weather was so contrary but now, seeing before him the new wooden fence, the neat poultry yard, the farm beyond it and, high on the hill behind, the white manor house itself, with its new pink roof shining through the bare winter trees, a fresh thought struck him. For a moment his face darkened with anger as he looked at everything that had once been his and then slowly a wicked smile appeared on his face. Between the laths of the poultry yard paling he could see a few hens peering at him and all too clearly searching for an opening through which they could reach the tempting worked soil with its wealth of fallen seeds that was waiting for them on the other side.

Laszlo looked around. There was no-one in sight, and even old Marton had his back to him.

It was obvious that he would only need one snare, and that the hedge would hide him as he set it. He hurried back to the house, collected a snare, and a steel screwdriver from the gun case, and in a moment or two was back by the fence. He bent down and with a swift turn of the screwdriver forced one of the wooden palings out of its lower socket. Then he grasped a live twig from the hedge in front of the opening he had just made, bent its end back in an arc and attached his snare to it. All this was done so swiftly that in a couple of minutes he was back beside the house apparently just idly looking up at the sky. For a while he stood there, every nerve taut. He listened hard. Dusk was falling and this was the moment when all the birds usually found their way back to the henhouse. In less than half an hour they would all be inside again and so there was not much time left for one of them to discover the trap that had been set for it. Laszlo then began to wonder if a trapped bird would make such a noise when the noose tightened that the farm people would be alerted and discover what he had been up to … and then the shame of being found out. The shame!

For what seemed like an eternity he heard nothing. Then there was a sudden brief fluttering of wings, and then again nothing. The trap had been sprung.

It was almost more than he could do not to run down excitedly. Nevertheless he managed a lazy stroll and, sure enough, from the branch he had so cunningly bent so as to be sprung by the snare, a fine fat Orpington hen was hanging, as dead as anyone could wish. Laszlo unhooked it swiftly, hid it under his coat, and then he did run, as swiftly as possible, back into the house. He felt no remorse at all for having caught one of Azbej's birds, and that what he had done was nothing less than common theft never even passed through his mind. If he thought of it as anything at all it was as a simple act of revenge and as such gave him the satisfaction of paying back in his own coin someone who had robbed him. The moment that this occurred to him Laszlo's heart took a great leap of joy and triumph; and if he had somehow regained all his lost inheritance it would have made him no happier than he was at that moment.

From that day on Laszlo set his hen trap every eight or ten days. He always did this on his own for it was obvious that old Marton wanted nothing to do with it. He never spoke his mind, or indeed said anything at all on the subject, but Laszlo sensed that in his book wild game was God's gift to whosoever might catch it but that poultry belonged to the man who raised and fed it. Accordingly, though he would cook any bird that Laszlo took, he would not eat it. He was even reluctant to pluck and draw such birds, so Laszlo found that he had to call upon young Regina to get this done. She came eagerly. All Laszlo had to do was to give the girl a little private nod when he was drinking his tot of brandy in the shop, or a discreet wave from over the hedge, and she would somehow contrive to come at once, no matter what she was supposed to be doing. Though no-one could have noticed that she was doing it, Regina somehow managed to keep a permanent watch on Laszlo's house and on him if he were out of doors. For her any reason was enough if she could be near him.

Sometimes when she disappeared from the store her father and mother would start calling for her, and then she would sneak home, making sure that she always appeared to be coming from somewhere quite other than where she had really been. When she went to Laszlo's she would cross the piece of empty land between the houses through the gate that her father had put in the hedge when he had rented it some years before; but she would never come back the same way, for if she had she knew her parents would guess where she had been. A moment or two after they started calling she would reappear as if coming from the stream, or from the roadway, or even from the house opposite; and even though she sometimes got a slap on the face she never let on where she had been.

Her love for Gyeroffy was like that of a faithful hound.

Of course she was still a child and the deep love she felt for the young man was utterly innocent, though she experienced all the ecstasy and suffering of a grown woman. If Laszlo spoke to her she was happy, and she suffered and felt excluded when he talked to other people.

She loathed Fabian. On those occasions when Laszlo and Fabian went into Ujvar together and did not come back until the next morning, she knew instinctively that they had been enjoying themselves with other women – horrible, coarse creatures, no doubt – and she was consumed by jealousy and hurt rage and cried all night. The following day she would try her best to be angry and not keep glancing at Laszlo's house; and she would decide not to go if he should call out for her. But a single word or a casual glance from him was enough to make her forget all her resentment, and then she would once again be his faithful doglike slave. And yet, behind this unthinking bondage, there was something else – a young girl's perennial curiosity about what the act of love was really like. On the days after his trips to the town Regina did all she could to get close enough to him, either in his own house or else in her father's shop, to be able to look closely at him, to study his face and hands and how he moved; and she would lift her delicate straight little nose and sniff the air around him: and when she thought that she had seen or sensed some legacy of that night spent away from home, a strange scent or a bite mark on his skin, she would become strangely upset and her throat would constrict. It was unspeakably painful ... and yet mysterious and attractive too.

Just after the New Year a covered carriage drew up outside Laszlo's house. It was nine o'clock at night, and Fabian had come to celebrate his Saint's Day. With him he had brought a huge cold turkey, some savoury biscuits and sweet cakes and a large hamper of brandy and cheap champagne. He also brought two women. The village gypsy musician was sent for at once and he played standing in the kitchen doorway as there was no place for him in Laszlo's room where the four of them dined and danced and sang. Fabian himself always needed plenty of space, for he loved to jump up and hurl himself about, sometimes dancing with both women at once, throwing himself about with wide-flung arms and all the time yodelling at the top of his voice.

News of the party spread quickly through the village and soon there was a group of neighbours gathered near the house to listen to the music and find out what was going on. They were mostly women, and they cross-questioned the driver about the loose women he had brought and were deliriously scandalized by what he had to tell. Some of the younger boys and girls started dancing on the frozen snow-covered ground but it was bitterly cold and soon they all went home.

After dinner was over the Bischitz family always sat in the large room behind the shop in which the family lived and ate. Here the shopkeeper kept his account books and also any special delicacies such as sugar and spices and dried figs which might have absorbed the smells of dried fish or pipe tobacco if these had been kept in the storeroom next door. On this evening old Bischitz sat reading a newspaper while his fat wife dozed in an armchair, worn out from the heavy labour of the daily chores. Regina had already put her younger brothers and sisters to bed and was folding away the tablecloth and napkins when their servant Juliska rushed in and disturbed this peaceful domestic scene with the scandalous news of what was happening over at The Count's house. Neither of the old people were in the least impressed, and indeed the shopkeeper himself, angered at the thought that the drinks had not been bought from him, bawled out the servant for having left the washing-up to go sightseeing, promised her a good slap, chased her back to the kitchen and then turned to his wife and said: 'Come on, bedtime!'

Regina stood by the cupboard rigid with shock. She was very pale and her parents had to call her twice before she heard them.

Regina lay quite still next to her sleeping six-year-old sister, but she could not sleep. One o'clock went by, and two o'clock, and still she lay there, her ears straining for the faint sound of the violin music. At length that stopped and for a long time she could hear nothing, not even the sound of her parents' breathing.

What was happening over there? What could be happening?

At length Regina could stand it no more. She slipped out of bed, very carefully so as not to wake her sister, felt for her clothes and somehow managed to get into them in the dark. Then she felt for her mother's shawl which was always hung on a hook behind the door, wrapped it round her and stole to the front door.

It was a dark night with no moon and all that could be seen was a faint bluish glow on the snow. So as not to wake anyone in the house with the sound of her steps on the wooden floor, she put on her shoes only when she was already outside and on the last rung of the veranda steps. The shoes she wore were a pair of once fashionable high-heeled but sadly worn ladies' button boots which would have reached up to mid-calf if most of the buttons had not been missing. They had previously been worn by her mother until it had not seemed worth mending them anymore.

Regina moved slowly across the frozen yard, her feet skidding on the hard-trodden surface of the snow. She reached the corner of the woodshed and, from the gate in the fence, looked across the empty field towards Laszlo's house. There was a light in the window, a sinister reddish light; and to the girl it seemed as if the wicked flames of hell were beckoning to her and calling for her to come and look.

Clutching the heavy shawl around her she stumbled across the field in which her father had been growing potatoes. Where these had been lifted the earth had been left in uneven little mounds and ridges and holes so that, as the young girl headed straight for the light in the window, she stumbled and slipped and fell frequently to her knees, as her thin, dark figure made its tortured way across. If anyone had been watching it would have looked as if she were battling against a hurricane, staggering to left and to right as she struggled on through the dark night.

Finally she got there. There was not a sound to be heard and only the light that filtered out through the flower-like hoarfrost on the window-panes showed that anyone was still awake inside.

Regina crept up and pressed her face against the lowest pane, despite the fact that it was almost opaque from the ice crystals that had formed an incrustation of dense arabesques on the glass. Obsessed by the need to know what was happening inside she would have broken the glass itself if that had been the only way. She had to know, she had to! That was why she had come. She started to breathe on the windowpane and then to rub it with a corner of the shawl. Several times she had to repeat the process until at last a small patch at the centre began to come clear as she managed to melt a square no larger than her own little hand.

With searching eyes she looked round the room, her body rigid with emotion and excitement, her hand tightly grasping the window ledge. She stretched up her neck with the folds of the shawl falling like mourning bands on each side of her face.

She was very pale, except for her blood-red lips, and it was some time before she was able to see clearly what was happening in the room. It was even longer before she realized what it was, and longer still before she really understood.

For a long time she stood where she was, as if turned to stone. Then, overcome by deep disgust, she started shuddering and at length was able to force herself to turn away. Then she reeled from the window and started to run for home, heedless of how she fell and stumbled and tripped in mindless panic. She ran with eyes wide open as if by so doing she could run far away from what she had seen. She ran as a deer pursued by hounds ...

In Regina's head was nothing but the thought of escape. She clattered up the wooden steps of her father's house, fell against the door and then, though somehow she succeeded in opening it, fell senseless across the threshold.

Regina was ill for days and during all this time, though her parents looked after her with loving care, they never discovered where she had been that night. As it happened they never even asked her for they assumed that it was all the result of a fright she had had for, either as a result of being over-excited, or from the effects of her fall, that night she stopped being a child and became a woman.

As for Laszlo he hardly noticed Regina's absence. For some days after that evening's drinking he had lazed about, tired and listless. Fabian had left behind three bottles of brandy, perhaps on purpose, perhaps merely from forgetfulness; and so Laszlo had enough to drink without going to the shop. For some weeks he did not think about setting his traps and so had no need of Regina.

Now he started to cough rather more than before.

When Regina got better their relationship was unchanged. Once again she was ready to do anything he asked but she was, if anything, quieter than before. She was also very pale, and her large brown eyes seemed framed in some bluish dew.

## Chapter Two

The general peace that Europe had known since 1878 finally came to an end in the summer of 1911. The year began without any apparent change but then gradually a few hardly noticeable signs appeared whose significance was only understood much later and then only by those whose business it was to search out the truth of what had occurred. Though these little signposts were so scattered and apparently trivial, for the few who understood such things they showed only too clearly that the general air of calm throughout Europe was at best only an illusion. They were like the faint grey mist on the horizon at sunset or the soft mysterious murmur that precedes an earthquake.

Nothing that happened early that year seemed to suggest that the general confidence in a perpetual peace was not entirely justified. When Prince Nikita celebrated the fiftieth anniversary of his reign by declaring Montenegro to be a kingdom, and the monarchs of Italy, Bulgaria and Serbia all attended the festivities, it seemed to be no more than a family get-together ... and there was nothing to foretell the coming alliance. A few months later there was another outbreak of unrest in Albania – but no-one thought there might be any connection with what had transpired in Montenegro, for was there not always unrest in Albania? When, from the other end of Europe, the news came that the Dutch, that most peace-able of nations, were fortifying Vlissingen, there was a universal outcry, with the English press seeing the sinister hand of the Emperor Wilhelm, who no doubt envisaged a new base for his growing fleet that was only an hour or so from the coast of Great Britain and the English Channel. And when, some months later, the Dutch government countermanded their orders, it was everywhere said that this was forced on them by strong protests from England and France. Accordingly when this little tempest blew itself out, just as had the much bigger one provoked by the annexa-tion of Bosnia-Herzegovina a year or so before, it seemed that all such affairs were but storms in teacups which were bound, sooner or later, to be settled amicably by all concerned. A few discussions over a green baize table, an exchange of diplomatic letters, and all was as it always had been. Even most of the diplomatists thought of international affairs in this way and so it was natural for the general public to follow their example. When it was announced in Vienna that the army was to be increased and the navy given a grand new ship-building programme, most people read the news with indifference, believing it all to be little more than just one more manifestation of *folie de grandeur* on the part of the Emperor Franz-Josef.

In the Budapest Parliament all went smoothly enough, and even the prolongation until 1917 of the Austro-Hungarian banking law passed off with little more than the expected public bickering between Justh and the People's Party on one side and the Economic Minister Lukacs and Ferenc Kossuth on the other. However, as this all seemed merely part of the aftermath of the Coalition period, nobody showed any interest. That these old rifts in the former Coalition were now seeing the light of day for the first time, and were shown to be little more than the private dis-putes of professional politicians, once again only proved to most people that what the former leaders of the Coalition said and what they did were quite different matters.

oIt was typical of that long period of international calm that one of the French princes, Gaston d'Orléans, Comte d'Eu, should choose that moment to launch an anti-duelling league! To round up support he travelled all over Europe, stopping in every provincial capital where he thought a branch should be founded. Anyone who joined had to pledge themselves to take any affair of honour to some predetermined court and to abstain from having recourse to sabres or pistols.

The idea was sensible and the prince's motives commendably lofty. Gaston d'Orléans himself was an eminent and distinguished personage whose wife would have become Empress of Brazil if her father, Pedro II, had not been overthrown by the ungrateful Brazilians. He was received everywhere with the courtesy and ceremony to which his rank entitled him; and wherever he went a branch of his anti-duelling league was founded at once with its full complement of president, general-secretary, statutes and plans for regular meetings. It was of course most flattering to be able to refer to this royal prince, the grandson of King Louis-Philippe no less, as one's colleague and chief, and it was nice to be known to share the opinions of such an eminent person. The Comte d'Eu lived in Paris and no doubt, if under his wing, one would soon find oneself received in the most select houses in the Faubourg St Germain.

In Budapest the league was headed by some impressive names and, through the Countess Beredy's influence, her brother, Fredi Wuelffen-stein, was made the general secretary. From Hungary the prince was going on to Bucharest and so it was arranged that he should stop on the way at Kolozsvar so as to found the Transylvanian branch of the Anti-Duelling League.

There too he was received with honour and on the evening of his arrival a 'brilliant reception' (as the newspapers called it) was given for him at the Casino. It was followed by a banquet. Everyone with any pretensions to social prominence in Transylvania took care to be there.

An enormous U-shaped table had been set up in the hall. In the centre of the top table sat the prince flanked on one side by Sandor Kendy (Crookface) wearing the Cross of St Istvan, and on the other by Stanislo Gyeroffy (Carrots) who, when he had briefly been a member of Szapary's cabinet, had managed to be awarded the Grand Cross of Alexander for having participated in the negotiations which had led to the signing of a trading agreement with Bulgaria. In addition to the cross itself Gyeroffy was swathed in the wide red, green and white ribbon of the order. By right of these impressive decorations, which entitled their possessors to be addressed as 'Excellency', Crookface and old Gyeroffy had the places of honour on each side of the royal guest and they, in turn, were flanked by all the other local notabilities placed according to the strictest rules of precedence. Among them were the prefect and his immediate predecessor, the Sheriff, the Mayor, the Rector of the University and various prominent churchmen, as well as most of the provincial titled folk. They made a fine display and as background to the top table had been hung a magnificent Gobelins tapestry.

Facing the guest of honour were the other Sandor Kendy (known as 'Wiggles'), the elder Adam Alvinczy and Major Bogacsy, now retired from the army and acting as chairman of the Orphans' Court of Chancery. These were the official hosts.

Now that Bogacsy was no longer a serving officer he was dressed in civilian evening dress and the only thing left to remind one of his belligerent past was an enormous pair of moustaches which resembled nothing so much as a large black pudding suspended over his mouth. He wore the insignia of the Order of Maria-Theresia, which had been awarded him for some deed of bravery in the Bosnian war though what that had been no-one knew, for he never alluded to it himself. When Bogacsy did talk about his past he only referred to his prowess at innumerable duels where he had always been much in demand as a second.

Bogacsy was very angry. No-one had told him why Transylvania was being honoured by the visit of this foreign prince and until he had arrived in the hall all he knew was the name of the guest in whose honour the town was giving a banquet. As a director of the Casino he had naturally taken his place at the head of the stairs to welcome the distinguished visitor and then, as they were waiting for the dinner to be announced, stood for a while chatting with him in the smoking room. The Comte d'Eu was at his most affable as he talked to the three official hosts and then, in tolerably good German, he started talking about the league for which he was seeking support:

'*Es ist eine verachtenswürdige Sache, dass man in unserem aufgeklärtem Jahrhundert noch immer duelliert. Das Duell ist pure Barbarei – nicht wahr? Und ausserdem auch ein schrecklicher Blödsinn! Das ist wohl auch ihre Meinung?* – it is a disgraceful thing that in this enlightened age men still go in for duelling. The duel is pure barbarism, is it not? Apart from being frightfully stupid! I'm sure you agree, don't you?'

This was said directly to Bogacsy, and the prince then went on to explain how utterly idiotic duelling was: the winner was naturally the man who was a better shot or who knew best how to wield a sword, and what had this to do with who was in the right? It was stupid and unworthy of sensible men and a shameful legacy of the past!

Bogacsy was outraged and almost apoplectic with rage. It was not for him to start contradicting such an eminent guest and yet he knew that everyone within earshot was watching his reactions and with their true Transylvanian sense of the absurd were inwardly laughing at his predicament. Despite the restraint that was imposed by good manners Bogacsy was so angry at the thought of all that silent mockery that surrounded him that he would have exploded in protest if dinner had not then been announced. A difficult moment was somehow avoided; but the duelling major was still so upset that he could hardly touch any of the delicious dishes put before him, even though he had had to fork out twenty-five crowns for his dinner, which even then was by no means cheap.

At the end of one of the wings of the great U-shaped table was seated old Daniel Kendy. Remembering that he spoke French fluently as a result of having once been an attaché in the Austro-Hungarian Embassy in Paris in the last years of the Third Empire, the organizers had decided that he ought to be invited so that when dinner was over they could introduce him to the prince who would therefore be able to talk to someone who knew Paris well. As the old man had no money his nephew Crookface Kendy paid for his ticket, but as a broken-down old fellow of no importance he was seated some way away from the guest of honour. It was important to see that old Uncle Dani did not, as he usually did, drink too much. On this occasion the old man swore that he would not, and indeed was full of good intentions, so happy was he at the thought of coming again into his own and being made much of as the old social lion who had once been a favourite at the court of the Empress Eugénie and well known as a man-about-town in Paris in the years that followed. He decided that this night he must do all in his power to be at his best.

He had shaved and dressed with great care, and indeed the effect was impressive. Count Daniel Kendy for the first time in years looked truly distinguished and many eyes were upon him. His slightly thinning silver-white hair was parted in the middle and set off his jet-black eyebrows and aristocratically aquiline nose. His moustaches had been curled for the occasion and beneath his lower lip was an elegant little goatee. The whiskers on each side of his face were long but neatly trimmed, and with the low folded collar, wide lapels and broad starched white shirt and old-fashioned evening suit, he seemed the perfect evocation of the dandified *boulevardier* of half a century before. His appearance was so striking that the prince immediately asked who he was; and when told his name and history by Crookface, at once declared that he remembered him well from the days when the French royal family had first returned from exile abroad. 'Of course!' he cried. 'Le Comte Candi!' (which is what all the susceptible ladies in those Parisian drawing rooms had called him). The name still seemed to have a dreamy, erotic ring to it.

Uncle Daniel also recognized the prince, but he could not remember if he had seen him at the Rochechouarts' or at the Princesse de la Moskowa's. At that time Daniel Kendy was a young man with great expectations for whom everybody predicted a brilliant future. If he had not wasted his fortune on drink he too would have been addressed as 'Your Excellency' today. He would have been seated at the right hand of the royal guest, covered in orders and ribbons and distinctions, and not where he now found himself, in an insignificant place amid a noisy rabble of ill-behaved young men. Looking up at the notabilities in the place of honour, all resplendent in their decorations with the noble Gobelin tapestry behind them, Uncle Dani's heart was filled with sorrow and remorse.

As the dinner progressed he became sadder and sadder and sadder.

And what does one do when one's heart is filled with sorrow? One drinks: there is nothing else. And so the old man drank and, once started, he did not stop and the inevitable happened. When the time came for that meeting to which he had so much looked forward and they called to him to come up and be presented, the old man was already so drunk that he could hardly put one foot in front of the other. Then, once again, the sad thought of what he had once been and what, through no-one's fault but his own, he had thrown away, once more pierced his poor fuddled brain and all that he was able to do was to stagger towards the prince, weaving from right to left and bending double at every step in a humble parody of a bow, waving his arms, and stammer out sorrowfully in Hungarian, 'K-K-Kendy! … n-n-nothing more … K-K-Kendy … n-n-nothing more …'

He was incapable of uttering another word. As the Comte d'Eu turned away, two young men grabbed Uncle Dani by the arms and carried him out; for everyone knew what was likely to happen when he started bowing so obsequiously.

At one of the side wings of the table sat Balint with Gazsi Kadacsay. Because he was a Member of Parliament and also an imperial Court Chamberlain the organizers had wanted to place him with the other important guests, but he had refused, preferring to remain with his own close friends to being put on parade at the boredom of the top table. Furthermore when they had met that evening Gazsi had said that he wanted to have a talk with him.

They had not seen each other for some time. At the beginning of the Carnival season Gazsi had been in Kolozsvar for a week or two, and then he had disappeared and been seen no more. At that time everyone had decided that he would shortly announce his engagement to Ida Laczok, for he had dined there three times, danced with her often, and called daily at the Laczok house at the hour when they drank coffee topped with whipped cream. He had even serenaded the girl twice in a week, and so everyone had said that the engagement was imminent. Then he had suddenly returned to the country and was seen no more.

At the beginning of the dinner the conversation where Balint and Gazsi were sitting was all about the royal prince's tour to promote his famous Anti-Duelling League. As they were all young and high-spirited, as well as being from Transylvania, their talk was full of mockery. Among them only Isti Kamuthy and Fredi Wuelffenstein, who were sitting just opposite Balint, took the matter at all seriously; Fredi, not only because he was the league's general-secretary in Hungary but also because he always liked to know better than anyone else; and Isti, because he had recently become even more anglophile than ever. 'There are no duelth in England,' lisped Isti, and for him this settled the question and therefore there could be no further argument about it. Fredi was in perfect agreement, but he was out of temper because he had also thought of the same argument but had not been able to get it out first.

The general conversation was not able to continue for long, for almost at once Laci Pongracz and his musicians entered the hall and started to play and from then on it was only possible to talk to one's neighbour.

It was Kadacsay who started.

'I think I owe you something of an explanation,' he said to Balint. 'I only came this evening because I knew you'd be here.'

'Why?' said Balint, surprised. 'What about?'

'About Ida. I know there's been a lot of talk, and that it's not been all that flattering as far as I'm concerned. I don't mind what other people think, but I'd hate you to think badly of me too.'

Balint protested that he had no reason to think badly about Gazsi, but the latter went on, saying that when he had returned home from his visit to Denestornya he had thought a lot about Abady's suggestion that he should get married and that this would be a solution to many of his problems and perplexities. Finally he decided to try out the idea. He had already decided that young Ida was the only girl who might suit him and who, as a woman, he felt he could bring himself to love. Accordingly he had come to Kolozsvar in the middle of January and at first everything had gone swimmingly. The old Laczoks seemed pleased at the idea of having Gazsi as their son-in-law, so much so that Gazsi admitted to have been quite taken by surprise. 'To think that of an ass like me ...' he had said to Balint in a self-deprecating manner. But though everything went exceptionally well, they never seemed to get further than just dancing together and exchanging jokes. The girl was pretty enough, but somehow this had not seemed quite enough to Gazsi. Surely, he had thought, there must be something more if one was to spend a lifetime together. One would have to know what she thought about things, what interested her, and what her opinions were.

'Well,' he said. 'That was really the problem. The poor girl is very, very stupid!'

He had tried her on all sorts of subjects, some of them quite serious; but when he had started like this, all the silly thing could do was either to stare at him stupidly or start to giggle. She had seemed to think that he was trying to make fun of her and so replied 'What an odd question!' and changed the subject to cooking, or poultry, or even horses as if she knew that that was all the poor boy really understood. When he had asked what she was then reading, she would answer 'Nothing! Nothing at all! After all what's the use? A good housekeeper doesn't have time for that sort of thing!'

'It was terrible,' said Gazsi, and went on to tell Balint how he had finally revolted and dropped his pursuit of the girl. 'Could I take

99

someone like that into my home? Could I really live my life with such a goose ... and go on breeding brats even more useless than me ...?'

He said he had decided he could not bear the thought of someone who just could not understand what he would want for his children. She would destroy everything for which he had struggled; and this was what he had felt he must explain to Balint, lest his friend should think he had behaved badly in making people think he had pursued the girl and then abandoned her.

'I shouldn't think badly of you,' said Balint. 'Who am I to judge other people? Nobody has that right, nobody! And I least of all!'

As he said this Balint's own face clouded over for he was reminded of the time when he had made that sweet little Lili Illesvary think that he was about to propose to her and had then let the opportunity go by without saying what had been expected of him. Suddenly he remembered how she looked in the library at Jablanka and how she had gazed expectantly at him with her forget-me-not blue eyes ...

After that Gazsi and Balint did not speak for some time, so engrossed were they in their own private thoughts.

All at once Gazsi made a gesture with his hand as if he were brushing away some depressing thought. Then he drained his champagne glass, cleared his throat and turned back to Balint with the cryptic phrase, 'I've had Honeydew serviced!'

'Good God, why? She's your best hunter, isn't she?' Balint was taken by surprise at this statement until he reflected that this was not the first time that Gazsi recently had no longer seemed so keen on what everyone had thought to be his only interest. Perhaps this was just one further example of his newfound disillusionment with horses and sport? Whatever it signified it seemed to Balint that somehow Gazsi's pronouncement was connected with that unexpectedly deep strain of bitterness he had shown each time the two friends had met during the last year.

'Yes, last week. I sent her to "Gallifar" who is standing at stud at Kolozs. He's got a good line – by Gunnersbury out of Gaillarde – quite worthy of my good Honeydew.'

Then he went on, speaking in a low voice as if confiding deadly secrets, to give his reasons in a most unnecessarily complicated way, with much repetition and circumlocution. He said that Honeydew was already seven years old which meant it was high time she foaled, and the right age to produce something good and healthy. She was anyhow no use as a saddle horse for anyone except himself as she would tolerate no-one else on her back. It had recently, he said, become an intolerable slavery for him as he had always to be there to exercise her, for he couldn't entrust her to anyone else and it was no life for a horse just to be lunged for a couple of hours a day. This was much the best solution, for she'd calm down as soon as she was in foal. Then her temperament was sure to change and she'd no longer be so dependent on him.

'What on earth would become of her if I wasn't there ... I mean, if ... if I were to go off on some tr-r-rip. As a r-r-riding horse she'd just die ... At least in this way she'll be of some use.'

Balint found these words disquieting, for he seemed to see in them some connection with their talk at Denestornya when Kadacsay had talked about making his will and about his attitude to death. So as to lighten the mood he answered as if he had taken literally what Gazsi had said about going off on some trip.

'If you're thinking of being away some time, which I think would be a thoroughly good idea, then I'd suggest Italy. It's already spring there, especially down in the south, at Naples and in Sicily. You could have Honeydew sent over to Denestornya while you're away and we'll give her a paddock all of her own so that she could run free all day long. We often do this with new mares who don't know the other horses.'

'Could I really? Do you mean it?' cried Gazsi joyfully. 'Are you really sure? Do you know I was just working up to asking you if it might be possible ... not now, of course ... not yet. But, but, later ... if the situation arises ... well, it would be wonderful.' And then, seeing the concern in his friend's expression, he started to talk about all sorts of technical matters concerned with the treatment of mares in foal. He told Balint that he really didn't have anyone at his own home who was properly qualified and experienced, not like the stud groom at Denestornya, and all the others who had worked for Countess Roza for so many years. A first foaling was always a bit tricky, of course, and quite a delicate matter, especially with such a highly strung animal as Honeydew. Then he started to praise all his mare's good points and went out of his way to say that problems only arose when one put a saddle on her or tried to ride her; then she would grow wild, but at all other times she was as tame and docile as anyone could wish. If she didn't have a saddle on her back then she would never kick out, not at man or beast, never!

He talked on for some time having apparently entirely recovered his good humour. Then he reached for his glass, filled it to the brim and lifted it to Balint, saying: 'Servus – greetings! My appreciation and thanks ... in Honeydew's name.'

While Balint and Gazsi had been talking about the problem mare, on the other side of the table Isti and Fredi had been ever more heatedly discussing their favourite topic – England. They both worshipped England and all things English, the country itself, English gentlemen, English horses, English sports, English clothes and footwear, English girls, English bandages for horses' tendons, English guns and cartridges, English razors, English gardens and English dances. All these things they praised, sometimes in unison and sometimes antiphonally, and for a long time all went smoothly. Gradually, however, this harmony somehow produced discord and by the time coffee was served a real quarrel had started. It all began because Fredi, though he spoke English well and knew many English people, had never set foot in the country and so had had to adore his beloved one from afar, and content himself with what he heard second-hand. Isti Kamuthy, on the other hand, spoke English deplorably and had not only been in London the previous year but had also managed to be made a temporary visiting member of that eminent gentlemen's club, the St James's.

It had come about in the following way. Isti had been extremely active in helping the government candidate at a by-election at Szilagy towards the end of the Coalition. The man had been elected, and when they were all back in Budapest Isti had been singled out for praise by the then Minister for Internal Affairs. Isti, seeing his advantage, had at once stammered out, 'I h-h-have a r-r-request!' and, when encouraged by Andrassy to blurt it out, said that he would shortly be going to London and would be most grateful for an introduction to the Austro-Hungarian ambassador. Of course he had got his letter and had presented it to the ambassador, Count Mensdorf, as soon as he arrived. Mensdorf asked Isti how he could be of service and it turned out that Isti had only one request and that was somehow to be invited to join the St James's Club.

The request had verged on the absurd for, in the view of most foreigners and especially of the diplomatic corps, the St James's was then thought to be the most exclusive club in England to which very few Englishmen aspired even if they possessed the most exalted social background. To be admitted one had to fulfil the most stringent, even if unwritten, conditions; and these applied as much to foreign diplomatists as they did to native Englishmen. A few diplomats had been accepted, but so few that it had been taken as a special mark of distinction. Mensdorf did his best to explain all this to Isti, adding that, according to English etiquette, new members must not speak to any existing member until the other had first introduced himself. This meant that even if Isti did get in it might still be several years before he managed to make any friends and so, the ambassador suggested, it would really be more sensible if Count Kamuthy dropped the idea altogether. He proposed a wealth of other, most tempting, ideas – invitations to spend the weekend at the houses of well-known peers, shooting parties in Scotland, a car trip through some of England's most beautiful countryside, house parties for the famed Cowes Regatta. Isti was unimpressed. He wanted only one thing, to be elected to the St James's, and this was his only request. Nothing else. Absolutely nothing else!

It happened that Mensdorf was closely related to King Edward and so he had considerable influence in social affairs. He bestirred himself and the miracle happened: Kamuthy was accepted.

So, for the two weeks that Isti was in England he was to be seen, day after day, from morning till evening, sitting at one of the first-floor windows of the St James's Club gazing proudly out into Piccadilly. No-one spoke to him and even the club servants hardly tried to conceal their contempt. Isti did not care. He could sit there in the window, surrounded by huge mirrors, happy in the knowledge that the thousands of people who passed along the street in front of him could look up and envy him and that, among all the more than seven million inhabitants of London there was barely one who was so privileged as to have the right to sit there behind the glass and drink his tea in the sight of all. It was a heavenly feeling.

After his two weeks Isti had come home. Though he had studied his Baedeker until he almost knew it by heart, all he had seen of England were the rooms of his club. It is true that he had marched through some of the museums, not because he was interested by anything he saw there but rather so that he had something to talk about when he returned. And talk he did. Even now he was telling Fredi about his experiences; and this was the origin of their quarrel. When Isti said that he had become a member of the St James's, Fredi was so jealous that he turned as yellow as if he were suffering from jaundice. From then on if Isti used an English word, Fredi would correct his pronunciation. 'You don't say "Anglish" but "Inglish", "Waterloo" not "Waterlow", "mew-seum" not "mooseum".' Fredi became insufferable and Isti couldn't bear it. He spluttered out that 'thomebody who had never been in England shouldn't prethume to correct him', and at this Fredi rejoined that if one didn't speak English it was ridiculous to go there.

The quarrel got noisier and noisier and Laci Pongracz, who was not far away, heard it and promptly switched to an even louder csardas in an attempt to cover up what was happening. Even so some of those sitting nearby were beginning to notice, and Kadacsay called across the table, 'Watch it, you two! People are listening.'

Whereupon the two would-be Englishmen stopped arguing and sat next to each other in grim silence. Before long Wuelffenstein could stand it no longer and, so as to have the last word, turned to Isti and said scornfully, 'Anyhow I don't believe you ever set foot in the St James's!'

Kamuthy swelled with rage and, scarlet in the face at being denied his triumph, jumped up and lisped at the top of his voice, 'Thatth nothing but ungentlemanly intholence! Intholent and ungentlemanly!'

'How dare you?' cried Wuelffenstein, also jumping up and at the same time banging the table with his enormous fist so that a coffee cup was overturned and went clattering onto the floor. It was fortunate that Stanislo Gyeroffy chose the same moment to rise from the table and with considerable presence of mind guide his royal guest away from the scene of battle into the quiet of the smoking room. Amid the noise of everyone getting up from table the Comte d'Eu himself was quite unaware that anything untoward had happened. Posting himself in front of the fireplace he proceeded to give a long scholarly dissertation on the history and development of duelling to the group of obsequious old gentlemen who had accompanied him out of the hall.

Bogacsy was there too, sitting facing the prince. He did not remain there long because almost as soon as he had sat down Farkas Alvinczy came up to the back of his chair and whispered a few words in his ear. Then he vanished. The retired soldier's eyes glinted but he did not move because at that moment the prince was looking in his direction. Somehow it seemed that his great handlebar moustaches had grown even longer as Bogacsy's mouth widened in a smile of pure joy. As soon as the Comte d'Eu's attention was engaged elsewhere Bogacsy got up and quietly left the room, leaving an empty place in the royal circle.

Kamuthy's seconds were already waiting for him in the so-called Ladies' Dining Room on the other side of the stairway. They were Joska Kendy, who stood there silently sucking on his pipe, and a mild young man called Garazda who came originally from Western Hungary and was now in his third year at the university in Kolozsvar. The usual stern greetings were exchanged with much formal ceremony but no shaking of hands. Then Fredi's seconds, Bogacsy and Alvinczy, sat down on one side of the table and Isti's on the other.

Then the traditional words were uttered, 'Our client, Count Nandor Wuelffenstein, demands satisfaction.'

All went according to the customary procedure, and in a few moments everything had been settled. There was no question of a reconciliation, nor of a Court of Honour as was recommended by the Anti-Duelling League to all its members. Armed satisfaction then? Of course! Swords? Naturally! Both sides agreed to light cavalry sabres. Up to what point? Disability, of course! When ...?

This was a problem, for Fredi, as general-secretary of the league in Hungary, was expected to accompany the prince as far as the Romanian border; and the prince was due to leave at five a.m. It was too late to change any of these arrangements.

'Well then,' said young Garazda, 'what about when he gets back from the border?'

'Certainly not!' said Bogacsy peremptorily. 'The Code Duverger expressly states that if both parties to a duel are present nothing shall prevent the meeting taking place. The duel can take place at once, tonight. It isn't even eleven yet; by midnight the whole affair will be settled.'

'Very well, but where? The Gymnasium is now closed and there is no other suitable hall.'

'But there is!' roared Bogacsy triumphantly. 'Right here! This room is quite big enough if we push the table to one side. The floor isn't too slippery, in fact it's just right. As one of the Casino's directors I hereby give my official permission.'

Then they got down to details. Two medical men would have to be routed out of their beds and made to attend. Bogacsy had a pair of light cavalry sabres at his apartment and Farkas Alvinczy two more. They would send for them and the two opponents could draw lots as to which pair was used.

Then Farkas said, in a worried tone, 'Where on earth can we find a sabre-sharpener at this hour? Mine are as blunt as anything.'

Here the major interrupted, saying proudly, 'Mine are sharp as razors! And my man can sharpen the others. He's very good at it: I taught him myself.'

To make sure that all went smoothly certain responsibilities had to be allocated. Garazda undertook to rouse Kamuthy's doctor, while Farkas agreed to get the other, and also to collect his two swords. Bogacsy, as a director of the Casino and one of the hosts at the banquet, could not leave the building while the prince was still under its roof, and so he asked Joska to go to his flat and wake his valet who would collect everything necessary and bring it all over, the sabres and the honing instruments. And so it was arranged that everything could be done at once and precisely as it should be.

Bogacsy now returned to the smoking room and, finding that no-one had usurped his chair, sat down again where he had been facing the prince, who was still in full flood. The duelling major listened with joy in his heart.

'... and from where, I ask you, does duelling stem? Who started this barbaric habit? I tell you, gentlemen, it is the last survival of the medieval *auto-da-fé*. In those benighted times people still believed that God would intervene and give victory to the one with right on his side, to the gentle and true in heart, while the sinner would perish miserably. Even then, of course, they were apt only to let the most experienced swordsmen take their chance with God's judgement. But today, gentlemen, today? Who believes that Divine Providence has anything to do with the outcome? Who on earth would be bothered with such nonsense? Nowadays we all know that the victor is he who has had most practice, be it with swords or pistols. Why, the vilest man can kill the most honest! It is terrible, really terrible!'

An approving murmur greeted these words. Even Crookface belched out something, but whether it was in agreement with the royal proposition remained doubtful. Bogacsy, however, nodded his head vigorously at every word.

This was only to be expected for the battling ex-officer had been uncomfortably aware of what a ridiculous figure he had cut before dinner when all the young men, especially those who were now standing about in the background, had been mocking his predicament. Now it was his turn to lead their silent mockery of the philanthropic prince; and the turn of those mocking young brats to admire him, Bogacsy, the perfect second who could listen so impassively to the royal visitor's absurdly inopportune speeches. Nothing showed in his expression, for it was a golden rule where duelling was concerned, that no-one spoke of the encounter until after it had happened. So he sat there stiffly, with his legs stretched out and his paunch protruding, the very picture of authority and elegant sangfroid. He knew he was doing it right and that everyone else knew it too.

It seemed that the royal guest would never stop. On and on he talked – for about an hour and a half – in good German and well-turned phrases. Of course his fluency was helped by the fact that he had said all this many times before, in several different languages and many different countries. And of course, too, he was listened to in deferential silence. There were no interruptions and no disturbances; how could there be?

After half an hour had passed young Garazda came quietly up to Bogacsy's chair and whispered something in his ear. Later Farkas Alvinczy did the same thing, and later still it was Joska's turn. There was nothing conspicuous about it, for each message was delivered discreetly and quietly. Bogacsy himself merely nodded acknowledgement of whatever he had been told, and these nods could equally well have been taken as tacit approval of the prince's plea to end duelling in Europe.

At long last the Comte d'Eu got up, and so did everyone else, straightened his elegant figure, looked with his sad grey eyes at the people near him, thanked them for their hospitality and warm welcome, and said how touched he was to find himself surrounded by so many people in tune with his philanthropic movement. He had hardly, he said, expected to meet with such success, such understanding and such sympathy among the people of a nation so traditionally warlike as the Hungarians and was surprised, as well as delighted, to encounter such support from those whose habit had always been to settle everything with a sword. And yet, here he was and everybody he met seemed to be in perfect agreement with him and to be only too happy to join the league against duelling. He said he felt filled with renewed strength and confidence and was now quite sure that very soon duelling would disappear for ever and be thought of only as one of the errors of the past.

'Dank, meine Herren. Dank, Dank, Dank – thank you, gentlemen, thank you, thank you, thank you!'

These words were greeted by well-bred, if slightly muted, applause; and nobody seemed to notice that at the back, from the direction of the card room, came some hastily suppressed giggles.

Surrounded by the Casino's three directors and, as befitted his exalted rank, preceded by two footmen carrying tall candelabra, the prince was escorted down the stairs. Just as he reached the swing doors into the street there was a moment's interruption as a little man with a turned-up collar and carrying a small Gladstone bag scurried in. The newcomer quickly effaced himself, flattening himself modestly against the dark wall of the vestibule. No-one noticed that he carried a bottle of disinfectant under one arm and that his pockets were stuffed with bandages!

He was one of the doctors that Bogacsy had sent for to attend the duel.

Though he was a trifle late Wuelffenstein managed somehow to get to the train on time. He was wearing what might have been a white turban on his head and his suddenly swollen nose was decorated with a wide Leukoplast dressing.

He was in a thoroughly bad temper for young Kamuthy had not only opened up his scalp but also slashed him on the nose, which was far more humiliating. Stupid ass! thought Fredi. Dwarfish little beast!

It so happened that, on the command to attack, Wuelffenstein, awkward as some tall men sometimes are, swung out his sword-arm in a wide arc, and little Isti, like an enraged hamster, had jumped in, hit him on the nose with his sword-hilt and given him a nasty slash on the forehead which had needed eight stitches to patch up. But that was not the end of it. The worst moment came when Fredi's nose started to bleed and that was when the fight was stopped, though not the nose-bleed which continued ignominiously until the flow had been stemmed by two huge wads of cotton wool which nearly suffocated him. Now he could only breathe through his mouth and he was racked with anxiety as to how he would look the following day with his nose all black and blue. It was a dreadful thought.

It did not help Fredi's good humour that the Comte d'Eu, instead of going at once to his grand sleeping compartment, insisted on waiting on the platform for Fredi to arrive, and when he did plied him with such solicitous enquiries that Fredi was forced to go into endless untrue explanations to excuse the condition he found himself in, for it would hardly have done for the general-secretary of the Anti-Duelling League to admit to having settled an affair of honour with sabres on the very evening that the league had held its first meeting in Kolozsvar. Up in smoke would have gone Fredi's pride in his new royal acquaintance, gone the dreams of success in the exclusive drawing rooms of the Faubourg St Germain, gone the thought of royal protection. Fredi's snobbish little soul had been seduced by the thought of meeting grand French duchesses in Legitimist salons, and being on nodding terms with rich manufacturers of champagne; and he knew only too well that none of this would ever happen if it were known what he had been up to that night, which it well might if Bogacsy had not insisted on accompanying Fredi to the station.

But Bogacsy was there with him, for it was the belligerent little ex-major's pride that he took his duties as second with deadly seriousness and would never abandon them until the affair was over and done with. This was especially true today when he could add his own flourish of mockery to the whole ridiculous affair. When he found the anti-duelling prince still on the platform at the station, old Bogacsy was overjoyed and his black-pudding moustache fairly bristled with pride. Though his German pronunciation was appalling, he was still able to give the prince an adroit and acceptable explanation for Fredi's appearance, declaring that his good friend Wuelffenstein had tripped on the Casino stairs, fallen against the balustrade, damaged his forehead and broken his nose.

'Iss grosze Maleur, Hohayt, iss grosze Maleur ...' which even the prince managed to grasp meant 'What bad luck, Highness, what bad luck!' Bogacsy repeated this several times, bowing each time so deeply that it was possible no-one saw the triumph in his eyes.

Only when the train had rumbled out of sight did he straighten up. Then he gave an extra twirl to his moustaches and marched off the platform as if he were Caesar and had just conquered Gaul.

# Chapter Three

Adrienne came back to Kolozsvar at the beginning of November. She arrived on the early morning express from Budapest, but that was only the end of her journey for before that she had been both to Lausanne in Switzerland and to Meran in South Tyrol. Adrienne had gone to Lausanne to visit her daughter Clemmie, who had been sent to the same boarding school that Adrienne herself had attended. She had found to her relief that some of her old teachers were still there and that they seemed to be just as wise and clever and sympathetic as she remembered them. The headmistress was now Madame Laurent, who had just started her career when Adrienne had been a pupil and who had always seemed to Adrienne to be more of a friend than a teacher. It was because Madame Laurent had taken over the school that Adrienne had decided to send Clemmie there, for she had every confidence in the wisdom and understanding of children's needs that Madame Laurent had always possessed. Now that her daughter had been there six months Adrienne had been to see her and also to discuss with her old friend what could be done with a child who had such a strangely withdrawn and unfriendly nature. Madame Laurent had explained the little girl's problems with such clarity that Adrienne, who had been worried and perplexed, now began to understand more clearly what was needed.

She had been thinking about this for most of the journey home. First of all she had reviewed all that had happened to make her take that painful decision to send her daughter to a school that was so far away from her mother. She knew it had been for the best and that there had not really been any other choice.

Until her husband had finally gone mad the child's grandmother had brought her up. Adrienne had been allowed no say whatever in little Clemmie's upbringing. She had even had to fight with her husband and mother-in-law to be allowed to nurse her when she had measles. The girl had been ill for an unusually long time and when some months had passed Adrienne had come to believe that in reality the little girl did love her mother but had been made to hide her affection because of the iron will of old Countess Clémence. She had been mistaken. When Pal Uzdy finally had had to be removed to the madhouse the emotional shock had completely broken the old lady who stayed in her own room, as motionless as a living statue, staring with unseeing eyes straight ahead of her and hardly ever speaking let alone taking any interest in whatever happened around her. She had withdrawn into herself and everyone else had been kept at a distance: not only Adrienne, whom she had always hated, but also her grandchild whom she was thought to have loved. When the child had been brought in to see her, she had just gestured for them to take her out again, and it had then been clear to Adrienne that Clemmie must be removed from Almasko as soon as possible. Two days later the French governess and English nanny had brought her to the Uzdy villa outside Kolozsvar.

Soon afterwards Countess Clémence also left Almasko. With Maier and her elderly maid she took off for her villa at Meran and had been there ever since. She never wrote and any news that Adrienne had of her came from the servants when they wrote to thank her for the monthly cheque that Adrienne sent them.

For the first time since her birth Adrienne's daughter belonged solely to her mother.

For a little while Clemmie had been her only joy, for their coming together coincided with Adrienne's second separation from Balint, a separation that she then believed was for ever. And so Adrienne lavished on the child all the love of which she was capable, for she felt that now there was no-one else. She spent all her time with her, and tried hard to win her love.

She did not succeed.

From the moment that it was clear that the grandmother was no longer there all signs of love for her mother also vanished. Those little shows of affection that had so heartened Adrienne while Clemmie was recovering from measles were seen no more, and it was not long before Adrienne had realized with a pang that what she had taken as a growing love for her mother had been nothing more than the child's desire to vex her grandmother.

Until Countess Clémence had left for Meran the little girl had always lived with her in the main house whenever the family had been in Kolozsvar. As soon as she had gone Adrienne moved her into Pal Uzdy's rooms in the one-storey wing next to her own bedroom. They were large rooms filled with light and air, but though her mother soon fixed them up as a nursery suite filled with expensive dolls and other toys, Clemmie ignored them all and never played with them. The most beautiful, an engaging and tempting clown, had barely been glanced at as it sat under the Christmas tree and when finally it had been picked up and given to her, the child had solemnly offered her polite thanks – as she had with every other toy given to her – picked it up and placed it at once on the nursery shelves along with all the others: and there they had stayed, lined up in exact order. If they were picked up when the room was dusted and not replaced exactly in line as they had been Clemmie would at once pick them up and replace them carefully in their proper place. Otherwise she never touched them. They simply did not interest her.

However, she did show interest in reading and so was given all the best children's books that Adrienne could lay her hands on – the volumes of the *Bibliothèque Rose, Alice in Wonderland,* and many others. These too she would accept coolly and always thanked her mother with formal politeness, though never with any sign of joy or pleasure. Once a box of coloured pencils had somehow inadvertently got among the other presents and, though she gave no sign of interest at the time, after a few days Adrienne noticed that whenever Clemmie had a spare moment she would get out the pencils and start making strange designs with them. She never made any attempt at figures – the sort of awkward men and animals that other children did – but instead would carefully and deliberately draw exaggerated coloured contour lines around the capital letters of her books, contours that were filled in with backgrounds of blue, red or green and which were sometimes three times as large as the original letters. Sometimes she would add meticulously drawn hatching to give solidity and depth, and here and there would add a huge eye or some horns. A little later she started doing similar drawings in her school copybooks, all just as precise and careful as if they had been part of her schoolwork. However, if someone called her she would put it down at once, as if she had no real interest in it, and if her mother tried to make some light-hearted comment, or enquire why she was doing it and what it meant, the child would merely reply with cold indifference 'I just do it' or 'It doesn't mean anything' or even, with studied politeness, 'I don't know why, I just do it!'

Clemmie never said anything about herself or her feelings. She never confided in anyone and it seemed as if nothing ever stirred her heart. She was never anything but polite and well-mannered; but she was always reserved and distant. The expression on her pretty, slightly Tartar-like features never changed and she always kept her brown eyes half closed, as if she were being careful not to reveal anything of herself. Her hair was very black and straight, just like her father's; and indeed she seemed to be completely Pal Uzdy's daughter not only in physical resemblance but also in character. In her there was nothing of her mother and nothing of that robust joy of life that characterized her mother's family.

For nearly a year Adrienne fought hard to find the way to her daughter's heart. She fought with love and tenderness and she sacrificed every minute of every day to gain her daughter's love and confidence. Eventually Adrienne realized that all these months of emotional struggle and effort had produced no result at all except perhaps to make matters worse between them. Everything she had done had been in vain and it seemed as if in some way it was those same efforts, that constant care and constant attention, that had somehow provoked even more withdrawal on her daughter's part. Adrienne could not put her finger on whatever it was that was wrong: she could sense it but she could find no reason.

It was then that she had made the painful decision to separate herself from little Clemmie and send her to school in Lausanne.

Now, coming back from her first visit to her daughter, she knew that it had been a wise decision, and not only because for the first time Clemmie had seemed pleased to see her mother; she had also shown signs of real affection. It had clearly done her good to be among girls of her own age who enjoyed life and played boisterously all around her.

What the headmistress had reported to her had been reassuring, even if not completely so.

Clemmie, she had been told, was an excellent pupil, obedient and industrious. At first, the headmistress said, she had been worried that, although always polite, Clemmie had been exceptionally unfriendly towards the other girls, but this had gradually begun to disappear, especially after she had begun to take part in the school sports. The girl had been taught tennis, rowing and a number of other ball games and, so as to put her more at her ease, she had been given five companions of her own age and it had been with the same five that all the games were played. These other girls had been specially picked because they were quiet and well-behaved and even-tempered. Clemmie played tennis with them, rowed with them and indeed spent most of her leisure time with the same little band. And, if this companionship had not actually ripened into real friendship, it was still companionship and the girl certainly seemed to get on well with her new little circle. In this she was helped by the fact that she was more intelligent than the others and this, together with her reserved manner, made the others – all naturally affectionate girls – look up to her as their leader and try to win her affection.

'Normally,' said the headmistress, 'I do all I can to prevent the formation of little clans among my pupils, but here, for once, I encouraged it. There seemed to be no other way if your daughter Clémence was not to start shutting herself off completely from the others … and that would have been really bad for her … most harmful.'

Madame Laurent was silent for a moment or two. Then she added, '*Car naturellement c'est une enfant assez difficile* – of course she is naturally rather a difficult child.' It was just this sentence that had worried Adrienne, for it had seemed to point to the possibility of an innate, inherited, danger. Then Madame Laurent went on: 'I firmly believe,' she had said with quiet confidence, 'that with constant attention and a lot of patience we will be able to bring her to a state of mind in which she will be able to cope properly with adult life. I am glad that you brought her to us so young.'

For Adrienne these last words had been a real encouragement and even more so because before she had brought Clemmie to Lausanne she had written fully to Madame Laurent telling her the whole story of the Uzdy family, of Pal Uzdy's madness, of Countess Clémence's decline into silence and melancholia and every detail that could in any way be of use to her.

Adrienne had not come straight home. On the way she had changed trains at Innsbruck and gone to Meran.

She had gone with a heavy heart, but she had gone because she considered it her duty to take care of old Countess Uzdy. It did not matter to her that the old woman had hated her from the day she had married her son, nor that she herself had detested her mother-in-law just as heartily during all those years that they had been forced to live in the same house as undeclared but nonetheless implacable enemies. Now that Adrienne was the only stable element left in the wreck of that sad family she knew she must put all her personal feelings and resentments aside and see to it that the old lady was properly looked after and lacked for nothing. Before leaving Transylvania she had written to the Uzdys' old retainer

Maier, who had gone with Countess Clémence to Meran, to say that she would be coming, and she had also sent a telegram when she left Lausanne. So, when she arrived at noon, the old man was on the platform to meet her.

Maier had not changed since those traumatic days when she had last seen him. It was as if neither time nor tragedy could touch him. He was still the same powerfully built, stocky man with a clear complexion, calm expression and intelligent eyes that she had always known. Now he must be over seventy, for his service with the Uzdy family had started when, as a fully qualified nurse, he had come to Almasko to look after Pal Uzdy's poor mad father. After his death he had stayed on until Pal Uzdy himself had been taken away hopelessly insane and now, for the last year and a half, he had looked after the old countess. She was the third member of that unhappy family to be served by him with a devotion and discretion that was almost saintly.

'And how is my mother-in-law?' asked Adrienne, as she shook hands with the powerful old man. 'Can she see people? When would be the best time?'

His answer was slow and ponderous, 'As your ladyship will see there has been no visible change, but then that is only to be expected in cases of mental illness. I think …' He hesitated before going on to say, '… perhaps it would be best to do it as soon as your ladyship arrives at the house.'

It was a wonderful day, and the autumn sun was as hot as if it were already spring. The snow-covered mountaintops seemed far closer than the row after row of foothills from which they sprang. It was as if they had somehow floated free of the ravines and pine forests below, and the great peaks of the Order range hung weightlessly like vaporous clouds in the azure purity of the Italian sky. Adrienne walked slowly up the hill behind the town's old fortress and all around her were orchards and vineyards and groups of dark evergreens like laurels and cedars that were interspersed with jasmine and camellia. Below her path the valley spread out, rich and fertile, and was dotted with small castles, churches and convents crowning each hilltop. A river threaded its leisurely way through velvet meadows. The whole landscape seemed to smile with peace and happiness.

Countess Uzdy's villa stood a little to the right of the road. Its entrance was on the north side but the main façade looked over the valley to the south-west. Like so many Italian houses built on a hillside it had been set in the centre of a large square stone terrace like an iced cake upon a tray, and from it steps led downwards to other terraces and gardens below but from the entrance all the visitor could see of this was the tops of the trees planted at a lower level.

It was only as Adrienne passed through the entrance gates that she realized how apprehensive she was. On her way to the house all she had thought was that this was a routine call and that it was her duty. It was her first visit to Meran and as she strolled up from the station she had been thinking only of how beautiful everything was. Now, as she stood on the threshold of her mother-in-law's house, she was suddenly aware how much she dreaded meeting the old woman again. It was not simply that in a few moments she would once again be face to face with the person with whom, despite Countess Uzdy's never concealed hatred of her, she had had to spend so many years in the same house; it was also that this confrontation would entail explaining why she had come and giving her news of Pal Uzdy and of her little granddaughter. She would once again have to put up with the old woman's icy stare and her probably offensive and unwelcoming remarks. Of course Maier had told her in several letters that nowadays the old woman sometimes did not utter a word for days on end, that she was usually listless and would sit quite still for hours without apparently noticing anything that went on around her; and that they even had to remind her to get up to go and wash, or take her meals, or go to bed. She had become, it seemed, little more than an automaton and had to be urged and encouraged to go through the ordinary motions of everyday life. Though Adrienne did not for a moment disbelieve any of this, she still wondered if it would be the same when they actually met or whether, at the sight of her, the old woman's venomous nature would overcome her depression and bring her back to life.

And this was not the only thing that made Adrienne suddenly afraid: she wondered too if she herself could muster enough self-control to appear natural and friendly and to talk as lightly and calmly as if that old hatred had never existed. She was desperately worried lest all those years of resentment would rise up and betray her into anger.

As these troubling thoughts flashed through her mind, she turned to Maier and said, 'I think it would be best to prepare her, and so, my good Maier, I should be grateful if you would go ahead and see her first. I will just stay here quietly for about a quarter of an hour. Then you can come and take me in. I'll be sitting on that stone bench.'

The old man said nothing, either in agreement or contradiction, but just looked at Adrienne with understanding. Then he nodded and disappeared into the house. The door closed noiselessly behind him.

When Adrienne found herself alone she sat down in the shade on the stone bench by the door and waited deep in thought. However, she only stayed there for a moment or two. Perhaps because it was cool in the shade she began to shiver slightly and so got up and walked round to the front of the house which was in full sun. She went very slowly, assailed by old and disturbing memories, memories that went right back to the first days of her engagement to Pal Uzdy when she had met his mother for the first time. She thought, too, of more recent times at Almasko when, after that dreadful moment when Uzdy had rounded on his mother and attacked her viciously, she had, out of pity for Countess Clémence, gone to be with her in her room only to be screamed at and greeted with the awful and wholly unjustified accusation 'It is you that turned my son against me! You poisoned him! You!'

Adrienne was thinking of this as she turned the angle of the house. Then, still very slowly, she started to walk along the broad terrace that stretched the full length of the south front of the house. On this side there were five long windows overlooking the town. The shutters of four of them were closed and the bright sunlight painted lilac-blue shadows below each of the louvred wooden slats. One window was open and when Adrienne reached it she found herself face to face with her mother-in-law who was sitting, barely five paces away, just inside the room. The low windowsill barely reached the level of her knees and she sat there, bolt upright, dressed entirely in black, like a statue of mourning. One shrivelled mummy-like hand lay in her lap. That, and the narrow lace collar at her throat, were the only touches of light to relieve the darkness of her figure. Even her thin face seemed almost as dark as her dress despite the sunlight which lit up her uplifted chin and prominent cheekbones. It was like light on dull bronze, and in some frightening way she had an ancient Egyptian look, calm, mysterious and menacing. She could have been an icon carved from granite so black that it absorbed any light that fell on it.

Adrienne stood in front of her as if petrified; but the old woman's Tartar-like eyes never moved and never showed any glint or sign that she even noticed that anyone was there.

Adrienne did not know how long she stood there, but it felt like an eternity during every minute of which she expected to hear a sharp reprimand, evil malignant words that would be followed by the old woman's leaping to her feet uttering a curse. But Countess Uzdy remained as mute and motionless as if carved from stone.

Gradually Adrienne realized that her mother-in-law was not looking at her and probably had not even seen her. Her eyes were fixed on something infinitely far away, beyond the far horizon and, like a stone idol, saw nothing that was in front of her. Even so Adrienne did not move. She stood there mesmerized as if bewitched by those sightless pebble-like eyes.

Someone touched her shoulder. It was Maier; and only then did Adrienne come back to reality. Silently she backed away and only when the old woman was hidden by the window frame could she bring herself to turn around and follow the old servant back round the corner of the house. Then she turned to him and said, 'Let us go inside where we can sit down and talk over what is to be done ... I must leave again this evening.'

They went indoors to the room which Maier used as an office. Here the old maid came to pay her respects to Adrienne who then went over all the accounts, checking the bills and receipts more as a matter of form than necessity, for Adrienne knew how trustworthy both these old retainers were. It was a welcome relief to have to think about such humdrum matters for, as she did so, all the accumulated tension slowly left her so that she was able to discuss in a matter-of-fact way everything that concerned the future running of the house, the expenses, the sending of the necessary funds, in fact everything that was needed for Countess Clémence's continued residence at Meran. Finally they discussed her medical needs, the nursing, the doctors' visits and how they diagnosed the old woman's condition. Now Adrienne was at last able to ask Maier what the outlook was and whether there was any likelihood of recovery.

Maier, who was sitting on the other side of the table tidying away the papers he had just been showing his mistress, looked up sadly and in a slow ponderous manner explained that the specialist who had been attending the noble countess had said that when old people developed this sort of melancholia there was rarely any hope of improvement. The patient could live on to an advanced age, for the body needed very little nourishment when it was not called upon to make any effort. With proper nursing the noble countess would continue in the same state for many years to come. Of course it was always possible that some sort of crisis might occur and then they would have to be very watchful and careful because in such cases patients sometimes became suicidal.

'We are always on our guard,' said Maier, 'though up until now there has never been any sign of anything of the sort. It seems that even if there should be some sort of nervous crisis the patient usually soon reverts to apathy ... so she would once again be as your ladyship saw her today, to all intents and purposes unconscious of her surroundings. This can last for years until such time ... such time as the body just wears out and starts slowly to ... to ... crumble away.'

Once alone again in the darkened sleeper Adrienne had thought about everything that had happened during the two weeks she had been away from home; about Lausanne and Clemmie and the talks with the headmistress, and, of course, about that sombre visit to Meran. She had been thinking of nothing else since she had got into the train long before night fell.

But, though Adrienne had gone over and over it all in her mind, repetition had not had the effect of making her memory of what had happened any clearer or more vivid. On the contrary, the closer she came to Kolozsvar, to home, so all the depressing events of the whole trip paled into insignificance compared with the sense of joyful expectation she felt arising in her.

When the train emitted a long whistle and for a few minutes all other sounds were drowned by a deep thundering reverberating rumble, Adrienne smiled happily to herself. They were passing through the Sztana tunnel, the last before she reached her destination. Home! Home! In an hour she would be home! In just an hour she would be lying back on her great white carpet covered with red cushions in front of a roaring fire.

There she would wait, gazing into the flames, until about midnight she would hear a little sound from the latch of the French window that gave onto the garden and her lover would come to her. Then, and only then, as she lay in Balint's arms, would she really feel at home. Then she would forget all her cares, her sorrows and worries, and the memories of the cruel days that were now past. Everything would vanish in their triumphant reunion. And this was the only reality ... only this.

## Chapter Four

A few days after Adrienne's return to Kolozsvar there took place one of the season's most elegant balls. It was a Bal des Têtes at which all the women were required to wear elaborate headdresses.

The idea had come from Elemer Garazda, the young man from the district of Tolna in Western Hungary who was in his third year studying law at the university. In Transylvania he was known to everyone as 'the Garazda Boy', or just 'Boy' for short, for one could hardly see his light-blonde moustache on his youthful pink and white face and also because it seemed amusing to address such a tall robust young man as 'Boy'. He had been chosen as leading dancer and organizer (*elotancos*) of all the dances and balls; and this in itself was a tribute to his popularity and efficiency as well as being an unusual compliment to someone who was not born in Transylvania. In recognition of this he had been doing his best to show his gratitude for the honour done to him, and so he had put forward the idea of the Bal des Têtes so as to show that he was full of energy and enterprise and capable of organizing something new and beautiful and amusing. He wanted to justify the confidence they had put in him.

The Garazda Boy had seen similar balls at the exclusive Park Club in Budapest where they had recently been introduced and had become very popular. The Kolozsvar Bal des Têtes was a charity ball given in aid of some Szekler villages that had been devastated by fire. It was the first ball to be organized in the new ballroom of the Central Hotel rather than in the old Redut Room where all the balls had previously been held.

The occasion had been eagerly awaited by all those who would attend; by the men because they would not have to make themselves ridiculous in some idiotic costume, and by their womenfolk because they could go in a classic ballgown and not spend a fortune on some elaborate fancy dress; and also because they would be able to dazzle their friends, and hopefully outdo them, with some amazingly original and magnificent and hitherto undreamed-of ornamental headdress.

For weeks before there had been to-ing and fro-ing and thought and planning and much pleasurable secrecy as to what all the fashionable ladies would wear. While everyone tried hard to find out what the others had chosen each was determined to keep their own ideas secret lest anyone should try to imitate what they had planned, thus leading to that social disaster when two or more women were dressed alike.

Nevertheless, in spite of, or perhaps because of, all this manic secrecy several women found themselves in just the situation they had most dreaded. There were eight Turkish turbans, five Dutch bonnets, three Andalusian headdresses complete with high tortoiseshell combs and lace shawls, six country maidens from the Kalotaszeg district, two Cleopatras and four Little Red Riding Hoods. Not a few extremely cross society ladies had to console themselves with the thought that they had been first in the field with their wonderfully original idea and that somehow and with low cunning the others had stolen the idea from them. The one to be blamed was always their closest friend – that two-faced snake in the grass!

At one end of the ballroom there was a platform on which were the chairs reserved for the lady patronesses. There they sat in a half circle beneath a bower of potted palms brought in from elsewhere. Here was to be found the wife of Kolozsvar's mayor, the wife of Stanislo Gyeroffy who had been Laszlo's guardian. Countess Kamuthy, Countess Jeno Laczok and the young wife of Dr Korosi who had recently been appointed Rector of the University, a position which conferred a new distinction on his pretty wife so that, whether she liked it or not, she was stuck with this distinguished group of older women. In the middle of them all was Countess Sarmasaghy, who was almost everyone's Aunt Lizinka, and who had been given the place of honour because all the others were terrified of the old woman's evil tongue and mischief-making ways.

All of these wore headdresses made of old lace, white or black, with the sole exception of Countess Laczok who had brought out a family heirloom, a cap of pearls stitched with other precious stones, which had once belonged to the wife of a former ruling prince of Transylvania, Mihaly Apaffy, and which had passed to the Laczoks by inheritance through the Bornemiszas. It was a unique object and in it Countess Ida, who was liked by everyone, looked like an ancient portrait brought to life.

On the platform with this group were the ball's official sponsors, a mixed group of local aristocrats and middle-class businessmen such as the mayor himself, two chairmen of local banks, the ex-doyen of the court pleaders, and some others. Old Carrots Gyeroffy was there sporting his famous orange wig, as was Crookface Kendy with his eagle's beak nose, the elder Count Adam Alvinczy and the inevitable Major Bogacsy. There were some others too, like Uncle Ambrus, who decided that the official platform was the best place from which to ogle all the pretty women as they entered the hall and so boldly walked the length of the room, and mounted with the official party as if he had merely come to pay his respects to the patronesses.

Joska Kendy also managed to get himself on the platform, but he did this not to ogle the women but to get as close as possible to pretty young Mrs Korosi, find a chair beside her and whisper sweet nothings into her receptive ear. Mrs Korosi, for her part, did not mind at all the opportunity to tell Joska her woes, which principally consisted of feeling neglected by her husband, the Rector, who in addition to his political activities as leader of the town's opposition was constantly occupied with attending meetings, making speeches and lecturing and administering to the point that his poor little wife was left quite disconsolate. All this she poured out to Joska in a soft voice so that he, moved by her sorrows, from time to time took his pipe from his pocket, jammed it between his teeth, then stuffed it angrily away again.

Many people arrived early and so the long-legged Garazda Boy was fully occupied from the start in showing people to their places, running constantly from the head of the stairs to the official platform and back again. He was very conscientious and felt it important, if he was to make a success of the evening, that each lady as she arrived should be seen to be escorted the full length of the hall down the double line of the other assembled guests. His assistant was the young Dezso Laczok, who was only in his second year at the university and hero-worshipped his superior; these two young men hurried alternately up and down the room anxiously trying to keep order and see that everyone was in their proper place before darting back again when a new headdress swam into view at the head of the stairs. The Boy, with his long legs, managed it at a run, while Dezso, who was smaller, practically skated across the polished floor. Then, with the new arrival in tow, they would bow ceremoniously as they made the necessary presentation to the patronesses. All in all they managed it very well. It was not an easy task to keep order with such a throng, but they carried it off with only one mishap. This was due, not to any female guest, but to Isti Kamuthy.

Plump little Isti, when in London the previous summer, had had made a pink hunting jacket by one of the most fashionable tailors in Savile Row. It was a marvellous coat made out of some material that was as hard and stiff as zinc. He had been anxious to have it generally admired and had thought of wearing it at Zsuk for the St Hubertus Day meet. Then someone had told him that in England pink coats were not worn when hunting with harriers and so, after repeatedly telling this to all his friends, he had had to be content with wearing an old green coat when out with the hounds as he realized he could not himself now break with such a hallowed tradition. It was a painful decision for young Isti, but the marvellous pink coat – which had cost all of eight and a half guineas – had had to stay unused hanging in his wardrobe. Then the opportunity came. He heard of the Bal des Têtes and decided that if he could not wear the coat in the hunting field he would wear it to the ball, regardless of the fact that all the other men would be in classical black evening dress. If challenged he would say he thought it was a costume ball and so, that evening, he pulled on his white breeches, a pair of riding boots, and donned the pink masterpiece. He himself knew that he would outdo everyone by the splendour of his coat and that all the girls would admire him. And he would cut such a dash that one or two of them might even fall in love with him.

When Isti first set foot in the hall everyone's amazement was everything he could have wished. There was a sudden hush, and then a clamour of joy broke out and he found himself surrounded by a bevy of young girls who crowded round him to touch and admire and giggle ... and make fun of him. Everyone talked at once, all demanding to know why he had thought to come dressed like that. For some moments Isti thought that he had all the success he had hoped for – but not for long. In an instant the great cluster of girls fell back with an expression of disgust; and then his dreadful outspoken little niece, Malvinka, said out loud what everyone else was thinking.

'Isti! You stink of the stables!'

This was something that he had never thought about; but the moment it had been said he knew how true it was. The much-used leather-patched breeches and the boots which had been impregnated with horse sweat passed without notice in the hunting field; but in the scented ballroom they reeked of horse; and for Isti the effect was awful. Wherever he went everyone fled from him, and it was the same the whole evening. No girl would let him come near her, or dance with her; and most of the men, in true Transylvanian fashion, started to tease and mock him, making elaborate gestures of disgust while muttering 'stink of the stables, stink of the stables, stink of the stables'. For as long as he could bear it poor Isti wandered about alone, chased away from every corner, feeling lonely and persecuted, as indeed he was. Finally, after a long battle with himself, he admitted defeat, renounced all effort at cutting a dash at the ball and took refuge in the card room where the clouds of cigar smoke that hung over the gaming tables obliterated all lesser odours. Here, at last unnoticed and unsmelled, Isti collapsed into a chair, and nobody bothered him anymore.

As soon as poor Isti had fled, order returned to the ballroom. More pretty women kept on arriving, their heads covered with odalisques' veils or bull-fighters' hats. If they had come escorted by husbands, brothers or fathers these last went to stand with the other men at the side of the room while the lady, all self-congratulatory smiles, paraded the length of the room so as to show off her miraculous and completely original headdress. Sometimes it would happen, as she glided down the centre of the room, that an ironic whisper, none too discreet, would be heard. 'Do look! That's the third tulip!' or, when a white-powdered wig went bobbing by, 'Just like a poodle!' More rarely there was heard a soft murmur of pleasure and approval. This happened when Dodo entered bearing the towering feather crown of an Indian chief, and when the pretty little Mrs Fischer arrived with a complete circus carousel on her head on which the little wooden horses went round and round whenever she gave them a touch with her fingers. It was the same when Margit appeared. She still looked as girlish as always even though at the end of January she had given birth to a fat healthy boy, the first grandchild for old Count Adam Alvinczy. In her simple white dress covered in tiny embroidered flowers she looked like a girl at her first ball. On her head she wore a plain red kerchief completely covering her hair and tied just as young peasant girls did in the country. It could not have cost more than twenty cents, but it was tied so skilfully, with two corners erect at the back of her head, and it was so well-suited to her calm brown face, lifted chin and proud dignified walk, that when she went up to the patronesses and sank into a deep curtsy, everyone was captivated by her charm and grace and applauded loudly. Margit herself blushed with pleasure and stepped modestly aside.

When almost everyone was there and the Garazda Boy was standing by the patronesses, looking at his watch and wondering if he ought to get the first csardas started, there was a stir at the head of the stairs and Adrienne swept into the room.

There was such a mob of people around the entrance that until she arrived in the central aisle she could hardly be seen. Then the dense phalanx of men in their black evening dress parted in the centre and Adrienne stood in full view. For a moment she stood there without moving and then slowly with long strides started to walk down the hall.

Adrienne's dress was black and very long. It was made of some smooth material covered with tiny shiny metallic paillettes which shimmered and rustled with every movement she made. It was as if she were covered from neck to floor with some magic snake's armour. Her head was held high and on it she wore a wide oriental golden crown as seen in pictures of the Manchu empresses. It was made up of branches of golden flowers bent upwards in wide arcs the tips of which had been decorated with hanging fringes of tiny gemstones. The hearts of all the flowers were sewn with rubies which might have been drops of blood upon the shining golden petals.

Her eyebrows and lashes had been darkened and made longer as Chinese women did and indeed Adrienne, with her black hair, ivory skin and pale face which held no trace of colour apart from her vivid red lips, seemed a true evocation of the Far East. She was like the statue of some legendary goddess who had for once stepped out of her pagoda, and her head and shoulders rose triumphantly from the lowest possible décolletage.

Adrienne's skin glowed with a myriad tiny reflections from the bright lighting of the hall, so that her shoulders, neck and breasts gleamed like highly polished marble. In the proud fullness of her beauty there was no sign of the unformed, skinny schoolgirl she had still resembled long after the birth of her child; and no sign either of the prudish virginal air which for so many years she had adopted whenever some man looked at her with desire in his eyes. All this had vanished some six months before when she had become reunited with her lover and in his arms had been able freely to live the life of a truly fulfilled woman. Her beauty was so sublime that when she entered the room she was greeted by a sudden hush of awe which continued as she started to walk down the hall proudly conscious of the effect she was making.

Balint had been waiting for her not far from the top of the stairs and when she appeared he took an unconscious step towards her, but Adrienne checked him with an almost invisible smile behind which he sensed the unspoken words: 'Now you can see what it is that I brought from Vienna and which, despite your demands, I would not tell you about. I kept it secret even from you, so that you should see me like this, suddenly, unexpectedly, my tribute to you', and she continued her progress between the double line of guests, many of them clad in all the colours of the rainbow. And as she continued her queenly progress down the hall a soft murmur of admiration rose around her which mounted to a crescendo as the spectators caught sight of the cascade of thin golden threads which fell from the back of her imperial crown, some almost to the ground, and all of them ending in a golden flower with a ruby at its heart. As she walked these flowed behind her, each flower reflecting the red-hot desire that could be seen in the eyes of the men who watched her progress.

Finally she arrived at the platform on which the patronesses of the ball were seated. Then she sank into the deep curtsy of one being presented at Court, her supple body sinking and rising with all the calm and assurance of a panther; and her bearing was so regal that there was a burst of spontaneous applause.

Adrienne's sweet-natured aunt, Countess Laczok, cried out enthusiastically, 'Oh, how beautiful you are, my darling!' and for once even the spiteful old Countess Sarmasaghy, Aunt Lizinka, suppressed her natural malice and found herself saying: 'I must say I've never seen anyone so beautiful!' Uncle Ambrus, dazzled, roared out: 'Damned fine wench!' and in a few moments she was surrounded by a crowd of men, young and old, who would not budge from her side even though the music had just started. Many of them at once asked her to dance. Some she did not seem to hear, but to others she just gently shook her head, for she was waiting for Abady and when he reached her side she took his arm and the others started to melt away.

Recently it had always been like this. Since Uzdy had been taken away hopelessly insane Balint and Adrienne had made no attempt to pretend or hide their love for each other. They made no secret of it and everyone knew; though whether they really were lovers or not remained uncertain. It did not matter for they both held their heads high and everyone knew that they belonged to each other; and so society accepted the situation. Men no longer chased after Adrienne, even though she was now so much more beautiful than before, for they realized that she would never look at anyone but Balint, and to pursue her would be in vain.

Everyone knew that divorce was impossible for her and so her feelings for Balint, which neither of them made any attempt to conceal while at the same time conducting themselves with so much dignity and discretion, always together at every function but never arriving or leaving together, became an accepted fact. Even Aunt Lizinka stopped spreading her evil tales about Adrienne for there were no men chasing after her and no flirtations to gossip about. Uncle Ambrus stopped yearning after her and hinting that they were having an affair. Now everyone knew the truth, even if not all of it; and as the basis for gossip is conjecture and concealment, here there was neither and so nothing to gossip about.

Boldly and together Balint and Adrienne faced the world openly.

Deprived of her favourite object of malice Aunt Lizinka had had to look around to find another target. She soon found it in the person of Count Jeno Laczok's elder brother Tamas. After a riotous youth and several years of adventure abroad, Tamas had qualified as a railway engineer and had found employment with the Hungarian State Railways. His work had brought him back to Kolozsvar, and his predilection for very young gypsy girls soon became well known. Aunt Lizinka at once pounced on this juicy scandal and decided to become 'worried' about him. Now, sitting on the patronesses' elevated dais, she plunged into the matter with glee, explaining with zest and false concern, that she was terrified that her nephew Tamas would land in gaol. 'You know, my dear, that little gypsy girl he keeps isn't even thirteen! Think of the scandal! How dreadful this would be for the family! I know for a fact that the police are after him even now.'

Although Aunt Lizinka's high-pitched screech could be heard in most parts of the hall, Balint and Adrienne, who were strolling past, heard nothing of it. Other people's affairs were no concern of theirs and so they did not bother to listen. They walked together as in a dream, completely wrapped up in each other and in their own happiness. Soon they sat down together on a bench beside the wall and then Adrienne turned smiling to her lover and said, 'Do you like it?'

'Very, very much!'

'Really and truly?'

'Even more than very, very much!' he repeated warmly and then, very softly, in a low whisper that no-one could possibly overhear, he muttered into her ear a few words in English, words whose meaning was their own secret symbol of their love.

For a moment Adrienne lowered her eyelids over her big topaz-coloured eyes. She did not speak, for the little movement was her accepted answer; but her full lips opened slightly to show the gleam of her white teeth …

Then with joy in her heart she told him how she had devised her imperial headdress, how she had pored over illustrated books, and how, when she went to Vienna, she had somehow managed to have it made in the workshop of the opera house. Then she told too how she had secretly brought it home and how, because the hanging flowers at the back had tickled her neck, she had lengthened them herself to make that jewelled cascade that everyone had admired so much.

The ball soon got under way, and the opening csardas was followed by a series of waltzes. Just as Laci Pongracz, the popular band leader, swung his musicians into the new favourite, the 'Luxembourg Waltz', there was a new arrival. A powerfully built man with a black beard entered the room. It was Tamas Laczok, and his appearance was to cause almost as much stir as had that of Isti Kamuthy an hour before, especially among the lady patronesses and the other matrons on the platform. This reaction was not entirely unexpected, even by the subject of it himself, for he, as well as all the others, had been fully aware of all the tales that had been circulating about him. As an engineer of the State Railways he had been sent to take charge of some repair works on the line between Kolozsvar and Apahida and had taken up residence some three weeks before in a small peasant's house in the district of Bretfu.

Though he was not far from the centre of Kolozsvar he had not often come into the town, for his was a solitary nature and he liked his privacy

Even so the news of the ball had somehow come his way, and though this would not normally have attracted him, he had also heard that old Countess Sarmasaghy was to be one of the patrons together with his younger brother Jeno. To cap it all he had been at the station that morning and had seen the arrival of the banker, Baron Weissfeld, and his family, who had come to attend the ball. The presence of these three had made him decide to put in an appearance himself.

In this he was prompted only by the dislike, amounting to hate, which he felt for all three of them. He was convinced that his brother had plotted with the banker to deprive him of his rightful share of the Laczok forestry holdings and further, that it had been Aunt Lizinka who had played a major part in seeing that he had been disowned by his family at the time he had been sowing his wild oats. The result had been years of exile. It was, of course, true that this experience had made a new man of him, for it was this that had led him first to study in Paris and obtain his engineering degrees and then to find a position with an international firm that had first sent him to Durazzo on a construction job and later to work on the building of a railway across the Atlas mountains. He had remained in Algeria for many years and he could have stayed there with a position of great responsibility. But he had decided that he would rather hold some secondary post at home with the Hungarian State Railways, partly because he had come to realize that he only felt really at home back in Transylvania and also because if he were to return he would be able to haunt his much-hated brother and perhaps also find the means of revenging himself upon his old enemies.

If this was the main reason why he had decided to attend the ball, he had also got wind of the scandalous tales that his aunt was now spreading about him. He had arrived late because he had not at once been able to find his evening clothes, and when he had found them his gypsy servant had had to iron them and then he had had to come into town, locate a shop that would supply him with a stiff shirt and white tie, and then go back to Bretfu to dress.

All this conspired to make him late. Now that he had finally arrived he looked around, peering above the heads of the dancing throng, until he saw his aunt and sister-in-law on the official dais and he realized that if Ida Laczok was there her husband could not be far away. Then he saw Baroness Weissfeld fanning herself on a chair near the others. Screened by the multitude of dancing couples he threaded his way, stooping slightly like a big-game hunter stalking a pride of lions, towards his much-disliked relations, carefully keeping out of their sight until he could suddenly burst before them from among the throng of dancers.

The surprise he caused them was as successful as he had hoped.

A little while before, most of the older men had vanished from the official platform and taken refuge in the hotel's smoking room. It was one of the rooms put at the disposal of the Comte d'Eu during his recent visit. The patronesses, however, had not moved from their place of honour. There, right at the front, were Countess Kamuthy, Baroness Weissfeld, and Tamas's sister-in-law, Ida Laczok. They were listening open-mouthed to Aunt Lizinka who, since she had successfully fought, and won, a battle in the courts to regain her husband's properties during the repressive regime of Count von Bach after the 1848 uprising sixty years before, had prided herself on her knowledge of the law. Aunt Lizinka was now in full flood describing the criminal proceedings which, according to her, now threatened her nephew Tamas.

At this point she was saying, 'My dears, it is quite clear. The law says that such persons must not only be locked up but also condemned to five years' hard labour. I know for a fact that the police have already put out a search for the little whore's birth certificate and that her old clay-digging father, who sold the child to him, is already in custody.'

Countess Ida, who never thought or spoke ill of anyone and who found herself forced to listen only because she could find no excuse to move away, now started to close her ears from boredom and looked round the room to find some distraction. And the first person she saw was her brother-in-law himself, standing quite close and clearly able to hear everything that was being said.

There he was, the spitting image of her husband Jeno, if perhaps not quite so plump. He had the same Tartar features with a single tuft of hair on his otherwise bald pate. With his slanting eyes almost buried in folds of fat, with his wide-spread eyebrows which gave him the air of perpetual enquiry, he resembled more than anything one of those soapstone figurines to be found in oriental bazaars. In this he was even more like than his brother Jeno, for while the latter sported only a pair of imposing moustaches, Tamas also wore a long thin beard twisted to the shape of a lyre. He stood there, just in front of Ida, quite straight on his shortish legs, with his hands in his pockets, smiling up at her.

'Tamas!' she cried out in surprise. 'Where on earth did you spring from?'

'*Servus* – greetings!' he replied.

Everyone looked round, and Aunt Lizinka choked in mid-sentence. Then she too stammered out, 'You? You here? You! How did you get in here?'

'Because, my dear aunt, I am still at liberty to go where I please! *J'ai voulu vous tranquilliser à ce sujet* – I just wanted to reassure you about that!' and he mounted the platform, pulled up a chair and sat down beaming all around him in good-fellowship and high good humour.

Faced with such a *fait accompli* there was nothing that the others could do. Then Tamas turned to Baroness Weissfeld and, carefully choosing his words, said, 'Not everyone gets to prison who deserves it, as your good husband must know.' Then he turned to Ida and went on, 'How is my brother? I heard he was suffering from a slight Thief's Cold.' After this, with the others speechless, he addressed himself directly to old Countess Sarmasaghy.

'My dear aunt, have you heard of my latest troubles? Oh, nothing to do with that tale about the gypsy girl, nothing whatever. No, it is all because my second foreman has just got himself sent to gaol for slander. It's really been most annoying for he was such a good worker and I don't know how I'll manage without him. The fool said something scandalous about the head foreman and as he said it in front of several of his work-mates, one of them denounced him and the idiot found himself hauled before the court. Three witnesses swore that they had heard the slander and the judge believed them, saying that there was little he could have done if only one man had spoken but that three he was bound to believe. What an idiot the fellow was to spread slander in front of three other people!' and he gestured towards his sister-in-law, Countess Kamuthy and Baroness Weissfeld. 'They shut him up, my dear aunt, and you can imagine the trouble that has caused.'

For a moment or two he paused, a wicked look in his eyes as he looked at each of the ladies in turn. Then he rose and said, 'Well! As I'm here I might as well have a look round. *Ma chère tante, je me prosterne devant votre bienveillante attention* – my dear aunt, I submit myself to your ever-vigilant goodwill.'

Then he bowed and went on his way.

As soon as he had left all three women rose hurriedly and fled in different directions, and Aunt Lizinka was left to suffocate in her own venom.

Farkas Alvinczy, who had been the previous dance leader, and a Member of Parliament until the year before, stood in a small doorway behind the gypsy musicians. To emphasize the fact that he was not really attending the ball he had come dressed not in evening dress but in ordinary day clothes. This was to show everyone that he had now renounced the frivolous pleasures of the world. It was his pose that a man like him with a brilliant past, who had been the envy of all other men and the favourite of the most beautiful women in Budapest, who had been an eminent servant of the state and a prominent politician, would now choose to withdraw from society rather than take second place in such provincial revels. How could he, who had tasted every pleasure the world had to offer, now be seen courting the attention of a group of dowdy country-women? Naturally he had not said this to anyone, but his air of mysterious superiority just tinged with melancholy spoke only too clearly for him.

And yet it really was nothing but a pose. It was true that he had been a Member of Parliament, but he had had nothing to say. While in Budapest he had had no more social success than many other good-looking young men, and like other good-looking young men he had had neither more nor fewer adventures with women than had the others. But he had tried to lead the life he imagined and he had even begun to believe it himself to the point at which he now suffered as much as if it had been true. Since he had lost his seat at the last elections he had stopped going out in society and had gone out only to gamble the night away. During the daytime he had slept. He no longer went with the others to sing and dance with the gypsies and it had begun to be whispered that he had become a heavy but secret drinker. Looking at his puffy face and watery eyes people had begun to guess that the rumours were only too true. Still, even if he had started to run slightly to fat he was still exceptionally good-looking.

Young Ida Laczok caught sight of him from across the room and at once said to herself that he would do for her. Since Gazsi Kadacsay had so inexplicably faded out of her life, she would have accepted anyone who asked her, for by now both her sisters were married and she was the only one still single.

Stopping her dancing partner as they waltzed by the gypsy band, she bowed to him and went over and stood near Farkas. He in his turn stepped up to her and they shook hands just behind the double bass.

'What are you doing with yourself these days?' she asked. 'It is nice to see you again,' she went on with a sparkle of encouragement in her eyes. 'You can't imagine how much we miss you.'

Farkas made a somewhat disdainful gesture and said in a bored voice, 'I just wanted to see how the Garazda Boy was making out. I must say he seems to be doing quite well. He's a clever lad so I expect he'll learn.'

'Oh, but it isn't at all the same as when you did it!' said Ida in a flattering tone and went on with several remarks in the same vein.

Shortly afterwards they were joined by Margit.

'Have you seen Adam?' she asked her brother-in-law. 'He disappeared ages ago. Is he in the card room? Were you there?' and her voice held an unusually stern and demanding note.

'I was there alright, gambling if you want to know,' Farkas replied bitterly, 'but whether Adam was or not I really can't say, and I don't care. I'm not one to spy on others: they can do what they like for all I care!' This was intended as a gibe at Margit, for all three of Adam's brothers resented the young woman who had captured him. They were also afraid of her for they knew they could not compete with her practical brain and strong will. Even so Farkas would not have dared to speak to her like that if they had been alone.

Margit raised her little beak-like nose and looked up at her tall brother-in-law's face. Then, with the shadow of a smile, she said, quite calmly, 'In that case I'll go and look for him myself.' Then she turned and walked swiftly away.

Margit stepped out into the corridor. There she hesitated for a moment or two not knowing which of the four double doors led to the card room. Then a waiter appeared carrying an ice bucket and opened the third door. Margit followed him for she had heard the booming voice of Uncle Ambrus saying, 'Come on, me lad, shell it out! We don't play for peanuts here, you know. The bank is sixteen hundred. Who wants it?'

Margit looked around her.

The room was one of the hotel's grand sitting rooms, but the furniture had been pushed to the walls to make way for a large baize-covered table that had been placed directly under the crystal chandelier. It was surrounded by eight cane chairs for the players, but her husband Adam was not among them. She saw Akos, his youngest brother, but it was only later that she remembered how deathly pale he had looked. She was about to leave the room when she caught sight of her husband. He was lying in a gilt armchair just behind where she was standing. His long legs were stretched out in front of him and he was fast asleep. He was sleeping so soundly that his mouth was slightly open like a young child's and on his face was an expression of happiness and content. He was asleep out of sheer exhaustion, for although since his marriage he had never once gone out carousing with his friends, he had spent all the previous night carrying his newborn baby about who was suffering from colic and who started crying again every time Adam put him down. He adored his son and fussed over him like any nanny.

Margit moved silently over to her husband and ever so gently started to caress his forehead. Still half asleep Adam reached for her hand and brushing it across his face started to kiss her arm just as he might have if they were in bed at night. He did not try to open his eyes, imagining that that was just where they were.

It must have been a familiar movement for Margit broke out in soft giggles. Still, she had to see that Adam was properly awake.

'Anna Laczok, Countess Harinay, doesn't have a dinner partner. I told her you'd sent me to ask her for you. But it would be nice if you'd go and ask her yourself, just to be polite, you know. The dinner will be served in half an hour and it wouldn't look right to wait until the last minute.'

Adam jumped up. 'You're right,' he said. 'I'll go at once.'

As they moved away little Margit looked up at the great height of her husband and said, 'I hope you're pleased I got you such a pretty partner. You can't accuse me of being a jealous wife!'

'Why ever should you be?' he answered good-naturedly and they walked hand in hand out of the card room, their steps matching each other exactly as the steps do of those who have a total understanding of each other. And although there was no-one to see them in the deserted corridor the two of them, linked by their intertwined hands, made a picture of perfect happiness.

Tamas Laczok, having had his fun with Aunt Lizinka, went to look for his brother and Weissfeld. After all, he said to himself, he had gone to a lot of trouble and expense – ten crowns, no less! – to get to the ball so now he might as well see that he got his money's worth, and that meant teasing the others as well. He went in search of the smoking room.

There they both were, sitting with about twenty other men in a wide circle discussing politics, as Hungarian men always do when a group of them gather together. They were mostly the patrons of the ball, or the husbands of the lady patronesses, who were now condemned to wait until they had to escort their wives to the supper room.

Jeno Laczok, with his vast bulk, sat stiff and motionless, a prisoner of his own fat. He was like a statue carved from stone. Beside him sat the banker from Vasarhely who never left his friend's side in Kolozsvar, partly because he always felt the need of his support when among strangers but also because no-one here knew what an important person he was in his home town.

The Rector of the University, Dr Korosi (whose wife felt so neglected), was pompously explaining some abstruse point, when Tamas's rumbustious entrance interrupted what he was saying and so spoiled his carefully constructed argument.

'Servus Sandor! Servus Adam! Servus Stanislo! Servus everyone! Greetings to you all. What a long time since I saw you!' and he shook hands all round, introducing himself to some of those he did not know, but not all as they did not interest him much, and Tamas had never been a stickler for convention. When he had almost come full circle he came face to face with his brother. With glee he slapped Jeno's protruding stomach and, seizing his shoulders with both hands, gave him a good shake while roaring out, 'Wow! You look pale! Where did you get that yellow colour?' and though his brother started coldly to deny it, he went on: 'Oh yes, you are! You're very, very yellow. Of course you don't notice it as you see yourself in the mirror every day.' Then, turning to the others, he appealed to them all for confirmation, 'It's true, isn't it? Don't you see it? Of course you're all far too polite to say it out loud, but you can to me, you know. After all I'm his brother, and it's my duty to tell him the truth!'

Tamas turned back to his brother and without a word to Weissfeld, who had got up, took the latter's seat.

'You really should have yourself looked at, Jeno! It could be very serious, very serious indeed,' and he dropped his voice to a penetrating whisper and went on, 'Just think about it. Father died of cancer, didn't he? And they all say there can be a hereditary disposition … not that it's absolutely certain.'

'To hell with you!' said Jeno trying to laugh it off, but his laughter sounded somewhat forced. Tamas knew only too well that he had touched upon Jeno's weakest spot and that his attempt to scare him was not in vain. Ever since their youth Jeno had had this one fear and so, when Tamas knew that his drop of poison was working, he became all solicitous, and said kindly, 'Don't you worry, it's probably something quite different, too much acidity, or maybe gallstones. Anyhow I certainly should see a doctor!' Then he turned to the others. 'Do forgive me! I'm afraid I've interrupted a most interesting discussion with this family talk … you really must excuse me!' and fell silent. The two brothers who hated each other sat side by side, as alike as twins. Apart from one having a beard and the other not, they were almost identical, the same tuft of black hair on their otherwise shining skulls, the same enquiring eyebrows and high cheekbones. They even sat in the same way, solid and granitelike, with their hands planted firmly on their knees.

Dr Korosi now went on where he had left off.

He had been talking about the recent announcement that recruiting to the army was to be increased and its equipment modernized. This had happened in January but the details had only just been made public. It seemed that an extra 50,000 men were required and that the annual army budget was to be raised by 20 million crowns, 60,000 of which would be made available immediately. Three weeks before, Lukacs, the Minister of Finance, had given a most reassuring speech declaring that none of these new measures would entail raising taxes, though at the same time he said that more battleships were to be built. Lukacs had spoken with calm assurance and had explained that the Dual Monarchy's fleet was obsolete compared with those of the other great powers, and that they could not now afford to lag behind in the armaments race that was taking place all over Europe. Austria-Hungary's continued status as a great power, and as an equal partner with her allies, depended upon her armed forces being on a plane of equality with those of everyone else. He talked about the annexation of Bosnia-Herzegovina and the international crisis it had provoked, cited the build-up of the German navy, and referred to the importance to the nation of Hungary's commercial shipping interests. Dr Korosi went on to recount how the news of the increase in the army had been received with indifference by most people who had become all too accustomed to being told over the years that it would soon be necessary, just as they all knew that the real enemy was Russia and that the Tsar, aided by French millions, had for a long time been preparing for war. The question of the navy, however, was something new and very different. Why, people were asking, did the navy have to be built up? Who was the enemy?

Dr Korosi made the most of this last point, for he was the leader of the opposition party in Transylvania. Speaking with a broad, rather flat, accent, for he came from Szeged, he asked, 'Whaat therefore is the Naavy to us? Whaat is it for? Against whom should we use it?' and he went on to repeat what everyone present knew already, that Austria-Hungary had no colonies and no overseas interests, that the German navy was already far stronger than the French, and no matter how many ships were built by the Dual Monarchy they would never be able to compete with the enormous British fleet. That left only Italy, whom everyone knew to be Hungary's staunchest ally, and so no reinforcement would be needed there for it had already been agreed that Italy would participate in the defence of the Adriatic. Now, though Korosi ignored the fact, not everything could be discussed in political terms nor all official announcements be relied upon. It was not generally known that the Austro-Hungarian general staff had for some time been dubious about the strength of the Italian alliance, even to the point of preparing for the possibility that, in the event of war, Italy might quite possibly side with their enemies. Every alliance, they knew, stood up only as long as it was in the interests of both sides to maintain it, and only the strong kept their friends. The man in the street, however, who was always childishly naive in anything to do with foreign affairs, would never try to understand what might be going on under the surface. As a result people were now searching for concealed, secret and even totally absurd reasons for the modernization of the navy.

This is what most people believed and now they heard it confirmed by what Korosi was saying.

'It is obvious,' said the Rector, 'thaat the Heir simply wishes to indulge his ridiculous desire to be an admiral! Franz-Ferdinand wants only to emulate the Kaiser Wilhelm, and so he needs a squadron! Thaat, and thaat only, is why the government is prepared to squander all those millions. To satisfy the Heir's absurd ambitions they are only too ready to spend Hungarian pennies to build Austrian battleships!'

'Of course, of course, that's it!' said several of his audience.

Stanislo Gyeroffy passed his hand over his carrot-coloured wig, as if to make sure it was still firmly in place, and then added with an air of official authority, 'I'm not sure that is entirely true', but even if it is then surely it could do no harm to humour the archduke a little? After all one day soon he'll be our King!'

'He'll only be our King if we crown him!' cried someone impetuously.

'He'll be King anyhow,' said another.

'After the Pragmatic Sanction it needs a parliamentary decision.'

'I say: until it happens, fiddlesticks!'

'No army, no navy!' cried another, though no-one quite knew what he meant. Then followed a hot debate about the prerogatives of Parliament and what clauses should be added to what texts and what should be insisted upon and what ignored. Before long they were arguing hotly about the wording to be used as if it were they who would have to decide and as if it had to be settled right where they sat. They argued about the status of Bosnia-Herzegovina and some demanded that Dalmatia too should be annexed without delay. Others hotly disputed this, saying that it would lead to Trialism, only to find themselves contradicted at once. The battle of wits was as contrived and as synthetic as military manoeuvres and though the weapons may have been as impressive as political invective they could no more win the day than could cannons loaded with blanks. All the same tempers flared and eyes flashed as the armchair politicians snarled at each other. Every issue of the day was brought up and dissected – but no-one stopped to think of the welfare of the nation.

Above the hubbub could be heard the high-pitched screech of Stanislo Gyeroffy and the deep baritone of Dr Korosi, who were rapidly arriving at the point where personal insults would be hurled at each other. Then the unexpected happened. It started when someone unwisely suggested that the government might be intimidated by the rising power of the newly self-styled King of Montenegro, nicknamed 'Nikita'. This was picked up by Kalman Harinay, Anna Laczok's husband, who cried out arrogantly, 'Well, as for that, we might just as well be afraid of those apes in Albania.'

At this point Tamas jumped up and let out a roar, 'Don't you judge them by yourself, my lad! Those Albanians are tougher than you ever will be! I know them well!'

This was doubly unexpected: firstly because no-one had for a moment thought that anyone present would have any first-hand knowledge of Albanians, and secondly because this plump stocky man whom few of them knew, and who hardly ever spoke, should suddenly interrupt so passionately. Furthermore Tamas's scornful attack on Harinay impressed them because Transylvanians like nothing more than a well-justified rebuke. Some of them laughed, but they all looked at the newcomer with dawning respect.

Stanislo Gyeroffy, thankful to find a diversion from his deepening disagreement with Korosi, quickly picked up Tamas's last words, saying, 'Do you know Albania well? Hasn't there recently been some insurrection against the Turks?'

'There certainly has! It's a real war. According to the *Petit Parisien*, which I get regularly, the Malissors overwhelmed Torkut Pasha and were immediately joined by the Miridiots.'

This was greeted by a storm of ironic laughter.

'What kind of idiots?' cried Harinay, while the others shouted out, 'Is that what they are called? Are the Malissors idiots too? Is that really what they call themselves? Ho! Ho! Ho! That's wonderful, that is!'

'The Malissors and the Miridiots are the two fiercest tribes of Albania! And you, fellow-me-lad,' said Tamas coldly to Harinay who was laughing immoderately at his own pun, '*tu ne rigolerai pas comme une baleine* – you wouldn't be laughing like a whale, if you found yourself their prisoner. These are true men of the mountains, bandits all of them.' And he turned away because it had just occurred to him that this was a God-given chance to have a go at the banker Weissfeld. Smiling as if merely going on with his explication, 'This lot are far more than your well-born forest thieves, my banker friend. These are not men who polish the seats of their chairs in their nice safe city offices, no sedentary businessmen who plot behind the security of the limited companies that they have founded. No! Not at all! These are real fighting men, warriors who risk their skins every day of their lives!'

Some of his listeners, who knew something of the forestry combine between Tamas's brother and Weissfeld, realized what lay behind these last words and put their heads together chuckling at Tamas's audacity, while some of the others, not understanding but now aware what a sharp tongue the elder Laczok had, fell silent and for a while did not attempt any further interruption. Tamas went on with his tale.

He was standing at the centre of the circle, turning from time to time to one side or the other, and he looked extremely comical. He was dressed in an old tail coat cut in the fashion of many years before, which was now stretched tightly across his bulging stomach; and with his bald head and long wispy beard he was like an actor in a vulgar farce. This impression was heightened by his exaggeratedly upward-slanting eyebrows, by the tuft of black hair on the top of his skull, and by the droll way that he would twist round with tiny steps whenever Stanislo Gyeroffy, Sandor Kendy or Major Bogacsy asked a question. These mostly came from the ex-soldier, for though he was nowadays principally interested in questions of honour, he had once served in Bosnia and knew something of the Balkans.

The audience, mischievous as ever, soon started muttering behind Tamas's back; and one of them whispered, 'Looks like a blackcock calling for his mate!' at which the others barely suppressed their amusement for few of them were at all interested in what he was saying.

Nevertheless what he was saying was of interest. He must have been a keen observer who rarely forgot anything he saw and he could talk about his experiences with logic and clarity. He had not survived in the Atlas mountains for so many years without managing to keep his wits about him, and this was now clear from what he was recounting. The gist of his discourse was that this new rebellion in Albania was quite unlike any that had preceded it. Now, for the first time, several of the tribes that had traditionally been deadly enemies had joined together to fight the suzerainty of Turkey. Christians and Muslims were fighting side by side and what is more, they had somehow managed to obtain a supply of up-to-date guns as well as apparently limitless ammunition. Many people had been speculating where this came from, especially as the rebels had no funds. The money must have been given to them, but by whom? To Tamas the answer was obvious: it could only be Nikita, the King of Montenegro. One amazing fact led only to this conclusion. Since the anti-Turk movement had begun small bands of the insurgents had taken refuge from time to time across the Montenegrin border; and had swiftly come back. This had never happened before. If any Albanian had dared to set so much as a foot across the frontier into the border district of Chernagora, they were immediately slaughtered by the Chernagorians, while the Albanians did the same to anyone coming in the opposite direction. If this ancient tribal hatred had been abruptly changed to friendship, only one man could possibly have managed it, and that was the wily old Nikita. Therefore it must be he who was providing the ammunition and guns. But where did he get it all from? Well, a year before he had told the correspondent of the French newspaper *La Gloire* that Montenegro obtained her armaments not only from Serbia but also from the great international firm of Schneider-Creuzot. The question was, where did Nikita get his money from, for it was well known that the Montenegrin treasury was empty? Here again the answer was obvious to anyone with eyes to see: it must be Russia. It must be the Tsar who paid for Nikita's guns and therefore also for those of the Albanian rebels. There was something very sinister going on in the Balkans. It was significant that when Nikita, then merely Prince of Montenegro, proclaimed himself King, Russian grand-dukes were present at the celebrations along with the kings of Serbia and Bulgaria. This in itself was strange since a couple of years before the last two were hardly on speaking terms and were known to detest each other.

The final proof of all this was that Torkut Pasha had been doing all he could to close the Montenegrin border! It was this last move which had meant that the only route left open was to the north through the lands of the Miridiots. 'Wouldn't it be better from the south?'

'Perhaps, but one has to pass the Malissor territory above Elbasa ...'

At this the whole group burst into a storm of laughter for *'elbasa'* in Hungarian means nothing less than 'Fuck off'.

From time to time one of his listeners, bolder than the others, had ventured some mocking pun if only to make fun of the newcomer. The general restraint did not last long. Each time Tamas used some outlandish foreign name they did not know, someone would seize upon it, mispronounce it, and turn it into an obscene joke. And after the last remark they were almost falling out of their chairs with laughter, the same men who, a few moments earlier, had been making abstruse political arguments with such deadly seriousness that they were ready to fight one another to prove a point. The sad truth was that all of them found anything that did not concern their own country fit only for mockery and laughter. To them such matters were as remote from reality as if they had been happening on Mars; and therefore fit only for schoolboy puns and witty riposte.

Laczok looked around angrily and was about to castigate his audience when the door opened and a waiter came in.

'Dinner is served, gentlemen. The ladies are already on their way to the supper room.'

Everyone started to get up and the discussion was over. Most of those present hurried to the door for they were hungry after all that talk and laughter, and no-one wanted to keep his wife waiting. For a brief moment Stanislo Gyeroffy stayed behind and went over to speak to Tamas; but it was not kindness or good manners that prompted the gesture. In a haughty, pompous tone, he said: 'Personally I found what you were saying not without interest. If you'll sit with us at dinner you could perhaps tell us more?' and without waiting for a reply he strode out of the room, his orange wig resembling nothing so much as a banner of reaction.

For his part Tamas muttered an obscene expletive and started angrily to roll himself a cigarette.

It was then that he noticed that he was not alone. From a chair behind him he heard a faint whimpering sound, and turning he saw that old Count Adam Alvinczy was lying sprawled in his chair. It was obvious that he had tried to get up to follow the others when he had been stricken by a heart attack. He had fallen back onto the edge of the chair and only his head and shoulders touched the back-rest. His face was ashen and covered with beads of sweat, and his wide-open eyes held a look of terror.

Quickly Laczok reached his side.

'Here ... here ...' gasped Alvinczy with a rattle in his throat, '... on this side ... my drops ... in waistcoat ...'

Tamas acted swiftly. He snatched the vial from the waistcoat pocket, ran to the washroom for some water and a glass, and while hurrying back poured in the medicine. Then he helped the sick man to swallow it, pulled him up into a sitting position, loosened his collar and shirt-front, and, soaking his handkerchief with more water, pressed it to old Adam's heart. Then he sat down and waited.

He waited in silence, watching old Alvinczy closely.

The medicine acted fast. The old man relaxed as the pain subsided, his contorted face returned to its normal smoothness and he closed his eyes. His breathing was still rapid but he was no longer gasping for breath as he had been when the attack struck him.

Perhaps I needn't call a doctor, thought Tamas, as he took the old man's wrist and searched for his pulse. Then rhythmically he started to stroke the back of Alvinczy's hand.

For some time he sat there without either of them speaking.

Out in the corridor he heard doors being opened and closed and the sound of people walking about and talking. It must be the card players, thought Tamas; and, no doubt, the other man's two sons, Farkas and Akos, were among them not knowing that in the next room their father lay near to death.

Then again there was silence.

Much later Tamas heard the music being struck up again and realized that the supper must be over. Alvinczy seemed to be asleep and Tamas wondered if now he could go too; but he did not want to leave the other alone. Then, in a weak voice, Alvinczy started to speak, 'I don't know how to thank you ... but I do ... very much. If ... if you hadn't been there I'd probably be dead by now.'

'Nonsense!' replied Tamas, though he too had thought the same thing.

'Perhaps it would have been for the best,' said Alvinczy, pursuing the thought. Then after a long pause he said, 'Oh yes! It would have been better that way.'

'What sort of talk is that?' replied Tamas roughly, though with kindness in his tone.

'You don't know, you can't know,' the old man said several times in a low voice; and then, almost as if he were talking to himself, he went on brokenly, telling of his great sorrow and his disappointment in his sons.

He had been careful all his life, he said, denying himself any indulgence, any little luxury, so that when he died his four sons would inherit enough to keep them in the style to which his family had always been accustomed. They would not have great fortunes, but they would be able to live well if unostentatiously. He had looked carefully over his widely scattered estates and divided them into four units. Then, little by little, he had improved them by constructing new stables and farm buildings, and he had made them profitable. And what had happened? Before his eyes his sons had begun to undo his life's work. They had spent money recklessly, drinking and gambling as if there were no tomorrow. For years now he had lived in dread of what it would all come to, for hardly a month went by without one of them coming to him with debts to be paid – sometimes huge sums, thousands of crowns at a time – and each time he had paid up, though to do so he had to raise mortgages on most of his property. His finances were in confusion and he too was deeply in debt. Now, if there were any more demands on him, he would have to start selling everything that was left ...

'Perhaps it is my own fault. If I had brought them up better perhaps they wouldn't have turned out like this. I've got four sons, you know, and all of them ... well, three of them ... have proved worthless. They are as bad as each other!'

What on earth, he wondered hopelessly, would become of them? The only one he did not worry about was Adam, for he had married a sensible wife and seemed to work hard. He alone was saved.

'But, my God! What will happen to the others? Let me not live to see it! Let me be spared standing by while they destroy themselves!'

This was the only time old Alvinczy had bared his heart to anyone. Now he talked for a long time, but he had never before uttered a word of what was plaguing his heart. And it was strange that when he did so it should be to a man who was almost a stranger, someone he had seen perhaps three times in his life. His sorrow was something he had always kept to himself, holding his head high, alone in his dignity and despair. He had never spoken before because he had felt that to do so might harm his sons; but the iron discipline on which he had prided himself was, just this once, broken down by the pain and fear brought on by the heart attack. Even now, as soon as he had finished, he suddenly regained his confidence, straightened up, turned again to this stocky man he hardly knew, and with every sign of shame, said, 'I beg you, sir, to forget all I've just been saying. I was exaggerating ... I just blurted it all out.'

Tamas interrupted him. 'The important thing is that you're better now. Come along, I'll go home with you,' and he stood up, helped the old man to his feet, and led him to the door. They walked slowly down the corridor: Count Alvinczy, tall, elegant and distinguished-looking and Count Laczok, stocky and somewhat absurd in his old-fashioned evening coat.

When they reached the foot of the stairs Tamas asked for Alvinczy's cloakroom ticket and went to fetch his coat while the other rested on a sofa by the wall.

'You don't have to come with me,' protested the old man. 'I can quite well get home by myself.' But he seemed quite relieved when Tamas would not hear of it and said, 'Don't talk nonsense!'

When he had paid off the cab, woken Alvinczy's valet and seen that his companion was safely in bed, Tamas set off on foot for his home at Bretfu. After an hour or two in that smoke-filled room in the hotel it felt good to be walking through the cold air of a March night.

He walked in high good humour, pleased with the success of his outing, for had he not been able to torment his old enemies? He imagined that this joyous feeling sprang only from his having been able to annoy and embarrass his aunt, his brother and that rascally banker. As he chuckled to himself he thought how astonished they would all have been if they had seen him in the role of the Good Samaritan, he whom they had only known, especially his brother, in the role of the heartless old reprobate. Looking only at the ironic side of what had happened that evening it had never occurred to him that his feeling of well-being had sprung from the basic goodness which had prompted his care of the man whose life he had saved.

Walking swiftly along the empty streets he went through the Hidelve district and past the railway station, his fur hat pushed back and his short jacket swinging as he went. His thick country boots made a clatter as he stumped along happier than he had been for some time. And as he went, he sang. It was an old Parisian music-hall song that had been popular in the days of his youth:

> *Moi j'm'en fou*
> *J'reste tranquillement dans mon trou!*
> *Pourquoi courir ailleurs*
> *Pour ne pas trouver meilleur ...*
> *Moi j'm'en fou ...'*

On he went, swinging his arms and singing at the top of his voice just as if he had been on the stage ... but, as he had forgotten the rest of the once risqué little ballad, all that came out was '*Tara tara, tara tara, tara tara tara ...*'

The supper had ended long before with everyone in a good mood: everyone, that is, except Pityu Kendy. At supper he had sat next to Margit Alvinczy, with whom he had fancied himself in love just as previously he had swooned after Adrienne.

Then he and his bosom friend Adam had been able to pour out their

145

mutual but hopeless passion for Adrienne, discuss her heartlessness and bewail her cruelty while all the time enumerating her perfections. But since Adam had married Margit, Pityu had transferred his affections to his friend's new wife – for somehow it seemed only natural to imitate him in everything even to pursuing another unattainable woman. And so it was now to Margit's husband that he poured out his woes, complaining of his hopeless love in much the same words as they had both used previously in discussing her elder sister. And Adam just listened, serene in his own happiness, not minding at all that Pityu now sighed forlornly after his own wife. Nothing had changed. They still talked about the sadness of loving someone who scorned the adoring lover: only the object of adoration was not the same. Adam did not know the meaning of jealousy, but Margit's reaction was quite different from that of her sister. Whereas Adrienne had treated Adam and Pityu as if they had been dolls incapable of real feeling and had teased them both with the same remote playfulness that she had treated all the other men who had run after her, and then promptly forgot them, Margit decided to take Pityu in hand and make a man of him. Principally she wanted to wean him from the bad habits of drinking and gambling. In so far as the gambling went, she succeeded; but the drinking was another matter. Here her influence failed.

That had been the source of some trouble during the ball. Pityu drank too much at the supper table, and by the time they served the ices she had firmly turned her back on him. When the music of a csardas sounded from the ballroom upstairs and everyone started to get up, she turned back to Pityu and issued her orders.

'You're drunk again! Either stay here and stop drinking or go home! I don't want to see you in the ballroom!'

With that she got up, gathering her skirt behind her, and ran up the stairs. In a few moments she had disappeared among the dancers. What could Pityu do? Nothing would induce him to stay alone in the deserted supper room; so he went sadly to the cloakroom, collected his coat and headed for home.

Strangely enough, though his head was swimming from the quantity of brandy he had consumed, there was no trace of resentment in his muddled thoughts. What a woman she is! What an angel! But, oh, so cruel, so cruel! And he repeated the words to himself until he reached home.

*

None of the happy throng that went back to dance after supper had noticed that old Count Alvinczy was no longer among them nor had any idea that he had been taken ill.

Balint, who had been supping with Adrienne, escorted her upstairs with the others. When they arrived at the doors of the ballroom she left his arm and for a moment they stood side by side. Balint looked at her questioningly and almost imperceptibly she nodded. Her lips moved, but she said nothing that even he could have heard. Then she moved slowly on alone.

Balint remained at the head of the stairs until the last couple had come up from the supper room. Then he hurried down, collected his fur coat and left on foot.

## Chapter Five

It was well after midday. Through the wooden laths of the shutters the sunlight cast long narrow flame-coloured lines over the carpet, across the polished parquet floor and even vertically some way up the door. The room was filled with a golden radiance.

Balint awoke, rang for his valet and ordered his bath to be run. Then he closed his eyes again and sank into a half-slumber filled with tender recollections. In his mind he could see again a bright fire burning on the hearth, a fire which had thrown an almost blinding light on the deep-piled white carpet on which he lay but which left most of the rest of the room in mysterious shadow. He had lit the fire while waiting.

All at once the door had opened and Adrienne had stood before him, the shining paillettes on her dress reflecting the bright flames of the fire with a reddish glow which spread up over her shadowy breasts, under her chin and past the dark lines of her brows until it shone like a spotlight on the golden flowers of her oriental diadem. There she had stood, lit as if on a stage ...

For a moment she had not moved, until as Balint knelt before her and started to kiss the hem of her skirt she had spread her arms wide waiting for his lips to reach hers. Then, bending slightly, she had taken his head in her soft hands and bent down until their lips met. As her mouth, so vividly red and slightly open, met his in a long ecstatic kiss, the jewelled chains of her crown fell in a cascade over his face and ears and shoulders.

When the man returned to tell Balint that his bath was ready he announced also that a letter had just been delivered from Baron Kadacsay. 'A stable boy brought it, my lord. I have put it on your lordship's desk.'

'Very good,' said Balint, his head too full of the memory of his time with Adrienne to take in properly what he had been told. Then he sank into the hot water still thinking only of his mistress.

Around her slender ankles the dress, so like the scales of a snake, had lain in shining coils, from which had risen her alabaster figure, the fire etching every part of it with its roseate glow touched here and there with misty lilac-coloured shadows. To Balint she had seemed like some Hindu goddess, Parvati, Maya, or Brahmanaspati, crowned in gold with a shower of rubies and other stones falling over her breasts. And though she had said nothing she had been smiling in happiness and triumph.

She had been like some sculptor's masterpiece, a statue that somehow exuded joy as he knelt before her raising his hands in supplication and adoration. Later, as she had lain on the rug that so resembled the skin of a polar bear, naked but still crowned with that jewelled headdress spread in a wide arc around her jet-black curling hair, she had still seemed in some strange way statuesque. The fire had exploded with its own ecstasy as the flames reached the pine cones within it as if it too were consumed with the passion that enveloped the lovers who lay in front of it. As each new shower of sparks exploded, faster and faster, so had the passion of the two lovers as they moved together in a crescendo of love.

'When was the letter delivered?' asked Balint when he had dressed and gone into his sitting room.

'Yesterday, my lord. Quite late, after ten o'clock. A boy brought it on horseback.'

A letter from Gazsi? Sent quite late at night … by a man on horseback? It had to be something exceptionally urgent, something really serious.

'Why didn't you bring it to me at once? You knew where I was.'

'The boy just said to hand it to your lordship. I asked if it was urgent and if something was wrong, but he just said that Baron Gazsi had not said anything in particular and had seemed to be quite well. There was nothing out of the ordinary at home, the boy said.'

Balint hurried over to this desk. The letter lay there, an ordinary grey envelope with his name scribbled in Gazsi's awkward writing, and on the back were scrawled a few words that Gazsi had presumably added as an afterthought: *'I stupidly sent this to Denestornya, believing you would still be there – Gazsi.'*

The letter itself read:

*Dear Balint,*
*Before I leave I would like to talk something over with you. Could you come over here tomorrow before one o'clock … to Bukkos St Marton, as I shall be leaving then and do not expect to be back for a long time.*
*Sorry to inconvenience you – it will be the last time, I promise!*
*So long … Servus!*

What on earth could all this be about, Balint wondered. Where was he going? And what a strange little note. He looked at the time; it was already half-past one, so if Gazsi had kept to his plan he would have already gone.

Could he have caught the one-thirty express to Budapest? He hadn't said anything about it; and anyhow if that had been his plan he would probably have ridden over himself instead of asking Balint to come to him. Perhaps he had had some mishap on the road and gone straight to the station.

None of this seemed likely. Gazsi would never have written like that if he were just setting off on some everyday little trip. It had to be something else, something infinitely more serious. Balint thought back to their last conversation at the banquet and it occurred to him now that Gazsi had seemed unusually disillusioned and depressed, that most of his talk about his future plans could have been interpreted in more than one sense, and that everything he had said might perhaps have referred to his imminent death rather than to some imaginary voyage. After all, Balint reflected, had it not been he himself, rather than Gazsi, who had talked about going on his travels and who had even proposed it? Brushing away such morbid thoughts Balint once more convinced himself that obviously Gazsi had wanted to consult him further about possible travel plans. And yet this did not seem like his friend. No! It was far more likely that before going away he wanted to entrust something to Balint, to make some arrangement about the management of his horses or the administration of his property ... that would be it! That was why he had asked for him; and Balint believed in this happy solution because he was so happy himself that this was what he wanted to believe. All the same a little pinprick of anxiety remained.

Whatever the reason it was obvious that he must answer the summons at once, and ten minutes later his car was speeding along the highway that led up the valley of the Felek.

It was a day of radiant sunshine even though spring had not yet come. The snows had recently melted on the hillsides and now all the south-facing meadows and slopes looked as if they had just been washed. There was not a speck of dust anywhere and it was too early for the weeds to have started springing up. Everything had been sluiced clean by the melting snow, as if the countryside had just been prepared for some joyous feast. On the north-facing slopes the snow still lay, gleaming white in the sun and, as it too was now slowly melting away, everything that might have soiled its surfaces had sunk to the earth and from its edges tiny rivulets of water were now beginning the seasonal change that the sun had already achieved on the other side of the valley.

Balint fancied that he could already smell the first scents of spring.

The car purred effortlessly up the last incline in the road. Balint knew he would be at St Marton in another fifteen minutes and that very shortly afterwards he would be at Gazsi's place.

Once again he wondered what on earth it was that Gazsi could have wanted so urgently as to send for him like that. As he drew nearer and nearer to his destination all Balint's suppressed anxieties rose up and assailed him once more; and no matter how much he tried to reassure himself that he was being stupid and unreasonable he was unable to banish them entirely. Again and again he found himself thinking of those words in the letter: '*I do not expect to be back for a long time ... Sorry to inconvenience you. It will be the last time, I promise!*' Had he not also written: '*I don't know if I'll ever be back.*' What strange words they were! In themselves they may have seemed banal and without great significance, but knowing Kadacsay's bitter indictment of himself, Balint felt they must have some other meaning, ominous even if not obvious.

He remembered too that Gazsi had once said to him that in the life of a man troubles and joys are usually equally balanced, but when something occurred to so upset the balance that nothing was left but trouble and misery then the only answer was to kill oneself. Of course when he had said this Gazsi had seemed unusually disheartened and miserable.

Balint tried to go over in his mind everything that Gazsi had ever said to him and as he did so he tried to remember some words that might have been more reassuring. Try as he would he could not think of anything. On the contrary, thinking back to those discussions when Gazsi had asked him to be his executor, and also when he had arranged that Balint would take in his beloved mare, Balint now realized there had been a double meaning in every word that Gazsi had uttered.

For a brief moment Balint half closed his eyes so as to concentrate better, and as he did so the sunlight through his eyelids seemed rose-red and all his worries disappeared as he saw in his mind's eye the image of Adrienne as she had been in the firelight, with her parted lips and wide open eyes, with her expression of almost painful anticipation of that moment when all space and time were wiped away, when there was no past and no future and when time itself became an eternity. Her beautiful face, framed in those wildly tumbling curls, could have been that of Medusa or the Tragic Muse herself, and for a moment Balint saw only this and felt the surge of renewed desire ...

An instant later he was able to banish the thought as he forced himself once more to think about his friend and pray, as he sped towards him through that countryside halfway between winter and spring, that Gazsi had only written to him in that equivocal manner as a result of some passing fancy or fit of depression at being delayed in some ridiculous fashion, and that he was even now at home, laughing at his own stupidity, with his crow's beak of a nose tilted to one side as it always was when he was telling a droll story about himself and when nothing was seriously wrong.

The car turned into the narrow road that led to Gazsi's village. The road curved round one more snow-covered hillside and ahead, a little higher up, could be seen the roofs of the village and on one side, surrounded by tall elm trees, Gazsi's old manor house.

As Balint drove on towards the hedge that bordered Gazsi's property and the gates, which would shortly appear, he found himself passing several little groups of village people all going in the same direction, one ahead of the other as in Indian file. They were walking in silence and with the heavy tread of the Mezoseg people. He sounded his horn and as the men and women drew to one side, some of the men raised their caps in respectful greeting. Balint wondered why they all seemed to be going to the manor house, and why they all looked so sad.

A moment or two later he had arrived in front of the portico with its wooden Grecian pillars that framed the entrance to the house. Three steps led up to it and standing at the top were two men, Gazsi's estate manager and the local Protestant pastor.

'Where is Baron Gazsi?' asked Balint.

'He died, just an hour and a half ago!' said one of them.

Balint felt his legs giving way under him and he staggered to a bench beside the wall.

Then they told him what had happened.

Baron Gazsi had been writing something all morning. When he had finished he had folded up the sheets of paper and sealed them. A little later he had walked down to the stables and looked into every box giving a lump of sugar to each horse as he always had. Just as the clock chimed the hour of midday he sent for the pastor and the estate manager, sat them down in the sitting room and gave them his orders. To the priest he had given instructions that the church organ, which had been in bad repair for some time, should be put in order and told them that he accepted the estimate of 500 florins and that he wanted it done at once. He had discussed many small details of the work, told them that when it was done they must send for a man to apply the gold leaf and specified that it should be old Kas from Kolozsvar because he was the best. The elaborate decorations above the organ pipes, which were a disgrace, must be properly restored and he insisted that before that work was started the pastor should arrange a sensible price with the gilder because he did not want money wasted on anything that was not necessary. Then he had asked the estate manager to bring in the accounts, checked them through himself and drew a line across the last page just beneath them. Then he had written 'I have found everything in order up to this point' and added the date and his signature. Then he had turned to other estate matters, saying that the young calves that had been selected for the market should not be disposed of at once because the current prices were too low. They should wait until the new grass started to sprout in the meadows. On the other hand the buffalo cows should be sold soon before their milk dried up. Up on the Botos, where it was too cold for wheat, they should sow barley and, if the fields of rye which had been sown the previous autumn proved to be full of thistles in the spring, they should be carefully weeded. All these orders he had given in the calmest manner. Occasionally, as he had been speaking, he had glanced at the clock as if he were expecting someone or had shortly been about to leave himself. Just before one o'clock he had said that he had been expecting Balint, but that perhaps he would not be coming. As he said this he had gone to his desk and picked up a small parcel carefully wrapped in newspaper and handed it to the priest, saying that it should be given to Balint if he should turn up later. If he had not arrived by the evening it should be delivered to Balint's home. Then he had gone into his bedroom and rung for his valet.

The priest and the manager, though not understanding what all this was about, had not thought that there was any reason to be disturbed.

A few moments later Kadacsay had come back into the sitting room, followed by the valet and a footman who carried a mattress which he had told them to lay on the floor. When the servants had been dismissed he started to explain to his astonished audience why all this had been done. He had, he told them, taken a dose of strychnine and because he knew that this sometimes caused uncontrollable cramps, he had had the mattress placed there as it would be better and easier than writhing about on the wooden floorboards! Then he had started to give further instructions about suckling pigs and the sheep's feed ...

Shortly afterwards he had looked again at the clock and said, 'Strange! I don't feel anything yet, though I've taken enough to fell an ox!' Those had been his last words. A moment later he had lain down and, a few seconds later, had died.

'Is he very disfigured?' Balint asked when the pastor and the manager had finished their tale.

'Not at all, my lord. Please come and look.'

They entered the manor house living room, which was long and wide and obviously served also as a dining room. In front of one of the windows was a small writing desk and, pushed against one of the side walls, was a plain pinewood table that had served for Gazsi's meals. In the centre of the room, where this was usually placed, there was a mattress and on this lay the dead man covered with a white sheet.

Balint kneeled down beside him and drew back the sheet from his head. He looked at his friend's face for a long time.

Nothing seemed to have changed and if he had not been as pale as wax Balint would have thought that he was merely playing some trick on them. His mouth held his usual mocking smile, his woodpecker nose was tilted slightly to one side and his eyebrows slanted upwards just as they always had when Gazsi had been telling a joke. One could almost believe that at any moment he would jump up roaring with laughter as he had so often done. And yet there was a difference. Gazsi's face now held an expression of majestic calm, comprised of a dignity quite new to him – and of contempt, but mainly of contempt.

Balint was struck by the strangeness of it all, for this was not the Gazsi he had known in life. The dead man lying there was someone he did not know, someone who had appeared only in death.

He covered him again with the white sheet and got to his feet.

Then he looked around the room and realized that its simplicity and bareness also signified contempt. Though like every provincial manor house in Transylvania it must once have contained some good pieces of furniture, there was now nothing of value in it. It was clear that such things had meant little to Gazsi for he had given all his good things to his sister when they had divided their inheritance – furniture, carpets, porcelain, everything. For himself he had kept only a couple of threadbare armchairs and a worn sofa. But along the walls there were long low bookshelves made of bare polished planks of natural wood, and on them were great quantities of books untidily stacked, much used and obviously much read. Balint went up to examine them and found to his amazement that they were mostly philosophical works by such writers as Hegel, Wundt and Schopenhauer. There were also some historical works by Ranke and Szilagyi, and a copy of Renan missing its cover, and several volumes of some German lexicon. Most of the books were tattered and some torn in half ... and all were stained and dirty as if they had been covered in candlewax or thrown about in anger.

Balint started to pick some of them up, but when it was announced that the doctor had arrived, along with the coroner, the prefect and the village notary, all of whom were needed to make out the death certificate, he went quickly out into the open air.

*

Outside it was a perfect day. The sky was so clear that it was almost blinding, very pale, white-grey rather than blue, and so savagely bright that it might have been trying to compete with the snow beneath.

So as not to remain surrounded by the crowd of weeping women, or be stared at by the village children who were gathered outside the house, he walked round to the side and took a path that led up the hill. It was already clear of snow and slightly muddy. After he had gone some hundred paces he found a bench under three young birch trees and sat down. Then he undid the sealed package.

Inside there were two envelopes and also a silver cigarette box with an inscription in gold: 'The Ladies Prize, Debrecen, 1905'. He opened it and inside was a little pile of tobacco dust and a note which read *'I leave you this as a personal souvenir. It is the only possession I value'* and underneath, in brackets, *'You may think it ugly, so don't use it if you don't like it! Gazsi'.*

In the larger of the two envelopes there was a long paper headed AMENDMENTS TO MY WILL below which was a precise list of his wishes for gifts to each of his servants, some other special provisions, and the fact that he wanted 1,000 crowns to be allotted for restoring the organ. These details had not been itemized in the will held by the notary, though a lump sum had been set aside for them. The next paragraph dealt with arrangements for his funeral: he did not wish to be buried anywhere else but to be laid to rest somewhere in the garden near the house – and there was to be no memorial or epitaph. The last section dealt with his horses. Firstly he wrote that the little speckled gelding who was too old to work should be shot so that he would not fall into the hands of the gypsies in his old age. As to the thoroughbred mare Honeydew, Gazsi left her to Balint and asked him to take her away immediately. At the bottom of the page was that day's date, the date of Gazsi's death, and his signature, written in Gazsi's large awkward writing.

The second letter was for Balint alone. Enclosed with it was Honeydew's pedigree wrapped in a single sheet of writing paper, on which there were just a few lines about the mare. *'As you agreed to let Honeydew foal at Denestornya,'* he had written, *'I hope it isn't presuming to ask you to keep her.'* Then followed a few light-hearted, joking phrases ending *'... my sister is apt to be somewhat grasping, but I don't feel she'd want this wonderful animal as she wouldn't have much use for her!'* He ended with the words *'Please don't forget your promise about my nephews. I don't want them to turn out like me'.*

Poor Gazsi, thought Balint. In his last moments he had been thinking of his own great unquenched thirst for culture.

Balint's eyes filled with tears. For a long time he stayed where he was, sitting on the little bench and staring at the snow. He thought how marvellous it was as it slowly melted, disintegrating into tiny particles of ice, thousands of minute crystals gleaming like miniature mountain peaks all turned towards the rays of the sun. It was everywhere pitted with deep little crevasses like spear-thrusts from the direction of the south, deep little holes formed by the sun's heat. And as it was slowly being destroyed by that very sun so the snow resembled white foam inexorably drawn to that relentless implacable light, to that radiance it so much desired but which was to be the source of its own destruction. To Balint the process was like an allegory of all existence ... and he thought again about his dead friend.

On the same day another death occurred, that of old Adam Alvinczy. He was found dead in his bed in the morning, and this news and the social excitement it provoked drew everyone's attention away from Gazsi's suicide.

Since Count Alvinczy had been a prominent man there had to be an important funeral. A long line of carriages and cars followed the cortege to the family vault.

The following day the lawyer read the dead man's will in the presence of his sons, of his daughter-in-law Margit, and of Stanislo Gyeroffy who had been made executor. It proved to be a harsh and comfortless document. The old landowner had carefully recorded all the money he had had to pay out to settle his sons' debts and on the basis of these figures he had drawn up the inheritances of three of them in three separate columns – three because Adam had been given his share two years before when he had got married. It was a shattering experience for those who were left: Farkas was to receive only the house at Magyaro-kerek, with just eight hundred acres and three small forest holdings; and Zoltan the meadows near Magyar-Tohat and the house in Kolozsvar. All had been heavily mortgaged. The youngest brother, Akos, got nothing because only two months previously his father had settled debts that already exceeded his share of the family property. 'I regret having to do this,' wrote the old man, 'but I cannot deprive my other sons just because of him.'

This came as a mortifying shock to the three brothers, and most of all to Akos who, as soon as the lawyer had left the house, stammered out the confession that on the night of the charity ball he had lost sixteen thousand crowns at the gaming table and the winners had only given him an extra two weeks to pay up because of his father's death. He now had only thirteen days' grace. Thirteen days, that was all. If he couldn't pay then he would be finished!

There followed a terrible argument, long and utterly fruitless. There was no possibility of help. Farkas's and Zoltan's shares were both mortgaged up to the hilt, in addition to which they would somehow have to find money to pay the inheritance tax. They could do nothing. The only hope was that Adam would pay for the youngest.

This, from the goodness of his heart, he would have been willing to do, but Margit vetoed the idea at once. They had a child to think about, she said, so Adam's own small inheritance could not be squandered in this way. What would be the purpose of such a sacrifice, she asked? It would only be throwing money away, and in fact would not really help Akos, who would still have nothing and who could not live on thin air! He himself would not want to live for ever on his brothers' charity, an eternal guest! It would be far more sensible, she went on, if he were to go away somewhere and start a new life. The family could, at some sacrifice, manage to raise just enough to pay for his ticket: but to cough up money just for gambling debts? No! Never!

Margit was at once attacked by Farkas and Zoltan. They said that she was mercenary and without pity and, of course, as they too were deeply in debt, they felt that they could have been as magnanimous as they liked as any help for Akos would have to be paid for by Adam who, because of their insistence, was for once coming close to rebelling against his capable young wife. It was lucky for her that she was supported by Stanislo; and this settled the matter.

So they started to discuss where Akos could go. First, as a matter of course, they spoke of America. Then it was the turn of Java and, following that, of South Africa. But at each suggestion the same problem arose: what would he do when he arrived? Work as a shoeshine boy? Get a job hoeing the earth on some plantation? The trouble was that he had no qualifications for earning his own living. Of course he could become a soldier, and indeed had been quite good at it when doing his voluntary service in the army; but where would he be needed?

It was this last suggestion that led to the decision that he should join the French Foreign Legion.

Akos agreed at once, and almost seemed pleased at the idea: but though at last everyone was of one opinion, no-one knew how one went about it. What did one do? How did one get there?

Then someone thought of Tamas Laczok, he who had taken their father home after his attack at the ball. They had had a long talk with him after the old man had been found dead, and he had been the last of his acquaintance to see him alive. He had seemed full of goodwill and the Legion had been mentioned more than once when he had been telling them about his time in North Africa and how he had had to nurse sick soldiers in the desert. He would know what should be done, but who could find out for them without explaining why they wanted to know? The Alvinczy brothers refused at once. They would have nothing to do with making such embarrassing enquiries, not them! Neither would they lift a finger in such a matter; it would have to be someone else. Stanislo Gyeroffy also demurred, murmuring contemptuously, though in an elegant drawl: 'I really hardly know the man.'

The plan was on the point of being abandoned when Margit spoke up.

'I'll find out!' she said. By what means she did not reveal and the others did not ask. It was unlikely that she would have told them if they had. At most she might just have answered 'Somehow!', for she was a person of few words who did not take kindly to being cross-questioned about anything.

Margit had immediately thought of Balint Abady who was clever and discreet and who was on good terms with Tamas Laczok.

That very afternoon Balint took a horse-cab and was driven out to Bretfu. The coachman, who knew the area well, drove him to the foot of the hill that led to the village and stopped there because the horse would not have been able to manage the steep road that was now covered with melting snow.

'It's the little house you can see up there, your lordship, the one below the vineyard,' said the coachman, pointing the way with his whip.

It was hard work trudging up the hill through mud and slush, and it was nearly a quarter of an hour later before Balint found himself in front of the house. It was a modest little building which must have been either a small summerhouse or else a room for pressing the grapes, before being converted into a one-room dwelling with a kitchen. Lamplight glowed through the window. Balint knocked and from inside a voice cried, 'Entrez!'

Tamas Laczok was sitting on an upturned packing case. He was in his shirtsleeves doing calculations beside a drawing board that was supported on two trestles. He welcomed Balint with a smile of pleasure saying, 'Quelle charmante visite, cher ami – how kind of you to come to see me!' and he got up, cleared the only chair of his jacket, necktie and collar, threw them on the floor, gestured to Abady to sit down and, having guessed that the visit must have some purpose, at once asked, 'How can I be of service to you, my dear friend?'

Balint saw no reason to beat about the bush.

'How does one enlist in the Foreign Legion?' he asked.

His eyebrows slanting up even more dramatically than usual, Tamas winked at his visitor. Though he said nothing to show that he had guessed at once that Abady was enquiring on behalf of one of the Alvinczy boys, he answered in a matter-of-fact way as if it had been the most natural question in the world.

'The Foreign Legion? Oh, that's very simple!' And he at once gave Abady all the most important facts, namely that the candidate just presented himself at the recruiting office. No documents were necessary and no questions were asked. It was just like becoming a Carthusian friar. One could use any name one liked: the Legion did not care and indeed nearly all the men serving in it went under false names. There was a medical examination and once that was passed the candidate was offered a five-year contract. Promotion to corporal was fairly swift providing a man behaved himself, and it was by no means unknown for officers to be promoted from the ranks. After five years a man could leave the Legion or sign on for a further period.

'I know of several men who have quit after their years of service, bought a small farm out there in Algeria and now live happily at their ease. Of course the discipline is hard, very hard; but it has to be as the men are a pretty wild bunch, tough fellows, and rough too, though reliable comrades when the fighting gets grim and the patrols are ambushed. There is an iron tradition that no-one lets down a comrade, ever. The climate's not too bad: it's healthy, even if it does get hot in the summer.'

As always Laczok spoke in French, and he went on to relate many things from his own experience when he had been building the railway in the High Atlas and when he and his men had been protected by the Legion's vigilance. Laczok had been an exceptionally perceptive observer. Suddenly he stopped reminiscing and said, 'But I haven't offered you anything! Wouldn't you like some coffee? I'm always ready for a cup!' and without waiting for a reply he leaned back his strong, pillar-like torso, and called out in Hungarian, 'Rara! Rara! Where the devil are you, you little beast?' and, turning back to Abady, he explained, 'Her real name is Esmeralda, but I call her Rara for short. Perhaps it's a bit sugary, but you'll see it suits her!'

The door opened quietly behind him and a very young, very slim and very beautiful gypsy girl came into the room. She wore a red dress as bright as a fireman's tunic, which set off her coal-black hair. Her brown skin seemed almost to have a greenish glow and it was with pouting lips and a languorous glance filled with sensual invitation that, in a throaty voice that suggested that she was in fact offering herself, she asked, 'You wanted me?'

'Coffee! For both of us!'

'It's on the stove; I'll bring some straight away!'

She went noiselessly from the room and a few moments later returned just as silently. Her bare feet did not make the smallest sound on the floor, for she walked on tiptoe like a young deer; and she moved slowly just as if she were performing some ancient ritual dance to a melody only she could hear. As she put down the tray she looked again at Tamas's guest and, in her long eyes and in the smile on her now widely parted lips, the invitation was unmistakable.

If Count Tamas had noticed this he showed no sign but went on with his tales of the Legion. 'I should think it's probably a good moment to join, for they'll be wanting recruits just now; more and more of them from what my old friends write to me from time to time. I see from the Paris papers – though they always write in such guarded terms – that France has got great plans for Morocco too these days. You can always tell what the French mean when they start complaining about this and that and talking about the security of their borders and the necessity to safeguard their economic interests. It just means that one of these days they'll march in; and once there everyone else will be squeezed out! You mark my words!'

'But at the Algeciras Conference, and when the Franco-German agreement was signed two years ago, the French again confirmed their open-door policy as regards Morocco, just as they guaranteed the independence and authority of the Sultan. France's influence is surely limited to political matters.'

'Ouf! The French don't bother about little things like that! I'll bet you anything you like that something is about to break there; and all the more so since they've sent in Lyautey from Algeria. I knew him when he was a mere captain, and I can tell you he's a tough one!'

Old Tamas then went on to talk about North Africa and all its problems. He talked well because he knew his subject. No matter how complicated the issue Laczok understood it and knew the real facts. Abady listened fascinated as his host unravelled the involved politics of Algeria and Morocco with the same clarity as a few days earlier he had talked about Albania.

It was dark when Abady finally took his leave. Tamas accompanied him to the door, saying, 'Wait a moment! There's a little path round the side of the house. It'll get you down dry-shod,' and he called through to the kitchen, 'Lajko! Lajko! Come out here!'

A slender gypsy boy, about seventeen years old, came running out. His beard had hardly sprouted and he wore an assortment of discarded gentleman's clothes – a shabby smoking jacket and a patched pair of striped trousers – and his feet were thrust into an old pair of tennis shoes. Under the jacket his chest was bare. And on his finely carved Egyptian features was a sly smile of mock humility.

'At your service?' It was a question.

'You can show this gentleman down the side path.'

The youth started off but, noticing that Balint was not following him, stopped a few paces away.

Laczok, seeing the surprise in Balint's face, gave a roar of cynical laughter. *'Elle affirme que c'est son frère, mais je ne le crois pas* – she says he is her brother, but I don't believe it!'

He gave a hefty slap to Abady's shoulder, and then bade him goodbye.

Abady and the gypsy descended the hill, the lad leading the way. He had all the litheness and grace of a panther and the quick, neat movements of his nomadic forebears. After swiftly taking five or six paces he stopped and looked back and waited for Abady to catch up. For a moment his white eyeballs gleamed in the smooth dark face and then he turned and went on down as if barely able to curb his youthful impatience.

Abady descended the path at his own pace. The city's myriad lights glowed down in the valley and for a moment Abady found himself almost blinded by the arc-lights of the station at the foot of the hill. For a moment or two he paused to gaze at the beauty of the great spread of tiny lights in the dark night; and, as he stopped, he was thinking what a strange man Tamas Laczok was. He knew so much, he was filled with esoteric knowledge, he had gazed at wide horizons and not been dazzled, and he was also a man of culture and refinement. But he had used none of it: he had just let it go to waste, burying himself here in a ramshackle cottage with a little gypsy whore, and yet he showed all the signs of being a happy man.

Balint thought of poor Gazsi Kadacsay, who had killed himself in despair because he could not acquire what Count Tamas had carelessly tossed away. He wondered if Gazsi's fate would have been different if he had managed to learn all that Tamas had learned; and would Laczok be so carefree and merry if, with all his knowledge, he had not abandoned his origins and turned his back on power and worldly success? Was it some inborn wisdom that had given him the strength to throw all that away, or would he have been just as happy if fate had not made him leave his own country and go away to learn about the world elsewhere? Would he have been as jovial and contented if he had merely stayed at home, living in idleness and easy ignorance?

Was a man formed by his experience or by his natural talents? Can a man only give up calmly what he is already sure of possessing, and never what he has vainly longed to acquire?

# PART THREE

# Chapter One

Late in the afternoon of March 7th, 1912, there was an exceptionally large crowd of people milling about in the spacious reception rooms of the National Casino Club in Budapest. As well as the familiar group of card players and all those so-called *'szkupcsina'* – the disgruntled old armchair politicians who were forever complaining – on this day there was an almost complete gathering of the ruling party's political leaders. They were all waiting for the return from Vienna of the Minister-President, Khuen-Hedervary, who had let it be known that he was bringing important news and wished everyone to be present so that he could discuss it with them in confidence.

In those days the Casino Club was always being used for such meetings because anyone who was a member could go in and out without anyone else wondering what they were doing there and, furthermore, since those who were not members were permitted to use one of the restaurant rooms on the ground floor, anyone could be seen coming in without the press guessing that something was up and broadcasting the news to the general public.

Everyone realized the news must be exceptionally important: it was known that Count Berchtold, Austria's Foreign Minister since the death of Aehrenthal a few months before, was also coming from Vienna and would see Khuen-Hedervary that night.

And very important it was – sudden, unexpected, serious and astonishing. It was also alarming and seemed fraught with danger. It was simply that at the previous day's audience, Franz-Josef had instructed Khuen-Hedervary to inform the political leaders of Hungary that after more than half a century on the throne he was seriously considering abdication. He had informed the Minister-President that ever since 1867 he had faithfully and honestly respected the agreement drawn up in that year between the governments of Austria and Hungary, that he had done everything he could to humour the leaders of Hungary, always promoting Hungarian interests and honouring that country's great families and now, or so it seemed to him, it was the descendants of those very people who had turned away from him and left it to him alone to preserve the terms of that agreement. 'In these circumstances,' the monarch had continued, 'we authorize you to explain confidentially to your colleagues that if the Party of 1867 now in power decides to ally themselves with those who wish to erode our most important governing powers, then we are ready to abdicate at once and hand the throne over to our successor!' He had then added, with conscious irony: 'Then they'll see what they are in for!'

The King's words were a direct reference to the proposal put forward by Ferenc Kossuth which, if accepted, would have put an end to the commander-in-chief's right to mobilize the reserves should the politicians' obstructive tactics prevent the annual recruiting law being passed in Parliament. This proposal, after much debate, had been accepted not only by Andrassy, but also, and most unexpectedly, by Tisza and by Khuen-Hedervary himself – in other words by the majority of the 1867 Party. The reason was that the opposition's obstruction of the passing of the defence estimates had already kept going since the previous July, and Kossuth had made it clear that acceptance of his terms was the price that had to be paid if the obstruction was to come to an end.

Tisza and Khuen-Hedervary had been almost alone in realizing that, in the present deteriorating situation in Europe, the primary consideration must be the building up of the armed forces. Tisza also did not think the diminution of the commander-in-chief's prerogatives – which in any case he had planned to bring about in due course – anything like as important as bringing to an end the stalemate in Parliament. For them both the over-riding priority was to modernize the army.

Since the previous July the European situation had grown worse and worse.

The revolt in Albania had spread alarmingly. The rebels had been joined by several more tribes and even by officers from the Sultan's army. Everywhere Turks were being assassinated and the government in Istanbul had ordered up reinforcements to control the borders with Montenegro. Nikita had at once replied by mobilizing the Montenegrin reserves while at the same time cynically offering peace negotiations – this from the man who had aided the Albanian rebels with sanctuary and supplies of arms! In this he had not been alone, for it was known that aid also came, if clandestinely, from Italy, for many resident Albanians had re-crossed the Adriatic and joined their compatriots in fighting the Turks. No-one believed that this was done without the connivance and active help of the government in Rome and indeed it was the first tangible sign of Italy's going her own way regardless of the official policy of her allies in the Triple Alliance, Austria-Hungary and Germany, whose Balkan policy was firmly based on maintaining the *status quo* of the Turkish empire.

All these developments were but a foretaste of what was to come, a curtain-raiser, as it were, to events elsewhere.

At Agadir in Morocco a few German citizens were subjected to some insignificant barbarity, whereupon Berlin despatched a destroyer, the 'Panther', to demand satisfaction and, if necessary, to exact retribution. Making a show of force with no preliminary negotiations was in itself sufficiently provocative, but matters were made worse when the Kaiser Wilhelm, who was given to such over-hasty actions, sent a telegram to the German commanding officer: *'Panther! Fass!* – Panther! Catch 'em!'

The European powers, who had between them settled Morocco's fate at the Algeciras Conference in 1906, protested loudly at this arrogance on Germany's part, especially when Berlin declared it a matter which concerned France and Germany alone. At once the French and English standpoints were made clear to the world; France protested strongly and London declared it stood firmly behind Paris. In a few days, tension mounted so high that war seemed inevitable and, even though Reuters announced that Great Britain had no wish to be involved, the Atlantic Fleet was put in readiness and a flotilla of torpedo boats left Portland with sealed orders. Some saw all this as a God-given opportunity to destroy the German fleet whose recent build-up had been worrying England for some time. Had this been allowed to happen a general European war would have been inevitable.

As it happened the German chancellor, Bethman-Holweg, found himself forced to come to an agreement with the French. This was not easy, but after prolonged negotiations, during which the German demands grew progressively weaker, Bethman-Holweg was obliged to accept compensation in the form of a slice of the Congo which was riddled with yellow fever.

It was an ignominious ending to an enterprise which had started with such a high-handed flourish; but for all its comedy the affair had its serious side. Before the Agadir incident the open-door policy as regards Morocco had been generally accepted. Now it was clear that Germany had bought peace by abandoning a policy that was in everybody's interest. And this she had done by selling her commercial rights in Morocco in exchange for a dish of lentils, which is what her newly acquired colony in Africa was derisively named by the other powers. Germany's action in almost breaking the peace and then descending to diplomatic blackmail (even though it was clear to everyone that what she had given up in Morocco was far more valuable than what she received elsewhere) served as Bethman-Holweg's introduction to the stage of world politics – and it was also the first significant dent in Germany's prestige abroad.

The Moroccan crisis had lasted from July 5th, 1911 until the end of September in the same year, and coincided with the general mobilization in Montenegro. This marked the start, in Budapest, of the parliamentary obstruction of the Hungarian army estimates. On July 8th Asquith announced Britain's solidarity with France, and on July 11th Kossuth declared that he would fight the Hungarian government's defence proposals with all the means in his power: and it was on the following day that he put into effect the obstructive tactics designed to prevent the modernization of the Hungarian army.

On July 26th the British fleet was put in a state of readiness and on the 30th Gyula Justh held a public meeting at which he brandished the slogan of universal suffrage as infinitely more important to Hungary than the nation's ability to defend itself. The rabble, roused by this irresponsible speechifying, streamed wildly down Rakoczy Street and was only halted at the corner of the Karolyi Ring. This occurred on the same afternoon that the British torpedo-boat flotilla left Portland Harbour for an 'unknown destination', and when the prospect of a European war had been at its most menacing.

And so it went on. Parallel to every event of world importance was some manifestation of purely parochial interest in Budapest: and when the Agadir incident was closed and the revolt in Albania came to a temporary halt, then other sinister happenings disturbed the peace of Europe, many of them close to the borders of Hungary, matters so dangerous and so close to home that one would have thought someone in Budapest would have noticed.

The next move was once again in the Balkans, close to the Hungarian border.

The Franco-German agreement was signed on September 28th. Two days earlier two Italian fleets sailed from Syracuse, one to conquer Tripoli, the other to attack the Turkish empire. Both of these moves were unexpected and came as a surprise to Vienna as to Berlin. It had been long recognized that France had agreed to Tripoli being in Italy's sphere of influence, even after that country had seized upon Tunis; but no-one had thought of it as being anything more than a sop to Italian sensibilities, a sort of consolation-plaster to be applied to the Italian public's wounded heart, and of little importance as there were so few Italians living in that part of North Africa. And indeed few people had given it a thought for some time past.

Now, all of a sudden, Rome remembered she was short of colonies and declared war on the Sublime Porte. Of course, when Germany had seen fit to ignore the international agreements settled at Algeciras and took her own individual line at Agadir, a proceeding whose negotiated settlement effectively closed the old open door to Morocco, she did irreparable harm to Italy's trading interests. At much the same time Aehrenthal's sudden announcement of the annexation of Bosnia-Herzegovina had encouraged Italy to enter, even if somewhat belatedly, the European powers' race to acquire colonies. And this she did, independently of her allies and, as Austria had done with Bosnia in 1908, keeping her intentions secret until the last minute. Once again those international agreements, on which the peace of Europe had so long depended, were ignored.

This had happened in October, but despite the inevitable international repercussions, in Budapest no-one seemed to notice and in public life nothing was changed. Political argument and obstruction went on as before, with the political leaders all claiming to be acting in the nation's best interests. Public opinion remained unawakened to the implications of what was happening abroad; and though Apponyi asked the House to consider what would happen if the Turko-Italian conflict spread to the Balkans, in the very same session all that seemed to interest Mihaly Karolyi, one of the leading opponents of the government, was the possibility of obtaining cheap meat from the Argentine.

The Speaker, Berzeviczy, tried to arrange a meeting between the government and the opposition in the Karolyi palace ... but only three ministers turned up, and the negotiations and the obstruction continued for a whole month until Berzeviczy resigned. There was then a short truce so that the budget could be passed, during which time matters of defence were put on the shelf until, three weeks later, they were brought up again only to be the object of renewed obstruction. By this time it had become obvious that the *Entente Cordiale* – Britain, France and Russia – which had brought Germany to her knees over the Moroccan question, would present a solid front whatever happened and that Italy's war in Tripolitania was being backed by Britain and France: the proof, if proof were needed, was the occupation by Britain of the Egyptian port of Solum.

And in Hungary all went on as before. As the world situation got worse and worse so the politicians in Budapest buried their heads deeper in the sand and went to war only with each other.

Franz-Josef's threat of abdication came like a thunderbolt from a clear sky. He had ruled so long, become so associated with the very idea of monarchy, that it seemed that the man himself, and only he, was in fact the institution. Perhaps some people realized that one day a change would come, but few could imagine what it would be like. In Hungary some of the political leaders such as Justh and his followers had, through the turncoat Kristoffy, maintained some sort of contact with the so-called 'workshop' of Franz-Josef's heir, the Archduke Franz-Ferdinand, at the Belvedere Palace in Vienna, but it must be admitted that this was mainly a matter of political tactics, one of the backstairs routes to power. Such men hoped that by exerting pressure on the Heir they might finally not only gain some of their vote-catching aims (such as, for instance, the introduction of universal suffrage) but also that this would enable them to ride into office; but they never really grasped that a change of ruler might also involve other changes too. Some there were ambitious men who felt their talents had not been sufficiently appreciated, who offered themselves to the Belvedere with much the same desperation as a bankrupt foolishly spending his last penny on a lottery ticket expecting thereby to win a fortune! But it would have been difficult, among all the thousands of other politically minded inhabitants of Budapest, to find one who had really considered either the effects of change or indeed that change might come at any time, maybe today, maybe tomorrow.

Now, suddenly, this horrid prospect was upon them; and it had appeared in its most unexpected form, the possible abdication of the monarch.

While the Minister-President conferred with his colleagues behind the closed doors of the Deak Room, and while Count Berchtold, accompanied by a small group of old friends, strolled with insouciant elegance through the galleries of the club, more and more people came thronging into the public rooms. In little groups they discussed the terrible news in hushed voices and, at the bottom of the stairs, the newspaper men waited for definite news, and cross-questioned each other to find out if anyone knew more than they did. The telephone never stopped ringing, sounding as loud as a fireman's bell in the general hush.

Everyone was upset and worried, for to most of them the Heir represented the Unknown. Only one thing was sure, and that was that Franz-Ferdinand hated the Hungarians. Only that was certain, everything else was a mere question mark.

The government's supporters were filled with anxiety, but the opposition's reaction was one of anger. No-one dared say openly what they felt, but the unspoken thought was there behind their words and what they felt was anger, anger with the old monarch who seemed to have stolen a march upon them all by being so ungentlemanly as to make such a threat at such a time. Why, it was as if two men had been playing a friendly game of chess – only it happened to be the game of government – when suddenly one of them got up and walked away!

Indeed it was all a little like chess where the accepted rules make sure that bishops only move diagonally, knights can jump a square or two, and pawns, while they can be taken from the side, can only move forwards and then only one pace at a time: and every move has only one aim, to checkmate the opponent's king. For as long as anyone could remember politics in Budapest had been like that. By strictly interpreting the House Rules, by reviving forgotten procedures, by shifting loyalty and by endless declarations of vote-catching slogans, the opposition had for more than ten years obstructed all progress, especially delaying the modernization of the army, until they thought they had got the king surrounded and defenceless. This was how they themselves saw the situation in 1912. Their reasoning was thus: who needs an army? The country? Not at all: only the king needed an army. Who needs a navy? Well, the king needed a navy; and if he wanted it all that much then he must be made to pay for it and pay for it by conceding the opposition's just demands. Of course he would give in because the pressure of world affairs would make it imperative for him. The worse the international situation became, the more they would insist on their demands being met, and they would squeeze the old sovereign until he would be forced to concede all they asked. Now, just as they had come to believe that this policy was working and that the government was preparing to surrender, what happens? The king announces that he is going to quit the game and let his successor take his place at the chessboard. It was a hard blow; and as unfair and as unsporting as the player who slams his fist down on the table. It was more: it was not the act of a gentleman.

Though that is what everyone thought, no-one said it openly.

Fredi Wuelffenstein came as close as any to saying frankly what was in his mind. He was standing in the doorway of the Szechenyi Room holding forth to a group of younger men in the belief, not entirely justified, that they admired him. Noisily advancing the left-wing view, he said, 'We mustn't fall for this! The King is only bluffing. He just wants to scare us, which isn't at all what we might expect of him. Of course he won't abdicate! Never! Not he! It's bluff, nothing but bluff! He believes we'll all be so scared of what the Heir'll do that we'll just give in; but we won't. Anyhow, what would happen if Franz-Ferdinand did become King? All he could do would be to come to some arrangement with us. We wouldn't crown him if he didn't; and without a coronation there'd be no King! Even the Belvedere must accept that. It's one of Hungary's most sacred traditions …' and he went on, ever more loudly and brashly, and always repeating himself, as people do who have only a meagre vocabulary at their command. Each time he said the same thing again he beat his fist like a hammer as if this would serve to convince his audience.

Then Niki Kollonich intervened. At the last elections he had come into the House on the Popular Party ticket. He was just as prying, insolent and insincere a man as he had been a boy; and he loved to stir up trouble. Now, he asked mildly: 'Surely I remember you saying last autumn that we ought to pay court to the Heir, to His Highness the Archduke Franz-Ferdinand?'

Wuelffenstein nearly exploded with rage because what Niki had said was only too true. Not long before, through his sister the beautiful Countess Beredy, he had managed to wangle an invitation to shoot at the archduke's place at More; and all that had happened had been that his host had completely ignored him, failed even to give him the time of day and indeed had not appeared even to notice his presence despite the smart English clothes he wore each day. This had continued for the whole three days of the shooting party – not a word, not even a glance. The only result of the whole expedition had been that back in Budapest, where the news of his presence in the enemy's camp had been widely trumpeted, poor Fredi now found himself an object of suspicion in his own party.

'I never said any such thing!' he shouted. 'All I said was that the Heir should be kept informed, that we should see that he knew what we wanted. Someone ought to tell him that we'll never give in, and that we won't yield an inch. He's got to know that without our co-operation the Crown gets nothing! That's what I said. Without us there'll be nothing, no army, nothing, just nothing!'

Niki then added, in admiring tones, 'Of course you told him that when you were shooting together, didn't you?'

'I've always said it, and to him too ... at least I would have done if the occasion had arisen ... but he doesn't impress me, I can tell you that! Nor anyone else either for that matter. And as for the archduke, well, he has no say in the matter until he becomes King; and when that time comes he can only rule if we want him to!'

Even Fredi might not have argued so passionately, nor uttered such idiotic remarks, had he seen who was standing behind him.

It was Slawata, adviser to the Austrian Foreign Office and an intimate of Franz-Ferdinand. Behind his thick glasses his eyes seemed to gaze into the distance and the bland expression on his face gave away nothing of what he might be thinking. He stood there, apparently somewhat bored, as if he had simply strayed there by chance. After a moment or two he wandered off to see what he might overhear elsewhere.

At that moment Abady arrived at the club and almost collided with Slawata at the door. The latter at once brightened up as if thankful at last to meet someone he knew.

'Komm! Ich muss mit dir reden! – come with me, I want a word with you. At last I've found somebody I can talk to. Let's find a quiet spot!' And so saying he took Balint's arm and led him away.

For some time Balint had tried to avoid Jan Slawata's confidences, because Slawata frequently said things that offended Balint's patriotic feelings. Yet it was difficult to avoid meeting this old colleague – for they had both started their careers in the Ministry for Foreign Affairs in Vienna – and there was something about having worked in the Ballplatz that formed a bond between its alumni that often lasted a lifetime. So it was with Slawata and Abady. Whatever their differences there always remained this old link, which was something more than mere friendship for it was based less on mutual attraction and more on the fact that, diplomatically speaking, they spoke the same language. Usually Abady's reluctance to listen to Slawata's often tactless opinions had led to his avoiding the diplomat's company, but on this day he welcomed it, for he was anxious to hear something more authoritative than the gossip and rumour that were flooding the Casino at that moment.

'You can imagine,' said the friend and confidant of Franz-Ferdinand, 'the emotions produced by the Old Man's announcement. For years we have been waiting for our turn to come and now we are not even ready for it! Nothing is prepared, we have no definite programme and no men trained and ready to take over the reins of government. Of course His Highness knows what he wants, but the details still have to be worked out. The "workshop" is feverishly busy, but I can tell you it's chaos, absolute chaos! Personally I could wish for some other solution to this crisis … we're simply not ready! I've been sent to see how the land lies, find out what people are thinking, judge everyone's reactions, their moods, what their reactions are … It's not a nice job, and I don't like it one bit. And it's a dreadful responsibility. If anything goes wrong then I'll get the blame and His Highness, as you know, can be pretty ruthless. He doesn't play games, that one!'

'Well, I for one don't think there'll be any change,' said Abady. 'As I see it Khuen-Hedervary will resign and whoever succeeds will simply back down and withdraw the resolution. After all the government only adopted it as a means to stop all this obstruction.'

'That might be so had Tisza not accepted it too; but with him involved things are much more serious. The resolution is now his baby. Of course I now see what a mistake we made in telling our Defence Minister Auffenberg to protest to the Hungarian government. That's what has made Tisza so angry; you know how touchy he can be about anything that seems like an infringement of Hungary's independence. Anyhow we think Tisza has an ulterior motive in supporting the resolution: he wants to use it against us as soon as there is a change of ruler. The theory at the Belvedere is that Tisza believes that when this happens there won't be any more bargaining; just a clean break with the resolution remaining but with the obstructionists removed. If, when the Heir ascends the throne, he finds himself opposed by a majority in the Hungarian Parliament, then he'll find himself up against the Constitution. In our view Tisza is the true enemy, not those loud-mouthed demagogues in opposition. He is a far more serious opponent than the others, much stronger – a real hard Hungarian, that one!'

Slawata could not leave the subject of the dangers he saw in Tisza's surprising support of the resolution; neither could he conceal his deep anxiety. He was clearly worried by what Tisza might obtain in a private audience with Franz-Josef. Indeed he might even persuade the old monarch, who had always appreciated his brilliance and charm of manner, to give way, especially if he could convince Franz-Josef that Auffenberg's unfortunate intervention in Hungary's parliamentary affairs had been instigated by the Heir, which, of course, it had been. If Tisza was able to make it seem that the resolution was the logical outcome of Franz-Josef's own work, and was designed to protect the 1867 Compromise against the destructive plots of the Heir, then it was by no means unlikely that the monarch would withdraw his threat of abdication. 'And then,' went on Slawata, 'we shall really find ourselves in difficulties; and we've already got enough as it is.'

Balint had never seen Slawata so worried. He, who had never been anything but sure of himself, of the rightness of his view of things, of the ineluctable truth of his own judgement and the sureness of his political analysis, now seemed so hesitant and so unsure of himself that he was reduced to seeking advice. To Balint it looked as if Slawata had at last grasped what an abyss yawned before the politician who had pronounced judgement on political affairs when he had no responsibility for their conduct, and was then forced to stand by what he had said.

The envoy of the Belvedere sighed deeply, took off his thick spectacles, wiped them on his handkerchief and replaced them on his nose; and Balint, who had long before noticed that Slawata always did this when he was about to say something important, turned to him expectantly just as the politician looked Balint full in the face and said, 'If there should be a change of monarch, would you consider the offer of a portfolio in the new government?'

This was quite unexpected, and a thin crease of anxiety appeared on Balint's forehead. What he already knew of the Heir's plans for the Dual Monarchy – and most of it had come from Slawata himself – was utterly opposed to Abady's most cherished belief in traditional values. He had been revolted by what Count Czernin had written some years before, when he had prophesied that Franz-Ferdinand would transform the loose conglomeration of independent countries that had formed the Habsburg empire into a huge monolithic authoritarian superstate with an all-powerful central government. This was just what the youthful Franz-Josef himself had once proposed long before he had accepted the 1867 Compromise. At that time Balint's own grandfather, Count Peter, had been nominated without his consent to the proposed new Upper House and had, scornfully, refused to have any part in a project which would have imposed Austrian authority throughout the Balkans; and even, eventually, to find his beloved Transylvania handed over as a dowry to whatever Habsburg princeling found himself nominated to the throne of Romania! Memories of what his grandfather had told him flooded through Balint's mind until his blood boiled with anger.

Even so he remained outwardly calm, and answered the question put to him with another.

'I would have to know first with whom I would have to serve; and, of course, what programme was envisaged.' Abady's voice was suddenly very cold.

'Kristoffy is the only man who has His Highness's confidence.'

'Kristoffy! Why, that's ridiculous! Apart from anything else there isn't a man in the country who'd consent to work with him!'

'Oh, but perhaps there is,' and Slawata smiled knowingly. 'We have reason to believe that Lukacs would ... and maybe even Justh.'

'Justh is a radical Independent and it was Kristoffy who destroyed that party when he was Minister of the Interior. They're deadly enemies! Nothing would make those two work together!'

'You perhaps do not know that they have been in secret contact for quite a time. They came together over the universal suffrage proposals, and those form the first part of the Heir's programme for Hungary. Other things will come later.'

'What "other things"?'

Franz-Ferdinand's confidential envoy barely hesitated before he uttered that old diplomats' familiar plea for secrecy, '*Unter uns natürlich* – just between ourselves, of course!' and then started to explain:

The first step, he said, would be a manifesto from the ruler. The principal item would be the introduction of universal suffrage. The importance of national defence would be touched upon, as would the need slightly to modify the terms of the Compromise so as to put an end to all the current bickering. The existing Parliament would be asked only to pass the necessary legislation for the suffrage proposals and the defence estimates – both with validity for one year – and the government, which would have been in on the planning of this programme, would then prorogue Parliament as soon as these two measures had become law. Everything else, the coronation and the proclaiming and passing of the laws needed for bringing about the centralization of the Monarchy, would be the task of the next Parliament.

'In that case,' interrupted Balint, 'the first thing is to make sure that whatever proposals Kristoffy makes to the House are accepted by a decent majority. Frankly, I find that most unlikely.'

'Lukacs will bring over the radicals in the government party and Justh will be followed by the whole Independent clan. When that happens the People's Party would naturally join us too. All that would be left against us would be Tisza and his lot.'

'Just let us suppose all this happens. Do not forget that with this political grouping Justh would be the only leader with a majority; and can you imagine him voting for an increase in Austrian power and centralization, and not for his own programme based on the union of our two countries only through the person of the monarch who sits on both thrones? Justh will be careful to see that the suffrage proposals, and the redrawing of constituency boundaries, are all to his own party's advantage. And I'm sure that even if today he seems to agree to accept revision of the Compromise and the centralization of the Monarchy, even if he goes so far as to give in over the army proposals, he'll only do it with the secret reservation that the revised voting laws ensure the supremacy of his Independence Party. In the case that the future reforms have to be introduced by Justh, then the future ruler will find himself in a far greater predicament than Franz-Josef has ever done. And, even if this does not happen, any collaboration between Lukacs, Kristoffy and Justh is bound to fall apart at the first strain put upon it. What then?'

'Then we would bring in our own voting laws and proceed accordingly!'

'Do you really believe it would work? That you'd be able so easily to create a majority that would approve …', and here Balint paused as he searched for some ironic phrase to clothe his real thoughts, '… would approve of what you have planned so neatly?'

'*Mein Gott* – my God!' replied Slawata forcefully. 'The Belvedere "workshop" certainly believes it possible. We count on Lukacs to carry at least half, possibly two-thirds, of the government party: Kristoffy the radicals – though it's true there are not many of them and those mostly intellectuals – and most of the minorities. So Justh would just have to join in, and the socialists with him. That's how Kristoffy sees it … and also Milan Hodzsa.'

'Hodzsa? Is he part of all this too?'

'Of course! His Highness has much confidence in him.'

For a few moments there was silence between the two men. Then Abady spoke, and his manner was both serious and unusually dry.

'I find all this alarmingly adventuresome, and very dangerous, as much to the archduke as to anyone else. The mere fact of a change of monarch constitutes a crisis. To add to it a general election, with all its attendant clash of chauvinist slogans and demagoguery, would be nothing less than madness. It would be sheer chaos, it couldn't be anything else. The monarch could never work with a Parliament opposed to all he stood for. The new ruler would find himself in a hopelessly false position, and helpless with it. There'd be no question today of imposing a repressive regime like that of Count Bach after 1848. The old emperor could only do it then because he had Russia behind him and peace everywhere else. Today it would be unthinkable. Anyhow it couldn't last and would soon end badly. Only chaos would remain, with all the various parties at loggerheads, desperately jockeying for position. What a picture to show the world! Especially now when we're already pretty near to chaos at home and the Balkans are ready to flare up at any moment! What a time to start provoking even more turmoil in the country!'

Slawata replied pensively, 'Well, it's the only thing against it.'

'It certainly is not! There are far deeper and more serious matters at stake. The very stability of the Monarchy lies in its respect for tradition. It rests on tradition and in turn is upheld by it. The ties between the monarch and the different strata of society and of the administration of the country are legion. The ruler who ignores this, and starts to destroy these links and replace them with something altogether less ancient, reputable and respected, will destroy the foundation on which his kingdom rests. A dictator thrown up by a revolution can do this because he owes his pre-eminence to his popularity. A successful general can do it because he is supported by his troops. But that sort of power rarely outlives the man who creates it. Such a dictator can try to make all men equal, and indeed he is wise to attempt it, if only because such potent personal rule will always be more effective if it is imposed on a homogenous society than on one based on a historic class structure, which is the historic rock on which hereditary monarchy is built. Hereditary power is only possible when it rules a society that is itself built up in layers whose traditional apex is the Crown. There is nothing logical in this. It is a historical and emotional acceptance of an illogical fact; that is all. The monarch who turns demagogue and who puts himself at the head of popular revolutionary movements may fancy that he's feathering his own nest, but what he's really doing is preparing the way for a republic, or for the ruin of his country!'

Slawata smiled ironically as he said, 'All that is sheer Montesquieu – *esprit des lois!*'

'Of course! But it is no less true, however long ago it was written. Anyway we are only guessing. All this is purely hypothetical and I, for one, don't believe His Majesty has any intention of abdicating … so all this talk is really about nothing, at least for the moment. Khuen-Hedervary will resign and a new government will be formed which will reform the suffrage laws, which in my opinion should have been done long ago. I hear that Justh is quite ready, at least for a year, to drop all that tiresome obstructionism, especially as regards the army estimates. So, if the army question is out of the way, the other reforms the Heir wants to see could well be presented without upsetting anyone.'

Slawata's reply took Balint by surprise.

'But we don't want anything while Franz-Josef is still on the throne. Indeed we'll make quite sure no real reform is possible. Perhaps some little concession here and there, but only if it proves unavoidable. His Highness wants to do it all after he succeeds to the throne, and until then he'll do everything in his power to prevent any changes. If Laszlo Lukacs becomes Minister-President, which seems likely, he'll forbid it outright!'

'Even if that means holding up the defence proposals?' marvelled Balint.

'Even that!'

'I just don't understand! Surely, in these critical times, the country's military readiness is vital to the Monarchy itself? Isn't that just what the Heir has been trying to achieve?'

'Of course, but not at that price! Just think,' the Heir's trusted adviser went on, 'when the archduke succeeds to the throne the most important card he'll hold will be the introduction of general suffrage. And it must be he, and he alone, who gets the credit. If it is introduced now, before his time comes, he at once loses his trump card and with it the handle which will open the door to his other plans. Therefore nothing must be done now, nothing. Under no circumstances. Under no circumstances at all! Better for everything to stay as it is.'

Balint jumped up unable to conceal his anger.

'What insufferable egotism! Here is our country behind all the other powers in military preparedness. We are in the middle of an appalling international crisis, and our beloved archduke is prepared for purely selfish reasons to hinder what is in his and the country's best interests!'

'No need to flare up like that!' said Slawata. 'After all the Old One can't live for ever ... and perhaps in a month or two ...?'

'In a month or two you'll be able to embark on these dangerous adventures you speak of ... is that it? I can see that nothing else is important to you now. All you want to do is to destroy what we already have – and the more brutally the better – only to replace it with some ill-thought-out and thoroughly nebulous super-monarchy. And that is why, as you yourself admitted, you can't find any supporters who are worth a tinker's cuss! The only men you'll find to support such a plan are those who have nothing to lose or those who fancy they'll benefit even if everything else crumbles.'

'I'm most disappointed that you should take it this way,' said Slawata morosely. Then he too got up. 'And I'm sorry, because in you I had hoped to find a colleague and sympathizer.'

'You have nothing to be sorry about! I should never ever have supported such a plan. Indeed, you have nothing to be sorry about ... *Servus!*'

'*Servus!*'

Balint turned away and left without offering his hand.

# Chapter Two

In the following weeks Balint often recalled his talk with Slawata.

For the moment everything remained much the same as before. The government resigned but was re-formed almost as it had been after some three weeks of argument and, as a result, the resolution which had so provoked the ruler was dropped. Khuen-Hedervary agreed to continue in office so as to get matters cleared up but, after another three weeks of renewed and gleeful obstruction from the opposition, gave in his final resignation and withdrew from politics. So, in the middle of April, Laszlo Lukacs became Minister-President.

Officially his programme barely differed from that of his predecessor, but he had surreptitious negotiations with Justh even before he took office. It was much the same with other grandees of the opposition, but it was soon clear that such interparty contacts were purely formal and had little significance.

Gossip about the news now became ever more confused and confusing, to the point where the most unlikely and impossible was everywhere believed. It would be declared as gospel truth that Lukacs and Justh, those dedicated left-wing reformers, were forming a right-wing lobby with – or without – the support of Tisza, their archenemy. There were even some developments which seemed to lend credence to this unlikely tale, such as when the followers of Kossuth sent a delegation to Vienna to protest that Auffenberg's message to the Budapest Parliament constituted an infringement of Hungarian sovereignty, only to find that the Austrian minister's action was defended by one Tivadar Batthyanyi who belonged to Justh's own inner circle. This represented a complete volteface, and it was followed by others. Mihaly Karolyi, the president of the OMGE – the reactionary landowners' agricultural association – who had always been a member of the Independence Party and who only two years before had been campaigning at Tisza's side on the suffrage issue, was now known to have switched allegiances and, as a radical, was acting as go-between between Justh and the heads of the government.

Though gossip was rampant, no-one knew anything for certain: except, of course, that the atmosphere behind the scenes was becoming stormier and stormier while all the old obstruction went on as merrily as ever. Public interest in what was happening in Parliament was steadily being stifled, for all that anyone could find out from reading the newspapers was that the country's elected legislators either met in closed session or else were insisting upon voting only about trivialities. This was all too boring to be of any general interest.

During this time Abady only came to Budapest when it was necessary for his work for the Co-operatives. His mother had planned to return home at the end of April so as the weeks went by Balint spent much of his time travelling between Transylvania, Budapest and Abbazia, where Countess Roza still was.

Now, just when she was about to come home, something occurred to delay her. Her room at the Hungaria Hotel in the capital had already been reserved and her son daily expected to hear when she would arrive. The telegram came, but it was not what Balint was expecting. It read: 'CAN'T TRAVEL NOW. LETTER IN POST. MOTHER.'

Two days later the letter arrived. It proved to be a large hotel envelope with the address written by some hand Balint did not know instead of his mother's slanting spidery handwriting. Anxiously Balint tore it open to find two letters inside.

The larger one read:

*My dear boy,*
*I am dictating these lines; but do not be disturbed as I am not seriously unwell. I have had a slight mishap in that when I woke up this morning I found I could not use my right hand properly. It is limp, rather as if it were asleep. As it did not get any better during the morning, at midday I sent for a doctor – though you know how much I dislike them. He has diagnosed circulation trouble and says it will soon be better. He has ordered me to have alcohol compresses and massage. It is all quite trivial, but I did not feel like travelling in this rather helpless state. So I shall stay on here for a couple of days, really only because it would be difficult in the wagon-lit train compartment with only one hand working, and it would be hard to dress and undress in the sleeper. You know how I dislike being helped.*
*Please don't worry. There is no need for you to think of coming here.*
*A thousand kisses.*

Countess Roza had dictated this letter to her old personal maid Terka, who had herself written the second letter. In this she said:

*I am only writing this to your lordship to let your lordship know that this is really so and that her ladyship is not worse than she says. I was rather scared this morning when I saw that she could not use her arm, but there is nothing else wrong, your lordship, only this, and the doctor told me himself what he told her ladyship, that it will get better gradually. Please excuse the liberty in writing to your lordship, but I thought you would want to know.*

*I kiss your lordship's hands. Terka.*

Balint left for Abbazia the same day even though he had promised Adrienne, who was going to Lausanne to visit her daughter at the beginning of May, that he would meet her in Budapest and go with her to Vienna, where they could spend a few days together. He sent an express letter to Kolozsvar to explain why he had had to abandon this plan, and left on the evening train.

He found his mother exactly as she had described herself. She could move her hand and fingers a little, but had no strength in them. Balint went to see the doctor on his own and the latter told him: 'It is arteriosclerosis. She will get better, though it is possible that she will never be quite the same as before. All the same it must be taken seriously if only as a sign that there is a tendency to apoplectic strokes. Some people are prone to this, and there is really no avoiding action we can advise. Perhaps it might benefit your mother to go to Bad Gastein in the summer.'

Countess Roza did her best to put on a show of crossness because her son had come when she had said it was not necessary: but it was obvious that she was really very pleased and happy. They spent sixteen more days together on the Quarnero coast.

The doctor's prognosis turned out to be correct. The old lady recovered the use of her hand, but even though she was soon able to write with it after a fashion, it was never quite the same as before.

During these days together Balint felt himself closer to his mother than he ever had been. It was as if a certain hardness in her was now dissolving. It may have been that in a hotel that regal arrogance was not so marked as at home at Denestornya where it never left her. There was nothing that Balint could put his finger on, nothing obvious, especially in the old lady's attitude to her son, but there was something gentler and softer about her, almost as if the trouble with her arm had given rise to a foreboding that had caused her, for the first time, to look into herself. Somehow Balint was aware of this. It was not just a suspicion, he knew it; and as a result he tried himself to be just that much warmer with her than before, only a little, just enough to please her, but not too much as he knew how much his mother detested anything that smacked of sentiment or effusiveness.

In the middle of May they started for home; and Balint, who thought that it must be about then that Adrienne would be returning from Lausanne, sent a telegram to tell her their plans.

The day they arrived in Budapest – though Balint had argued against it because such fashionable places were sure to be crowded at that time of year – they went to have tea at Gerbeaud's. Countess Roza insisted; Balint had noticed at Abbazia that his mother had recently shown a liking for being surrounded by people. It was an unexpected change in the old lady who had always avoided crowds, rarely went out to other people's houses and never went to restaurants or tea rooms.

Now, all of a sudden, she seemed to want to be surrounded by people. It was as if the bustle and turmoil of everyday life brought her joy, as if what had happened in that hotel room by the sea had reminded her that her life was passing inexorably.

As they always did now Balint and his mother walked arm-in-arm.

Of course Gerbeaud's was very crowded. Every table was occupied and every chair taken, and in front of the long counter customers were standing two or three deep. Finally they found a place just beside the door, Countess Roza with her back to the wall and Balint on her right. They were so close to the doorway that many of the people crowding in at that fashionable hour brushed against their table.

Countess Roza did not mind at all. Smiling with good humour she sat there patiently until at long last her coffee topped with whipped cream was brought to her. Then, slowly stirring it, she watched the mob flow to and fro as the throng of society women almost fell over each other as they fought their way in and out. The old lady's slightly protuberant grey eyes watched it all with amused tolerance, even though some of the customers were only inches from her chair.

It's amazing, thought Balint, as he bent forward to sip his tea. How she would have loathed all this only a month or so ago!

A tall young woman dressed in rust-coloured linen appeared in the doorway.

It was Adrienne.

She could hardly get through against the rush of those trying to get out, and had to stand by the door to let the crowd go by. She stood there, beside the door, with her back to where Countess Abady was sitting.

She was already standing patiently there when Balint looked up and of course instantly knew who it was.

Joy flooded through him ... and then fear of what would happen next. If Adrienne did not see them, even though she was so close, and so did not greet his mother, Countess Roza would assume that it was done on purpose. Also it was unthinkable that, finding themselves so close to each other, they could make do with a formal greeting. A few words, however trivial, would have to be exchanged, or it would be ruder than if they managed not to see each other at all. He knew that Adrienne would do whatever was necessary, but how would his mother react? After all she had hated Adrienne for years, and for a long time the two women had not met. Before that, if they had somehow encountered each other at a charity bazaar or in the house of mutual friends, Countess Roza would nod icily and turn away. What would she do now? It would be dreadful to have to stand by and see his mother, by her manner if not in so many words, insult and hurt the woman he loved.

All this flashed through his mind, and his heart constricted with pain.

And then the unexpected happened.

Roza Abady touched Adrienne's sleeve with her left hand and in gentle tones said, 'Why, Adrienne! Didn't you see me?'

The younger woman turned, startled by something so unexpected. For a moment she was lost for words, but she quickly recovered herself, greeted the old lady in her turn and lifted Countess Roza's hand to her lips. There was more in this spontaneous gesture than the mere politeness of a younger woman for an older, for in those days grown women kissed old ladies' hands only if they were close relations. In Adrienne's gesture gratitude was almost equally blended with humility. Then, across the table, she greeted Balint, who had risen when she turned towards them.

Countess Roza waved to Balint's empty chair and said, 'Won't you join us? We're rather squeezed, but do come and sit with us ... or are you with friends?'

'Thank you. I'd love to for a moment if I may. I just came in to get something.'

Adrienne spoke hesitantly in rather an embarrassed tone, but the old lady was completely calm and as cheerful as if nothing had ever come between them. She even seemed happy, and indeed she was happy because her desire to play the role of the gracious royal lady always surged up in her whenever she had a chance of giving, and especially when that gift would be unexpected and surprising, and appear to come from the great height of her queenly throne. In her happiness now there was also mingled a real element of goodness as well as a certain faint and forgiving irony for the obvious embarrassment of her son as well as that of Adrienne, though she was careful not to let any of this appear. She rambled on naturally – perhaps indeed almost too volubly – so as to help the others regain their equanimity, telling Adrienne all about Abbazia and how she had spent the winter there, and then asking for news of Adrienne's father, Akos Miloth, of her sister Margit, and even of her little girl Clemmie who she had heard was at school in Switzerland – so sensible to have her brought up there!

'I came here to buy her some chocolates,' said Adrienne, 'and also some for the headmistress and her room-mother. I always do, every time I come back, just to show how much I appreciate them.'

Then, apparently without any reason, she added, 'I only just arrived – on the five o'clock train this afternoon,' and Balint wondered if she said this so as to show that she had known nothing of the Abadys' movements and so had not contrived this meeting in collusion with him.

They exchanged a few more words and then Adrienne got up and said goodbye, disappearing into the throng of busy shoppers at the counter. A little later they saw her go out carrying three parcels. As Adrienne passed near Countess Roza she bowed her head gracefully to the old lady ... and in her eyes Balint could catch the glint of tears.

A quarter of an hour later Balint took his mother back to her hotel. They walked in silence and they did not speak, even when they separated in the great hallway of the Hungaria, except merely to confirm what they were doing that evening. Balint was anxious to look in at the Casino to hear all the latest news. When they said goodbye he kissed her

186

hand but held it in his for a fraction longer than usual. Countess Abady patted her son's cheek with her chubby little hand.

These two almost imperceptible gestures were all that was needed to mark the gratitude of the son and the acknowledgement of reconciliation by the mother. It was enough for both of them.

When Balint arrived the Casino was crowded. Storms were brewing once again.

During the previous weeks Lukacs had been doing everything he could to get the army estimates passed with only a year's validity. To get Justh's co-operation he had made two different offers on the suffrage question. Both had been turned down. Neither did he get very far elsewhere for Apponyi, in a public speech, declared that neither he nor any of his followers would even discuss what Lukacs was proposing, while Justh let it be known that he found even the suffrage concessions inadequate.

The chances of reaching general agreement were still further reduced by a split in the Independence Party, for just when it had appeared that an agreement with Justh was imminent, the Kossuth–Apponyi group brought up an absurdly far-fetched set of nationalistic demands. Then, as Justh did not want to be made to appear less patriotic than the others, he in turn put forward some even more radical suggestions – and only Lukacs knew how his hands had been tied by his secret allegiance to the Heir's policies which left him with no room for manoeuvre. The Justh party now put forward ever more stubborn and revolutionary demands for reform in the mistaken belief that the Minister-President had the power to grant them. They had the means to obstruct the passing by Parliament of any measures with which they did not agree, and they used this power relentlessly. All that was done in the House in those days was endless voting on trivialities ... voting, voting ... closed sessions and more voting.

At this point Tisza once more emerged into the limelight.

Though it had not yet happened, it was everywhere believed that soon Navy, who had succeeded Berzeviczy as Speaker of the House, would resign and that Tisza would take his place.

This would mean a violation of the Rules of the House for only a few years before, in 1904, Tisza had himself been at the head of affairs.

Abady moved from group to group, saying nothing but listening to what everyone had to say. He only stayed about fifteen minutes listening to each discussion before moving on to the next: but everywhere he heard the same thing, hatred for Tisza, hatred and more hatred, hatred from every kind and shade of opinion in the opposition, hatred from faithful believers in the 1867 Compromise, hatred from the followers of Andrassy, from members of the People's Party and even from those unrepentant old politicians who still brandished the banner of 1848 and revolt against the Habsburgs. There was no difference anywhere.

On the other hand there was no such unanimity in the government's own ranks. Those few supporters of Tisza who were present kept their mouths firmly closed and stood about in frigid silence. The rest of Lukacs's supporters belonged to that familiar type of politician, inane and passive like so many who blindly follow where they think the majority are leading and who are only happy when betting on a certainty. Such men are dismayed by the hazardous and they were now restless and anxious, shaking their heads and vainly trying to reassure themselves by repeating to each other what they firmly believed to be words of ponderous political wisdom. They were obviously scared, for they remembered what had happened in 1904, and the memory of the disastrous days that followed now made their very bones ache. They tried to bolster up their courage by telling each other that Tisza's force of will would overcome all difficulties and that it would be done peaceably and with none of the violence of those other days. The mere fact of having a strong man like Tisza controlling the business of the House would be menace enough to keep the troublemakers in their place. Hedging their bets, as such politicians are wont to do, a number of them went round whispering in the ears of anyone who would listen, especially their political opponents, that should there be any repetition of violence in the Chamber, they personally had never approved of such methods and indeed went so far as to oppose them!

Balint found all this deeply disheartening. He thought of Tisza, whom he greatly admired, risking his entire political future faced with the deadly hatred of his opponents and backed only by a mob as treacherous as the men he was trying to confront. The more he thought about this appalling situation the more worried he became.

He had no doubt that the policy of forced votes would win the day. If Tisza managed to bypass the Rules of the House and succeeded in getting the necessary legislation passed, he would be applauded by the majority and, though the opposition might rant and rave, that was all it would amount to. But afterwards? What would come later? All Balint could see was that Tisza would pile up such a mountain of hatred against himself that he would find himself permanently consigned to a political no-man's-land. What a tragedy if his powerful presence were to be forever lost to Hungarian public life, especially if that loss came about because he had been sold down the line by his own followers, maybe even by this present government, or by its successor, as soon as it might seem expedient to return to the rule of law! Nothing would ever wash away that legacy of hatred, for not only would the opposition do all it could to keep it alive but the government's own supporters would do the same if only to make sure that the most eligible candidate for the office of Minister-President was squeezed out of the race. No-one else would suffer in the same way, but Tisza could find himself excluded for life from any high office. Could it be coincidence, Balint wondered, that this fate was reserved for the man Slawata had declared to be the most serious obstacle to the Belvedere's adventurous plans?

But what other solution was there? At present effective government was impossible for, if the rule of law was to be respected, then this irresponsible handful of obstructionists could continue indefinitely to hold up implementation of everything the country so urgently needed. To break down this obstruction, the only course seemed to be to ignore those very rules which for centuries had guaranteed the freedom and integrity of the Hungarian Parliament. The pity was that it looked as if no-one but Tisza would shoulder the responsibility for doing this and that he and he alone would afterwards be blamed. Was it not possible that some other courageous, hardheaded politician could be found? Someone not so important to the state, who would not be such a loss if he found himself cast out into the wilderness? That would at least be better; for the cynical truth is that the man who acts is blamed, not he who gave the order. The man on the platform gets the rotten eggs, the brains behind him are forgotten.

Balint thought he should speak to Tisza on the subject.

For a long time he wondered if he really should mix himself up in all this. Wouldn't Tisza think he was just pushing himself forward? But what he had thought made him so anxious that it seemed more important to pass it on to Tisza himself. The next morning he asked when he could see him and was given an appointment that afternoon.

Balint talked at length. He told the ex-Minister-President that he agreed with the need for bringing an end to the present impasse and that to bypass the Rules of the House was perhaps the only way. He told the older man of the hatred for him that was already being shouted out loud and which would become far worse if he put his plan into execution. Taking into account Tisza's well-known puritan disregard of his own best interests, he said nothing about personal unpopularity and indeed emphasized what he honestly believed, that personal advantage must always give way to the nation's best interests. But, and he said this roughly lest it might be taken as an ill-judged attempt at flattery, there was another aspect to this matter which was of over-riding importance. The question was not whether Tisza would suffer personally by being cast out of political life, but whether the country would suffer by losing him. He was, said Balint, the only man of sufficient stature and experience to stand up to the demagogues who surrounded him. Therefore a man so important to the future direction of the nation's affairs should not be expected to undertake, or indeed be exposed to, a task that a lesser and more disposable politician could do just as well. Balint begged him not to accept the nomination for Speaker. Surely, he said, there must be someone among Tisza's followers who would be eager for the post and who would do everything that Tisza asked of him?

Tisza listened attentively. He never once interrupted the younger man, but he looked closely at him through the thick glasses which made his grey eyes seem so enormous.

When Balint finished he answered him point by point with circumstantial detail to reinforce what he was saying. He conceded that Abady was in many ways right in what he said and particularly that anyone who succeeded in bringing down the obstructionists was putting his head on the political block. But ... but ... over-riding all other considerations was the vital necessity of restoring order to Parliament. He did not deny what Balint had said about his own pre-eminent stature, it was so self-evident that to do so would have been a pose unworthy of him; and Tisza was no poseur. He knew that his country would probably have need of him in the future, but despite the risks he had decided that now it was for him to act. He alone had the prestige to carry it off and no-one else could shoulder that particular burden. He would not regret it, even if it meant that afterwards he would have to abandon public life. It was necessary for the country; and the cause was worth the sacrifice.

'If I have to I will then go quietly into retirement.'

His reasoning was like a well-forged chain. There was not a single flaw, nor an unnecessary word. Every phrase was as solidly cast as bronze.

Tisza then got to his feet and as Balint was escorting him back to the corridor of the House he thanked the younger man for his good wishes in the most friendly terms. Then, tall, erect and broad-shouldered, he walked calmly to the head of the stairs and disappeared from Balint's sight.

Tisza was elected Speaker on May 22nd.

The socialists, who saw in this the death knell of all their plans, at once announced a general strike. The factory workers turned out in force, joined up with the city rabble, and started overturning trams and trucks so as to build barricades. The mob was heading for the Parliament building but was stopped by the police at the corner of Alkotmany Street. Stones were thrown at the police and a few pistol shots were heard. Then the police fired back: six dead, 182 wounded.

While this was happening in the square outside, the legislators in the House were still voting for or against a host of unconsidered trifles.

Throughout the country it seemed as if a storm was brewing.

That was what each man felt and fancied he saw. Behind Tisza's back all sorts of surreptitious discussions were taking place. Secret messages passed between Laszlo Lukacs and the Independents and, though it never became known exactly what happened, it seemed likely that the Minister-President was still seeking a peaceful solution through agreement over the suffrage question. What was certain was that Kossuth and Justh believed that such an agreement, whether based on law or not, existed. Only that could explain why, on June 1st, Kossuth demanded to be heard in debate and offered, in the name of the Independence Party, to abandon all obstructionist activity if the number of those to receive the vote was increased by 120 per cent. Lukacs at first gave an evasive answer but on the following day he refused categorically to accept Kossuth's proposal. Some people thought then that he must have been influenced by fear of Tisza, but it is more likely that he had had to stall so as to have time to consult the Belvedere, and that the Heir refused his agreement because he had set his face against all radical reform until he succeeded to the throne.

The disappointment aroused a storm of indignation in the ranks of the Independence Party and their next meeting was held in an angry mood.

This was the situation which Balint found on his return to Budapest with his mother on June 4th. He had already realized that whatever he found going on in Parliament would be distasteful to him, for he had grown up with a belief in the sacredness of Hungary's constitution and respect for its traditions. It had been painful to read about recent events in the newspapers, but now, seeing it for himself, it was worse. All the same he had to be there, just as eight and a half years before, when the derisively named 'Darabont' (or Bodyguard) government had sent soldiers into the House to enforce its will. Balint sensed that something of the sort might happen again, now that passions were even more inflamed than before and there had been shooting in the streets outside. If the same sort of thing occurred in the present session then Tisza was not the sort of man to cower before the guns of the military, and if he were bold enough to stand up to them then Balint felt it would be cowardly not to do the same.

The signs of the coming storm were all there when the session began. From the outset the opposition brought into play one of its oldest time-wasting tricks, the filibuster. A Member whose ability to spin any point out for an unconscionable time demanded to be heard on a point of order concerning the Rules of the House. Traditionally such a demand must be given priority, and at least three-quarters of an hour or more could be satisfactorily wasted in this way. Tisza merely dismissed the request in the most summary fashion. Bedlam at once broke out on the left, with members drumming on the benches and demanding an immediate closed session.

From where Balint was seated he could see Tisza clearly. The newly elected Speaker sat there motionless, waiting for the hubbub to subside. The sun glinted on his short greying hair and his eyes were hidden by his thick glasses which were like two shining discs placed just under his forehead. At last, when it was possible to be heard, he said in a serious tone, 'I must ask the honourable Members to abandon the course they have adopted, a course which is bringing our country to ruin.'

Undoubtedly he knew in advance that so mild a rebuke would be in vain and that his request would be greeted, as it was, with whistles, drumming on the benches, stamping and loud irreverent shouting.

Tisza called for order, and again started to speak. His voice was solemn and his manner calm, and only when he quoted back at his political opponents some of their own words did he allow himself some ironic overtones.

'My duty,' he said, 'as guardian of order in this House, is to bring to a definite end all obstructive tactics and technical objections which, as Count Gyula Andrassy has said, can be forged into an effective weapon by a mere twenty ill-intentioned Members, and which, Albert Apponyi has declared, constitute usurpation of the nation's age-old liberties ...' but he was not allowed to finish the sentence for his voice was drowned by the uproar his words had produced. Men jumped to their feet from the benches on the extreme left and howled their anger, then, above it all, Tisza somehow again made himself heard. 'I ask the House now if it accepts the Defence Estimate Bill or not? I wish for an answer: Yes or No?'

The majority of those present at once stood up to show their acceptance and Tisza declared the motion passed. The opposition was now powerless to do anything but continue to howl their fury, cursing and raging and hurling insults in every direction, insults which never reached their mark for the noise was such that no-one could hear what they were shouting. While this was going on Tisza closed the session, got up and walked out as slowly and as calmly as if he were merely out for an afternoon stroll.

This all happened before midday.

Abady went to the House again for the afternoon session. It was barely half-past three when he looked into the Chamber and saw that the opposition was already there in force. They had heard that Tisza had ordered a police cordon and had been afraid that they would not be allowed into the building. And so it happened that, with only a few exceptions, all the seats on the left-wing benches were already occupied. Everyone there seemed happy, even merry, exchanging jokes and laughing as if they were expecting something exceptionally amusing to happen. Some had brought whistles, others bells; and they were busy showing each other what they had brought and gently trying them out. What fun we'll have, they muttered to each other; what jolly, jolly fun!

At four o'clock the government party took their seats and there was an ominous hush which lasted until Tisza rose to open the session. Then bedlam broke loose again with the sound of whistles blowing, bells ringing, voices shouting and crowing with manic laughter. No-one could hear a word the Speaker uttered, though everyone could see his mouth open and shut. Then he stopped trying to speak, noted something with his pencil, rose and left the Chamber, all members of the government party trooping out after him. The noisemakers thought that they had won that round.

But not for long.

A moment or two later the red plush draperies over the door to the Chamber behind the left-wing benches were drawn aside and the chief usher entered with a paper in his hand. Behind him could be seen a high official of the Parliament in his gold-braided uniform, and behind him row after row of policemen.

From where Balint stood it was difficult to see exactly what happened next, but behind the dense phalanx of policemen there seemed to be some heated discussion, perhaps even a brawl. What happened was this. Mihaly Karolyi, who found himself in the corridor just as it was filling up with policemen, pushed his way into the Chamber through the central door on the left, jumped up onto the writing desk of the first bench in front of him, stepped over the shoulders of those sitting there and ran, white shoes flashing and arms spread wide, along the bench-tops until he found himself in front of Justh. Then it seemed that he struck out at the nearest policeman with both fists – though it was impossible to see whether they reached their mark or not for at that moment expert arms caught him and lifted him in the air, and four stalwart policemen carried him bodily outside. He was the only one who physically attacked the police that day, though strangely enough his name never figured on the list of those who were arrested later.

The others merely adopted an attitude of passive resistance. When the man in gold braid touched them on the shoulder, they got up quietly and were escorted out by two policemen.

Abady left after the first of the obstructionist Members had been ejected from the Chamber.

He had come to the session because he considered it his duty: and he remained until the police arrived because, though he knew that he would be deeply shocked by what was going to happen, he agreed that it was necessary. While all this was going on he just stood like one mesmerized, for though his innermost feelings were outraged and although he was horrified by what was happening, he could not tear his eyes away but felt impelled to stand there and watch the horror as it happened.

With a bitter taste in his mouth he stepped out into the corridor. It was empty, for Tisza had evidently given orders to his followers that on this day they should keep discreetly in the background and not wander about as they usually did. Even the ushers had disappeared.

Balint walked swiftly downstairs. In the hall on the ground floor a small group of ejected Members stood nonchalantly at one side surrounded by policemen; they were still there when Balint returned from the cloakroom having collected his hat and stick.

Now they were crowding around the main entrance and Balint wondered what on earth they could be waiting for. Could it be checking of their papers, or were their captors expecting others to join them before they were all hurried away in one large group?

Abady was soon enlightened: the ejected members were having their photographs taken. Eager newsmen were standing outside beside the pillars of the portico, and each group of three or four arrested men paused on the threshold as they came out, their guards flanking them, and moved on, only to have their place taken by the next group, as soon as all the cameras had clicked.

Soon it was the turn of Marton Kuthenvary, who had had more experience of newspapermen than most. He knew exactly what was needed and asked his escorting policemen to take him out into the sun before stopping for the picture-taking ritual. He wanted to be sure that the picture was a good one and knew that anything taken in the shadow of the portico might be too obscure for the 'victim' to be immediately identified.

The police, whose orders, it turned out, had been only to escort the recalcitrant Members to the door but no further, demurred, but Kuthenvary insisted, cunningly pointing out that the colonnade of the entrance was an integral part of the building and that they would not be infringing their orders if they came with him as far as the outer pillars. The argument was reinforced with a couple of good cigars, and the astute Kuthenvary got his way.

The published picture was one of the best. There the 'victim of tyranny' stands framed by agents of authority, the very picture of outraged, dignified righteousness. Since he was being forcibly removed from the building Kuthenvary had asked the policemen to hold both his arms as if pinioned and, even when the photographers were on the point of getting their distances right, he had stopped everything, crying 'Wait!' as he took off his hat and handed it to one of his attendants. This done, he had again struck a pose and said, 'Alright, I'm ready now!'

The result was everything Kuthenvary could have wished. His flowing hair, cut to look like that of the great poet-patriot Petofi, waved dramatically in the wind and his tall figure looked at its most impressive between two little short men in uniform.

Balint reached the square just as the photograph was taken. Then Kuthenvary came down the steps.

'Hello! Balint, my dear fellow!' he called out. 'I'll send that to my constituents in Gsik ... a hundred copies ... it'll be excellent propaganda, don't you think?'

From that afternoon the Parliament building was surrounded by a police cordon.

Nevertheless, three days later one of the excluded Members, an obscure, little-known MP called Gyula Kovacs, managed somehow to climb in over a balcony, jump into the Chamber, fire three shots at Tisza and aim a fourth at himself.

Tisza was unhurt and remained standing calmly at his place. Seeing his assailant fall and assuming that he had killed himself, he continued what he was saying, adding in his precise everyday manner:

'This is just the doing of some poor miserable madman, who has himself anticipated his just punishment. We should all look upon his action, and his fate, with the compassion due to those who lose their wits.'

From that moment the opposition members did not even try to attend the House. They had a 'Manifesto of Protest' published in the papers; but it was received by the general public with lethargy and indifference.

The session was brought to an end as soon as some amendments had been made to the House Rules and some minor legislation passed, unanimously of course. Then followed the summer recess.

Balint did not wait for the official end of the session. He went home to Transylvania.

# Chapter Three

The steam-saw's rhythmic whirring could be heard all over the sawmill compound, through the mountains of sawdust, through the neat stacks of prepared planks which rose in high regular blocks beside the tar-covered roofs of the motor shed, the canteen and the manager's offices, through the dense pine forests which covered the surrounding hillsides, and far down into the valley of the Retyicel at the head of which the Abady sawmill had been built. The timber-fenced compound was as large as a mountain village.

It was midday and the sun's bright rays were almost perpendicular. There was no shadow anywhere and on the smooth pillarlike trunks that had been stripped of their bark in the forest the sunlight glinted with a shimmering yellow glow. The newly cut planks could have been made of yellow-gold velvet and the piles of sawdust were like saffron-coloured snow ... and, as always wherever a steam-saw is in action, everything looked as clean as if it had just been scrubbed. About half an hour before, Abady had ridden down from the ridge of the Fraszinet where he had been inspecting a new plantation in the forest. There, the forest manager, Winkler, and the head forest guard, Andras Zutor (Honey), had walked the plantations with him. A few hundred yards away was the forest lodge of Szkrind where they would all eat before starting off for the mountain pass of Kucsulat. Balint's tent was already on its way with two other foresters – the *gornyiks* – and a supply of fresh horses because they would have a long way to go if they were to arrive that evening near to the source of the Beles which rose just below the southernmost part of the Abady forests on the slopes of the Ursoia. Balint was to start after the others, and with his fast horse he expected to catch them up about halfway; but in the meantime he had come down to the sawmill where he had to meet one of the directors of the Frankel enterprise to whom Balint was contracted to sell all his timber.

As Balint emerged from the labyrinth of woodpiles a young man appeared, somewhat stealthily, less than a hundred paces away where the compound almost touched the surrounding woodlands. It was Kula, whose full name was Lung Nyikulaj, the grandson of the old headman of the village of Pejkoja whose inhabitants Balint had been trying to protect from the extortions of the local officials. He was a well-intentioned youth and for some time had been Abady's confidential informant.

Kula had hurried down from his village and disappeared across the willow-fringed stream marking the boundary of Pejkoja into the dense woodlands behind. He did not go directly to Meregyo, which was his ostensible objective, but had started from home saying that first he had to visit the canteen manager at Szkrind who wanted to buy some cheeses. From there he would go on to Meregyo to see the judge who had two horses for sale. All this was because everyone in the mountains knew everything about everyone else, and had he been seen at Szkrind without good reason, especially when he was supposed to be going to Meregyo, news of this unusual detour would have spread abroad just as if it had been reported in the newspapers. And nobody must get to hear that he had had a clandestine meeting with the *mariassa* – the lord – for, in that part of the mountains where all the peasants were of Romanian stock, a Hungarian landowner who was also an aristocrat was inevitably an object of suspicion.

Because of this, Honey Zutor and Kula had concocted the plan between them that the only way such a meeting could be kept secret was if it should take place, apparently by accident, in an alleyway between those towering blocks of wood where nobody would see them. The *mariassa* would stroll casually out from the side of the mill and Kula would come in from the other side. The day and exact time were settled in advance and, as at midday the Fraszinet ridge could be clearly seen from Pejkoja, all Kula had to do was to keep watch and set out as soon as he saw Balint leave the ridge. Everything had gone according to plan and Kula was already there waiting among the trees when Balint rode into the sawmill compound.

Young Kula was taking a great risk. What he had to tell Abady concerned the nefarious activities of Gaszton Simo, the Hungarian notary for the Gyurkuca district, whose unscrupulous dealings had caused much misery and hardship for the men of the mountains, and who saw to it that no-one crossed him with impunity.

Among those who had suffered most were the people of Pejkoja. What Simo had done, and was still doing, was to give aid to the moneylenders so that they exacted extortionate rates of interest when the villagers had had a bad year and needed money to tide them over. Then when they could not repay the loans, he arranged foreclosures. In this he was partnered by the rascally Romanian *popa,* the parish priest of Gyurkuca. Some years before the worst of the moneylenders, one dark snowbound night, had been brutally murdered, and his house, with all his papers, burned to the ground. Despite this setback Simo had not ceased to plunder the ignorant peasants in the mountain villages, until most of the poor people of Pejkoja had been dispossessed of their land and had been forced to pay rent for what had formerly belonged to them. Abady had tried his best to protect them and had offered to take up their case himself and pay any legal costs, but the villagers had refused, partly because they did not trust the *mariassa*'s motives and partly out of fear of the priest. Even so Abady had tried to take the matter into his own hands and file a complaint against Simo, which, he had hoped, would lead to the notary being transferred elsewhere. This had failed because Simo's superiors in the county town had told Abady that he had no legal grounds on which action could be taken. So, until now, all his well-intentioned efforts had been in vain.

Most of this had happened more than six years before. Since then Abady had not let up in his search for evidence which would condemn the rascally notary, but so far he had not been able to find anyone among the men of the mountains who dared provide him with what he wanted.

Now it appeared that something else, nothing to do with the money-lending racket, had at last come to light.

For many years it had been the custom for the peasants to pay their taxes to the notary's office, a practice which Simo had always maintained was not an obligation on his part but merely a service he was glad to be able to provide. Recently there had begun to be trouble and several of the mountain farmers had received 'reminders' from the tax office that the last demands had not been paid. Simo told everyone concerned that this must be due to some clerical error and that he would take care of the matter for them. No-one knew what he had done, but at least the threatened bailiffs did not appear. Now, suddenly, the situation got worse and in Pejkoja alone three men found themselves faced with having their belongings seized and auctioned if they did not immediately disgorge what they had already handed over to Simo. One of them was Kula's grandfather.

The proof of Simo's guilt was what he now handed to Abady. It consisted of a receipt signed by Simo, the order for seizure and sale from the bailiff's office, and a power of attorney for Balint on which old Juon aluj Maftye had put his mark.

The midday siren had just sounded when Balint bade farewell to his employees at the sawmill, mounted his dappled grey horse and trotted swiftly away. In half an hour he had arrived at the pass.

He had gone alone without a groom or forester, partly because he knew the mountains so well he did not need a guide, and partly because no mountain pony could have kept pace with his horse. He always did this when not on official business or out stalking, for the forests seemed to him at their most beautiful when he rode through them alone. So he would send the packhorses on ahead and follow at his own speed.

On this day the ostensible reason for the expedition was to hunt wolves. Reports had been received from shepherds grazing their flocks on the clearings high on the Ursoia that wolves had been seen prowling at night and that they had already done much damage. It was true that this report was ten days old when it reached Balint in Kolozsvar and that wolves rarely stayed for long in any one district. Still, it was just possible that they might still be there and so Balint had thought it worth a try. It was sheer chance that wolves had been reported on the Ursoia at that moment, but there was nothing haphazard about Balint's desire to spend a few nights alone in the mountains. If this pretext had not come his way he would have thought up something else ... anything that could be used to camouflage his real reason for going there which was simply to meet Adrienne where they could be alone in a place they both loved.

They had planned a visit to the mountains long before, but every time they had talked of it, it had been as of some unrealizable dream, some bliss that the unknown future might hold for them; for until recently they could find no way of arranging it without news of their tryst in the mountains being everywhere noised abroad. Now, at the beginning of summer, an opportunity had suddenly and unexpectedly presented itself.

Since Margit Miloth had married Adam Alvinczy and moved to a small manor house her father owned at Magyar-Tohat, she had begun to poke her sharp little beak of a nose into the running of her father's estates. Old 'Rattle' Miloth, as he did about everything, complained loudly, shouting to all and sundry that he was being robbed by his own daughter; but Margit took no notice and arranged for her husband to look over all her father's holdings explaining that Adam must have some occupation and that this was as useful as any. As a result she had discovered that Count Miloth owned some forestland high in the Upper Aranyos, not much, a mere 900 acres, mostly of apparently unprofitable mixed beech forest. Of course Adam had to go and inspect it and it proved to be quite a nice little forest with a lot of handsome beech trees, which had little value up there, but there was also a smallish stand of pine, most of it young, for the local peasants had long ago taken to stealing any timber worth felling. This, Margit decided, must be changed and the Miloth forests properly guarded. It was, she declared, a wicked waste to abandon their property like that, and if not properly guarded the next thing would be that the young saplings would be stolen for sale as Christmas trees. A forest lodge was built on her orders and an experienced forest guard was engaged and installed there.

All this had happened the previous year.

At the beginning of May Margit's small son developed whooping cough and the doctor recommended that as soon as he was well enough he should be taken to the mountains for a change of air.

Margit had seen no reason to go to some expensive resort miles away when they had their own little lodge at Albak which, at an altitude of twelve hundred metres, was certainly high enough. The little house there was clean and new, and it had a marvellous view. They would be able to stay there for two or three weeks, which would cost them nothing, breathing in mountain air that was as clean and fresh as any in the high Alps.

And so it turned out that at the end of June Margit and her son, together with the maid, who was also the child's nurse, and the cook, moved to the lodge for two or three weeks. The forest guard went to sleep in the stable, and a summer oven was built close to the house. The lodge only had two rooms and a little kitchen, but it was quite enough for the three women and the child.

It was Margit's visit to the mountains which had made it possible at long last for Balint and Adrienne to make their dream come true. Adrienne would go up to visit her sister for a few days and then, saying that she wanted to go on directly to Almasko, which would take her by way of the Beles and Banffy-Hunyad, she could easily slip over to meet Balint on the Ursoia which was near the source of the Beles and only some three hours' walk from the Upper Aranyos. There she would be able to sleep in Balint's tent, and the following day walk down through the Valko woods to the government mill on the Szamos river where the carriage from Almasko would be waiting for her.

They had just worked it all out when news came that wolves had been seen on the Ursoia. This delighted Balint as it gave him a perfect reason to go up the mountains and to go alone ... for it was still important that Adrienne's name should be protected from common gossip.

It was quite a distance to the high ridge of the Kaliniassa. They had to go up the valley of the Szamos and through the Valko estate lands, and even then there was another ridge to pass. It was dusk before Balint's little group arrived on the Ursoia and darkness had fallen by the time his tent had been erected. Then Honey Zutor and the *gornyiks* set off once again for the Kaliniassa with strict orders not to move from there or wander about in the forest until Balint came down himself. At the Kaliniassa there was a log cabin and a barn where the horses could be stalled, for after the news that wolves were in the area it was too dangerous to turn them loose to graze in the forest meadows. On the way wolf tracks had been seen, though it was impossible to say if they were new or a few days old. When Balint was alone he dined by the light of a small lamp off the bread and bacon he had brought with him and then sat outside the opening. He did not light a fire, but just sat there quietly. It was a glorious starlit night with the countless stars of heaven shining brightly in the dark sky. He thought he had never seen so many, and the Milky Way was like a vast river of light – its darker patches like islands – that wound its way from one horizon to the other. The great constellations were like letters of fire in the sky and, in Balint's imagination, seemed to be making their way ever closer to him so as eventually to disclose some ageless secret message even to that worm-like creature that was man, the secret, perhaps, of life and death ... and of eternity ...

The distant horizons could still just be made out, especially where it seemed that some tiny reddish star could be glimpsed trembling through the tips of the sharp fang-like pines that covered the mountain ridges in front of him. Occasionally, and very far away, a dog could be heard barking in the valleys below. Then silence, only silence: but it was not the silence of an empty room, solitary and deadly; rather was it a living silence, a silence that pulsated with the life of the great forests.

Balint stayed where he was for a long time, alone outside his tent in the cold quiet night. His soul was filled with the beauty by which he was surrounded; and he fancied that he could almost hear Adrienne's light steps as if she were already hastening towards him along forest paths paved with stars. Though they would not be together until the following day it was as if their desire for each other throbbed in unison on the mountain ridges that lay between them.

Two days before, Adrienne had arrived at Margit's little lodge. She was not the only guest. Pityu Kendy was already there and making himself extremely useful because, with the family there, there was too much work for the forest guard who found himself not only having to look after the two ponies, scythe the grass and bring it in for their fodder and bedding, but also to go down to Albak to fetch milk and poultry and Margit's letters. So Pityu was at once put to work cutting wood and splitting kindling for the fire, cleaning the horses' tack and also, which was far more important, pushing the perambulator along the mountain paths, seeing that it was first in the sun, then in the shade, and then in the sun again. Here in the mountains this was no longer women's work, for there were more stones than soil on the rough tracks round the lodge. Pityu did everything he was asked with joy in his heart, for since he had transferred his hopeless love for Adrienne into an even deeper devotion to Margit, he was in total bondage to her. It was a happy bondage because Margit never teased him, as her sister had done, or saddened him by seeming to flirt with other men, as Adrienne had, but just accepted his hopeless devotion and listened to his litanies of love with an almost motherly tenderness and sympathy. Sometimes she would scold him, taking him to task for his tendency to drink too much, but she always treated him as a human being worth scolding and not as some sort of toy, which was how Adrienne had treated all her admirers. And the more she scolded the happier he was, because it meant that at least she had some use for him even if it was only splitting logs. As a result Pityu was happy; and it did not matter to him that he had to sleep at the other end of the barn from the forest guard, nor that he had to wash at the well as he was not allowed in the house until the rooms had been cleaned.

Adrienne's coming did not make him any happier, for it was difficult for him to forget that, before Margit had married Adam Alvinczy, both men had vied with each other in their protestations of eternal love for her elder sister. Pityu was always embarrassed when he found himself in company with the two sisters together. He was afraid that Adrienne would laugh at him. He was afraid to open his mouth in front of her, afraid to remain silent, and afraid even to look at Margit lest his love for her should be too obvious. He felt very awkward.

It was a great relief to Pityu when, on the second day of Adrienne's stay, a little mountain pony arrived from the Szamos brought by a lad employed as a servant by one of the Gyurkuca farmers. The boy said that the pony had been hired down in the valley for some *doamna* – lady – so that on the following day she could ride down to the Beles where her carriage would be waiting.

A relief that Adrienne would be leaving? Yes, thought Pityu; but that night, lying in the darkness of the barn, the dismaying thought came to him that of course he would be expected to act as Adrienne's escort and so it would be most impolite of him if he did not at once offer to go with her.

What a disaster! Two precious days of his stay with Margit would be lost, for he certainly wouldn't be able to get back before the evening of the next day at the earliest. It was also a very long walk. Not so bad while they were going downhill, but afterwards, climbing up again – why, it would take at least six hours! Pityu was all too conscious that with his increasing girth and short fat legs he was no mountaineer. Moreover he would probably get lost: and even if he didn't he would be dog-tired by the time he got back. Worse than that was the realization that he would have to spend hours alone with a woman with whom for years he had fancied himself in love and to whom he had spoken only of love. What could he do now? What could he say to her? How should he behave? Should he try to justify his desertion in favour of her sister? It seemed to him that whatever he might say would only be an admission that all those sighs of love and years of adoration had been no more than moonshine and empty rhetoric!

Poor Pityu did not know which way to turn; and it weighed on him all the more that he did not want to admit to himself that neither the old love nor the new had ever been real, that it was all a pose, and a habit. When he and Adam made such a performance of being in love with Adrienne, they could console each other with mutual complaints about how cruel she was to them both. Even now, when the adoration had been transferred to Adam's wife Margit, he could still pour out his heart to Adam who was not in the least jealous anymore than he had been when they both fancied themselves in love with her sister. If he were now to face up to reality he would have to admit to himself that none of it had ever been more than play-acting. Poor Pityu lay awake racked with the impossibility of finding any solution to his problems, and logical thought was not made any easier firstly because at the far end of the barn the forest guard Gligor was snoring loudly, and secondly, because though the straw bed was comfortable enough, the old blanket that covered him stank of stale sweat and there was an equally noisome smell from the boots of the boy from Gyurkuca that were hanging up to dry nearby.

It was so difficult to think straight in these uncomfortable surroundings that Pityu found himself repeatedly reaching under the drinking trough for the sizeable flask of old brandy that he had hidden there. It had had to be hidden because Margit had forbidden him to touch a drop while he was there; but it was his only comfort, and after several generous swigs he finally fell asleep – though still without finding any solution to his woes.

He was up at dawn. His first job was to rub down the newly arrived pony, brush it and prepare the animal just as he had been taught during his period of military service as a Hussar. When Adrienne's bags were brought out from the house he fastened them with professional skill to the wooden saddle and then stood there, in hobnailed boots and with a rucksack on his back, waiting for Margit and Adrienne to come out. Gligor, also dressed ready for a journey, and the boy from Gyurkuca, waited with him.

It was eight o'clock before the sisters came out of the house and walked over to where the pony was waiting.

Pityu at once offered to go with Adrienne. He begged her to accept his services, perhaps a shade too fervently for during the long wait he had paid several swift visits to the barn to get some Dutch courage from the clandestine brandy flask.

Margit did not give Adrienne time to reply but answered swiftly, 'Certainly not! You're not leaving here!' Then she laughed and said, 'What an idea! Leaving two women alone without a man to protect them! It'll be quite enough if Gligor goes.'

'I don't need him either,' said Adrienne. 'The boy knows the road; he came up it only yesterday.'

But Pityu insisted. 'Impossible! Going alone through the forest with some lad you don't know! I can't allow it, I can't! I can't possibly let you go like that, I can't!' And, holding his beaky nose high in the air, he started gesticulating wildly.

Margit turned sharply towards him and said, 'What a way to talk! If I didn't know there was no liquor in the house anyone'd think you'd been drinking!'

Brought up short by such a suspicion Pityu stopped insisting at once, and from then on concentrated so hard on being careful that he hardly said another word.

The sisters said their goodbyes and Adrienne set off on foot along the ridge. The forester went first, followed by Adrienne and behind them the boy leading the pony.

Margit waited until they reached the second turning on the path and then called out after them, 'Addy! When you get to the top, send back Gligor if you don't need him anymore. The post arrives today and I'd like him to go down to the village.'

'Alright, I'll send him back,' called Adrienne, and the little band disappeared from view. Young Countess Alvinczy gazed after them for a moment or two, a tiny smile on her face. Then she turned abruptly to Pityu and said roughly, 'Well? What are you standing about here for? Take off that rucksack and split some wood. No lunch for anybody who doesn't work!' Clumsily the young man started to take the bag off his back, and as he did so Margit looked hard and suspiciously at him.

Balint had been waiting since dawn at Piatra Talharilor – the Thieves' Stone – just where the Abady forests met the common lands of Valko and the district of Ambak. The four towers of rock dominating the steep hilltop meadow gave the place its name.

He stood there watching the little road which started far away down by the bed of the Aranyos, wound its way along the ridge which marked the watershed between the valleys and, about two kilometres from where he stood, dipped suddenly down beside the edge of the sheep pastures and disappeared towards the upper stream of the Beles. With his binoculars he could see a long way.

Finally, at about ten o'clock, what he was waiting for appeared: there, in the far distance, was Adrienne riding the pony, and the lad from Gyurkuca was leading the way.

He left the rock and met them on the saddle of the ridge. After a brief greeting, Adrienne dismounted and Balint led the boy and the pony to the shepherds' hut at the bottom of the meadow and told him to wait there until they came to fetch him in the morning. Then he came back to Adrienne and at once they started upwards on the mountain path which wound its way ever higher, round a dense stand of pines which covered the upper slopes, through labyrinths of huge rocks and scattered junipers, until they arrived at the summit of the Ursoia.

As they mounted ever higher so the landscape widened until they could see ridge after ridge of tree-covered hilltops. The bald slopes on the Albak side had long disappeared from view on the other side of the ridge and, from where they now stood, nothing could be seen but seemingly endless forest. Deep shadows marked the valleys between the peaks and everywhere else it was as if the mountains were covered by a dense coat of dark green fur. There was little to be seen except the centuries-old primeval forest, the sharp tips of the treetops pushing ever upwards, jostling each other in their efforts to reach the sky. Upwards, always upwards. The steep slopes might have been etched with blue-green arrowheads so regular, so uniform that they were as unreal as a geometrical drawing or an embroidery pattern. In contrast, just below them, a green meadow could be seen beyond the sheep pens until it too was bounded by the dark of the forests.

This meadow was a bright angry green on which the sun shone so brightly that silvery reflections danced over the virgin blades of grass, for here the shepherds had cleared the meadow, burning away any small trees, juniper bushes or shrubs leaving only the precious grazing for their animals. The meadow was like a carpet without a fault.

High above, where Balint and Adrienne had stopped, the ground was littered with stones and between them were dwarf pines, silky tassels of broom, and grey and lilac thistles in profusion.

It was hot, and as they went slowly onwards by the edge of a steep cliff Balint, carrying Adrienne's bag, went ahead to lead the way. Here the going was not easy for the path was often barely more than a foot wide and creased with the deep furrows made by the winter storms. Sometimes they displaced stones which rolled swiftly down the rocky slopes below, and sometimes they had to pick their way through steep twisted steps of granite. It took some time to reach the forest and, when they did so, entering the trees from the blinding light of the open mountaintop, it was like stepping suddenly into night. After the shimmering heat of the Ursoia's stony summit, the cool heart of the forest was a welcome relief.

Covered in perspiration they sank down on a bed of moss.

'Oh, how hot I feel!' said Adrienne. 'Wouldn't it be wonderful if we could bathe!'

'There's a rubber tub in my tent; but I've not much water.'

'That doesn't matter as long as it's icy cold.'

After a few moments Balint, hesitatingly and slowly, as though for some reason he felt impelled to hide the desire he felt rising within him, said, 'If ... if you don't mind the cold ... and it really would be icy ... there's something else we could do. There's a mountain pool not far from here, just fifteen or twenty minutes' walk, where one of our fast mountain streams is partially blocked. It has a sandy bottom.'

Adrienne opened her golden eyes wide.

'Here? In the forest ... in daylight ...?'

'There'll be no-one about.'

'No-one?'

'No-one! Just us ... alone in the forest.'

They gazed deeply into each other's eyes. Adrienne's full lips slowly curved back and she lifted her chin and spread out her fingers as if she were counting with them. Then, very softly, she uttered just one word – 'Good' – very slowly; and her warm deep voice prolonged the word with sensuous languor. The path they took was a mere deer track through the trees. Underfoot was deep moss as resilient as a sponge and their legs were brushed by the cranberry leaves that grew everywhere around them. They descended a steep slope beneath trees like giants, and here and there a ray of sunshine penetrated the thick foliage overhead, irradiating a tree trunk until it glowed like the embers of a fire, or struck vivid green or red reflections from the leaves of burdock and the shy flowers of the forest. Otherwise all around them was in deep black shadow.

The air grew markedly moist, for though they could not yet glimpse the stream they were now very close and the sound of rushing water grew ever louder.

And then there it was before them.

They emerged out of the thick trees onto the bank of a sizeable basin of water, almost circular, with steep banks dipping down to it that were so regular that they might have been carved by the hand of man himself.

Here the cranberries tumbled in tropical profusion; and here and there could be glimpsed bluebells, buttercups and pale green ethereal ferns. In the middle of the basin some rocks rose above the surface of the water, heavy black rocks, glistening with the water that flowed around and over their smooth polished surface. Around them were little flecks of foam left by the swift-flowing stream.

The basin had been formed by a natural obstruction in the stream's path and into this little pool the water cascaded over some other rocks some two and a half metres above its surface. Unusually the water fell not vertically but diagonally, hitting the side of other rocks that projected from the mountainside until it divided into countless little rivulets all casting upwards a spray as fine as powder.

The patches of foam glinted snow-white in the sun, but almost everything else was in deep shadow. The steamy vapour was steel-grey, the pond black as the rocks and, on the bank opposite, the sand was so covered in thick moss that it too seemed as black as the dense vault of the foliage of the maples overhead, which, with the faint blue tinge of the pines that surrounded them, closed off the sky like the roof of a tent.

'Stay where you are!' commanded Adrienne as she started to climb down.

Balint stretched himself out on the top of the bank some way above the surface of the water, and fell at once into a profound daydream, in which it seemed that around him was neither forest nor rocks, no rushing stream, no space and no distance. Everything was two-dimensional, with narrow rays of sunlight like ephemeral shafts of transparent gold-dust that glimmered faintly here and there, the only light in a world of shadow where thin clouds of greyish vapour floated weightless like a veil designed to disguise and soften the almost theatrical regularity of some lilac-coloured columns which were, in reality, the tree trunks around him. Everything seemed unreal and insubstantial.

Now, at the base of this magic picture, there appeared concentric rings moving ever outwards on the smoked-glass surface of the water and, in their centre, the vapour clouds swirled around the naked ivory-white limbs of the woman who was making her way to the centre of the pool, shoulders thrown back and alternately swinging her stretched-out arms behind her. Her hair seemed even darker than the surrounding rocks, or the moss and lichen and tree trunks, and it too seemed to float like a cloud above her pale body. Where she walked the shallow pool grew gradually deeper so that, as she approached the waterfall, the foam which had at first just gathered only around her ankles, started to cling first to her thighs and then, as she was descending ever deeper into the water, mounting higher and higher over her body, to swirl in mounting confusion as if crazed by desire for what it touched and by what it was parted and embraced.

She stood there like a vision of some figure of legend, of a wood nymph bathing herself in the wild deserted forest, perhaps even of the goddess of all forests, Artemis herself. She stretched her arms far above the black crown of her hair and, very slowly, started to turn towards him, the lacy foam sometimes reaching even to her chin as the rushing water swirled round the nipples of her breasts and concealing, but not entirely, the dark triangle of her womanhood. It was as if she were standing in a translucent case of shimmering glass.

One of the sun's rays fell just where she stood, and where the jet of water splashed fiercely over her shoulders it put up a spray that might have been composed of innumerable tiny diamonds. At that moment a small almost circular rainbow appeared in the air above her head and, as Balint watched entranced, it seemed to be being held high above her head in her own upstretched arms.

The way to Balint's tent was along a wide but abandoned forest road that wound its way through thickets of young trees. For most of the way they walked hand in hand, only separating for a moment from time to time where the young saplings had invaded the path and blocked their way or when they had to climb over a fallen tree.

They walked without speaking, instinctively feeling that it would have been a sacrilege to break the primeval silence which remained with them until they reached the tent. And even there, in the peace of their refuge, they barely said a word.

They ate a simple meal in the open space in front of the tent, sitting on the edge of the little meadow that lay between the trees and the edge of the cliffs from which the view seemed so immense.

It was like being high above the open sea; for the horizon, now itself only a vague outline in the haze of the afternoon's heat, seemed unattainably far away. Then for a long time they lay there in each other's arms, gazing at the sky above.

Huge tumbling clouds sailed lazily above them, sometimes seeming hardly to move at all.

Around them nothing moved, not even the air.

At the same time Margit and Pityu were also having their midday meal some miles away. The child had been fed earlier and was asleep in his pram not far from where they sat under the lodge's wooden portico.

Pityu was nervous and worried because Margit had been even cooler than usual towards him all morning. At first he had thought that she had been angry only because he had offered to accompany her sister, forgetting everything that he was supposed to do about the house. Accordingly he tried to make amends by taking his axe, going to the woods and felling three young beech trees, carrying them back to the house and cutting them up into firewood. It had been heavy work that had made him sweat and blistered his hands; and he had hoped that, seeing this, Margit would have uttered some consolatory words of appreciation. She had done nothing of the sort. Instead she had looked icily at what he was doing and then, announcing that she had some letters to write, disappeared into the house and only emerged at midday. It had been a bad omen and Pityu knew instinctively that there was going to be trouble.

He was not mistaken. Trouble indeed there was. When he had been chopping the wood with such zeal Margit had gone into the barn and found the hidden brandy flask. She said nothing until they had finished their meal. Then she spoke her mind.

'You have broken your word to me. You promised you would not drink anything here; it was the only condition I made when you asked if you could come. This was vile of you and particularly base to me. Not only did you break your promise, but you also sneaked the brandy up here yourself. I would have been angry enough if you'd gone down to the village and got drunk there. Maybe I'd have forgiven you if you'd done it openly ... but, oh no! You tried to trick me in my own house. It was vile of you, and so you can pack up and be off ... this instant!'

Pityu tried his best to interrupt her, to no avail; and when she had finished he still tried to justify himself, to excuse himself and to make promises never to do it again. Young Margit remained unmoved and inflexible, and after Pityu had tried to stammer out his regret she interrupted him and called to Gligor the forester:

'This gentleman is going down to Albak. Saddle one of the ponies and put his bags on it!' And without another word she turned and went back into the house.

And so Pityu had to leave: he could do nothing else. At least she had not humiliated him by entrusting her letters to Gligor, and it was some consolation, indeed the only consolation, that when he was about to go she handed them to him, explaining which was to her father, which to her husband and which to the estate manager at Varjas, saying as she did so that she could rely on him to put them safely in the post at Torda and that they would thus arrive all the sooner. It wasn't much, but it was something!

So down the mountain road he plodded with a heavy heart, that rocky, steep path that only eight days before he had mounted in such happiness. Now he stumbled and tripped and was miserable, for clambering about in the mountains was not something he enjoyed at the best of times, and on this day it was worse than ever. Somehow he had never mastered walking with a heavy iron stick and now, with his hands raw from all that axe-work, the more he grasped it the more it felt as if he were picking burning coals from the fire. He had not minded the blisters when he thought he was being useful to her by cutting the wood, but now it was different. He had been turned out of Paradise, however modest it had been, and now every painful step took him further and further into the wilderness.

A strip of light appeared under the canvas door of the tent. It was dawn. Balint woke first and then Adrienne. One of them murmured, 'It's the dawn,' and then the other repeated, 'the dawn', and together, as if by a mutual impulse, they started to get up.

The pale light called them outside and there the air was cold, with the steely cold of the high mountains that stimulated and invigorated like a draft of cool champagne. They stood together, arms entwined, breathing in deeply.

Just above the far horizon a narrow strip of yellow light outlined long lilac-coloured clouds. The sky was violet and hanging in it was the sickle moon. As they watched the sky lightened to mauve and then to grey, and from grey to palest green, except high above them where it seemed to have no colour at all. The outlines of the mountains were etched strongly against the light sky but seemed paper-thin, those closest to them, those which were covered by the pine forest, jagged like the teeth of a saw, but the furthest away rounded, as if cut from metal discs. These were the great curves of the Magura of Gyalu, or the pyramids of the Triple

Mountains and the flattened summit of the Dobrin. But no matter how different these ranges were in reality they now all seemed the same, ridge after ridge of them, as harmonious as the rhythms of a great symphony, cutting into the sky like giant knife blades projecting from earth.

Nearby, in the slight dawn breeze, the ink-black branches of young pines moved slightly to and fro; but everything was still in shadow, showing no sign of colour except in the sky, shadows, darker or paler, but still shadows as in a faded drawing in pen and wash.

The light increased, not steadily but seemingly in rhythmic steps that could almost be counted. A siskin started calling from a thicket of dwarf pines. Then from far away another responded, to be followed by the morning song of the blackbirds. A tiny titmouse was to be seen flitting from branch to branch, and then another, and another …

Silently watching, Balint and Adrienne stood at the edge of the cliffs waiting for the sun to rise. It was like being in a new world of which they were the first inhabitants, watching for the first dawn of Creation.

The long horizon blazed into red and gold, and long shafts of sunlight rose from the hilltops, racing across the sky until vapoury shreds of cloud, hitherto unseen, shone blood-red. Higher still other clouds appeared, in long strips like celestial ribbons, the highest and nearest edged with silver and those furthest away glowing orange, saffron and an incandescent green. It was as if behind the horizon some giant furnace was being stoked into flame and was pouring out streams of liquid metal.

Now the light seemed to rush upon them for, as if touched by a magic wand, the shadowy outlines of the mountains took on the colours of day, light blue in the far distance and nearer at hand a rich spectrum of different greens. A rosy enamel illumined the bluffs of rock, but still there were no shadows, only nature's own colours, and it seemed to the watchers that the whole world was waiting with a throbbing heart for the eternal mystery of sunrise.

Then the veil of clouds was shattered, torn apart and annihilated, and in its place the sun rose, triumphant, so bright that it could not be looked at. As they turned away the couple saw that at long last the growing sunlight cast its shadows on the earth, shadows that lay prostrate on the ground, at the foot of cliffs, trees and shrubs, as if in homage and gratitude for the renewal of life.

Homage and gratitude were what Balint and Adrienne felt too as they stood, arms enlaced, at the edge of the cliffs. Almost as soon as the first ray of sun had touched the crown of the trees above them, they felt its warmth first on their heads, then downwards across their bodies to their feet until it was also there on the meadow grass and the wild flowers and in the branches of the dwarf pines that surrounded them.

The birds now came to life, swarms of them, crested hoopoes on the tree branches, blackbirds pecking on the floor of the meadow, and woodpeckers running up and down the tree trunks. Below them a king-fisher darted from the depths of the valley and settled in a tree nearby. Somewhere a squirrel started its morning chatter.

For a long time they stood there, still motionless, alone as if they had been Adam and Eve, the first couple on earth, surrounded by the joyful chorus of the birds' morning song.

Entranced they stood there, gazing into the radiance that surrounded them and engulfed their world with transcendental beauty, a beauty so strong and intoxicating that they felt that at any moment it would, like a magnet, draw them ever upwards, soaring into the infinite.

Adrienne took a step forwards and in ecstasy spread her arms out towards the rising sun …

# PART FOUR

# Chapter One

Shortly afterwards a meeting was held at the local headquarters of the Denestornya branch of the National Agricultural Association. The association's affairs were discussed first, and afterwards, as was the custom, the local officials of the Co-operative held their own meeting. They did so because both organizations' committees were made up of much the same people – the Protestant pastor, the chemist and ten or more local farmers. The meetings were held every other Sunday, after church. Arpad Pelikan was there in his dual capacity as manager of the Agricultural Association's storehouse and also as treasurer of the Co-operative. Two others were there, Abady's secretary Miklos Ganyi, who always attended if he was not away on some business of his employer; and young Aron Kozma, who represented the head offices in Budapest of both organizations. It was his responsibility to oversee all business transactions.

Kozma had been Abady's confidential adviser for some years and his right-hand man ever since Balint had started to interest himself in the formation of rural Co-operative societies in Transylvania. He was the perfect foil to Balint, for his practical knowledge and common sense complemented Abady's enthusiasm, which was all too apt to lead him into impractical adventures. As a result Balint had learned to entrust complete control to him, and so, whenever he turned up at Denestornya, the Co-operative meeting was hastily convened so that Kozma could be present when important decisions had to be made. On such occasions it was better that Balint should be absent because his impetuosity had already led him into some unfortunate scrapes.

One of these had recently occurred at Denestornya itself. An eighty-acre farm had come up for sale in the district and Balint had insisted on it being bought by the Co-operative to be split up and resold to the people of the village. There was nothing wrong with the idea and it would probably have worked well if the farmland had gone to those who could pay for it. This had been the intention of the local committee, but Balint, through the goodness of his own heart and blind trust in the goodness of everyone else's, had supported the claims of the poorest of those offering to buy the land. The result had been that some of the poorest farmers, though getting their little parcels of land and at once occupying them, either did not repay the purchase price at all or did so only in part. Had Balint not offered to pay for them, the Co-operative's committee would have been in trouble.

Similar things had happened elsewhere: there had been a foolhardy purchase of a harvesting machine at Haromszek and an ill-considered construction of a building for the Co-operative in a village in the district of Gsik. These too had proved expensive adventures destructive of the idea of self-help and co-operation which was the basis of the whole educational movement.

When the meetings were over Kozma shook hands with the other committee members and started to walk back to the castle with Ganyi.

For the first part of their way they were accompanied by old Gergely Szakacs, Roza Abady's pensioned-off head groom whose house lay in that direction, and by Pelikan, who walked with them out of courtesy to the visitor from Budapest. They went on foot because Countess Abady did not like to have her horses put to on a Sunday unless it was necessary. The weather was beautiful, although it was already mid-November, a real Indian summer, and so no-one minded walking despite the distance; and indeed it was quite a walk for the Agricultural Association's headquarters lay at the far end of the village which consisted of a single very long strung-out street. Most of the houses were lined up on the left of the millstream and, on the right, the land rose steeply to the hills. It was a good mile from the meeting place to the church beside the old manor house where Abady was waiting for them. This old mansion, though quite close to the castle itself, had been where Balint's grandfather, Count Peter, had lived. After the old man had died Countess Roza had allowed her rascally agent, the lawyer Azbej, to take up residence there, but when he had left some years before, Balint, whose work for the Co-operatives had vastly increased, had given over three rooms in the house for the movement's archives and secretariat.

As the four men walked down the long street they met many of the village folk out walking. The village girls, arm-in-arm, all dressed in their Sunday finery, separated to make way for them and then joined up again as soon as they had passed, whispering to each other and giggling as country wenches always do.

All the young men were out too, strutting proudly together and occasionally tossing joking remarks in the girls' direction but not joining them, for that would come later in the afternoon when the dancing started. They lifted their caps respectfully to Kozma and his companions, as did the older men who stood chatting in front of the village hall. Kozma and the others, though deep in conversation, greeted everyone with equal courtesy.

They were discussing the meeting they had just attended and especially the bungled distribution of the recently purchased farmland.

Aron Kozma could not disguise how annoyed he had been, and how dismayed, when he had discovered how stupidly Abady had blundered by getting involved at all. It had been foolhardy, he said, and worse, it had done harm.

Countess Roza's old groom echoed Kozma's words. 'I said right at the beginning what a nonsense it was, but the young master is not one to listen to anyone else's words, however sensible. He just bangs on and storms his way into trouble, that one does! He's not cautious enough. It was a big mistake, a very big mistake in my opinion!'

For a little while Aron and old Gergely discussed what they both thought of Balint's credulity and of how he was so easily carried away by his own enthusiasm. Miklos Ganyi listened nervously until finally he felt impelled to interrupt. Then he spoke up most respectfully but still with determination.

'You gentlemen must excuse me, but ... in my opinion we should look at it differently. There are aspects which should not be forgotten. I don't think we should judge it quite as you gentlemen have been doing. Of course I admit that this business of the farm got out of hand; and also that Count Balint doesn't know enough about human nature. Perhaps it's just as well he doesn't. It may be for the better that he does let his sympathies run away with him from time to time. Yes, that has its good side too.'

'In what way?' enquired Kozma.

'Just think of it,' said Ganyi, his bony face suffused with enthusiasm. 'If Count Balint didn't always try to help everyone, where would our Co-operative be? It's only his enthusiasm and drive that gets so many people to work for him.'

He turned his thin brown face to Aron. His thick glasses glinted in the sun.

'Take me, for instance,' he went on. 'I was an assistant notary in Kis-Kukullo. I had six years' seniority and it wouldn't have been long before I'd have been a fully fledged notary myself, if I'd stayed on. But Count Balint came to us one day and told us of his hopes and the great goal for which he was working … and I left my job, my excellent little job, which would always somehow have given me a modest little income, and went to work for him. It wasn't so much what he said, for he's no great talker, but it was the faith behind it; you can almost feel the faith in him! And it's been the same for others too, lots of them.'

'He's right, you know,' said Arpad Pelikan, a short stocky man with a direct look. 'Indeed he is. I had a successful little store here; but when the count wanted a manager for the Co-operative warehouse, I sold my shop and accepted the job. I would never have done it if I hadn't known that someone like Count Balint was behind it all. But I'm glad I did.'

'You're both right, of course. It's most interesting,' said Kozma, and he burst out laughing. 'I never thought about it like that before. Anyway, who am I to argue the point? Wasn't it the same for me? The devil take me if I'd have worked for nothing if Count Balint hadn't talked me into it.' He paused, and then he added, smiling, 'And now, God help us, he's got hold of my young brother as well.'

Still talking of Balint they went on their way through the village.

As they walked they kicked up little scuffs of pale sand-coloured dust which rose like tiny pennant-like wisps at their heels until it was scattered by the wind.

When the morning service had ended and Kosma and Ganyi had set off from the church to attend their meeting at the other end of the village, Balint passed through the cemetery to the little door that led to the manor house. Every time he went that way, which was at least once a day, he thought about the old man and even fancied that Count Peter was there, waiting for him either among his beloved rosebushes or else, further up, standing between the Doric columns of the portico. He could see him even now, with his fine features, neatly trimmed pointed moustaches and silver hair, a sweet smile on his face and wisdom in his eyes.

The place had been run down while the lawyer Azbej lived there, but as soon as he moved out Balint had taken the neglected garden in hand and planted new roses – standards along the path and climbers to cover the front of the house – so that now the place was nearly the same as he remembered it; not quite, for he could not give the roses the same loving care as had his grandfather. Balint had also had the outside of the house restored as it had been in Count Peter's day, so that the white walls and columns, divested of Azbej's lurid repainting, were now just as they had been. Inside it was different for, when the old man had died, all his furniture had been removed and stored at the castle for now, with one exception, it was not needed as the main rooms of the house were only used as estate offices and for the headquarters of the Co-operative. Only Count Peter's writing room had regained its old aspect with all his furniture replaced as it had been. The walls were lined with book-cases made of cherrywood, of middle height and decorated with finely wrought columns topped by Egyptian-looking heads of gilt and green-ish bronze with, at their base, gilded eagles' claws clutching golden balls.

In this room everything was once again as it had been except for the pictures – the watercolours by Barabas and the portrait of Balint's great-grandmother by Isabey. Balint had taken them to his own room in the angle-tower in the castle and there they had remained, for Count Peter's workroom was now used only as Balint's personal estate office.

The old desk stood in its original place in front of the windows but Balint only used it when studying reports or signing papers, for though its smooth leather top, black and polished and surrounded by a deli-cately wrought safety rail, was an invitation to work, the drawers below had been found to be locked when the old gentleman had died and no-one knew how to open them. The keys to the side drawers were, it was supposed, in the centre drawer, but though the key to this was in its place and was the right key – for it bore a tag in Count Peter's writing – and although it turned quite easily, the drawer still did not open. Balint was sure that somewhere there was a secret catch, but he had never been able to find it. After many attempts he had finally given up the struggle and indeed had been happy to do so for he felt instinctively that this drawer probably held some special memories, some long-dead secrets better left undisturbed. In any case he did not need those drawers, for near the door there stood a modern rolltop work table with its drawers of files, and this Balint used for his daily correspondence.

It was at his grandfather's old desk that Balint sat when Aron and

Ganyi had gone to the meeting. His letters and a pile of newspapers had been put there for him and he at once took that day's paper and turned to the news from abroad. He had been doing this every morning for the past six weeks – ever since the Balkan war had started. Every day the news was increasingly unexpected and confusing, and Balint read it all with growing anxiety. He was only too aware that the official policy of the Ballplatz was to maintain the *status quo*, but also that, on the contrary, the Heir himself planned to increase the direct rule of the Habsburgs and to extend it by enslaving the southern Slavs. The twists and turns revealed in the papers therefore baffled and confused him. That Russia wanted war was certain, for her power and influence were everywhere to be seen. But Vienna – what was her part in all this? Was Austria tacitly following her lead? Balint grew increasingly sure that somewhere, somehow, some fatal error was being compounded.

Austria-Hungary's Foreign Minister, whose authority and power could easily have put an end to the fighting, turned instead to subtle diplomacy and induced the other great powers, in apparent but deceptive harmony, merely to give a little rap on the knuckles to the heads of the warring Balkan states by letting them know that, whatever the result of the fighting, Vienna would never consent to any diminution in Turkish authority. This mild and ineffective warning was not issued until October 8th, 1912, by which time it should have been obvious to all that it would have no effect.

The only concession the great powers would allow, it seemed, was that Turkey must be induced to grant essential reforms in her administration of Macedonia. The news of this important climbdown also came too late: it arrived in Cetinje only on the afternoon of the day on which Nikita had already declared war on Turkey and sent his troops to invade her borders.

Balint could not conceive how all this muddle had been possible. It was not to be believed that Vienna had not known in advance what was being plotted in Montenegro. Even if the Ballplatz's own intelligence service had failed to pass on the news, they could easily have been informed by merely reading *The Times*, for the great London newspaper had published, as early as the end of August, the full text of the Balkan Pact. To imagine that, when Turkey had been defeated, anyone would be able to induce the victorious armies to retreat behind the ancient boundaries was an absurdity hard to credit. There must, therefore, be some other explanation, and it could only be that the central European powers took a Turkish victory for certain and that Vienna was looking forward to the defeat of the Balkan states. At any rate it was clear that this was the view of the Prussian Marshal von der Goltz who had himself, a few years before, planned the reorganization of the Turkish armies.

The Sublime Porte thanked the great powers for their interest and promises of support, but clearly did not have much faith in them; while the Balkan states paid no heed at all. Then the war started and the Turks were chased from the field.

Barely ten days had passed before the Bulgarian army had reached Adrianople and the Serbs, skirting the borders of Montenegro, had arrived at Uskub and entered Albania. They laid siege to Scutari and were now nearing the Adriatic at Durazzo. The Greeks were at Salonika. The race was on and it was no longer a question of where the Turks would take up a stand but rather which Turkish stronghold would fall first.

It was at this point that at last the Dual Monarchy seemed to wake up to what was happening. Though indifferent to the fate of Macedonia and Rumelia, that of Albania was a very different matter. A Balkan Albania was not at all what Vienna could contemplate or permit, for it would be an intolerable invasion of Austria's own interests if Serbian power was allowed so to extend itself. Strong protests issued from the Ballplatz and also, though in a lesser degree, from Italy who was alarmed at the prospect of Serbian control of the eastern shores of the Adriatic.

The newspapers reported these disconcerting developments with excited glee and, as Franz-Josef was at that moment in Budapest, his Foreign Minister Berchtold hurried there to be with him, as did the Heir, Franz-Ferdinand, and Schemua, the head of the Austrian general staff. The latter left on the following day for Berlin, and three days later Conrad left for Bucharest with a personal letter, written in his own hand, from Franz-Josef to King Carol. At the same moment a semi-official statement appeared which announced that Austria-Hungary, should it be necessary, would use force to ensure the independence of Albania. More was to follow.

A large portion of the Austro-Hungarian army was put on the alert and a million men were sent to the Russian border on the pretext of a trial mobilization.

Today there was even more disturbing news. At Mitrovica and

Prizren in Serbia the Austro-Hungarian consulates had been invaded by the mob, Austrian flags torn down and the premises looted.

Balint sat at his desk staring moodily before him. The news of the previous few days had been alarming enough, but this was far worse, for an attack on any power's consulates, if it had been as reported, inevitably meant war, for no power, unless bent on *hara-kiri*, would let such a provocation pass.

He gazed out of the window with eyes hooded by anxiety.

Outside all was bathed in brilliant sunshine. The lawn which sloped down in front of the house was still as green as in summer but the leaves on the trees were already turning brown or reddish bronze. In front of the window a leaf, saffron-yellow with sharply serrated edges, floated in the slight breeze like the trembling flight of a giant butterfly.

It had come from the maple which grew at the corner of the house and for a while continued to float there, hesitating, balancing in the air, brightly lit by the autumn sun, until finally it fell to the ground to join, with an almost imperceptible rustle, its already fallen sisters. And, as it fell, another took its place before the window, held for a moment in the air until it too fell to the ground. Balint fancied for a moment that these dying leaves were conscious of their beauty as they prepared themselves for the death they knew would follow.

The garden was so peaceful that it was hard to believe that anywhere in the world there could exist hatred or war or destruction. It was as if such beauty must exist everywhere and as if peace must be universal.

Watching this Balint felt his heart constrict.

It was not only anxiety for his beloved country and for the fate of its simple people; something else worried him deeply. What was to become of his mother if war did break out?

Lately Countess Roza had been having sudden attacks of dizziness. She had done her best to prevent anyone knowing, but Balint had divined her secret and was sure that something of the sort must have occurred the previous night, for in the morning she had sent him a message saying that she would not be going to church with him but intended to spend the morning in bed and to get up only at lunchtime. There had to have been a serious reason for this, for Roza Abady, when at Denestornya, laid great store on being seen in her pew every Sunday morning. Balint had questioned her maid but the girl had not seemed to know anything and, though he had tried to see his mother himself, she had merely sent word that she wanted to sleep until midday and did not want to be disturbed.

Now all his thoughts were concentrated on what would become of her if there was a general mobilization and he had to go to war. If that happened he would certainly be away for several months, with no news of her and in a constant state of worry.

He was so agitated that he got up and walked about the room for a while before sitting down and taking up the newspapers again. He could find only one item that seemed even slightly reassuring. Sir Edward Grey had offered to mediate in the dispute and try to find a formula for restoring peace. That England was prepared to take this line seemed, at least, hopeful.

Then he turned to the home pages, but found nothing reassuring there.

Since Parliament had reassembled in mid-September, the loose coalition of the parties in opposition had changed its tactics. While most of its members had absented themselves from the summer debates, now they reappeared in force, for in their private meetings held in early autumn it had been all too clear that their policy of boycotting Parliament had passed almost unnoticed in the country. Something else would have to be tried. They were now again present in force, making provocative declarations which they read out with a lot of noise, scandalizing the more conservative members with noisy interruptions, blowing whistles and toy trumpets before again retiring *en masse.* Their well-publicized attitude was that all the sessions held since June 4th had been illegal and therefore invalid, and so there was nothing scandalous about their repeated clashes with whoever presided at the debates and with the parliamentary guards. On one occasion a large band entered the Chamber so tightly clasped together that they were able to occupy the floor of the House without the guards being able to reach those who should have been excluded. They stood there, between the ministers' seats and the stenographers' desks, from noon until the evening; and this heroic opposition lasted until eight p.m. when they decided to leave.

Later they tried something else. The guards had become more adept at keeping out those who were proscribed by the exclusion decrees, so the opposition cliques started to search for new ways round them. Someone found out that the kitchen staff could move freely in and out of the Parliament restaurant where no guards were posted. The plan was soon made: into the building by the kitchen entrance and up in the kitchen lift, which carried the paprika chicken and the veal fricassee to the restaurant floor close to the Chamber itself! What a surprise for everybody! There they'd be, and there they'd stay until in due course they were hustled out again, as they undoubtedly would be; but what did that matter when the great Tisza, to his shame and annoyance, would for once have been outwitted? The plan was put into action at once ... and failed. They were seen sneaking in, it seems, or perhaps one unwisely talkative Member let out the secret which reached the officials in time. Whatever the reason, they were stopped before getting to their places, and the escapade was the talk of the day just when the Serb army was standing before Durazzo and the spectre of a world war was stalking the Danube basin and the foothills of the Carpathians.

At this same time other absurdities were being perpetrated in the Hungarian capital, and the newspapers lost no time in passing on the news to their readers.

The opposition leaders – Kossuth, Justh and Andrassy – seemed suddenly to become aware that all was not as it should be in the Balkans and felt they owed it to the people to make public their point of view. The opposition had to have a voice, they said; to make a stand, let their views be known. And in this they were, of course, right to recognize that they had gained nothing from their passivity and their refusal to attend debates. The general public had failed to appreciate the great moral lesson of their abstention and had not even realized that in this great dispute the opposition itself was really the injured party! It was, of course, the same realization that had brought them back into Parliament, which had prompted the renewed rash of obstructionist tactics, and led Zoltan Desy openly to attack Lukacs claiming that the Minister-President was the 'world's biggest Panamist', though few people knew what he meant by the epithet except that it was rude. This had all been good clean fun and, they said, completely justifiable, even heroic ... until now, when the Balkan crisis seemed to deserve something more.

The opposition had to have a voice, they said; to take a stand, make a speech! Some cogent expression of opinion was necessary, something to show how original they were and how different from the government in power, how statesman-like, how much more intelligent and understanding!

It would not be enough merely to take part once more in the

parliamentary debates on foreign affairs, and in any case if once they gave Tisza an opportunity to allow their members to speak it would be tantamount to recognizing his authority, to accepting his appointment as Speaker and his right to interpret the Rules of the House in his own way, all of which they had until now steadfastly refused to do. Why, someone might even interpret such a move as accepting the legality of Tisza's position, and that was unthinkable.

Instead they searched around to find another solution which, to them at least, appeared very droll and witty.

The opposition therefore proclaimed that 'Parliament' – their own self-styled Parliament, not the one that met in the official House – was the only true parliament and would hold its sessions in the ballroom of the Hotel Royal. There, they declared, the real Parliament would meet, complete with Speaker and Legal Authorities seated on a dais high above the members, a President, two Vice-Presidents and other necessary Officers of State.

The first member to speak was Albert Apponyi. In a speech redolent of sweet reason, he outlined recent political events in the capital and declared that all those gathered together that day in the hotel ballroom were the country's true representatives and that in their name, and that of the Hungarian nation, he saluted the heroic struggle of the Serbs, Greeks and Bulgarians. He talked about the right of all nations to determine their own affairs, and of the right to independence, and he therefore proposed that Hungary should make a noble gesture to those enslaved peoples and stretch out the 'hand of friendship' to Belgrade. This was the tenor of the motion he urged the delegates to accept.

Other speakers followed him. Among them Lovaszy and Lajos Hollo went even further. Both had for some time been outspoken critics of Austria-Hungary's foreign policy. Now they came out as outright partisans of Serbia, stating that Viennese pretensions to the status of a world power were ridiculous and based on nothing but foolish vanity. It was nothing to Hungary, they said, how affairs in the Balkans were settled; and nothing but folly to intervene in any way: it would be mere meddling in other people's affairs. It was here that it was stated for the first time, although still in somewhat veiled terms, that the alliance with Germany was a harmful one and served only Germany's interests. The general feeling that surged through all the speeches, and which was expressed in vague terms of brotherly sympathy for oppressed nations, was that the Hungarians were loved throughout the Balkans while the Austrians were universally loathed. Apponyi's motion was accepted unanimously, and everyone thought that by doing so they had made a 'heroic' protest against the pretensions of Vienna.

Balint put down his paper with a gesture of contempt, deeply shocked by everything that he had read. This pseudo-Parliament was crazy, he thought, and it was nothing short of sheer folly to act so lightly when at any moment Hungary might be involved in a war and the nation forced to fight for its very existence.

It was unbelievable, Balint reflected, that those so-called political leaders, Apponyi, Kossuth and Andrassy, could have been so irresponsible as to permit such a declaration without realizing what an effect it was bound to have abroad. It was tantamount to an invitation to Russia to attack their beloved country, and it would encourage all the petty Balkan states to underrate the power of the Dual Monarchy and to scorn its warnings and authority. And in Paris and St Petersburg it would look as if the Austro-Hungarian empire was on the point of disintegration with a revolution in Hungary as the first step. How was it possible that none of them had paused to think of such consequences?

Balint got up again, went over to the window and opened it. He stood there for a long time without moving and allowing the cool air to circulate around him and calm him down.

Outside the dew still lay on that part of the grass that the sun could not reach, and there, too, the unmelted hoarfrost lay like milky glass. Elsewhere the lawn was dotted with fallen leaves, coppery-red from the plane trees and butterfly-yellow from the maple. The leaves were still falling, very slowly and floating in the air like a light mist of golden smoke in front of the open window ... But Balint saw nothing of this. He merely stood there, staring sightlessly before him.

He came to himself only when the door opened and Aron Kozma and Ganyi entered the room. They gave him their report of the Co-operative meeting and told him that the bookkeeping was in order and that they had found no faults in the society's management. Then Kozma outlined the present state of the problems attendant on the distribution of the newly acquired farmland, and said he was glad to report that the former muddles had been satisfactorily cleared up. Owing to the diligence of the more reliable members, the late-payers had been obliged to settle their debts and so the society was now in a position to repay the few thousand crowns that Abady had advanced. Kozma explained all this in great detail because he was anxious to make Balint understand how much trouble he had caused by his well-meaning but thoughtless intervention.

Balint nodded and seemed to be listening. Now and then he said something to show appreciation of what had been done, but though he was as polite and considerate as ever, his mind was not in it. All the time that Kozma was speaking Balint was still seeking to understand what lay behind that pseudo-parliamentarian debate that had so angered him.

Soon he believed that he had discovered what had led people who should have known better to act in that ridiculous way. It was nothing more than the almost universal belief of Hungarian politicians that their voices could only be heard inside their own country. Their whole conception of politics was based on this, and nobody for a moment believed that their actions and words were watched or heard by anyone abroad, not even Apponyi whose brother-in-law was ambassador in London and who presumably wrote home from time to time, nor Andrassy, whose father was close to Franz-Josef's intimate circle and who had for a while been a diplomat himself. In the heat of domestic passions it had never occurred to them to think of such matters as anything but the skirmishes of party politics which no-one outside Hungary could for a moment understand or even be interested in. To these men the horizon extended no further than Vienna and outside this circle, this little Hungarian globe, there was nothing! The motion passed in the Hotel Royal's ballroom was not in reality meant even for the Balkan states, but only for the government in Budapest, or at best, for the monarch so that he might see how discontented its authors were.

The general public, which for centuries had had no interest in world affairs and had never even grasped the importance of the Balkan conflict, now showed no more interest in the opposition's motion, and in any case would never have believed that any reaction outside the country could have any more relevance than if it happened on the moon.

While these matters were passing through Balint's mind, he had been nodding approval of everything Kozma told him but in fact paying less and less attention to what was actually said. So now, when Kozma suggested that when they made their next tour together Balint should not only refrain from accepting any personal financial responsibility but should promise him never in any circumstances to do such a thing again, because such an action was the very negation of the idea of self-help and co-operation, Balint, who had heard only the last few words, at once replied, 'Of course I'll promise … of course, you're quite right!' and Kozma grinned at the secretary in triumph as if saying, 'You see how easily he can be convinced! He has even given his promise!'

It was now getting close to lunchtime. They got up and were about to walk up to the castle when Balint realized that he had not even glanced at his mail. Accordingly he asked Kozma to go on to entertain his mother while he and the secretary went through the letters together. He would join them in a few minutes.

The first few letters dealt only with Co-operative business and so, after briefly scanning their contents, he handed them to Ganyi saying how they should be answered. The next letter was in a grey envelope and was from Honey Andras Zutor.

It concerned the notary Gaszton Simo and recounted how the young forester Kula had come to find him in the woods and had recounted that while he, Kula, had been at the market at Hunyad, the Romanian *popa* Timbus had gone to Pejkoja and threatened Kula's grandfather, old Juon aluj Maftye. Angrily he had asked the old man why he had gone so far as to denounce Simo for malpractice and how it was that he had dared to appoint a Kolozsvar lawyer to represent him. The old man had been badly scared and had told the priest that he had understood nothing of what was happening, that it was all in the hands of his grandson and that, as he was very infirm and could not read or write, he had merely signed whatever had been put before him. Old Juon had apparently said that he was guilty of nothing and that there was nothing of which he could be accused. The priest had then taken out some paper and tried to induce the old man to put his mark on it, but the grandfather, despite the priest's menaces, had resisted and had not signed. Kula now wrote that he feared the old man would not be able to hold out for long because he felt death approaching and Timbus had threatened him with eternal damnation. The young man did not know what was in the paper the priest wanted signed but thought it probably countermanded the lawyer's appointment, though of course it might have been something else, perhaps some appreciative statement about Gaszton Simo. The old man had not been told.

'… *and this is why I am writing to your lordship*' ended Honey's letter, which as usual was clear enough even if lacking in punctuation, *'because some big trouble may come of it Kula is frightened and sure that Timbus and Simo will certainly shake the old man and he said I saw Simo yesterday he is not an easy man to deal with and he may have been going to say something else but I looked hard at him and perhaps he thought I was going to hit him but it is certain that now he is in a good mood though only three weeks ago he talked about being fed up and wanting to move away but now he doesn't say this anymore but quite different things ...'*

Balint's face clouded. When he had left the mountains in August he had looked for a lawyer who spoke Romanian and who could not only plead old Juon's case at the tax office but who could also speak with the country people when the inspectors came to make their inquiries on the spot. It had not been easy to find the right man because everyone knew that Simo and the head County Sheriff were close friends and that therefore everyone in the Sheriff's office would move heaven and earth to protect their colleague. He had had to find someone who had no ties, either of family or friendship, with anyone in the Sheriff's office.

Finally one such had been found and the denunciation of Simo officially deposited with the authorities. As yet there had been no hearing and though an inquiry was bound to be held sooner or later, it was obviously in Simo's interest to do everything he could to postpone matters until he had had time to make the plaintiff withdraw. If he could achieve this then he would win the case.

It was not, however, only a case of clearing Simo's good name. If he were to be exonerated then it would be Simo himself who would have his hands on the steering wheel. He could then file a complaint for malicious prosecution and the honest young Kula would find himself hounded and persecuted in his turn.

Balint grew ever more depressed at this terrible thought, for it would be a heavy responsibility if the young man should get into trouble because of his confidence in Balint. Looking up from Honey's letter Balint looked at Miklos Ganyi, sitting beside him at the desk. Through his thick black-rimmed spectacles Balint fancied he could see a look of compassion and an eagerness to be of help. It was as if Ganyi already knew what was worrying his employer, and it occurred to Balint that as the secretary had spent six years in a country notary's office he would be sure to know exactly how such inquiries were carried out and so perhaps would have a useful idea of what the consequences might be.

Turning to Ganyi he gave him a brief account of the affair and also told him that the accused was doing all he could to persuade the plaintiff to withdraw.

Ganyi listened attentively, his long bony face tilted sideways as was his habit when listening to something important.

'I have heard about this case,' he said, when Abady had finished. 'I had it from Winkler, the forest supervisor, when he was last here. Simo will certainly be dismissed if the case is proved. This is automatic in cases of tax fraud. However, if they can persuade the old man to declare that his grandson never explained what he was being induced to sign, and especially if he were to say that the receipt he produced had nothing to do with the tax demand but was for something quite different, there could then be some very serious results.'

Ganyi paused, and then went on: 'Since the old man cannot read or write then no retribution would fall on him; but the grandson could be made to seem responsible and could be accused of slander and of falsifying legal documents. For these crimes he might well be convicted ... and ... and perhaps not only him. Simo is quite capable of spreading his net further and indicting Andras Zutor as an instigator of the crime, and ...' – here Ganyi again hesitated before plucking up courage to say what was in his mind – '... and perhaps even your lordship.'

'Really? Me too? Why?'

'Because it was your lordship who recruited the lawyer and instructed him to proceed. Of course your lordship's actions can easily be explained and defended for it would be clear that, no matter how the situation turns out, your lordship acted in good faith and for the general good. It is unlikely that Simo would go as far as that, but your lordship would certainly be subpoenaed as a witness and Simo would do all he could to drum up support in the press by posing as a martyr. You can be sure that the more trouble he can stir up the happier he'll be!'

'It would be ironic if Simo tried to act the sacrificial lamb! But what can we do? Go up and see old Juon?'

Ganyi's mouth opened until a glint of white teeth could be seen. Then, very slowly and with marked emphasis, he said, 'That I would not recommend. The old man is an essential witness and the accused would be sure to assert that a visit from your lordship constituted an attempt to persuade the plaintiff to bear false witness. Such an assertion would only complicate matters. There is only one thing to do: explain to the grandson that it would be fatal to him personally if his grandfather were to withdraw. A watch must be kept on him, and this can easily be done, up there in the forests, without attracting anyone's attention.'

Balint stood up. He thought for a few moments, then put out his hand to Ganyi. 'Thank you for such excellent advice. I'll write to Zutor today.'

'Your lordship should put nothing on paper. It'd be better not to write, for one never knows into what hands a letter may fall. Send for him and do it verbally; that would be better, far better!'

They went out, the secretary politely escorting his employer as far as the veranda steps. Then with a modest smile that pulled apart the line of his little black moustache, Ganyi added, 'Perhaps your lordship would like to entrust this matter to me? With your permission I could explain everything to Zutor personally. I have had some experience in similar cases, and it might be better than if your lordship ... it would give me great pleasure.'

When Balint questioned his mother, Countess Abady merely said that she had been sleeping badly which was why she had decided to stay in bed that morning. She seemed in very good spirits and talked animatedly to Aron Kosma. She had put on the silk dress she kept for special occasions, perhaps because it was Sunday or perhaps it was because young Kosma was there, for his father had been a childhood playmate of hers, though she had not seen him for more than forty years. On this day she was at her most vivacious and, though her manner always held something of condescension in it, it was with all her old charm that she talked of horses and their breeding and of the hunts of long ago. Balint felt reassured.

After lunch he sent a telegram to Winkler at the forestry headquarters on the Beles, telling him to send Zutor to Denestornya. Then, leaving Ganyi behind, he and Kozma got into his car and were driven away. That Zutor would find only his secretary there he did not mention. It was better that way.

As Balint got into his car Countess Roza came out on the balcony and continued to wave goodbye until the motor glided out of sight through the massive gateway in the castle's outer court.

Later Balint often thought of this moment and always in later years this was how he remembered her best, a diminutive figure standing very straight behind the carved stone balustrade, waving goodbye with her chubby little hand ...

# Chapter Two

The tour of the Co-operative centres in the south-eastern counties that Balint took with Aron Kozma lasted ten days. Their last stop was at Kis-Kukullo in a small village called Kis-Fuzes a mile or two from Dicso-Szentmarton.

All through the meeting, during the reading of reports and the checking of the books – and even more so during the voting which then followed – Balint and Kozma both noticed that everyone seemed to be in a great hurry to bring the meeting to a close. They whispered among themselves and glanced repeatedly at the clock on the wall. When asked the question that everywhere else had loosed a flood of suggestions and endless discussion – 'Are there any complaints or special requests?' – everyone at once had said, 'No, nothing! ... Everything's fine! ... Nothing at all! ... No, nothing!' and looked eagerly towards the door.

Neither Abady nor Kozma could make out what could be going on. They were both sure that there was no dark secret about the bookkeeping that had to be kept from them, so they assumed that the village people were merely anxious to go somewhere else and were afraid that any prolongation of the Co-operative meeting might mean their missing the fun.

The general air of gloom and dismay that had seemed to mark the meeting vanished immediately when, about midday, Balint brought the discussion to an end and headed for his car. Then it was as if a heavy load had been lifted from everyone's shoulders and, wreathed in smiles and merrily shaking hands with the visitors, they escorted Balint and Kozma to their motor, happily closed the car doors upon them and waved goodbye with such enthusiasm it was as if they were calling out with one voice, 'Now it's time to go! Go! Go now!'

In the Kukullo valley the villages were so close together that it seemed that each one started where the last left off. The next on their route was Gyalfalva where the manor house belonged to Pityu Kendy. They reached it after a drive that took only a few minutes despite the fact that the road was crowded with pedestrians, many of them young men, girls and children and all of them from Kis-Fuzes, who were hurrying along as merrily as if they were on their way to a country market or a travelling circus.

The village street of Gyalfalva was no less crowded and everyone smiled and waved at the car's passengers, assuming, no doubt, that they were all bound for the same festive destination. Held up by this happy crowd Balint's car crept along until it was nearly opposite the entrance to Pityu's house. Here, in the curve of the wooden palisade that flanked the gates to the Kendy manor, the crowd was so thick that they were forced to a halt. The chauffeur sounded his horn and the crowd at once gave way, but not along the road, only towards the Kendy gates. The driver started to explain that they were on their way to Dicso only to be faced by Pityu Kendy himself, dressed in a leather jacket and fur cap, who ran to the car, and shook hands with Balint and Kozma, crying, 'You can't shame me by passing my door and not coming in!' and went on to explain what was happening.

What he said was far from clear. Today, he declared, was a great day, an important day, which was why he had invited so many people. In fact he had invited everyone he knew, including Balint and Kozma. Hadn't they had his letter, he asked, and then answered himself saying that of course they had not been at home, but that he had written. Balint enquired what it was all about, and Pityu explained that it had all been in the letter. He had, he said eagerly, condemned Brandy to death and today was the great day when the Court would pronounce sentence; now, in a quarter of an hour, the Court would be in session. They were only waiting for Balint's arrival, and that was why he had been at the gates, because he had heard they were in the district and was on the lookout for them.

Brandy? Court? Pronounce sentence? Balint and Kozma were still as much in the dark as if Pityu had never launched into his breathless attempt at explanation. All the same it was now clearly impossible to continue on their way without stopping, all the more so because at that moment some of the other guests came crowding out of the gates, among them the two young Laczoks and Zoltan Alvinczy, who at once launched into further explanation telling all over again how Pityu had sentenced Brandy to death, while from the steps of the portico inside old Uncle Ambrus bellowed out, 'Stop fooling around out there and drive that spittoon of yours in!'

Balint was in no mood for any sort of party, for his tour of the village Co-operatives had been exceptionally exhausting, involving as it had daily discussions lasting from morning till night. By the time he had got to bed in the evening he had still not had time to read the daily papers, and with the continuing Balkan crisis to worry him – for though it had recently calmed down somewhat, it was still menacing enough – all he wanted to do now was to get home. The idea of this jolly celebration appalled him: but it would have been churlish just to drive on and, besides, Balint had no desire to cause offence. And so, with his companions, Balint got out of the car and walked up to the house.

The large dining room in the centre of the house was packed with guests. There were the three Kendys, old Daniel, Uncle Ambrus and Joska; Farkas Alvinczy, Kamuthy, and several neighbours including Todorka Racz, all drinking cronies of Pityu's.

Everyone was in a happy party mood, which had been reinforced by copious draughts of wine and brandy. The dining table was littered with empty and half-empty glasses.

Everyone, too, knew what this feast was about, for Pityu had taken care to explain the joke in detail and in his letters of invitations he had slipped a paper listing the crimes for which Brandy was to be arraigned and sentenced. Pityu clearly thought it was all a huge joke, of which he was proud to be the instigator, and now, in typical Transylvanian fashion, all his guests were drinking and laughing and teasing each other and their host.

Soon the great moment arrived.

Pityu Kendy called out, 'Guards! Do your duty!'

The two young Laczoks, Dezso and Erno, stepped forward wearing ancient military shakos, which Pityu had found in some drawer, and hung around with rusted sabres and dilapidated sabretaches. Both men were short and stocky with markedly Tartar features. They were as alike as twins. Standing strictly at attention they made an impressive pair with their gold-fringed headgear, even though this was somewhat moth-eaten.

Then came the command, 'Bring the accused up before the house!'

The two Laczoks clattered away and the guests followed them out onto the long stone terrace in front of the house. There they settled down in a semi-circle, on chairs that the footman and maid brought out from the dining room. The chairs wobbled a little on the uneven paving stones, but the guests were in no state to notice. The sun was shining, the lovely pale sun of the beginning of winter, and everyone was eager for the fun to begin.

As the gentry settled themselves in their chairs, two gypsy bands took up their positions, one on each side, holding their instruments at the ready, and the village folk crowded together on the lawn in front of the house, all in festive clothes, young and old alike, the girls in their most elaborate finery. Among them a swarm of children tumbled about, sometimes running up close to the terrace and having to be dragged back before they reached the terrace steps for they were too young to know their place.

Balint saw that among the crowd were all the men who had seemed so eager to get away from the Co-operative meeting.

Everywhere there was an air of expectancy and excitement, especially down on the lawn for they all knew that later there was to be a barbecue in the farmyard, with quantities of wine and gypsy music.

Now the gentlemen gaolers brought up the accused. It was a large wooden five-litre wine jug and they were carrying it by two handles that looked like arms. The belly of the jug was painted with flowers of all colours and the dome-shaped lid represented a face with wide slanting eyes and a huge moustache made of some kind of fur.

The culprit was carried up with stiff formality, in a most soldier-like manner, and placed on a bench that a footman hastily slid under it.

The arrival was greeted with cheers and, strangely enough, squatting there on the bench between two guards, who stood erect with drawn swords, the accused had an air of knowing malice, seeming to challenge everyone present, guards, judges and spectators alike with a look of pride in his own wickedness.

The trial started, not in the usual way for Pityu himself was to be prosecutor, witness and judge and also, as everyone could see, executioner too, for strapped to his waist was his officer's revolver in its leather holster.

Pityu rose to his feet and, to a flourish from the gypsy bands, waved in the air the prosecution's crime sheet.

'You vile scoundrel!' cried Pityu, and after this unflattering start proceeded to enumerate the crimes of which Brandy was accused: that he made men unsteady on their feet, that he caused dreadful headache, that he made noses swollen and empurpled and, finally, made men drunk so swiftly that there was no joy in it.

After these generalities Pityu turned to more personal charges, himself appearing as chief witness.

'I shall now testify,' read out Pityu, 'how many crimes have been committed against myself, how many times you have muddled my brains while I have been at cards and made me stake my all on a single ace. Time and time again you have encouraged me in foolhardy bids so that I have lost money. More than that you have so fuddled my wits that I have insulted my friends to the point that I have had to fight duels with them, slashing away with sabres for no good reason. And each time I have begged to be left free of you and so commit no more idiocies. Right up to this very day you have kept up this evil course. This summer, when I was a guest in the high mountains, I was thrown out in shame because you had furtively crept back and insinuated yourself once again into my confidence. Well, that was the last drop, I mean your last drop, and you deserve the penalty of death! Does everyone agree?'

'Death! Death! Death to the horrid criminal!' cried the guests on the terrace; and from down below, amid guffaws of laughter, the crowd echoed, 'Death!'

'And so, you horrible scoundrel, you see your last hour has come. But, so that no-one can say you had no chance to defend yourself, I now invite you to offer your excuses. If you have anything to say, speak now!'

Pityu's manner of shouting at the accused was so stern and convincing that everyone was struck dumb and waited expectantly for the jug to reply. They listened in vain.

Then Pityu spoke again. 'Nothing to say? Alright. Then I will proceed to sentence. Brandy is hereby condemned to death by firing squad for the manifold crimes he has committed against honest Peter Kendy, who from henceforth will only drink wine!'

Great jubilation. Cheers, hand-clapping, hats thrown in the air and another flourish from the gypsy bands. Then above the hubbub came another shout from Pityu:

'To the scaffold with him!'

A procession formed up. First went the gypsy band from the village, immediately followed by Pityu's footman and valet pushing a small cart in which they had placed the condemned Brandy on a bed of straw. On each side walked the young Laczoks with drawn sabres and behind it, proudly erect, stalked Pityu, who in turn was followed by the chief guests, the gypsy band from the county town and the older generation of farmers. The boys and children ran forwards on both sides, eager to be first at the place of execution.

The procession rounded the house to the strains of a funeral march, and then wended its way up the sloping garden until it reached a giant oak tree standing close to the surrounding wall. This was the appointed place.

The music stopped and the jug was lifted up and placed against the tree trunk. The spectators formed a semi-circle with the two Laczoks at each end. Pityu stepped forward until he was about five paces away from the condemned. Then he took out his revolver, released the safety catch, and called out, 'Now I shall send your guilty soul to Hell!'

Uncle Ambrus, who, the older he got, liked less and less for anyone else to steal the limelight, tried to spoil the effect by muttering, 'What rubbish! How can a jug have a soul?'

Pityu laughed back, 'But it can … the spirit of cherries!' and fired straight at the wooden jug.

The force of the bullet made the jug wobble twice on its little wooden legs before falling forwards on its belly. From beneath it spread streams of red liquid which collected in little puddles between the massive roots of the old tree.

Everyone now crowded around Pityu, cheering and applauding him while the gypsy band struck up the well-known aria 'The intriguer is no more!' from the opera *Laszlo Hunyady*. Old Daniel Kendy, oblivious of everything else, shuffled up to the toppled wooden jug, crouched down slowly and painfully and dipped his fingers in the spreading crimson stream. Then he licked his fingers twice and, with the air of a great connoisseur, said quietly to himself:

'Kirsch! Kirsch! *Quel dommage* – what a pity! Such a noble kirsch!'

Accompanied by the town band, who were now playing a selection of joyful tunes, the guests walked slowly back to the house and crowded once more into the big dining room. The villagers were taken round to the farmyard by the estate overseer and his assistants and there they found meat roasting on spits and cauldrons bubbling away. The local gypsies struck up and soon all the younger people were dancing. Wine flowed from a barrel that had been tapped in the entrance to the barn and they could all knock back as much as they wanted.

In the dining room too there was a lavish collection of Rhenish and other fine wines, as well as an imposing array of locally produced wines, new and old, and all of them so potent that the executed Brandy would have hidden himself in shame. Soon the food was brought in, simple country food, filling but unsophisticated, cabbage with smoked pork, and sausages of many different varieties, for it was just after the first pig-killing of the winter. Everyone ate heartily and laughed and joked … and they all drank heavily.

In half an hour several of the guests were drunk, but none more so than the noble host himself who was by now quite cross-eyed.

Otherwise the tipsiest of the older men, as might have been expected, was old Daniel and, among the younger ones, a neighbouring land-owner, Vince Himleos, an extremely polite young man whose widowed mother had impressed upon him what an honour it was to be invited by Count Peter Kendy and had made him promise to mind his manners and to introduce himself to everyone present, especially to the older men.

With this motherly advice ringing in his ears, he was obsessed with the thought that maybe he was not doing this properly. The more he drank the more convinced he became that perhaps he had not been doing all that he should; indeed, he decided, after much agonizing, that more was needed, something that would save him from the awful fault of not knowing how to behave in noble company.

Accordingly he got up and staggered to the head of the table where Farkas Alvinczy and Kamuthy were sitting, clicked his heels and announced: 'I am Himleos!'

'*Servus* – how do you do?' they both responded politely, as did Uncle Ambrus, who was sitting next to them, for no-one in such company minded a man being drunk and not fully in control of himself.

Then poor Himleos, whose old Hungarian name meant 'pox-ridden', reached old Dani, clicked his heels again and said his name once more.

As the older man did not turn around and answer, probably because he had not heard him, young Vince introduced himself again, more loudly and then, seeing that he still got no response, touched old Daniel's shoulder and yelled in his ear, 'I am Himleos!' and put out his hand.

Old Dani still did not turn fully to face him but briefly looked him up and down and then peered into his proffered palm. Then, under Dani's red nose, a wicked smile spread across his face and, stuttering badly as he always did when drunk, he said very slowly, 'I hope you g-g-g-get well s-s-soon!' and, chuckling to himself, turned back to his glass.

Young Vince staggered at this insult as if he had been struck. Though mild and inoffensive by nature the one thing he would never have accepted, even when sober, was that someone should make fun of his ancient family name ... and now he was drunk. He stepped back and swung back his arm to strike out. Luckily Uncle Ambrus sprang up in time to grasp him in a powerful bear hug so that Himleos could do nothing more than scream out. 'Monstrous! I protest ... protest ... I protest!'

The gypsy musicians fell silent and many of the younger men, Pityu among them, ran forward, surrounded the irate Himleos and dragged him to the other end of the room where they all, especially the two young Laczoks who knew him well, did their best to hush him up and calm him by telling him about old Dani. Others busied themselves with Daniel Kendy himself, who now rose to his feet and, swaying as if caught in a gale, started to bow repeatedly in every direction and, in elegant French, stammer out:

'À v-v-votre d-d-disposition ... v-v-votre d-d-dis ...' but got no further for he was grasped by several strong arms and carried out into the garden, for it was well known what followed when Dani was in drink and started to bow to everyone present.

Abady took advantage of the general confusion to leave the room. With Kozma in tow he quickly found his chauffeur who was waiting for them just outside the main gates.

They drove swiftly through the village, which was now completely deserted because every man, woman and child was up at the Kendy manor house carousing and dancing to the gypsy music.

Balint left with a bitter taste in his mouth for it had been some time since he had attended drunken revels of that kind. At the mock trial and execution he had laughed with the others at the humour of it all, but now, as they drove through the darkening afternoon, he looked back with concern and bitterness at the waste of talent and energy that had been lavished on such a lark. Now, he thought, they would talk of nothing else unless it was equally trivial. It was as if none of those people could ever for a moment be serious, even when the country was threatened by something as potentially dangerous as the Balkan crisis. Not a word had been uttered about that, not a single word. And it had been the same all through Balint's tour, during which he had met all sorts of people, officials and men of all different stations and standing in towns, villages and country districts. And these were people who professed, in their own fashion, an interest in politics and world events ...

Kozma sat beside him, silent and apparently so wrapped in thought that Balint wondered if he was thinking the same.

On reaching Dicso-Szentmarton they drove straight to the hotel where they had intended to spend the night before visiting three more villages the next day; but Kozma had to continue the tour alone. At the hotel a telegram was waiting for Balint which the porter explained had come from Denestornya at midday.

Balint's heart constricted with anxiety as he opened it and all his fears were confirmed for Countess Roza had suffered a stroke that morning.

Balint returned at once to the car, hardly pausing to say goodbye to Aron.

'Denestornya!' he said. 'As fast as you can!' and the car sped off into the coal-black night.

Days passed without change. Winter set in and soon it was Christmas, the first Christmas in four years that Balint and his mother had spent at Denestornya and not at Abbazia.

Outwardly the festivities were conducted as they always had been.

Roza Abady sat in the centre of the great hall on the first floor of the castle facing the stairs. The dining table had been extended to its full length and on it had been placed a huge tree decorated with angels' hair, paper garlands, golden stars and a host of tiny candles. All around it were stacked high piles of winter clothes which Countess Roza and her two housekeepers had been knitting during the previous twelve months. These were for the children in the village and would not be distributed until after church on the following day. They were displayed now because Countess Abady somehow felt they were not really Christmas gifts unless they had first been placed around the symbolic tree.

Also on the table were a quantity of parcels all labelled with a name. These were her gifts for everyone of her household staff and their families, and consisted of shawls, dress materials, warm vests, coats and jackets without sleeves ... and a lot of children's boots.

As had been the custom throughout Countess Roza's time, each recipient came in from the staircase where they had been waiting, in a rigid order of precedence, the children accompanied by their parents. 'Enter the hall, bow to the gracious countess, receive your present, kiss her hand and then leave quickly so as to make room for those who are waiting!'

This immutable ceremony proceeded as it always had. The two housekeepers, Mrs Tothy and Mrs Baczo, stood on each side of their mistress, pushed forward the children when they had to, and handed up the appropriate presents. The butler stood by the door to see that the right people came in, and also that they went out again.

Only one thing was different – the role played by the countess herself. In previous years she had personally given out each present; now Balint did this instead, for the old lady's right side was paralysed.

This year, too, she no longer spoke a few friendly words to each of her dependants as they stood bowing before her. Now she just nodded to them, for she did not want them to hear the few almost unintelligible words that were all she could utter, and offered them her left hand to kiss for she could no longer raise her leaden right arm. Even so, she still sat upright with her back like a ramrod, propped up by cushions. Now she sat in the wheelchair in which she had been propelled from her own rooms, for it would have been too awkward to lift her into the throne-like armchair she had always used before. The wheelchair had been pushed forwards just in front of the tree so that she had the light behind her, casting shadows so that no-one should see her distorted face. To make quite sure of this she wore a lace bonnet that was tied with extra-wide ribbons. This helped to support her chin.

Countess Roza had ordered all these arrangements herself, explaining to her maid and to the housekeepers, in the babble of sound that only they had learned to understand, when they had dressed her for the feast. Even so her eyes sparkled angrily for a moment when she fancied they had not fully understood what she wanted, for to her it was of the utmost importance that nobody should be shocked by her appearance nor for a moment feel sorry for her; no-one, not even her own faithful servants. While she was still living she must remain what she had always been, a great lady with her head held high, a sovereign queen in her own right, wrapped in indomitable pride like a robe of purple and ermine.

And so, outwardly at least, all was as it always had been on every Christmas Eve at Denestornya for the last forty years. But the myriad candles in the great chandeliers and in the sconces, and all those tiny flames that covered the tree and which were reflected in cascades of polished crystal, sparkled in vain. The Shadow of Death lurked in the immense hall and everyone who stepped inside that resplendent room could feel his presence. Perhaps he was lurking in the gilded display cabinets or in the deep window embrasures, or even in the next room, in the darkness of the neighbouring drawing room which could just be glimpsed through the tall glazed doors. Wherever he was he was there, waiting; and at any moment he might step forward. Even now, or in a few moments, there would be a faint tinkle from the glass doors and he would be there before them ... Everyone felt it: while coming forward, bowing and kissing their mistress's hand, they would send covert frightened glances to the far end of the hall where the white doorway and the black squares of glass hid something frightening and unknown.

There were few of Countess Roza's retainers who did not feel a wave of relief as they regained the great stone stairway and could steal away.

## *Chapter Three*

In the new year, at the end of February, the affair which had led to the formal denunciation of Gaszton Simo by old Juon aluj Maftye, of Pejkoja in the mountains, took a new turn.

To recall what had led to this we should remember that in the spring of the previous year – 1912 – old Juon had received a tax demand which claimed the payment of some 286 crowns for arrears dating back to 1909. At this point he was not unduly worried. A year and a half before, he had received a similar reminder which had not been followed up since old Juon had at once complained to the local notary Gaszton Simo, to whom, when the demands had first come in, he had paid the tax money and from whom he had received a receipt. The notary had expressed himself outraged that the tax office should be in such a muddle and promised to go himself to the county offices in Banffy-Hunyad and see that the misunderstanding was cleared up. When no further demands had been delivered by the village policeman the old man assumed that Simo had been as good as his word. For eighteen months there was official silence until in that fateful spring of the previous year there had come a new demand for the same arrears, and in August this had been followed by an order for the seizure and sale of all Juon aluj Maftye's possessions.

At that time old Juon's affairs had been looked after by his grandson, Kula, who had at once taken the papers to Honey Andras Zutor, Abady's trusted chief forester, to ask his advice. In his turn Honey had reported the matter to Balint because he knew that for several years past his master, knowing how Simo had exploited the simple people in the mountain villages and extorted everything he could from them, had already once tried to have the notary removed from office. Now Balint had acted again. He had got young Kula to obtain from his grandfather a blank power of attorney, which had been delivered to Count Abady together with the notary's original receipt.

Balint had then found a lawyer in Kolozsvar who was willing to handle the matter, had the power of attorney vested in him, and arranged for Simo to be denounced for embezzlement and false pretences at the appropriate office of the Ministry of Finance. And so the matter took an official turn.

However, wheels grind slowly and the inquiry by the tax inspectors became more and more strung out. The ball was thrown from court to court – but each time only after another long delay. Five weeks would pass before a letter received any reply. Then the men in the Ministry wrote to the county tax office which passed the letter on to the Sheriff. The Sheriff eventually returned the papers to the tax office saying that it was their responsibility, not his. The tax authorities wrote once more to the provincial county office stating that this matter came under their jurisdiction, not that of the tax office, since there was nothing on Simo's receipt to say that it concerned anything to do with taxes. The finance office therefore disclaimed all responsibility in its turn, as in their opinion this was either a disciplinary matter for the county's administrators or else a case to be heard in the criminal courts. The papers were then sent once more to the County Sheriff to determine whose responsibility it all was. In the meantime Gaszton Simo offered himself for a disciplinary inspection, but cunningly sent this offer to the wrong office. He did not approach the Under-Sheriff as he should have, but instead approached the association of local notaries of which he himself was president.

The notaries' association refused Simo's request to be investigated saying that it had authority only in internal disciplinary matters, not in

245

anything that concerned members of the public. At the same time they held a special meeting and unanimously passed a vote of confidence in Simo's probity: thereby making it clear to Balint that Simo had somehow manipulated the whole cadre of county notaries into taking his side.

This had been the situation at the beginning of March. Until then, though nothing definite had transpired, it had seemed as if Damocles sword was suspended over Simo's head. But then matters took a very different turn.

Gaszton Simo himself filed a complaint for false accusation, denouncing in his turn old Juon's grandson, Kula, and accusing Honey Zutor not only of complicity but also of having instigated a plot against him.

For proof he offered a declaration from old Juon that his grandson had deceived him, that being unable to read or write he had had no idea that the paper on which Kula had forced him to put his mark had been a power of attorney, that he had only recently learned this and wished at once to disclaim any such intention, that the receipt from Simo that the boy had taken from him did not apply to anything to do with tax payments but only to an old debt that he had repaid and furthermore that he had never said anything against the notary Simo whom he held in the greatest esteem and respect. He ended by begging forgiveness, saying that his grandson had abused his trust, and that he was nothing but a simple helpless old man who had known nothing of what was happening.

It was a good document, well-written, clear and wonderfully precise. And not only precise but also very much to the point, for every accusation against the notary had been logically disposed of and refuted in advance. The declaration had been countersigned by two witnesses, Timbus, the parish priest of Gyurkuca, and one of the churchwardens. In a postscript the old man stated that he had dictated the declaration to the priest, and this too was countersigned by two witnesses, the same churchwarden and the village schoolteacher. Nothing could have been seen to be better nor more seemingly in order.

The news of Simo's counter-action reached Denestornya without delay in a letter from Kalman Nyiresy, the pensioned-off forestry director of the Abady estates, who wrote a fulsome and repetitious account of what had happened. It was clear from the letter what joy Nyiresy took in passing on the bad news, despite the terms of flattery and simulated homage in which it was phrased.

Nyiresy had never forgiven Balint for having enforced his retirement, even though he had been presented with a large house at Banffy-Hunyad with a garden that reached down to the river Koros, and a pension amounting to half his former salary. The reason was that for more than thirty years he had been able to lord it up in the mountains, doing no work but living well at his employer's expense. He still lived well at Banffy-Hunyad, giving parties and entertaining his friends as if he were a country gentleman. But this was nothing compared to his life up on the Beles where he had been overlord of sixteen thousand acres, where he could shoot what he liked, eat as much venison as he wished, fish for trout in and out of season, and use the meadows for his own grazing; for, until Balint himself took an interest, no-one had ever asked him to account for his stewardship.

In sombre mood Balint read Nyiresy's letter. He was disgusted by it, for he could almost see the outrageous old man with his white beard, sitting at his desk and pulling at a long pipe, smiling wickedly under his huge tobacco-stained moustaches as he contemplated with what displeasure his former master would read what he had to tell. He was certain that the news came direct from Simo, for the two had been friends for many years; and indeed it was more than probable that they had composed the letter together, chuckling with joy as they poured out more wine and champagne and drank toasts to the notary's certain triumph.

Throwing down the letter Balint tried hard to banish this disagreeable picture from his mind lest it should cloud his judgement.

The Juon aluj Maftye affair had now become serious. That Simo had embezzled the old man's money was certain, and would remain so; but that the young Kula, with this new evidence, would be found guilty seemed equally certain. What else could the County Court do? And Zutor too might well suffer.

Balint knew that he could never let this happen. He could never sit idly by, doing nothing, while simple people who had trusted him and acted on his orders found themselves in trouble because of him. That was unthinkable.

And yet, what could he do?

There was only one thing, and that was to insist upon appearing as witness for the defence. In this way he could tell the whole truth and shoulder any blame that might come his way. If he went into the witness box he could tell the world everything he knew about the criminal alliance between Simo and the *popa* Timbus, and how for years they had extorted everything they could from the mountain people. It was true that he could prove nothing, but what did that matter? He would also make it clear that the denunciation of Simo had been his idea, and that he had organized it from the start. Let them condemn him if they wished. It did not matter so long as Kula and Zutor went free, for they had only acted on his orders.

It was an ugly and indeed dangerous situation, even though, as a Member of Parliament, he was immune from prosecution in the county courts. In such circumstances he would be allowed to resign his seat – and of course would himself insist on his release. Then a few weeks later he would find himself in the place of the accused. In the meantime what a picnic the scandal-press would have, dragging his name in the mud, vilifying the lazy aristocrat who had dared to slander the clean-living notary who worked so hard in his humble country post! Weeks and months of insult and shame would be his lot until the case was finally heard and then, if the Minister of Justice declared a 'non-suit' in recognition of his years of unselfish public service, which was by no means certain, he might avoid a prison sentence though nothing would wipe away the stain on his name.

None of this was as important as the fact that he must stand up for those who were only involved because of him.

Only one consoling thought came to him at this bitter moment. He need no longer worry about his mother's feelings, for the stroke had mercifully so incapacitated her that they could keep from her all knowledge of what was happening to her only son. She would not have to know how their good name was being besmirched.

But what if matters went so far that he was sent to prison, what would happen then? Could they keep that from her too? And, with a shudder, the wish arose in him that his mother should never live to see that dreadful day.

Two weeks went by, two weeks full of dismal foreboding, during which everyone at Denestornya, the secretary Ganyi, Peter the butler, the two housekeepers, Mrs Tothy and Mrs Baczo, and the other servants, even the retired stable manager, Gergely Szakacs, went about their work with worried faces. Everyone knew that the Simo affair had taken a sinister turn, though no-one dared mention it.

Abady himself spoke of it only to Adrienne whom he used to visit from time to time in the evening at the Uzdy villa just outside Kolozsvar. Then, as they lay in each other's arms, he would talk over with her all the horrible possibilities of the forthcoming case. Adrienne had at once approved of everything he intended to do, saying that he really had no choice, even if it meant going to prison. They had talked over the case from every angle, but never found any other solution. Even so Balint returned from his visits to Adrienne with renewed hope for, despite the fact that everything seemed against him, Adrienne could never bring herself to believe that things would end badly. It was impossible, she said, impossible. It was a moral impossibility and so it just could not be! Faced with this intuitive certainty Balint somehow managed to keep up his own courage.

On the evening before the case was to be heard the principal actors were all in Banffy-Hunyad, even young Kula who was spending the night at the house of Honey Andras Zutor. Everyone would be taking the early train to Kolozsvar where the county courts were held.

Old Juon aluj Maftye did not come because the notary Simo, afraid that he might blurt out the truth under cross-examination, had arranged a medical certificate for him. The old man was glad to stay at home because he was worried about the paper that the priest had made him sign, and yet knew he would never dare to revoke it and state it had been forced out of him. The other accusers were there in force, Gaszton Simo and the *popa* Timbus, the witnesses to Juon aluj Maftye's disclaimer, and three others who had been brought in to bear witness to Kula's connection with Zutor. These last were spending two nights in a shed at Nyiresy's house so as to make sure they did not stray off somewhere else.

The priest Timbus and Gaszton Simo were dining merrily at Nyiresy's table along with Simo's chief protector, the Head Sheriff, the stationmaster and two lawyers, all important local notabilities and all good friends with Nyiresy and Simo. Beside them the *popa* was only small fry, but he was there as an essential witness at the following day's trial.

The wine was flowing and a gypsy band playing for all its worth. The dinner had been lavish, as Simo had contributed a roebuck and at least thirty trout that he said he had confiscated from poachers.

'Luckily I caught them just at the right moment!' he said, winking at the Head Sheriff who knew all his little tricks.

'What a rascal you are, Gaszton!' he laughed back, even though these were things they never normally spoke about for the Sheriff liked to preserve his dignity.

Nyiresy owned a vineyard near Ermellek and the strong wines they were drinking came from there. It had not taken long before tongues were loosened and now there was no longer any pretence of talking of the forthcoming trial with impartial earnestness. Now they talked loudly and arrogantly, spicing their talk with obscene jokes, and no-one bothered to disguise his malice or his hatred of Count Abady, for it was not only the host who bore a grudge against Balint but all the others too. One or two resented the meddlesome aristocrat and were jealous of him, but most of them were only influenced by a feeling of solidarity with Nyiresy whom they regarded as a good fellow who liked his cards and wine and entertained them all so generously.

There were those who resented Balint because he had taken the Abady forests in hand and put an end to their poaching his game, but the main cause of their dislike was that they looked upon him as a troublemaker. This epithet, in their eyes, meant anyone who made the lazy work, who pressed them into service for the new Co-operatives, who was always having officious messages sent to them from the county offices or the prefect demanding speedy action, whose meddling sent them on tiresome and exhausting journeys connected with infringements of the forestry and game laws, and who was continually pressing for the Land Registry Office to keep its records accurate and up to date. In a word, he 'made trouble' – and now there was this unnecessary affair of the notary Simo which had entailed endless paperwork. Scribble. Scribble. Scribble.

It was this last which had enraged the chief judge, who liked to think himself sovereign in such matters. So what happens, he demanded? Along comes this young count putting his nose in affairs which do not concern him and who does not even live here but in the county of Torda-Aranyos miles away.

This judge was known as a hard man who liked his own way and before whom the whole county trembled. If he approved of someone, they flourished; but woe betide the man who crossed him. And now there had appeared this meddlesome aristocrat who had somehow stumbled in from an adjoining county and who dared denounce one of his own trusted notaries. Further he had seen fit to denounce him in the capital, thereby bypassing the judge's sacred authority. It was intolerable.

The host sat in the place of honour with his long-stemmed meerschaum pipe resting on the tablecloth in front of him. He was wreathed in smiles, delighted at the way everything seemed to be going. He did not say much but sat smiling under his huge tobacco-stained white moustaches. When he did speak thick clouds of smoke coiled upwards from his mouth as from the craters of Etna; but with him the poisonous gases were replaced by words of venom.

On his right sat the chief judge, who was a broad-faced, thickset man with a clipped moustache and greying hair cut to a short bristle. A vertical wrinkle separated his eyebrows, which everyone knew was the mark of a stern man. He too spoke seldom, but when he did, first slowly removing the leathery stump of a chewed cigar from his mouth, everyone else fell silent out of respect for his undoubted authority. His grey eyes were like ice, and when he smiled and showed a glint of white teeth, it seemed to stem not from merriment but only an intention to bite.

Next to him was the stationmaster and, across the table, Simo's lawyer, Dr Todor Farkas, who was known in Banffy-Hunyad, though not to his face, as 'Dr That-is-to-say', as he used this phrase at every opportunity. Beside him was Simo and then another local lawyer, Balazs Toth. Finally there was the director of the Land Registry Office, then the Sheriff and the *popa* Gyula Timbus.

Of course they talked of nothing but the case and the news that Dr That-is-to-say had brought, namely that Abady himself had come forward as a witness for the defence. Simo's lawyer had heard the news that morning in Kolozsvar and now it was being eagerly mulled over. The news was so exciting, and so unexpected, that the gypsies played in vain. Nobody listened to a note.

Everyone had something to say, but Nyiresy summed up all their thoughts in one phrase: 'What the hell is that rotten bastard up to now?'

Only Simo found it disconcerting. He felt it would have been better if the case had been heard without Abady, who was a Member of Parliament, putting his oar in and interfering. What the devil did he want? It was extremely disquieting. Anything could happen. He had always been against involving Abady ... and now? It was a bad business, he thought, but he was careful not to show his anxiety but laughed broadly and roared out, 'Well, let him appear! We'll push him around a bit!'

'I expect he just wants to pour some whitewash on that rascally forester of his, Andras Zutor,' said Balazs Toth.

'It won't be easy ... that is to say ... Kula Lung was induced to bear false witness either by Zutor or by the count himself. Nothing else is possible. Anyhow no-one is going to believe that an ignorant mountain lad could hire a lawyer in Kolozsvar all on his own.' And Dr Farkas went on to declare that he for one had always been sure that Abady was behind the whole thing: '... that is to say ... there is no doubt that the count is the real culprit. I was only in favour of leaving him out of the accusation because he is a Member of Parliament and, if we were out to get him, we'd have to wait ages while we had him unseated; and not only that but, well, that is to say, our friend Gaszton always said he wanted the case heard quickly. But there is nothing to worry about, indeed it is all for the best ... that is to say ... tomorrow I'll get him in a high old muddle when I question him. Then either he'll have to deny everything, which will mean his friends Kula and Zutor will be found guilty, or else it'll be clear to all to see that he himself was behind it all, and then we'll indict him too.' Dr That-is-to-say spoke with smug malice.

Huge puffs of smoke came from beneath Nyiresy's great moustaches and he said, 'That's talking, that is! Send the Noble Lord to gaol, eh? We'll all drink to that!' And he laughed loudly as he raised his glass high and touched all the others within reach. The gypsies, though not understanding what it was all about, played a flourish.

General hubbub broke out and when it subsided a little the Head Sheriff turned to Simo and, speaking very slowly, asked, 'You're sure that Abady doesn't have anything concrete, some other paper, perhaps? It'd mean trouble if matters were to take another turn, you know.'

'Of course not; what could he have?' said Simo quickly.

Then the lawyer interrupted, saying, 'It is quite impossible that he should come up with something else, quite impossible ... that is to say ... supposing – just supposing, mind you, not conceding – that the count tried to bring in other facts, things that had nothing to do with this case, the judge would refuse to hear them. The law does not permit it. Our evidence is clear, and we have written statements to prove it. These are quite straightforward. They cover the whole case and cannot be gainsaid. I ought to know; after all I drafted them myself. Faced with our evidence there can be no argument. In court tomorrow there will only be one issue and that is the degree of responsibility of the accused. Nothing else!'

'Why is that?' asked the stationmaster, just for something to say.

'These are the facts. Juon Lung aluj Maftye has made a legally valid declaration that he was misled by his grandson and that our friend Gaszton Simo has always behaved most correctly towards him. Therefore the author of the false accusation is Juon's grandson Kula. Now, what we wish to prove is that this Kula did not himself think up the idea but was pushed into criminal behaviour by Andras Zutor. Kula Lung, as the first accused, will certainly be found guilty, and most probably Zutor as well ... that is to say ... for Zutor was cognizant of, and indeed behind, everything that Kula did. What sentence these two get, light or heavy, will depend on whether we can show the count to have inspired the whole malicious proceeding. If we can, then Zutor's guilt will be to some extent mitigated because he is the count's employee, as will Kula's to a lesser degree, and the court will not be slow to appreciate the moral pressure that someone like the count can apply if he wishes. There is one possible outcome, but only if we can get the count to admit his part in the matter. Personally I don't think we will, that is to say, Count Abady cannot be such a fool as to fall into that little trap. But the alternative is much more certain. Abady will, of course, try to show that Zutor is not to blame. That is where I come in, that is to say, I know for a fact that it was Abady who enlisted the defence lawyer and who gave him old Juon's power of attorney. But I won't bring that up at tomorrow's hearing: all I will do is force him to declare that he had no part in the matter. It will be enough for the moment ... that is to say ... Kula and Zutor will naturally be found guilty and our friend Gaszton will immediately be vindicated, which is the most important thing.'

'Well,' interrupted Nyiresy furiously, 'and what happens to that highborn brat? Does he walk away free then? Nothing more?'

Dr That-is-to-say leaned back in his chair and waved a finger in the air with pompous self-righteousness. 'Didn't I say that was where I came in? On the following day we will accuse Abady of perjury, and won't that be a lovely thing to see? Eh?'

The host erupted in cheers and Simo's little shoe-button eyes sparkled with glee.

Now the chief judge decided to intervene.

'I wouldn't go as far as that – not that I want to see him go free, oh no! – but there are political considerations. If the two accused are condemned that will be shame enough for our noble count. No-one will ever speak to him again in those mountain villages. He won't be able to stick his oar in anymore or worry about things which do not concern him. We'll be free of him and that'll be enough. I'd hold on to that perjury charge for a while. With that in our pockets we'll have got him where we want him … for years to come; and if he ever again starts up his little tricks we'll let him know what we've got on him.'

'You old rogue!' cried Nyiresy as he exploded with laughter and slapped his neighbour on the back. 'Treat him like that pack of notaries you've got, eh? First catch 'em out in some fault, and then keep it dangling over their heads!'

Between the judge's thin lips his teeth gleamed.

'Exactly. That has always been my method.'

'But you can't seriously want me to abandon my plan?' cried Dr Farkas, outraged. 'Fail to catch Abady for perjury when he's practically thrown himself into our clutches? Oh no! Nobody can wish that!'

He was at once backed up by the other lawyer, Balazs Toth, and so went on, 'Is that what you want? In my client's best interests I forego the pleasure of calling the count as a witness, even though I always knew what a God-given opportunity it would be to start criminal proceedings which would have made me famous … that is to say, how did Karoly Eotvos make his name? With the Eszlar case! And Polonyi and other famous lawyers? Always through some great criminal proceedings. I've denied myself this until now because professional ethics make the client's best interests paramount and I will always be faithful to that. I will stick to that and get this Kula found guilty, but once that's done, it's time to do myself some good. Why, even the petition to Parliament to have Abady unseated so he can stand trial for perjury like anyone else – why, that will be advertisement enough. The press will be full of it! Then the case itself. Every word will be printed in the papers. There'll be reporters, interviews, a magnificent speech for the prosecution which will be printed in full … and at last the verdict. To bring an MP, who is also an aristocrat, to trial, sentence and prison, to stand before the world as the champion of honour and jus …! I will never give that up, never! I'll see it through to the end … and the end will be magnificent!'

He was so worked up and shouted with so much enthusiasm and sublime ambition that everyone started to cheer and the judge called across the table, 'Alright, I don't mind! Put him in prison then. Put him in prison!'

# Chapter Four

Balint spent the evening in his own rooms in Kolozsvar. He had arrived in the late afternoon and as soon as he got out of his car the hall porter told him that some man unknown to him had already called twice, asking for Count Abady, and had left a card.

It was just a little piece of cardboard on which was written *Koriolan Timbus*.

'He said, your lordship, that it was very important and that he'd come again in the evening.'

Timbus? Surely it couldn't be the priest from Gyurkuca, for his name was Gyula. But if not, who could it be? Was it perhaps his son?

'What sort of a man was he? Young? Slim?'

'Yes, your lordship, very skinny and didn't look at all well.'

Then it must be the priest's son, that fanatic young agitator with his head filled with irredentist pro-Romanian ideals. He was a sickly youth whom Balint had only seen twice; once lying on a couch at his father's house with hatred in his eyes, and then again at the railway station at Balazsfalva when he had surreptitiously handed some paper to the Romanian lawyer Timisan. It seemed most unlikely, thought Balint, that he would voluntarily come to see him, but then who else could it be?

'Very well then,' said Balint. 'Send him up when he comes.'

It would not really matter if the young man took up some of his time, for Balint had no plans to go out that evening.

Later, in his study, Balint paced up and down going over and over what he would say in court the following morning and how he would say it. Firstly it was necessary to put his thoughts in order and make a list of the points he wanted to make, saying what had prompted him to arrange for the notary to be denounced and making it quite clear that in his own mind he was working only for the public good. As he worked out what he would say he realized more and more how thin, from the legal point of view, was his evidence. It was more than possible that the court would not even listen to him, but if he was heard then it was at least certain that Kula and Zutor would go free. And then he'd have to bear the blame himself. That no longer mattered. He had to go through with it and accept whatever came his way. He could accept anything, even shame, ignominy and the destruction of his good name, rather than allow two men to be punished whose only fault was trusting him and carrying out his orders. The way ahead was clear; there was no way out.

He was so deep in these dismal thoughts that for a moment, when Timbus was announced, he had forgotten that he was expecting a visitor.

The door opened and a very thin, narrow-chested young man came in. A few sparse tufts of beard grew on his emaciated face and his long black hair stood up untamed and rebellious. Two red spots glowed on his cheekbones.

He came forwards very slowly to where Abady was standing by his desk, and when he stood before him he bowed stiffly but ignored Balint's outstretched hand. Then he sat down in one of the chairs placed beside the desk.

Abady followed his example and then asked, 'What can I do for you?'

The young man cleared his throat twice, hesitated, and then in a rush of words like a sudden flood, he croaked out, 'I ... I ... came about tomorrow, about tomorrow's case ... about the trial of Kula ...'

'About the case?'

'Yes, the case. I've thought about it for a long time because what will happen all depends on me. Do you understand? On me, only on me!'

'I must confess I don't understand.'

'Yes. On me, only on me!'

Timbus's burning eyes were full of hatred, but they never left Balint's face and it was obvious that he was having a battle with himself and had to make up his mind about something before he could go on. Then suddenly it all came out in a torrent of words that seemingly tumbled over one another.

'Yes, on me, for I have the old man's disclaimer, written by that scoundrel Simo, and Simo's letter, the one he sent to my father. He wrote it to my father and my father tore it up and threw it away, but that was afterwards, after he came back from Pejkoja, from seeing Juon aluj Maftye. Then he threw it away, but I found it. I read it. I read them both and I wish I hadn't. Understand? And since then I can't sleep, because it is a dreadful thing. Do you understand? A dreadful evil thing.'

He stared at Abady with a look that might have been taken for menace. For a moment he paused and then he went on, 'Yes, a dreadful, evil thing. Do you understand me? My father on one side and on the other young Kula, a poor simple Romanian. And the truth? Either

I betray my own father … or I suppress the truth … and you are on the side of the truth and so I have to save you, even you, of all people!'

He looked aggressively again at Abady and then added, almost to himself, 'I thought about it all night long, until dawn, but I can't do anything else. So I came.'

He reached in his inside pocket, took out a folded wad of paper and threw it on the desk.

'Here it is!'

By now Timbus was very short of breath and after panting out the last words he leaned back in his chair, exhausted.

Balint had listened carefully to what the young man had to say. Now he was filled with pity for him, for the internal battle which still raged within him sounded in every word he uttered with such passion and effort that Balint barely noticed his rude manner and obvious hostility.

'Well then? Read it! Why don't you read it, that's what I brought it for?' he shouted and, leaning forwards, pushed the papers towards Balint with thin dry fingers as if they were garbage he was reluctant to touch.

Balint opened the packet.

Inside were two papers, one a long double sheet, the other a short private letter.

Both had been torn and screwed up and one of them was held together only by a centimetre or two that had remained untorn. At the top corner of the larger sheet were printed the name and professional address of Dr Todor Farkas and below were some handwritten words which started 'I, Juon Lung aluj Maftye, declare …' It was the draft text of the declaration said to have been dictated by the old man to the priest in Pejkoja and was written in precise legal terms.

The smaller sheet was in Gaszton Simo's writing, and read:

*… since you told me last week that old Juon has now been persuaded to do what we want I am sending you a draft which I have had drawn up and which you must make the old man sign. Take this up to him in Pejkoja. Take with you also pen and paper and two witnesses we can trust. Leave these two outside and go in to see the old man alone. There you must write it down as if he had dictated it to you. Then put this draft in your pocket and call in the witnesses so that they can see that it was indeed there that you have written the paper. Then*

*the old man must put his mark on it in their presence. You do not
have to explain what this is all about* [this sentence was underlined
twice]. *We must be quick about this. I've had that good-for-nothing
wretch of a grandson, Kula, called in for questioning about his army
service. He'll be retained at the recruiting office for two days so you
must hurry over to Pejkoja at dawn tomorrow and do exactly what
I've told you. You won't regret it, I assure you. When you get home be
sure to destroy the draft and this letter. I would have come myself and
not written but my lumbago has come on again and I can't get out of
bed. It doesn't matter much, but take care to burn these papers when
you get home ...*

As he read these words Balint was filled with joy and relief. Salvation
at the last moment, salvation from the mess he had got himself into.
More, it meant that Kula and Zutor would be freed of all blame. All the
worries of the past weeks fell away like a heavy weight taken from him.
He looked up at Timbus and, filled with gratitude, he held out his hand,
saying, 'I don't know how to thank you!'

The young man's reaction was the same as before: he just looked back
as if he had never seen Balint's proffered hand. Then, venomously, he
said, 'You needn't bother. I'll take no thanks from you, not from you!'

'And why not?' replied Balint smiling. 'The mere fact that you've done
this today shows that good intentions will come together somehow and
will always prove stronger than hatred ... even that hatred you so obviously feel for me.'

'That's just it! Try as I may I have to admit that for years you've tried
to help my people. I've seen it for a long time. But why do you do it?
What is behind it? What are you up to? It's all just some trick, I know.'

'Oh, come! You don't really believe that, do you?'

Timbus's face darkened. Speaking almost as if to himself, he said,
'N-no, but I wish I did!' Then he went on angrily, 'It is absurd, ridiculous.
For a Hungarian lord to help our people, why it's the very opposite of all
I've been taught to believe. It contradicts everything I've ever learned
and what I want to believe, everything I've worked for, everything I
believe to be true. It's absurd ... just absurd!'

'Not at all. Why, old Juon himself, Kula's grandfather, told me that
there was a time when all the mountain people had the greatest faith and
trust in *my* grandfather. You must have been told of this too. I myself

remember, though I was only a child then, how often so many of your people came to him with their problems asking for his advice or getting him to settle their disputes. He acted as a sort of judge for them, and they always had faith in his judgement.'

'That's just what the old people say: but they're stupid, credulous. They understand nothing and they've forgotten that they were nothing but serfs, slaves who were forced to work and flogged if they didn't. And who exploited them? You did, you powerful Hungarian lords!'

'They were never slaves! Alright, let's talk about the serfs. They themselves were all equal whether they were Romanian or Hungarian. They hung together, like everyone of the same station in life. It was the same all over Europe and no-one then thought of it in racial or nationalistic terms. And it's pure legend that any landowner would exploit his own serfs. It would have been dead against his own best interests. What a landowner wanted was to have contented people working for him. In times of war the lords would fight with other lords and then they destroyed each other's lands, and your opponents' serfs would suffer too. But not your own, never!'

Timbus tried to answer Balint's words in a flood of exasperated argument, going over the whole hotly debated question of the ancient Dacians and their descendants, the Romanians, who had occupied that land since the times of the Romans. He quoted Sinka, Anonymus, Hasdeu and Xenophon. In broken phrases which poured out in confusion, new ones starting before the last was finished, he tried to evoke all those multifarious tomes of ancient political theory which had been written to prove what he had so eagerly absorbed, namely that a Latin civilization had flourished in Transylvania long before the arrival of the conquering Hungarian hordes. He spoke with such passion that he was soon shouting at his host.

He was stopped by a fit of coughing, a dreadful racking cough which seemed to break him in two, as he crouched in his chair with a handkerchief pressed to his mouth. It was a dry gasping fit which seemed to tear his lungs apart. When, at long last, it abated and he was able to straighten up again, he leaned back in his chair in total exhaustion.

Balint would have liked to reply that, long before the Hungarians arrived in the ancient province of Dacia, Transylvania had repeatedly been overrun by Goths, Vandals, Gepids, Avars and other barbarian tribes and a full six hundred years had passed between the time when the Emperor Aurelian withdrew his legions and the arrival of the Hungarians. And during these six hundred years the history of Transylvania had only been that of a highway whose path was trodden by countless nomads who came that way and then passed on. He would have liked to add that there existed no records and no traces of any indigenous culture, but he stopped himself because when Timbus dropped his handkerchief in his lap Balint saw that it was stained with blood, not just a drop or so but large spreading stains. Blood! The poor man was coughing blood, and Balint was stopped in his tracks by pity for the unhappy young fanatic.

'This is all very ancient history,' he said in a soothing voice. 'These things happened over a thousand years ago, so what good does it do to argue about it now? The truth is that only two peoples who are not Slav or Germanic live in the Danube basin now and those are the Romanians and the Hungarians; and they would do well to learn to live with each other. It is in the interest of both nations and we should never forget that. Of course mistakes have been made and are still being made, but it is surely the duty of every man of good faith to work for reconciliation. It will never be easy, because crimes have been committed and there are many wrongs to be righted. But all this hatred, this hatred that has built up over the centuries, must somehow be washed away. It must be!'

In the heat of his own conviction Balint managed to find many arguments he felt to be convincing. It was the first time he had tried to express in an organized way what he had long felt.

He ended by saying, 'I am sure that the time will come when all these past wrongs are forgotten and your people and mine will no longer be kept apart by hatred and resentment, but will live side by side together like brothers.'

Timbus, who had been listening in silence, now jumped up and shouted, 'Never! Never that! Never! Never!' He stood there trembling, with burning eyes.

'Why not?' answered Balint gently. 'To me it is a historic necessity. Our two peoples – and I ignore the Slavs and Germans – have no other true relations in this part of Europe. We must come together and trust each other if we don't both want to find ourselves the slaves of our neighbours. It must happen if we are to survive.'

'Maybe it's so ... maybe!' muttered Timbus. 'Maybe ... some day ...' Then he raised his thin arms in the air, gesturing with those emaciated talons, his hands, and a high scream, full of hatred, broke from him, 'But first … first we'll pay you back tenfold … a hundredfold, and after that … No! Not even then … Never! Never!'

Reeling, he turned about, ran to the door, wrenched it open and disappeared slamming the door behind him.

Balint did not attend the court. After Simo's lawyer, Dr Todor Farkas, had thundered out his accusations against Kula and Zutor, Abady's lawyer got to his feet; but instead of addressing the court he merely went up to the presiding judge and, without comment, handed up Gaszton Simo's letter and the draft of old Juon's recantation. This brought the case to an end with shame to the accusers and complete vindication and acquittal for Kula and Zutor. When the judge read out his findings he addressed scathing words to Dr Farkas, reprimanding him for unforgivably unprofessional conduct in writing the draft at all, and then for his audacity in declaring to the court that it was dictated by old Juon with no help from anyone else. The intimidation of the old man was so obvious that little more had to be said. It was the end of Dr That-is-to-say's career. He managed somehow to avoid disciplinary action from the lawyers' association, but he never again appeared in any but unimportant and insignificant cases.

Simo was dismissed from his post at once. To save him from prison some influential relations somehow found the money to repay not only what he had embezzled from old Juon but also many other sums which came to light as soon as his dealings were investigated. He was then sent far away to Borod where he earned a meagre living as a humble scribe paid by the day. That was the end of his self-created little kingdom in the mountains.

An honest notary was now sent to Gyurkuca. He had been recommended by Balint, and his appointment was made so as to honour Count Abady and thus show the world that the past was now forgotten.

This was the work of the chief judge, who was a clever man.

# Chapter Five

From the day that Roza Abady had her stroke Balint hardly moved from Denestornya. If he had to go to Kolozsvar for an evening he would spend the night there but always returned early the following morning so as not to be too long away from his mother's bedside. The longest time he ever stayed away was the day and a half that he had to spend in town dealing with the affair of Gaszton Simo.

At this time he was completely preoccupied with his mother's illness.

Every day Countess Abady spent more and more time asleep. Even when she was awake she could rarely pay attention for more than half an hour to anything Balint came in to tell her. He would recount news of the horses, or the fallow deer, or, in early February, of the newly born lambs and litters of piglets – every day something different and always something cheerful and amusing, something funny or unexpected, a little joke at which his mother might smile and even occasionally give a little laugh. It always had to be good news or some minor success, but even so she tired fast, and then her attention faded and soon she would again close her eyes.

Balint went to see her just two or three times a day; at midday before luncheon, again in the afternoon when they would have tea together on the glazed-in upper veranda, and sometimes in the early evening when she had been lifted from her wheelchair and put to bed. A young doctor was kept in permanent attendance because had there been any emergency or change in her condition it would have taken too long to get the country physician to drive over from Gyeres. Since the beginning of January there were also two trained nurses, one for the day and the other to watch at night. The two housekeepers, Mrs Tothy and Mrs Baczo, hardly ever left their mistress's side, for only they could understand her occasional mumbled words. Besides, they knew her habits.

There was little for Balint to do. Indeed his mother seemed not always to notice when he came and went. She never sent for him or spoke about him and often it seemed that she would not notice if he had been absent for several days. All the same he did not dare go away as he was convinced that if he did something dreadful would happen, as when he had gone to the Szekler country in December. During these long months he cut himself off from the world. All the Co-operative business was done by letter, and the Simo affair, serious and ominous as it had been, was the only thing to have dragged his thoughts away from his mother's condition.

Everything seemed unreal and remote. He even read the daily papers with the same indifference, only glancing superficially at what was reported each day, which at any other time would have interested him deeply.

The political situation in Budapest grew ever more fraught and potentially dangerous. Party hatred exploded into personal feuds and even Tisza found himself obliged to fight several duels with political opponents who had insulted him. It was always they who were wounded and retired, for Tisza was a better swordsman than most and always emerged unscathed.

Laszlo Lukacs was attacked even more frequently than Tisza. Zoltan Desy in a speech at a public banquet again unloosed the epithet 'the world's greatest Panamist', which everyone now knew to mean 'scoundrel' or 'unscrupulous crook', at which Lukacs, as Minister-President, took him to court. Whereupon Desy told the world that Lukacs, when Minister of Finance in 1910, had renewed a bank's salt-shipping contract in return for a donation of several million crowns to Lukacs's party funds, that he, Desy, knew all the gruesome details, and that this payment had financed Lukacs's election campaign. In turn Lukacs replied that the renewal of the bank's contract had in no way added to its profits, that the contribution to party funds had been from simple goodwill and political conviction and that furthermore he, Lukacs, never had, nor ever would have, profited by a single penny.

The publicity did no-one any good, even though Lukacs's personal integrity had been confirmed when Desy lost the case.

But that was not the end of the affair.

The very day the verdict against Desy was proclaimed, Andrassy, Apponyi and Aladar Zichy endorsed everything Desy had said; and the scandal thus reached monumental proportions. Even the foreign press reported the matter in full, though no-one at home seemed to pause for a moment to consider how Hungary's reputation abroad was being damaged. All these patriotic politicians seemed to think of was getting even with their opponents who had forced Parliament to accept the army estimates. Party passions obscured everything else.

From then on no-one in the House would speak on any subject other than the salt-contract scandal. In vain did the government try to introduce a bill for wider suffrage. The waves of personal hatred and malice were so strong that no progress could be made. One day in March the opposition appeared in force in the Chamber, and Lovaszy, backed by some seventy or eighty supporters, shouted out 'Stop for a moment!' and in the brief silence that followed all those behind him started calling out 'Salt! Salt! Salt! Salt!' Of course Tisza suspended the session and ordered in the guards. These were at once rounded on by the rebellious members, who tried to wean the guards from their duty by explaining to them that their military oaths were not valid and did all they could to get them too to mutiny and disobey orders.

This was the first time that these so-called politicians, who made great play of their patriotic duty, tried to incite mutiny. It did not succeed.

Now they looked around for new allies and even went so far as to make common ground with the most left-wing of the Galilei Club, with whom they organized a big meeting in the Vigado. At this rally the public were regaled with the unusual sight of the otherwise reactionary Apponyi and Aladar Zichy sitting side by side with Jaszi and Kunfi who some years later were to play a leading part in the October Revolution and the Bolshevik regime which followed it. Everything was forgotten except party hatreds and opposition to the government.

At the same time as this was happening at home the situation abroad was growing ever more serious.

Diplomatic activity had never been so frenzied. In London a conference was convened to heal the wounds and lead to peace, but it was held in vain. Even though Turkey accepted most of the great powers' proposals, peace seemed as elusive as ever. The much-vaunted disinterestedness of the great powers was clearly shown for what it really was by their insistence on Turkey's ceding the Aegean Islands to their own jurisdiction – a concession that was immediately granted but which led only to the peace talks being abandoned. Adrianople remained under siege while Montenegro never paused for a moment in the shelling and encircling of Scutari, cynically disregarding the fact that the London Conference had just confirmed Albania's right of ownership.

What impertinence! said the great powers. This cannot be tolerated, they muttered indignantly: but six weeks went by until it was already the end of March before they managed to agree upon any practical action. A resolution was made summoning Nikita to explain himself. Nikita refused to appear. Then, at the beginning of April, the Allied fleets demonstrated before Antivari. Still Nikita refused either to budge or to restrain his army. Then an international blockade against tiny Montenegro was declared; but even this had no effect upon Nikita, who scornfully ignored it while his armies occupied Scutari.

And they stayed there, regardless of the menaces launched from the London Conference. Nikita must have had secret knowledge that Russia stood behind him despite her ambassador's public support for the sanctions agreed in London.

The Dual Monarchy now found herself forced to take the initiative. In London she declared that she could not tolerate the Montenegrin presence in Scutari and would therefore 'act independently'.

War, which had been coming nearer and nearer for two months, now stood before the door.

Balint read all this in the newspapers, but he was not as affected as he used to be; for his anxiety was personal and near at hand. There was, firstly, his mother's uncertain condition, and then, for a while, the impending trial. Though this faded with the collapse of the prosecution, it did not alleviate Balint's anxiety. Indeed it rather increased it for now Balint had something else to worry about.

Only this was real to him: this and the beauty of Denestornya in spring.

By the middle of March the snow had vanished but for a few patches on the northern sides of the nearby hills. For a while some lingering traces of white remained on the banks of the streams but, when these disappeared, on the riverbanks and beside the paths, young grass started to shoot up and, in meadows which had lain asleep all winter, violets bloomed in their thousands.

One afternoon in early May Balint returned from a visit to the mares who had been put out at grass in the meadows near the castle until the summer grazing paddocks were ready for them.

On the steps of the main entrance he found the old butler Peter waiting to tell him that Countess Roza had been repeatedly asking for her son.

'Where is she? She isn't feeling any worse, is she?' he asked.

'Not at all, my lord,' replied Peter. 'On the contrary she seems suddenly to be better. In fact her ladyship is expecting you on the veranda. She has already asked for her tea.'

Balint ran up the stairs, passed through the billiard room and there, on the glazed-in veranda, sat his mother in her wheelchair. At first he could not see her face, for she was sitting with her back to him, but as soon as he took his place on the sofa beside her he saw an unexpectedly joyful radiance in her eyes. When the old lady saw him sitting beside her she put out her left hand – the only one she could move – and took his in her own.

'Ah!' she said. 'Here you are! Here you are!' The words were not quite clear, indeed they sounded more like 'He-y-Ga!' though to Balint's ears they seemed clearer than for many months. Her still half-frozen face was irradiated with a happy smile.

'Where have you been? I've been waiting for you ... waiting for you so long ...' and her smile seemed to suggest that she had been awaiting him for years, since time immemorial.

Balint did not quite know what to make of this, for he had been with his mother two hours before, just after lunch. And not only that but for some weeks she had received him with such indifference that this sudden warmth made him wonder in surprise whether she had really recognized him at all. Whatever the reason for the change he was overjoyed and started to tell her about the mares grazing in the meadow and how the new grass was already growing lush and appetizing, with plenty of clover in it. Everything he told the old lady was happy and encouraging, and she would squeeze his hand and interrupt, saying, 'Oh, I am so happy, so happy!', while the repeated little pressures of her fingers seemed to pulsate to the rhythm of his words.

As he spoke the nurse Hedwig offered the old lady the special cup with a spout from which she could drink her coffee and buffalo milk. Roza Abady allowed the spout to be put in her mouth and then, when she had drunk her fill, her lips to be wiped with a white napkin. On this day she let this be done for her without protest, though on all other days she had let them know that she hated to be helped and would herself hold the cup to her mouth with her left hand. Now she was using her left hand to hold Balint's and did not let it go for an instant. As soon as possible she turned towards Balint and gazed hard at his face as if she could never see too much of him. Soon, however, she started to tire, and then it was clear what had rejoiced her heart.

Countess Roza closed her eyes and leaned her head back against the pillow. Then, just before dozing off, she murmured, 'Tamas! I am so happy ... so happy that you came back! Tamas, my Tamas!' And she spoke quite clearly without even the hint of a slur.

For a moment Balint did not fully understand; but then it came to him – Roza Abady had thought that it was not he but his father Tamas who had sat beside her and held her hand: Tamas, who had died twenty-five years before, had come back: and that was what had made her so happy.

She did not sleep for long. In barely half an hour she was awake again.

Her first glance was at her son who had sat there without moving, his hand imprisoned in hers, all the time she had been asleep. Again she smiled at him.

Perhaps subconsciously recalling what Balint had been telling her before she drifted off to sleep, Countess Roza's first words were: 'Let's go ... to the stud farm ... to the stud ...'

Balint did not at once understand what she was saying, so the old lady shook three times the hand she still held imprisoned in hers, repeating, 'To the stud ... with you ... the stud!' and when Balint tried to dissuade her some nervous energy so took possession of her that again she said: '... to the stud farm ... I want ... with you ... to see the mares ...' and the veins stood out on her forehead.

The nurse ran to find the doctor, and when he came the three of them tried to calm her down and explain that it would be too tiring for her to visit the stud farm straight away, too much for her. In the end they succeeded, possibly because by then she was too tired by her own eagerness to argue further, but it was only after they had promised that they would take her to see her beloved horses in the morning. Then she dozed off again.

The next day the country practitioner from Aranyos-Gyeres was called in early and the two doctors discussed whether they should allow the promised expedition. In the end they agreed that if the patient still wanted to go out she should be allowed to do so, for the weather was exceptionally fine and surely, if she were carried carefully downstairs and pushed gently along the smoothest paths, no harm could come of it. On the contrary it might help renew her will to live, that will which until the previous day's miraculous revival had so noticeably declined.

Balint was still somewhat anxious, but felt unable to forbid it: all the more so because the previous evening, when he had gone to visit his mother in bed, and early that morning when he had looked in to see how she was, he saw in her such happy expectation and joy that he did not have the heart to disappoint her.

With a contented smile she had welcomed him to her side: and each time she had again called him by his father's name. Filled with renewed joy she told her maids, in his presence, which dress and which bonnet she would wear that day ... and what she chose was her finest.

As might have been expected the news had spread early that the old countess was going to visit the mares and so all the Denestornya employees gathered below the castle hill just where the great avenue of tall Hungarian oaks began.

The wheelchair was carried down the stairs by Simon Jager and Balint. At the bottom of the steps that led up to the castle's main entrance old Gergely Szakacs was waiting to ask for the honour of wheeling his old mistress along the paths of the garden and park.

So a procession was formed.

Balint took his place to the left of the wheelchair, his hand still held by his mother's. On her right was the nurse Hedwig and behind Gergely Szakacs walked the two physicians and the second nurse. These were followed by Peter the butler, holding a big box of sugarlumps, and Countess Roza's elderly maid Terka. Behind the group tottered the two housekeepers, Mrs Baczo and Mrs Tothy, overweight and struggling to keep up with the others. Breathless and flatfooted, these two were forced to give up before they were halfway to wherever their mistress was going.

On each side of the alley that ran between the great oak trees stood a line of the entire staff, indoor and outdoor, of the castle and estate of Denestornya. Everyone was there, even two of the park gamekeepers who, hearing that there was a chance to catch a glimpse of their mistress, had come to be there with the others. All the men held their caps in their hands and saluted silently as Countess Roza's chair was pushed slowly past.

Sitting almost upright, her slipper-shod feet placed on the footrest as if it were a footstool, the old countess passed between the two lines of her employees like a queen on a slow-moving throne. Even now, old and ailing and very, very weak, she was still the ruler. She was wearing the same lace-trimmed bonnet that she had put on to hand out the presents the previous Christmas. The wide ribbon was tied tightly with a large bow beneath her chin – for she did not want anyone to see how distorted her features had become – and as she passed she inclined her head slightly to left and to right and did her best to smile.

And in fact she did smile, a smile irradiated with happiness and triumph ... for she was thinking that all these dear people had gathered there not only for her but also to greet that beloved husband who somehow had come home at last and who was now walking at her side, and holding her hand, as he had done so long ago when they were both young.

The procession went on its way until it reached the bank of the mill-stream. There Balint took the box of sugar from old Peter and, alone with his mother and the nurse, and of course Gergely Szakacs pushing the chair, they made their way along the path that led across the great meadow. The others all stayed behind at the end of the oak avenue, while Simon Jager and the stable lads ran off towards the bridge over the river.

'Where are they going?' asked Countess Roza, smiling up at Balint.

'They're going to drive the mares over here.'

'Good! That's good!' the old lady agreed happily.

As they waited she looked to the right, towards a stand of tall poplars whose silver buds were just beginning to unfold, and to the undergrowth beneath them where the hawthorn bushes were covered with creamy white flowers. Then she turned her head to the left to look along the lines of lime trees and wide-spreading horse chestnuts whose great trunks were outlined by the morning sun. From where they stood the view extended into the far distance, which was why the meadow was known as the Meadow of the Great View – and now Countess Roza, her slightly protruding eyes opened wide, gazed over the vast extent of her domains before again looking up at her son, and saying, as she squeezed his fingers in hers, 'You see how beautiful, how beautiful it all is ... how beautiful!'

Balint could not reply. His eyes were full of tears and all he could do was to give her hand an answering squeeze.

Far in the distance the mares could now be seen coming towards them, galloping because the stable lads were cracking their whips behind them and this was something to which they were not accustomed. On they came, at a fast gallop, and only stopped about fifty paces away from the little group. There they stood, heads lifted high, with ears cocked as if asking who these people were who had strayed onto their meadow and wondering what was this strange little carriage they had never seen before. For a moment they stood in amazement, almost motionless, with nostrils distended ... but only for a moment, for suddenly one of the older mares came forward and advanced towards Countess Roza. Then came another, and another, and then, again another, until it was clear that they had all recognized their beloved mistress and were hurrying to her side.

In a few moments her wheelchair was surrounded. So close they came that their soft muzzles searched her face and rested on her shoulder, asking for the familiar lump of sugar. Balint and Szakacs had a hard time keeping them in order, but Countess Abady was laughing happily, 'See? This is Csujtar ... and Menyet ... and here is Borostyan ...' and with her left hand she gave them lump after lump of sugar. She gave and gave and gave: until at last her arm tired and fell into her lap. Then she closed her eyes and leaned back in the cushions murmuring, 'I'm so happy, so happy!'

She said it so softly that it was barely more than a breath. She did not move. Her head was inclined towards her shoulder.

'She's tired,' said the nurse. 'We should wait a little.'

Balint, helped by Gergely Szakacs, succeeded in driving the mares a little further away. Then they returned to his mother.

She was still in the same position, quite motionless, a smile upon her lips. For a few moments her son waited. Then he took her hand in his. It was already cold and she had no pulse. The two physicians hurried to her, but all they could do was to confirm that she had just died. The younger doctor suggested trying to resuscitate her by an injection, but Balint and the other doctor would not allow it, believing it a dreadful idea, just for a few hours, to bring the dying back from other shores only to suffer again before finally letting go. Why should they trouble her now, she who had died so beautifully and in such happiness?

Gently they lowered the chair's back. Then they raised the footrest until Countess Roza lay almost horizontally, her chin still supported by the bonnet's wide ribbon.

Slowly they started back.

Once again they passed under the great flower-laden trees where the birds were all singing their joy in this resplendent return of spring. Behind them the same procession re-formed, but it was now a funeral cortege.

Further back, just a few paces away, the whole stud followed, all of them, close to each other, their heads lowered as if in sorrow for the dead mistress who had loved them so much. It was as if they too wished to honour her last journey.

At the bridge over the millstream they were held back by the stable lads. Then one of them neighed. They remained there a long time.

# PART FIVE

PART TWO

# Chapter One

When the Balkan war finally came to an end. Leopold Berchtold, Foreign Minister of the Dual Monarchy, summoned a delegation of both Houses of Parliament to meet him on November 19th, 1913. The delegation included members of both the government and the opposition parties in proportion to their strength in the House.

In the previous year Berchtold had sent for a similar delegation so as to give the representatives of the Hungarian Parliament a résumé of the Ballplatz's view of the state of foreign affairs. This had not been easy the year before; in the autumn of 1913 it was even more difficult.

A year and a half had passed since Berchtold had first taken charge of the Viennese Foreign Office, and in this time all his efforts at diplomacy had ended in failure. When the Balkan war had started Berchtold had been so confident of a Turkish victory that he had then declared that, no matter what happened at the front, the *status quo* in the Balkans would remain unchanged. He had spoken recklessly, and too soon, for almost at once the rebels in the Turkish provinces had chased the Ottoman armies from the field, and so there had been no question, after such dizzying triumphs, of ordering the victorious insurgents to withdraw behind their former frontiers. Berchtold had then found himself in the unenviable position of having to go cap in hand to the London Conference, defend his now untenable former convictions and somehow save what he could from the debacle he had failed to foresee. His task had been to evict Nikita from Scutari and prevent the Serbs from obtaining such influence in Albania that they would acquire the use of an Adriatic port. His aims therefore had been entirely negative.

All this had formed the theme of Berchtold's address the previous year; and, because then the situation in the Balkans was still far from being settled, and also because the Dual Monarchy's relations with Russia had been particularly strained, he had managed to set forth his exposé without encountering undue criticism.

A year later the situation was very different. At the end of August the Bucharest peace treaty had been signed and so what had previously remained uncertain now had somehow to be explained away. As far as Austria-Hungary was concerned the profit-and-loss account showed a deficit, and Berchtold had the pitiful task of trying to make the best of it.

The truth was that the Dual Monarchy had everywhere been the loser, and furthermore the Balkan states had acted as if she did not exist. In May an agreement between Bulgaria and Romania had handed Silistria to the latter in return for Romania's neutrality during the hostilities; and it seemed that this must have been planned by a former secret agreement inspired by St Petersburg. Already, despite Romania being a party to the Threefold Agreement, Bulgaria, which with the help of the Ballplatz and Aehrenthal had finally become independent of Turkish suzerainty three years before, had also annexed Rumelia. As soon as these moves were made relations between the different Balkan states became soured, for they all aspired to a share of the disintegrating Ottoman Empire, and promptly quarrelled among themselves as to who should get what. Russia was asked to arbitrate, but when, encouraged once more by Vienna, Bulgaria refused to accept the Tsar's verdict, war again broke out. This time Russia encouraged the other Balkan states, now also including Romania, to turn against her disobedient former protégé Bulgaria.

The war was over in ten days.

On July 1st the Serbian army defeated the Bulgarians. On July 3rd the Romanian army marched south and by July 10th stood before Sofia. Meanwhile the Greeks chased the Bulgarians from the Aegean coast while the Turkish Enver Pasha advanced upon Adrianople, over which much blood had already been spilt, and reconquered it with almost no casualties.

In these ten days Austria-Hungary lost her last vestiges of respect in the Balkans. Something might have been saved, even at the last minute, if she had seen fit to intervene, but the Dual Monarchy made no move. This may have been wise, in that her intervention could well have provoked a war with Russia, but the real reason for this inactivity was that, after all the internal confusions which had obstructed the modernization of the army, Austria-Hungary was then even more unprepared for war than she was to be in 1914.

So, though she could hardly have done anything else, the end result was that in the eyes of Europe these Balkan wars were lost, not by Turkey but by the Austro-Hungarian Monarchy. Up to the last minute the Austrian Foreign Office did its best to camouflage the truth. Firstly the Ballplatz declared that, along with the other great powers, Austria reserved the right to approve the terms of the forthcoming peace treaty. It is probable that she imagined the London Conference would stand firmly behind her and thereby do something to save her good name. Unfortunately the great powers, including Germany, did nothing of the sort: they all approved the peace terms unreservedly.

This produced a new dilemma. Either Austria could pursue her aims unilaterally, which might lead her into war without the support of either Germany or Italy, or she had to renounce her claim to revise the peace terms in the way that best suited her. Faced with this impasse the Dual Monarchy withdrew from the London Conference.

From the beginning Austria had put herself in a false position. Her diplomacy was ill-thought-out and badly prepared; and it showed the world how many cracks there were in the Threefold Alliance of Austria, Germany and Italy. Above all it antagonized Romania, who in the end received more from the Bucharest Agreement than she would have been allowed by St Petersburg only a few months previously. Austria's claim to have the right to approve the peace terms therefore seemed to the Romanians to be an attempt to limit their share of the spoils, though that had never been Berchtold's intention.

Romania's revenge was to come in the following year.

The main result of this feckless muddling was that from the moment Austria-Hungary withdrew from the London Conference, the world got on quite well without her. Vienna no longer had any say in Balkan affairs. The Turkish–Bulgarian treaty, and that between Turkey and Greece, had both been settled and signed without anyone even asking the opinion of Austria. It was as if the Dual Monarchy did not exist. She did make one more attempt to retrieve her lost prestige by issuing an ultimatum to Serbia that Albania's independence must be preserved; but the effect of this was lessened by the fact that it was also the policy of Italy and England – above all of England, who did not relish the possibility of having a Serbian (which meant Russian) fleet at large in the Mediterranean.

This was what Berchtold had somehow to explain to the delegation from Hungary. His presentation of the disagreeable facts was masterly.

Firstly he emphasized that Austria-Hungary's foreign policy was based on the need to preserve peace. He spoke of the 'harmony' which existed between the great powers, even including Russia – though he did admit that in the previous years there had been 'some small differences of opinion' which had later all been smoothed away. This had been a definite success for the Monarchy's diplomacy.

He then spoke appreciatively of the Ottoman Empire. It had proved its continued power and vitality by the re-taking of Adrianople from the vanquished Bulgarians. That the Sultan had also lost two great provinces was, in one way, advantageous to Turkey for she was thereby relieved of some of her most unruly subjects … quite a happy result, in fact! It was, of course, true that when the war began Austria-Hungary's principal aim had been the maintenance of the *status quo*, but, as Berchtold's predecessor, Gyula Andrassy, had said as early as 1878, 'We mustn't prop up a crumbling house until the day it collapses'. So it was with the *status quo*. In this he took the same view as his great predecessor.

All this Berchtold told with great skill and authority. No-one could have bettered his air of effortless superiority. His distinguished appearance, with high balding forehead, recalled a stylized figure from a magazine devoted to men's fashions. He spoke as from a great distance, so *de haut en bas* that he left no doubt in his hearers' minds that he belonged to the inner circle of the Vienna 'Olympus', that social group so exclusive that only a few of its members were not born to the purple.

Indeed his exposé was masterly.

He represented the independence of Albania as a triumph of Viennese diplomacy and, as evidence of this, he announced that Austria had already found a suitable king for that new and still untamed country. This was the Prince of Wied, who until recently had served in a Prussian guards regiment, the so-called Yellow Uhlans.

There was also another extraordinary success to be told: it was the cession of the island of Adakaleh to Hungary. This, he felt sure, would please the Hungarians as it had figured so largely in the classical Magyar novel *The Golden Man*.

With the account of these two great successes Berchtold brought his address to an end. The meeting was then terminated and all discussion postponed until the following day.

In this way the Austrian Foreign Minister had somehow extricated himself from a most awkward position, though this, ultimately, was not because of the brilliance of his exposition, nor because of little Adakaleh, but because the whole affair was at once overshadowed by the unwise comportment of the opposition members of the Hungarian delegation who provoked a scandal by raising the matter of Tisza's use of the parliamentary guards in Budapest – this when discussion of all internal matters was forbidden to them. It had long been agreed that the delegation could discuss only foreign affairs, matters concerning the joint Austro-Hungarian army, and the general state of the economy. The intervention was all the more unexpected because it was those very members of the delegation who had so defiantly affirmed that internal matters were taboo, who now brought them up to the scandal of all those in the public rooms of the palais in the Bankgasse where Berchtold had given his address.

It was only after half the time allocated for the discussion had been wasted in this way that the delegation was able to turn to those foreign affairs which were, after all, the sole *raison d'être* of the meeting.

Now, finally, Berchtold found himself asked some very awkward questions. Was it true, someone asked, that Germany had abandoned the Dual Monarchy on the question of Austria's claim to inspect and if necessary revise the terms of the Bucharest peace treaty? Why, asked another, had Berchtold not spoken in warmer terms of the role played by France?

This last question was raised by Mihaly Karolyi, who by then had become the acknowledged leader of the Independence Party. Karolyi praised the part played by Poincaré and asked why there had been no criticism of the totally passive role played by the Ballplatz throughout the whole Balkan crisis and the London Conference which had followed. This attitude was not entirely logical, coming from the representative of those who had extended the hand of friendship to Serbia from the great height of the pseudo-parliament in the Hotel Royal's ballroom: for how could someone who saw no wrong in aggression emanating from Belgrade condemn the passivity of Vienna?

The presence of the delegation brought quite a number of Hungarians to the Austrian capital.

It was also the reason why Balint found himself there. He had been appointed in the autumn by Tisza who wished to reward him for having given up his non-party stand and joining the government party when Tisza took office.

Abady had thought about this for some time and the move had

made things easier for him, especially in regard to his work for the Co-operatives. Now he no longer had to apply for an audience with the appropriate minister but could buttonhole him at any time in the party's private rooms. Balint's change of heart had had nothing to do with his political beliefs. In the past he had remained free of party allegiances only because of his innate distaste for any restraint on his freedom of action. Now he overcame this.

He had not come to Vienna from Budapest with the others, but from Switzerland where he had just spent a few days with Adrienne on the shores of Lac Léman near Nyon. From there Adrienne had gone on to Lausanne to visit her daughter while Balint returned to Vienna. In their little pension they had registered as man and wife – which in those days before passports posed no problems – and indeed this is what they now considered themselves.

That terrible unbreakable chain which had bound Adrienne to her incurably mad husband had shattered of its own accord in the autumn. On November 2nd Pal Uzdy died suddenly.

He had been in excellent health until the end of the summer and indeed, throughout the four years of his confinement, and though his mind had gradually grown ever more clouded, his physical condition had even improved. He had put on weight and there seemed to be no reason why he should not live for years, even possibly outliving his wife.

In the middle of September, however, his persecution-mania took a new turn. He said nothing to anyone, not even to Adrienne who visited him often, but he began to imagine that his medical adviser was trying to poison him. Normally it was to Adrienne that he would confide his innermost thoughts, but not this time. It was his keeper who began to notice a change in the patient and soon diagnosed the trouble. Uzdy started by sniffing at his food suspiciously, and then leaving most of it on the plate until he was eating almost nothing. The doctor did his best to persuade him to eat but though Uzdy pretended to agree, he would tip the soup into the washbasin and throw the meat and vegetables into the lavatory pan. When this was discovered they tried installing a little electric cooker in Uzdy's room so that he himself could prepare the eggs that his keeper brought him telling the sick man, though of course it was not true, that he had smuggled them in from outside without the hospital people knowing anything about it. He also brought him apples and pears and a little silver knife with which to peel them himself. This worked for a few days, but proved to be a failure when Uzdy, from his window, caught sight of his keeper talking to the hated doctor. From then on he refused to eat at all, and would soon have died of starvation if Fate had not decided otherwise.

He grew very thin, barely more than skin and bones, and for hours he would pace up and down his room without stopping. Soon he could hardly keep himself upright, but reeled from side to side grabbing hold of whatever piece of furniture he found in his way. Though too weak to stay upright for more than a moment without support, nothing would make him stop.

On the last day of October he slipped and struck his back against the bedpost. The injury sparked off an attack of pleurisy which soon affected his lungs. In three days he was dead.

He was buried at Varalmas, where his own mad father had been interred. It was after this that Adrienne decided to visit her daughter.

It was still necessary in those days to do nothing which might cause tongues to wag and so Balint left before her, having arranged that they should meet in Salzburg and only from there go on to Switzerland together. They did this principally because it would not have been thought seemly, despite the circumstances, for Adrienne to have travelled alone with a man during the first weeks of mourning. They used the opportunity to talk over their future together. Adrienne was insistent that they should wait until the year's official mourning was at an end before they married. This, she felt, was for the sake of her daughter who would never afterwards wonder why her mother had not waited for the customary period. Balint felt obliged to agree.

In spite of the reason for this voyage it turned out to be like a honeymoon. Here, for the first time, they were alone, with no fear of discovery or exposure, and happy in the knowledge that their future together was at long last assured.

Balint's only regret was that his mother had not lived to see how things had turned out. He knew that she would no longer have opposed his marriage to Adrienne but, on the contrary, would have rejoiced with him. He remembered how sweet and welcoming she had been to Adrienne that time they had so unexpectedly met at Gerbeaud's. He knew that his mother would have approved.

Balint had chosen a small pension on the edge of the lake. It had only twenty rooms and had been converted from the country retreat of some patrician family from Geneva who had had it built at the end of the eighteenth century and named it, after the fashion of those days, 'Monbijou'. The name had been kept, and suited it well. It was designed in the French manner, elegant and stylish, and typical of the sort of modest, but not too modest, retreat built by the wealthy of those days. The house faced the lake. In front of it a wide lawn sloped gently down to the water's side and it was backed by giant oak trees. Across the lake the mountains rose, a wild jumble of rocky crags above which, whenever the clouds parted, could be seen the snow-covered triangular peak of Mont Blanc. This seemed to float so high in the sky that it was difficult to imagine that it was anywhere attached to the earth.

There they stayed for eight days, eight days of quiet joy and happiness far removed from the impassioned fever of their first coming together in Venice when every minute of that month of frenzied lovemaking had to be made the most of as both of them feared that any one of those days might have been their last on earth. Then every dawn might have heralded a parting made final by death. Now all was different. They lived together beside the lake in calm intimacy … and in the happy promise that soon they would never again be parted.

They made all sorts of plans, reaching out many, many years ahead. They would have a quiet wedding with only two witnesses, no-one else. Some modernization would have to be done at Denestornya; electricity installed and two new bathrooms, one for Adrienne and the other … the other for the future when their son, who had not been spoken of by them for a long time, not since Uzdy's madness, would then at long last have become a reality. This, they now felt, was sure; and the child would be the crown of their love, a descendant who would be the living proof of their enduring will to live.

## Chapter Two

After the meeting Balint went to a concert given by the Vienna Philharmonic Orchestra to hear one of the Beethoven symphonies.

It was quite late when the concert was over and Balint hurried to get to Sacher's before midnight when the public dining room closed. He was too late. The lights had been turned out and all the tablecloths removed. Balint found himself somewhat put out for he did not know anywhere else where he could get a quiet meal without music. He turned back from the dining room and had just entered the front hall when he met Peter and Niki Kollonich coming in.

'Have you come to get some food?' asked Balint. 'They've just closed here, so I've got to find somewhere else.'

'Come and join us then,' replied Peter. 'We've got a private room for supper. Kristof Zalamery and I booked it in advance!'

'It's really very nice of you, but if it's with gypsy music and girls then I don't think it's for me tonight.'

They reassured him. No gypsies and no girls, except for one who would be coming later. She was La Pantera, a famous Spanish dancer who had been appearing at the Ronacher Theatre for the last two months and who had thrown the imperial capital into a fever.

Abady had already heard of her. She was, he knew, beautiful as well as being an accomplished dancer – but she had become even more famous for her diamonds which had been pictured in every illustrated paper in the world. This had been done many, many times, since La Pantera, or her manager, used these famous jewels for the dancer's publicity. Just in case interest in the diamonds should wane, they were stolen every five or six months – only to be recovered a week or ten days later. Each time this happened they could be written up again, with every detail lovingly described and the enormous value greatly exaggerated so as to tease the respectable reader.

Balint and his cousins were shown into the private room where they found only Fredi Wuelffenstein, who had been invited by Zalamery. Fredi, who was also a member of the delegation, was admiring his tall, slim figure in the wall mirror. With his padded shoulders, pale blond hair and the face of a white negro, it looked as if he had been trying to emulate the statesmanlike poise he had so admired in Berchtold that afternoon.

Then Stefi Szent-Gyorgyi came in and they all started to talk. At first Fredi tried hard to get them onto politics but this did not suit either Balint or the Kollonich brothers. First of all each one of them wanted to know why the others were in Vienna. Stefi, it seemed, was going to England to hunt, while Peter and Niki were on their way back to Hungary after a visit to Upper Austria where they had been invited for the pheasant-shooting. At first the talk was all about guns and horses and gamebirds, but it was not long before they started to talk about La Pantera and Kristof Zalamery. They all knew that Kristof had fallen madly in love with the dancer the very first night she appeared; and since then the whole town had been talking about the fortune that he had been spending on her, and especially about the diamond dog collar necklace that he had added to her famous collection. Every detail was known to the good people of Vienna. It had been bought at Klinkosch's in the Mehlmarkt and had cost sixty thousand crowns. It was also known that he was ferociously jealous and guarded her like a dragon, and so, though he liked to show her off, he never left her side.

'At this very moment he's waiting in his carriage at the stage door of the Ronacher. He'll stay there until she's changed and then,' said Peter, 'he'll bring her straight here thereby making sure she doesn't meet anyone else on the way!'

Niki laughed. 'What an ass that Kristof is! All that money spent on the girl and all that trouble keeping an eye on her ... and she cuckolds him every night!'

'That can't be possible! Why, he lives with her at the Imperial Hotel!'

'Oh yes, but they have separate rooms divided by a sitting room. Kristof can stay with her only until three a.m. Then she sends him away saying she has to get her sleep if she's going to be able to dance properly the following night. That's when the others come in!'

'What rubbish you do talk!' said Peter, who was always upset by his brother's love of making mischief. 'That's far too complicated. Why would anyone else be there, ready and waiting? Where are they? In the corridor? In the hall? It's absurd: nothing but the usual lying Viennese gossip!'

'Not a bit of it. La Pantera has a confidante, half-secretary, half-procuress. She is older than the dancer and goes everywhere with her. Everyone calls her "Contessa", probably because it sounds well. Anyhow you strike your bargain with her, and you wait in her room, which is next to La Pantera's, until the coast is clear!'

'And how do you know all this?' asked his brother angrily.

'How do I know it? How? Everyone in Vienna knows it!'

'Everybody is ... everybody is nobody.'

'Well, if you really want to know,' chuckled Niki, 'it's because I did it only yesterday. It wasn't even very expensive, only five hundred crowns.

It was worth it just for the fun of it all. I rather like making a fool of that good old Kristof!' Abady felt slightly nauseated.

He got up to leave, but it was too late. Just at that moment the door opened and Zalamery entered with the dancer upon his arm.

The man was built like a Hercules, though slightly balding and beginning to run to fat. He was a heavy man and though his dinner jacket had been made by one of London's most famous tailors and was a perfect fit, on Zalamery it looked as if it had been rented from a stage costume shop. It was like this with everything he did. He owned a large stable of racehorses ... but never won a race. His forests in Marmaros were endless ... but he never shot a stag himself, though it was true that his guests had some good sport. He was a good-hearted man, but vain. He liked to be admired, and he liked to show off the splendour of his possessions. This was why he felt impelled to bring his mistress for his friends to see.

The woman was truly beautiful. She was tall and slim. Under a helmet of raven-black hair her face was one of classical beauty and her eyes sparkled under the thickest of black lashes. Her hands, feet and legs were perfectly formed, but her glory was her walk. She moved like one of the great cats, a puma or a jaguar, who seemed always ready to pounce. It was presumably from this quality that she had been named La Pantera, the leopard. Her look was cold as ice, like that of a wild beast.

She wore a dress of dark blue silk with wide sleeves. It was tied at the waist by a sash of the same material and seemed to be half evening dress and half tea gown. She wore only one piece of jewellery, the diamond collar that Kristof had given her. This was just to please the donor: the rest she only wore when she danced.

Introductions were made and she offered her hands for the men to kiss.

There was nothing to show that she even noticed Niki, and it is possible that she did not even remember him for it was obvious to Balint at least that she was not really interested in other people. To her everything was reduced to business, her dancing, her diamonds, her beauty and her fixed icy smile.

She talked coolly about all sorts of bland cosmopolitan subjects. Her manners were impeccable. Saying that she was tired after the performance, she asked only for a glass of champagne and a little cold fish, nothing more.

'We won't be staying long, will we?' she asked Zalamery humbly, as if to underline to the other men that she regarded Kristof as her lord and master. She then told how she had a rehearsal at midday because she was preparing a new number, a Russian dance which was very difficult but which would be very beautiful. She would have to work hard at it, she said, because she was going to do it at St Petersburg in three weeks' time. It would be just right for a Russian audience, and she was sure they were going to love it.

And so she rattled on. Everything she said was impersonal, even mechanical, and Balint was sure that this was how she talked in every city she visited, with hundreds and hundreds of adoring men whose names she may never have learned and whose faces she forgot at once. Then she would move on to another capital and to other men. If she had not been so beautiful she would have been essentially boring. As it was her movements were so fluid and so alluring that to watch them was such a joy that no-one noticed the banality of her conversation. Her hands, her fingers, her arms moved always in perfect harmony with the tilt of her head and the line of her shoulders. The picture seemed to have no flaw. It was as if a great artist had designed every pose she adopted.

Balint was wondering whether she had studied her effects, or whether they were natural and inborn, when across the room from him he saw an elderly woman come in and stand by the door of the apartment.

She was of middle height and rather thin. She wore a dress of smooth black silk. Her hair must once have been light brown but there remained now only a few strands of this colour: the rest was bluish silver and there was a great deal of it piled in two thick tresses into the form of a crown much in the style that can be seen in portraits of the Empress Elisabeth, Queen of Hungary. On each side of her face some tiny short curls framed her high, slightly oriental cheekbones. It was an interesting face, pale and elegant, and its pallor was accentuated by a startling pair of black eyebrows that just met in the middle. Though obviously no longer young, she held herself very straight, and so distinguished was her bearing that beside her the splendid La Pantera might have been just a pretty chambermaid. She greeted no-one and did not seem to expect to be greeted herself. She was like a soldier, on duty and waiting for orders.

'*J'ai tout rassemblé, madame* – I've collected everything. Here they are, *il ne manque rien* – there is nothing missing,' and she passed her hand over the sizeable Morocco-leather bag that hung from her arm. It was clear that she was speaking of the diamonds which were always in her charge. 'Do you need anything else?'

'No. Not now. You can go back to the hotel, Contessa ... No, wait a moment! Take this with you, please!' replied La Pantera. Then she turned to Zalamery and said: 'You won't mind if I take this off now, will you?' as she touched the diamond dog collar he had given her.

'Would you undo it for me?' she asked and bent her lovely neck to Zalamery's broad chest.

It was not easy for him, and a few moments passed before his thick fingers managed to release the clasp.

While this was happening the Contessa stood quietly by without moving. Only her eyes moved as she looked around the table and Balint felt that they lingered for a moment when they came to him. It was almost as if she would have liked to look longer at him. He was attracted by her looks and by those light grey eyes set under the dark eyebrows. He felt he had somewhere seen that glance before, but it was only a fleeting impression and soon passed away.

Kristof handed the diamond collar to the Contessa. The lock of the leather bag clicked to; then she looked once more at Abady and for a moment stared hard at him. Then she turned back to the dancer and said, '*Bonne nuit, madame. Bonne nuit, messieurs,*' and with a slight inclination of her head with its massive crown of silver hair, she left the room.

Balint was not sure if he had imagined it, but it had seemed to him that when the Contessa was saying goodbye to the men in the room she was really only saying it to him. Who was she? Who could she be? Had he ever seen her before?

All around him the conversation started up again, but Balint could think of nothing but the woman who had just gone out.

A few moments later a waiter came in and handed a visiting card to Abady. On it was printed the name 'Comtesse Julie Ladossa' and on the other side had been written a few words in Hungarian, '*Please come out for a moment*'. Julie Ladossa! She was Laszlo Gyeroffy's mother!

He went out at once and found her sitting on one of the sofas that lined the walls of the anteroom. The Morocco-leather bag was on her knees and resting on it were her hands, long narrow aristocratic hands that were still beautiful even if lined with age. They were an artist's hands, Laszlo's hands. Balint sat down beside her.

'Please don't be offended that I asked you to come out. It is such a long time since I talked to anyone from my own country. I recognized you at once – you're so like your father – and so as to be sure I asked the head waiter if it really was you.'

'What can I do for you?' asked Balint, but he found himself too embarrassed by the encounter to go on. It would have been absurd to greet Laszlo's mother with some polite formula like 'How do you do?' especially as he had met her acting as someone's servant, or was it worse than that?

He wondered what terrible times she had been through until she had finally ended up like this.

It was true that she showed no signs of degradation, no traces of the life she must have led unless, perhaps, it was to be seen in a faint cynical turn at the corner of her mouth, a little bitter smile that suggested that there was nothing and no-one she did not despise, least of all herself. A wilful, stubborn line rose where her eyebrows met.

Then she was asking him all about Transylvania, about her old acquaintances, about the Alvinczys, the Laczoks, whom she referred to by their full names as if they were no relation to her and as if they had not all been her childhood friends and playmates. Obviously she wished to make it clear to him that she no longer belonged to that world, that she no longer deserved to and would not presume even to think so.

All this was said in a calm conversational and conventional matter as if they were talking about matters that did not really in any way concern them. After a while she fell silent.

Then in a deeper tone, very softly but with an underlying force of barely suppressed passion, she asked, 'How … how is my son?'

It was difficult for Balint to find the right words with which to answer. If only she had still used the light, somewhat distant tones with which she had asked all her other questions he would probably have told her the cruel truth quite openly. He would have said that her son had turned into a depraved drunkard and was bankrupt. He would have told her in the baldest terms – perhaps out of anger, or resentment, or the desire for revenge – that Laszlo's tragic life had begun that day in his early childhood when he had been deserted by his mother. But Julie Ladossa had spoken to him in that passionate voice, that voice which came from somewhere deep inside her soul; that voice in which could be heard the echo of many years of guilt and remorse, of more than two decades of sorrow and humble acknowledgement of her own fault, and in those half-strangled tones he had recognized the force of her living tragedy.

Therefore he hesitated before answering her questions and, when he did, he did so with compassion. He told the truth, but he did it gently. He did not conceal Laszlo's sad situation, how he had sold the house and land and now lived on a small pension in one of his former tenants' houses at Kozard. He said that he had been ill but that Balint believed that he was now a little better, though it was some time since he had seen his cousin who had now broken off all relations with everyone he had known in the past.

'He too!' she whispered. 'So it has happened to him too,' and she stared ahead of her.

They did not speak for some minutes. Then she got up, saying: 'From here we are going to St Petersburg. Then to Moscow, Odessa and Bucharest. We shall be in Budapest at the end of February ... If you happen to be there ... and wouldn't mind seeing me again ... you might perhaps have some news. I would be so grateful!'

'Of course! I'll see you with great pleasure!'

'We shall probably be at the Hungaria, but I'm not sure because the agent arranges everything like that.'

Balint thought that Julie Ladossa would now put out her hand and leave; but she just stood there, without speaking, though she obviously had something on her mind. Her eyes were fixed far, far away and the vertical line on her forehead seemed even more deeply etched than before. Then, speaking swiftly and urgently, she looked at Abady and said, 'Tell me! Tell me! Do you sometimes see Sandor Kendy, the one they call Crookface?'

'Of course. Not often, but when I'm in Kolozsvar he sometimes comes to town.'

A strange, unexpected and cruel smile played across her lips. Then she straightened up so abruptly that she might have suddenly grown several inches taller. From under her thick lashes there flashed a look of uncontrollable hatred. 'Well! If you see him again, tell him that we have met ... and also what I'm doing now!' Now she did put out her hand, and then, from the door, she spoke again, 'Be sure to tell him that too

... that too ...' and she laughed as she went out, a laugh that to Balint seemed filled with cruelty.

Balint stayed where he was, rooted to the spot.

What had she said? Why on earth should she want that of him?

And why did she ask after Crookface only now and not when she had enquired after all her other old friends? Why this unexpected commission ... and, above all, why that demonic laughter?

How did it all fit together?

He tried to recall everything he had ever heard about Laszlo's mother. He had never heard any mention of Sandor Kendy when people had talked about Julie Ladossa. Neither her sister-in-law, Princess Kollonich, nor even Aunt Lizinka who never left any piece of evil gossip unsaid, had ever mentioned him. It was true that no-one had ever told him with whom she had eloped and it seemed that no-one really knew, for Aunt Lizinka told many different stories, at one time saying it was with a Hussar who happened to be riding by, or a waiter, or a tightrope walker, but it was clear she was just improvising for she really knew nothing and her candidates for the culprit were always unknown men, never anyone they all knew like Sandor Kendy. Crookface was surely above suspicion.

This was how Balint's first thoughts took him; but then other memories came into his mind. There had been that evening he had spent at Crookface's manor at Kis-Keresztur where he had seen the portrait of a lovely young woman he had taken to be Crookface's deaf wife when young. It was quite a logical assumption because the picture had been exactly like Countess Kendy dressed for a costume ball, for her gown had been in the style of the eighties, old-fashioned now and covered with the frills of the past. He remembered that he had asked about this but had not been given an answer.

Now he also remembered that the picture seemed at one time to have been damaged. There had been signs of a repair to a diagonal gash that had once sliced the picture almost in two, right down to the little painted bouquets on the skirt. He had noticed it then but something in the gruff old man's manner had prevented him from asking about it. Many years before he had heard that when Julie Ladossa had bolted Mihaly Gyeroffy had slashed at her portrait and flung it out of the window. Could Crookface's picture have been that portrait? And if it was, how had it got to Keresztur? And why?

Had Kendy married that gentle deaf girl who was not of his class just because she was so like that other who had flung out of his life with a peal of demonic laughter some thirty years before?

These were all unconnected fragments from an untold story. For a moment Balint felt almost ashamed of himself, prying into matters that did not concern him. Let it all pass into oblivion, he said to himself. Let nobody know. One shouldn't rake up the past. If there was one thing in a man's life that should remain strictly private, and which was no concern of anyone else's, it was his innermost feelings. Those were one's own: to others they should be taboo.

He thought of his own love for Adrienne, a love that had now lasted ten years, and he was filled with happiness and gratitude. They had never misunderstood each other no matter what storms had afflicted their lives. Now it seemed they had reached port at last.

Until death do us part.

## Chapter Three

Balint never gave Julie Ladossa's message to Crookface Kendy. In fact he had never intended to, but his conversation with the 'Contessa' did have one other result.

When the former Countess Gyeroffy was asking him about her son, Balint felt ashamed that he could tell her nothing about Laszlo except for a few generalities and ashamed that he had not thought about his cousin and childhood friend for many months. It was true that this was not his fault but Laszlo's, who had rebuffed every gesture made towards him. The latest rejection had come when Balint had sent him a telegram to let him know that Countess Roza had just died and to offer to send over a car so that Laszlo could attend the funeral. Laszlo had not replied, not even with a message of condolence, nothing. Balint had been so offended by this that at the time he had felt he would never be able to forgive the cousin who had once been such a close friend. Now, however, he decided to bury his resentment and go over to see Laszlo and try once again to become friends with him.

As soon as he got home to Denestornya he drove over to Kozard. The weather, as so often in Transylvania at the beginning of December, was sunny and mild.

He arrived about midday at the little house in which he knew Laszlo was living. The door of wooden laths that led through the crumbling fence was open. It looked as if it was never closed. Balint walked straight into the house. The first room he entered was the kitchen, and through this could be seen a room in total disorder, an unmade plank bed at one side, a rough wooden table nearby, a country cape of rough cloth hung on one wall and under it lay an ancient pair of peasant's boots. None of this, thought Balint, could have belonged to Laszlo, so he walked through to the next room.

This was not much better, though the pinewood furniture had at least been polished. It looked as if it had come originally from one of the servants' rooms at the manor house. On the chest of drawers lay a gun case of ornate brass-bound leather engraved with Laszlo's name inaccurately spelled 'Count Ladislas Gieroffy'. This room had been tidied, the floor properly scoured and the windows opened to let in the air.

Balint walked round the house hoping to find Laszlo sitting on the sunny side. He wasn't there. There was no-one there. Then Balint saw that there was a girl standing at the far end of the garden, an adolescent girl who was washing laundry in the stream. He walked down to where she stood on the bank dipping the clothes in the water, soaping them and then scrubbing what she held on a little wooden board.

The girl was astonishingly lovely, so beautiful that Balint was lost for words when he finally came face to face with her. She had large doe-like eyes fringed by dark lashes and her long eyebrows were so fine they might have been painted on with a brush. Her face was a perfect oval and her skin both pale and rose-coloured. Her red lips were full, as red as blood, and she was as slim as a reed. The sleeves of her dress were turned up to the elbow and her smooth satiny arms were as rosy as her face and neck. Only her hands were roughened by hard work. She wore a kerchief tied round her head like all the peasants of that region, but her clothes had been made to be worn in the city, even if now they were worn and patched. Her apron was in rags and her bare feet were slipped into an old pair of ladies' button boots which would have reached to mid-calf if most of the buttons had not disappeared years before. No matter how old and dirty her clothes the girl was so beautiful that one forgot everything but that.

Balint greeted her and then said, 'I'm looking for Laszlo Gyeroffy. Do you know where I can find him?'

The girl looked at him with a scornful expression on her beautiful face.

'What do you want of him? Why are you looking for him?' she asked sullenly.

'I am his cousin, Balint Abady.'

The girl made a little curtsy, as good manners demanded.

'I am Regina Bischitz.' Then she added, 'My father owns the village shop.'

'Well, now we know each other,' said Balint with a light laugh, 'perhaps you could tell me where Laszlo is?'

Regina shrugged.

'He's not here. They took him to Szamos-Ujvar.'

'They took him?'

'Yes. That Fabian, he took him ...' and grabbing a shirt that was both filthy and torn, she held it up for a moment before her and then plunged it into the stream, wrung it out and started to rub it with soap.

'Fabian? Who is this Fabian?'

'Ugh!' said the girl. 'He is a bad man, that Fabian! He always takes him with him ... and there he makes him drink, and ... and carouse ... and it is so bad for him. He's a worthless scoundrel, that Fabian!'

'If I knew where he was at Szamos-Ujvar I'd drive in and find him.'

'You can't go there, not there! It's terrible!' cried Regina, and her eyes filled with tears. 'That Fabian, he takes him to see bad women, wicked women ... that's how he's ruining him. The count is so ill, so very ill and that's why ... and he makes him drink and drink ... and ...'

She stopped without saying the last word but balled up her hand into a fist and made as if she were hitting someone with it. Then she picked up the shirt again and started to rub it with such fury that if it had been the hated Fabian it would have been as if she were doing her best to choke all life out of what she held in her hands.

She turned away from Balint and, as she did so, she bent forward and huge tears fell from her face like a rain of large diamonds on the wet cloth she was holding so fiercely. There was a fallen tree trunk facing the girl. Balint sat down on it and waited for quite a long time. Finally the girl finished her work and stood there panting in front of him. Then he asked again when Laszlo would be back.

'It's no use waiting for him,' said the girl. 'Even if he does come soon he'll be in a dreadful state, dreadful. He'll mess up the room again ... and I scrubbed it this morning early. Oh, I can do it! I do everything, the washing-up, the scrubbing, the airing, everything!'

She seemed overcome with sorrow. Then she sat down on the edge of a little bench, with her back very straight and her head inclined, staring at nothing.

'Doesn't he have any other servant?'

'I am not his servant, I ... I do it because I want to. I can't bear to see ... to see a gentleman like the Count ... such a great gentleman ... to see him ... so uncared-for ...'

'Didn't he have an old man called Marton looking after him? What happened to him?'

The girl waved her hand in the air.

'He's useless. He just cooks and cleans the Count's boots, nothing else. He's gone off again now, probably to lay snares in the woods. It's the only thing that interests him. I do everything here because I can't bear to see the filth he'd live in if I didn't. No-one knows I do it. It has to be in secret. I can only come when my father isn't around and can't see me leaving the shop. I can work here today because he's gone to Kolozsvar. Most times I can only do it at night, or very early in the morning, because if he catches me I get a beating.'

She stopped and again looked straight ahead of her.

The kerchief fell from her head and her long Titian hair fluttered in the slight breeze. Sitting on the bench she was like a statue with her firm breasts straining the thin cloth of her blouse. She was very beautiful, a rose of Sharon not yet fully open but no longer a bud. Tears brimmed under her long lashes and then again rolled down her cheeks.

'How old are you, child?' asked Balint, trying to distract her from whatever she was thinking.

'Fifteen,' she muttered, but still went on staring in front of her. Then suddenly she broke out in a wail of complaint, though Balint could not tell whether she had sensed the sympathy in him or whether she was so filled with sorrow that she could not keep it to herself. She spoke in broken phrases, with no words directly connected.

From her poured the story of how, some five years before, when Laszlo had been confined to his bed with pneumonia, she had watched by his bedside and nursed him back to health. Since then she had done everything for him, even stealing brandy when his credit at her father's shop had been exhausted. Soap too, and paraffin.

She did everything. Always more and more, but always in vain, quite in vain.

'In vain? What do you mean, in vain?' asked Balint in astonishment.

'Just that! In vain. He doesn't speak to me ... except when I bring him brandy. Then he just says "You're a good little girl, Regina!" or "I'm glad you came, Regina!" But it's not praise for me. It's all he says, ever ... and it's only for the brandy, not for me.'

'Are you sure?'

'I'm sure alright. He accepts everything I do, but I never get a word of thanks. To him it's nothing more than his due, nothing out of the ordinary that I should clean for him, tidy him up when he's dead drunk, rub his arms and his legs with that horrid black ointment he has to have for that ... that trouble he caught in Szamos-Ujvar.'

Now, at last, she jumped up, full with rebellion. 'But me? Why, he doesn't even pat my cheek!'

Balint wanted to reassure her and said, 'I am sure that's only because he thinks you're still barely more than a child, Regina. He's probably very fond of you in his own way.'

'Do you really think so?' she asked eagerly as she sat down again. Then, a shy smile came into her face and she said, 'Yes, I suppose so, in his way. To him I'm just a sort of household pet who's useful to him. I am the only person he talks to. He tells me – oh, so much about his life ... and to me it is some little reward because he tells me about such wonderful things, and in such beautiful words.' For a moment she seemed lost in thought, and then added sadly, 'But since he's got so thin he doesn't talk much anymore.'

Taken by surprise Abady said: 'He's got very thin? Since when?'

'Just in the last few weeks. Of course he hardly eats at all. It's hard for him to keep it down!'

Now Balint started to question the girl as to whether Laszlo was seeing a doctor and what were his symptoms? Did he, for example, have little patches of red on his cheekbones? Regina answered all his questions quite intelligently. The doctor, she said, came every week. The Count coughed a lot, but not more than before. Those red spots? Yes, they did appear if he had drunk a lot ... but otherwise? Maybe yes, at other times too.

Balint did not speak for a few moments. Then he said, 'We ought to get him into a sanatorium. I could see that he was taken good care of … and he'd get trained nursing.'

'Take him away? Away from here?' cried Regina, distracted with fear, with terror lest they should take him away from her so that she would never see him again, never ever again. No, not that! Never that, her heart would break.

Regina now sensed that she had said too much and that she'd somehow endangered the man who had become her only reason for living. Now, at once, she had to cover up the truth for otherwise they would take Laszlo away from her; and so the words poured out of her, swiftly trying to take the sting out of anything serious she might have said: the doctor had praised her nursing and said it was quite adequate, and not only the doctor from Iklod who saw Laszlo every week, but also the chief consultant from Szamos-Ujvar who came over from time to time; also there was somebody else who saw to it that the Count was properly looked after. Dr Simay he was called, the same man who sent her father twenty florins every week for Laszlo's food and who also paid the chemist's bills.

'Who is this Dr Simay?'

'He's a lawyer at Szamos-Ujvar. My father writes to him whenever … whenever something is needed.'

'So he really is being properly looked after? All the time?'

'Oh, yes! Ever since he was ill with pneumonia,' insisted Regina.

Until then she had stuck fairly closely to the truth, but now she felt impelled to lie. Resolutely she then said, 'All the doctors think he's getting on very well and … and soon will be quite himself again.'

Abady was surprised.

'But only just now you said he was losing weight and couldn't keep his food down and you were afraid he'd soon die?'

Regina smiled.

'Well, yes, I did say that, but I didn't really mean it like that.'

'Really?'

'Yes. I … I … was upset that he'd gone … gone there again … for that … and so I said more than I meant. But it really isn't as bad as that, really it isn't.'

Young Regina played her chosen part so well that Balint believed her when she made out she had exaggerated everything out of jealousy and anger. Still, he did not want to leave without establishing some sort of contact with his old friend.

'Look, my dear,' he said as he took some money and a visiting card from his wallet, 'I won't wait for Laszlo this time, but I'm going to leave these two hundred crowns with you because I know I can trust you to use it for Laszlo if something happens and then you'll be able to buy whatever he needs. And here is my address. If he does take a turn for the worse, or if I can be of help in any way whatever, please send me a telegram at once. You will, won't you?'

'Of course!' she cried. 'Of course I will; at once. I'll send for you at once!' and, as she spoke the words, inwardly she swore to herself, Never! Never! Never! Just so that you can take him away from me? Never that! Never ever that!

They shook hands near the stream. Balint had barely turned away when she was already back at work at her washing. Nevertheless she glanced covertly back at him several times, fearing that he might change his mind and wait for his cousin after all.

If he did that he would certainly take him away from her, especially if Laszlo came back dead drunk, for then it would be obvious that everything she had said about his getting better had been a lie.

She looked many times in the direction of the road until the engine had been started and the car driven swiftly away towards Kolozsvar. Only then did she relax.

## Chapter Four

That year, for the first time, Balint spent Christmas alone, but he consoled himself by thinking that it would only be that once.

In the years to come Adrienne would be there; and, if God was kind, others too, more and more.

For the great household at Denestornya everything passed as it always had, with the same ceremonies as there had been during Countess Roza's lifetime. Nothing had changed: the tree was placed in the centre of the dining table, around it heaps of presents on the white tablecloth that had been arranged, as before, by Mrs Tothy and Mrs Baczo. The old butler, Peter, stood by the door, as in every other year. There was one difference: Countess Roza's throne-like gilt chair was not in its usual place.

Instead Balint stood, slightly to one side just as if his mother had still been there, and handed out the presents to the women and children who came in one by one just as they always had. He wanted no break in the tradition so that next Christmas Adrienne would continue what Roza Abady had done all her life.

When everyone had left and most of the myriad candles in the chandeliers and in the sconces had been snuffed out, Balint stayed there for a long time. He walked from end to end of the immense hall, stopping before the display cabinets, gazing deeply at all the family treasures they contained and also at the objects on the tables that had been placed in the deep window embrasures. They all had their part in his past and that of the family. He looked at everything pensively, almost absent-mindedly. It was a strangely varied collection ranging from exquisite pieces of china from Meissen and Vienna to a huge ancient lock of rusty iron which had once fastened the castle's portcullis. There were also some things which were frankly cheap or ugly, but these were souvenirs of Countess Roza's youth and had been kept for the sentimental memories they evoked. There was a pottery figure of a girl whose skirt would oscillate if touched, a china pug with bulging eyes which had been given to his mother as a child and treasured by her ever since and so placed side by side with the precious cups of gold and silver and the pieces of fine porcelain – objects that had been handed down from generations of former Abadys.

Balint knew the history of each object: and he swore then that everything must always stay as it always had been.

After a long time he went down to the ground floor. There he put on a warm coat and went out into the dark night. Across the courtyard and down to the churchyard where a new Abady vault had been built up against the church when, at the end of the eighteenth century, there had been no more room in the crypt beneath the nave. Here were resting the remains of Balint's grandparents, of his father and, since the previous spring, also of his mother.

The vault was locked, but Balint had had no intention of going in. He only wanted to go as far as the door so as, symbolically, to tell Countess Roza that the Christmas Eve ceremony had been held and that he had done it, and always would do it, exactly as she had. He remained there only for a minute or two. Then he said a silent prayer and walked back up to the castle.

Time went slowly by. Adrienne came back from Lausanne rather later than she had planned because little Clemmie had had some recurrent bouts of fever and Adrienne had not wanted to leave until the girl had been thoroughly checked by the doctors. Finally they declared that there was no cause for anxiety, that this sort of thing often occurred with growing girls and soon would disappear of itself. Nothing to worry about, they said.

So Adrienne came home reassured.

There was a great deal to do as soon as she was back. She and Balint had many plans to make. With their architect they worked on the detailed plans of that part of the castle in which they were going to live. Discussions were held with contractors for installing running water and electric light, hitherto unknown at Denestornya despite the family's great means. Decisions had to be made about whether the necessary power should come from motor generators or from turbines driven by the mill. All sorts of new projects occupied them every day.

In the great world outside there was a lull, even in the Balkans. Only the Albanians were still in turmoil. Oddly enough they did not seem at all to appreciate the new Prussian guard's officer king that the great powers had so carefully chosen for them. It was true that the excellent Prince of Wied was hardly known to his new subjects for in the last two months, ever since he had become King, he had barely set foot in his new country but had preferred to make a round of the courts of Europe, great and small, to offer thanks for his elevation to royal status. Wherever he went he was greatly admired. He was tall and slim and powerfully built and boasted a full set of white, if somewhat equine, teeth. Such a tour was an excellent opportunity to show off these physical advantages and make himself admired, for as a ruling monarch he was able always to stand in the middle of the room, thereby making sure that he was the centre of attention and that everyone would be able to see what a fine upstanding lad he was; and, as all the parties were given for him, all he had to do was to smile continuously with a benevolent, if not very intelligent, expression on his face. And how was he repaid by those vile Albanians? Only two months out of the country and revolution broke out. Not only that but in January those ungrateful rebels announced that the Prince of Wied had been deposed and replaced by a man of their own choice – one Izzet Pasha. The great powers declared that this was beyond endurance and sent a fleet to demonstrate off Valona. At the same time they bade the Prince of Wied to hurry up and take possession of his throne. 'At once!' the new king cried: but then found that his country's new coat of arms was not ready.

He had ordered it to be prepared by some of the world's leading experts on heraldry, and naturally could not present himself to his new subjects without it, for how could a man be a real king if he had no proper heraldic insignia? Not only that but he had to form a royal guard, and although he had issued a tempting invitation to the adventure-hungry young aristocrats of Europe, no-one had yet come forward; and how could he set foot in his kingdom without a guard? So he continued on his travels, always smiling, and went to Rome, Berlin and London.

While the 'pacification' of Albania found no smooth path, the solutions proposed in the Aegean proceeded without a hitch. The islands of Imbros and Tenedos were given back to Turkey while the rest were handed over to Greece. It was true that these were still occupied by the English, but as this was said to be only a temporary arrangement, it seemed that peace had been achieved there too.

All the same there were a few signs that something disquieting was moving under the surface, and this not only in the Balkans. It was rumoured that a Russian secret agent, one Count Dobrinsky, was travelling about in disguise on the Hungarian side of the Carpathians.

It seemed that he had already been in Ruthenia for some little time and that his presence there had only become remarked when, instead of the old-style little wooden chapels, there had been erected many new churches built of stone in the Russian manner with money from an unknown source. Wherever such a new 'Russian' church appeared so at the same time did a portrait of the Tsar, Father of all the Russias. But Dobrinsky was not only there to build propaganda churches, his real function, it was reported, was to draw strategic maps of the passes over the Carpathians and to recruit a network of confidential informers, about fifty of whom had been arrested and brought to trial at the end of December. This was the calm before the storm. It was the beginning of 1914.

Society in the Hungarian capital did not seem to be aware of any of these things. Nor did Parliament. Nearly everyone was interested only by whatever scandal came their way. Only Tisza was doing everything he could to make up for lost time. Only he saw how necessary this was. Even though it was so late in the day he did all he could to bring peace to the controversy over the status of the ethnic minorities in the kingdom. He alone, it seemed, realized how essential it was to get these troubles settled before some world crisis would test the country's mettle. He initiated talks with the influential Romanian politician Maniu – and was promptly attacked by Justh and other chauvinist demagogues for so doing. The county of Pest reacted stormily. The discussions went on for some six weeks, until, in the end, the Romanian 'national committee' rejected the Minister-President's overtures. Despite their refusal to co-operate Tisza declared that for his part he would be as good as his word and continue to hold out the hand of friendship whether it was grasped or not.

It was the last very late attempt to solve a problem that had dogged Hungarian politics for more than a decade. It was, perhaps, a trifle shop-soiled too, because of the irredentist pretensions of the Bucharest peace treaty. But Tisza, even if he had wanted to, could not then have offered more. His hands were tied, firstly by the fact that public opinion was against him and secondly because there were so few others in public life sufficiently clear-sighted to realize the seriousness of the international situation.

At the end of February Balint again found himself back in the Kalotaszeg. He had to go to Magyarokerek to deal with a most interesting situation that had developed there. After a series of abortive attempts a Co-operative society had been formed in the villages in the mountains where the only work was in forestry. This was not unlike the one of two similar societies which had already been formed in the Szekler country. Abady was anxious to persuade this new Co-operative to affiliate to his national movement. This was no easy task, especially in the bigger villages like Kalota-Szentkiraly, Valko and Gyero-Monostor who had all rejected the idea of affiliation. However, the people of Magyarokerek were more flexible in their ideas and accepted Balint's proposition within a month of forming their Co-operative. Balint therefore felt himself bound to find them a forest, for though the villagers were honest, and full of goodwill and joy in their work, they had no money with which to pay for the standing timber on whatever land might be made available to them. This was the custom, but it was difficult to find a landowner willing to forego the profit on land which he had always regarded as there only for his personal profit.

Balint accordingly had decided to give them one of his own holdings which was separate from the other Abady forests. It was situated on the south side of the Kohegy on the boundaries of the county of Szekelyjo. Balint's idea was to allow the villagers to owe him the purchase price until they could start to make a profit from felling the adult trees. Accordingly he went there with his own forest manager, the engineer Winkler, and his secretary Miklos Ganyi, to advise the Co-operative on how to plan the felling and also how to run the new society.

It was pouring with rain when Balint's little party arrived. Everywhere was water and mud and their only consolation was that most of the snow had already disappeared from the mountains.

They walked the boundaries of the forest and checked that they were properly marked; and in the afternoon they sat down in the judge's house and saw that the contract was properly drawn up. At the same time they drew up a schedule of when the timber should be sold and what its price should be. Then they estimated how much would be left, when the land price had been paid and the cost of the labour settled, to form the society's capital. This last had been Abady's express wish and would be his gift.

When all these things had been settled and there only remained some minor details and the preparation of fine copies of the agreements – work which would take an hour at most and which could best be done by Winkler and Ganyi – Balint realized that he had time to call on Farkas Alvinczy, whom he had not seen for a long time.

Since old Count Adam Alvinczy had died and his sons divided up their diminished inheritance, Farkas had hardly stirred from Magyarokerek.

Balint had last seen him at Kis-Kukullo when he had found himself dragged in to attend Pityu's party to celebrate the trial and execution of Brandy. Even there Farkas's presence had been exceptional; and since then he had not stirred from home. Balint had to climb a steep path to reach the Alvinczy manor house. It was perhaps just as well that it was already evening and that night was falling, for the state of dilapidation of the handsome old house was not as obvious as it would have been by day. As it was, one hardly noticed that the plaster was falling away in great patches and that one corner of the house was crumbling.

There were no servants to be seen but a light shone from one of the ground-floor windows. Balint stepped up onto the columned portico and opened the door.

Inside he saw Farkas Alvinczy, sitting at a large dining table on which was spread a huge map lit by a single lamp. Farkas was leaning over the table and was apparently so deep in a book that lay beside the map that he did not notice Abady until he was standing in front of him.

'Why, Balint!' he cried. 'Whatever are you doing here?'

It was obvious that he was delighted to see his visitor, though his greeting was elegantly moderate and free of effusiveness. Balint was at once offered some refreshment, and it was no homebrewed beverage, but a choice of the best liqueurs.

'What would you prefer?' asked Farkas. 'Would you like Benedictine, Cointreau, Chartreuse, Maraschino di Zara? Or something else? I think I've got everything.'

Indeed all these elegant bottles stood nearby in a row on the sideboard.

'You know it's the only thing I spend money on now. Since I gave up the great world – and the high life of the capital – I just don't have the means anymore. This is my only indulgence. For a man like myself ... used to only the best ... well ...'

They touched glasses and sat down at the table. Balint explained what brought him up to the forests and then they talked of some of their mutual friends, of economics and the prospects for the next harvest. These subjects were soon exhausted, for it was obvious to Balint that none of this really interested his friend anymore for Farkas treated it all with haughty contempt. With a dismissive wave of his hand and a mocking smile he said, 'None of this is very important; just little things for little people!'

After more somewhat desultory talk between them Farkas finally spoke of the map that covered the table and which had been carefully attached to it by metal clips. It represented the Indian Ocean, from Aden to the Malacca Straits. When Balint asked why he was studying this map Farkas for the first time became quite animated and eloquent. 'That is where I'm travelling at present! You see? Today my ship arrived here!'

'Your ship?'

'Yes, my ship. This is it!' and he pointed to a steel pen head which had been placed on the blue-coloured sea, pointing to Ceylon at the foot of the pink-coloured sub-continent of India. 'This pen here, that is my ship. Every day I push it forward the distance travelled in the previous twenty-four hours, according to this book. The day before yesterday we left Bombay, and tomorrow we shall arrive at Colombo.'

He told how he had travelled like this for the last two years. He had ordered accounts of voyages and the corresponding maps, and each day he read just as much as was covered by that day – no more, for that would be cheating. Like this it was just as if he were making the voyage himself. If the traveller wrote that he had spent five days at sea with nothing to relate, then Farkas waited five days before reading on or marking the map.

'But isn't that rather dull, making yourself wait five days?'

'Not at all! Time goes by. Sometimes faster than you'd imagine. I think about the sea and about my travelling companions. I dress for dinner in the evenings – you always do on a luxury liner, you know.'

He told Balint he was now a much-travelled man. The previous year he had rounded Cape Horn, visited Terra del Fuego and indeed 'done' South America. He had also been to the South Pole and back. It had been beautiful and most interesting even though it had been a shorter trip than he really liked.

'This one is very good. The weather's lovely and so far the sea has been quite calm!'

Balint looked hard at Alvinczy wondering if he was making fun of him and was just saying all this for a joke, but it was clear he meant everything he said and took it all very seriously. On Farkas's classical features, on that still beautiful if now slightly puffy face, there was an expression only of calm honesty. None of the young Alvinczys had ever shown any sign of a sense of humour and now it was obvious that the man was simply telling the truth. Looking at him Balint noticed how well-turned-out and soigné Farkas still was. He was freshly shaved, his hair had been brushed smooth; and he was wearing a well-cut double-breasted dark blue smoking jacket with gold buttons, just what an elegant man of fashion would wear while cruising the world's oceans. 'Where is your ship going?' asked Balint, so as to make him talk on.

'Tokyo. Then from Tokyo down to the Philippines and on the return trip we shall call at Java and Sumatra. I need another map for that part of the voyage, of course, but I've got it here all ready. Would you like to see it?'

He was about to get up to fetch it when Miklos Ganyi appeared at the door seemingly rather agitated.

'This urgent telegram was brought up from Hunyad by a special messenger. He had to ride up. I'm sure it must be important or Zutor wouldn't have sent it on after us.'

'Please excuse me!' said Balint to Alvinczy as he opened the envelope. It had been sent that day at midday and read:

THE FOLLOWING TELEGRAM CAME TODAY FROM SZAMOS KOZARD:
THE COUNT IS VERY ILL. PLEASE COME AT ONCE. REGINA.

Balint jumped up. Laszlo! Laszlo, his Laszlo, was dying and was perhaps already dead. He would have to start for Kozard at once. Balint read out the message to Farkas and for a few moments they discussed the sad news. Then Balint and Ganyi set off.

Alvinczy came with them only as far as the door. He said the proper words of condolence: 'What a pity – a real shame – he was such an old friend!' but one could tell that the news had not really meant anything to him. As soon as the others had gone, he turned on his heel and hastened back to his book and his map.

Balint caught the night express to Kolozsvar. There another telegram was waiting for him. It came from Kozard and read:

THE NOBLE COUNT LASZLO GYEROFFY WENT TO A BETTER WORLD
AT FOUR P.M. THIS AFTERNOON. I CONSIDER IT MY SACRED DUTY TO
PROVIDE EVERYTHING NECESSARY. PLACING AT YOUR LORDSHIP'S
FEET MY DEEPEST CONDOLENCES I REMAIN YOUR LORDSHIP'S MOST
HUMBLE SERVANT – AZBEJ.

Early the next morning Balint left by car for Kozard. Before leaving he remembered that La Pantera should have been in Budapest since the previous Saturday and so Julie Ladossa would be there too. So he sent a telegram to her at the Hotel Hungaria.

He reached Kozard just before eight o'clock. Old Marton Balogh was sitting on the doorstep. He looked old and worn and he just sat there looking glumly ahead of him. He did not get up when Balint came up, nor did he touch his cap: and when Abady questioned him, he merely pointed with his thumb to the room behind him and muttered, 'There, in the back room. The young Jewess is with him,' and then went on staring into space.

Regina sat by the window at a table she had pushed there so as to make more space in the room for the moment when they would bring in the coffin. She had been alone with Laszlo when he died. She had shut his eyes, tied up his chin, washed the body and shaved his previous day's stubble. Now Laszlo was lying there covered with a sheet. His two pillows had been placed on the chest of drawers.

In front of the girl was some bedding – three towels and two blankets, some shirts, too, and handkerchiefs and socks. She was making a list so that everything could be accounted for, though to whom and why she had not thought. The important thing was that everything should be in order; and so there she was, stub of pencil in hand, making a list of the clothes in the pile in front of her.

Her red hair flamed in the light from the window.

She replied to all Balint's questions calmly and intelligently. Her large doe-like eyes seemed even larger as a result of her long vigil, but despite all her hard work she did not seem tired. Calmly she told what had happened.

Laszlo, she said, had just wasted away. Sometimes he had taken just half a glass of milk, but latterly not even that. He had not been in pain and recently had hardly even coughed. He had slept more and more, and in the last few days had only been awake for a few minutes at a time. He had slept quietly until the moment when he had turned to the wall and died.

'Why didn't you let me know earlier, as you promised?' asked Balint crossly.

Regina did not answer, but just looked at him with pouting lips. Then she said, 'Would you like to see him?'

They stepped over to the bed and she folded back the sheet.

It looked as if Laszlo were asleep; even though it was the sleep of death. To Balint, looking at his fine aquiline nose and long moustaches, it was strange to see him so calm, which he never had been in life. His waxen face was barely more than skin and bone but about his mouth there still seemed to linger a faint mocking smile, while those eyebrows which met in the middle were raised at the edges as if in contempt.

Abady somehow resented his unexpectedly strange expression and was relieved when Regina covered his face again.

'In this cupboard there is a lovely suit. He told me to put it on him when he was dead.'

Balint was startled.

'Did he know he was dying then?'

'No, not now, anyhow. He said it a long time ago.' She opened the cupboard and hanging there was an iron-grey morning coat, a double-breasted cream-coloured waistcoat and a pair of striped trousers. Under the suit was a pair of black and beige buttoned boots. 'He once said that though he'd sold everything else he ever possessed he would never sell this suit no matter how much he needed the money!'

Regina then took the suit out of the cupboard and laid it out neatly on the chair.

'They said yesterday evening, the men from Szamos-Ujvar, that they'd bring in the coffin at midday. He ought to be ready by then.'

Balint offered to help her.

They slit each piece of clothing down the back so that it would be easier to put on. As Regina was cutting the waistcoat a small blue card fell from the pocket. It was a tote ticket from some long-forgotten race meeting. Abady picked it up and saw that on it was printed the letter nine. It must have been a losing ticket for if it had won then surely Laszlo would have handed it in, despite the fact that it was only for quite a small sum, just ten crowns, no more. Balint wondered what to do about it. His first thought was to throw it away, but then it occurred to him that it might have had some special memory for Laszlo and that that was why he had kept it.

It was true that that ticket had meant something special to Laszlo, though it was doubtful whether he ever realized he still had it in the pocket of the suit he had never worn again after that day at the King's Cup race in Budapest when he had promised Klara Kollonich never again to gamble. In the grandstand he had said to her 'I promise!' and they had shaken hands on it. So as to mislead anyone who was standing near and might have heard these solemn words and seen the mysterious handshake and wondered what they signified, she had given him ten crowns and asked him to put them on a horse for her, just as if they had only been discussing a bet. He had put the money on Number Nine.

The bet had been lost … and the girl too. Laszlo had broken his word to her and had gone on gambling. To him that ticket had been the symbol of the day the Fates had turned against him.

Abady knew nothing of this, but his instinct told him to put the blue ticket back in the pocket from which it had fallen.

Outside the house Bischitz saw the car and asked the chauffeur about his master. When he learned that it was Count Abady, who was rich and important and a close relation of the dead man, he at once began to wonder if he might be able to get him to pay for all the soap, paraffin and brandy that Regina had stolen from the shop. He knew he could not send in an account for these to Dr Simay, who was hard and severe and would only say that he was not responsible for what the shopkeeper's daughter might have pinched on the sly. Bischitz was not even sure that it had been Regina, for all he knew for certain was that he had missed some stock that he thought ought to have been there, and he could not even say how much had been taken. Still, he now thought, such a distinguished gentleman as Count Abady was certain to have a softer heart than the stern lawyer, for wasn't he even now inside the house and, as he had seen through the window, talking kindly to his daughter?

Accordingly he hastened back to the shop and started to make out a bill. Being an honest shopkeeper he was careful not to add anything extra – though he did round off the total – but added it all up more or less to what he thought had disappeared.

When Abady came out of the house just before midday Bischitz had already been waiting for him for some time. Hat in hand he introduced himself and, after a lengthy explanation, offered Balint his account. He never mentioned how many times he had slapped Regina when he fancied she had taken something, but spoke warmly of her as if she had done it all with his approval. He even managed to give the impression that he had encouraged her.

Balint was about to take the bill, which amounted to a few thousand crowns, when a carriage with jangling harness drove up from the north and stopped beside them. A short, stout man with greying hair stepped out. He was aged about sixty and wore a short imperial and thick glasses. Peering at Abady with the slightly squinting gaze of the shortsighted, he spoke directly to the shopkeeper. 'What sort of a bill is that?'

Bischitz started and then, rushing his words, he began to explain that there had been certain expenses which, merely out of discretion of course, he had not mentioned before for, still out of discretion of course, there had been some old debts of Count Laszlo's ... and some new ones ... and he hadn't wanted to trouble anyone with them.

There was nothing soft about the lawyer, for it was Dr Simay who had arrived, and he at once called the shopkeeper to order.

'I gave strict instructions that you were to give no credit. Further I forbade you to turn to anyone else in anything that concerned Count Gyeroffy's needs. Give that to me,' he ordered, 'and I will look it over.' He then went up to Abady and introduced himself, 'Dr Geza Simay, at your service.'

They shook hands and Balint then explained that he had come at once to provide whatever was necessary for Laszlo's funeral, and added that he had brought the necessary funds with him.

'That won't be necessary, my lord,' replied Simay. 'I have already made all the arrangements. The announcements have been sent out from my office. The coffin will be here in half an hour and the service and interment will take place tomorrow morning at ten o'clock. The local pastor has already agreed to conduct the service.'

'But the costs? My cousin had no money, and the small annuity that he has been receiving from Azbej ceases with his death. I would never agree that the man who deprived Laszlo of everything should now wish to appear generous and pay for his funeral.'

Simay smiled.

'Azbej is paying for nothing, my lord. There has been no annuity or anything else from him. Up until now it is I who have provided everything for Count Laszlo, and I shall settle these costs as well.'

'What? No annuity from Azbej? But I thought ...? Well then, where did the money come from?'

Simay paused for a moment, as if he had just realized that perhaps he had said more than he should. Then, unperturbed and unhurried, he went on to tell something, if not all, of the truth.

'I used to look after all the late Mihaly Gyeroffy's affairs; so it was quite natural that I should see to his son's interests too.'

'So it was you who provided for Laszlo?'

'Not I myself. I merely arranged what had to be done,' said Simay hesitantly. 'I had my orders. It is the same with the funeral.'

'You had your orders?'

'Exactly. I am a lawyer, you know, and this had been part of my legal work.' Simay spoke somewhat drily, and then, to cut short any further enquiry, he turned to Bischitz and said, 'The coffin will arrive at any moment. Please have a few strong men ready to carry it into the house!' To Abady he said: 'I hope your lordship will now excuse me. I have to go up to the family vault,' and after a brief farewell hurried off up the hill towards the manor house.

Balint was surprised by what he had just heard and asked himself who then could it have been who had kept Laszlo from starvation. Could it have been his aunts? Surely not Agnes Gyeroffy, Princess Kollonich? Or her sister Countess Szent-Gyorgyi, the gentle Elise? That was more likely; and yet how could she have organized all this so quickly when she lived so far away at Jablanka, in the Slovakian province of Nyitra? It was possible, he supposed, that she had given her instructions in advance; and yet it seemed unlikely. It was all very mysterious.

There was nothing more for Balint to do at Kozard that morning so he got into his car and was driven back to Kolozsvar where he found a telegram waiting for him. It was from Julie Ladossa, saying that she would arrive by that evening express from Budapest.

So she really was coming!

Balint at once wondered if her arrival would make for any problems with the others who would be coming for the funeral. How would they behave towards the notorious former Countess Gyeroffy? Would they greet her correctly … or cut her dead? That would be dreadful, no matter how justified. Balint now realized that it had been thoughtless of him to have sent off that telegram; but as he had he would now have to suffer the consequences. As to himself he decided at once that he would behave towards Julie Ladossa as if he knew nothing at all about her past. He would give her all the respect that was due to her as Laszlo's mother, just as if she had never abandoned the position to which she had been born. That, he decided, was the right thing to do.

He went to meet her at the station. The train was on time. Holding herself as erect as the last time he had seen her she got down from the carriage with head held high. She was wearing the same black dress as she had that night in Vienna and Balint wondered if it was the only good dress she possessed. She held out her hand, explaining that she would have been there in the morning but that as they were staying at the Royal Hotel and not at the Hungaria she had not received the news at once.

She spoke calmly, in even natural tones. She showed no signs of sorrow or tearfulness. In fact there was no change in her manner, though Balint felt that if anything her face was even more expressionless than when they had last met. Was the vertical furrow on her forehead a shade more pronounced and her lips even more compressed, as if she was consciously clenching her jaws? It was so uncertain that Balint was not sure if it was really there or whether he had imagined it.

He took her to the Central Hotel and saw her to her room, saying that he would fetch her in his car at eight-thirty the following morning.

'Are you taking anyone else?' she asked.

'No. Only you, Aunt Julie.'

At that last word she turned her head away abruptly. Then, very quickly, she muttered, 'Goodnight!' and disappeared into her room.

Balint returned home on foot. As he went he was assailed by many memories of childhood and of his years at school when he and Laszlo had lodged together at the Theresianum in Vienna. His heart contracted with sorrow and he was so overcome that tears filled his eyes. He longed for Adrienne's comforting presence, but she had had to leave again for Lausanne some five days before as they had wired her that her daughter was ill again and that she should come to be with her. If Adrienne had been at home he could have gone straight to her and told her of his sadness, and she would have listened and understood and comforted him; but she was not there and he had no-one to whom he could pour out what was in his heart.

He walked on until he reached the Abady town house, but when he reached the entrance he stopped, knowing that he would not sleep. Perhaps a long walk would help calm him, he thought, and so, even though a slight rain had started, he turned away and quite involuntarily headed for the Monostor road, towards the Uzdy villa. For a long time he stood there, by the bridge that led to the park, and then, after wandering for a while down the tree-lined alleys, he made his way back to the centre of the town. He had been walking for more than an hour and a half.

As he entered the market square he stopped, startled. A tall dark woman was standing on the sidewalk in front of the church. She just stood there without moving, apparently staring at the main entrance, lit up by one of the streetlights.

Balint had recognized her at once: it was Julie Ladossa.

Holding her voluminous coat tightly around her, she stood there like a figure of stone; and Balint wondered how long she had been there and if, like himself, she had been wandering about in the dark night ever since they had parted earlier that evening.

He turned swiftly away in case she should catch a glimpse of him and think that he was spying on her. Balint now took a turn through the streets of the old town and when he finally found himself in the passage beside the Town Hall which gave onto the market square, he looked again towards the church.

The dark shape was still there, just as before, motionless in the slight drizzle. Was she going to stay there all night?

The street in front of the little house at Kozard had been deserted when Balint had arrived the previous day: now it was thronged with people. All the village folk were standing there waiting.

The road was muddy, but the rain had stopped and so everyone could wait without getting wet.

The Bischitz husband and wife were there, dressed in all their finery as if for the Sabbath; and Fabian was strutting about giving orders in a stentorian voice. Old Marton was hovering disconsolate near the house. Only Regina was nowhere to be seen.

The entire Azbej family had turned up – Mrs Azbej, short, fat, full-bosomed, with several double chins; the Azbej children, short and dark, with eyes like tiny black plums, the image of their father; and the dishonest little lawyer himself, all self-importance, strutting about playing the host and receiving the eminent mourners as they arrived.

He had already welcomed the chief judge of the district and the doctor from Iklod and led them towards the ramshackle barn that stood in a corner of the manor house grounds.

That morning the coffin had been brought there and set up on a bier, according to Dr Simay's instructions. He had ordered it so because there would not have been enough room for the mourners to pay their last respects in Laszlo's little cottage. The inside of the barn had been decorated, again on Simay's orders, with branches of pine cut from the woods that Mihaly Gyeroffy had planted but which now belonged to Azbej, as the little lawyer did not fail to point out so as to show everyone what a generous fellow he was.

When Abady arrived with Julie Ladossa, Azbej hurried forward on his short legs to greet them, bowing obsequiously, the image of grief-stricken sorrow, even though he had no idea who the lady was that Balint had brought with him. 'Such a blow! Such a terrible blow!' he whispered with his tiny mouth, holding his hat in one hand and with the other repeatedly wiping his eyes with a huge handkerchief. Backing before them with more bows and protestations of devotion to the deceased noble count, he led them to the barn. They could see little more of him than the top of his round bristling pate of black hair.

At the door two gendarmes in full-dress uniform stood at attention. They were there not only for good form but because the coffin had not yet been closed. Its lid was leaning against the barn wall. The chief judge and the doctor stood together by the hedge smoking and nearby were the dark-clad employees of the funeral director.

Only Dr Simay was inside the barn. He had had the chairs from Laszlo's house brought there and placed in a line in front of the open coffin. He was sitting on one of them.

When Balint and Julie Ladossa came in he stood up and went to greet them. Suddenly he stopped in his tracks and with both hands touched his glasses as if he could not believe what he saw. Julie Ladossa stopped too. For a few moments they stared at each other, then Simay bowed coldly. She nodded in acknowledgement.

Now they stepped forward to the bier, Abady and the unknown lady to one side and Dr Simay to the other. He stood there for a moment at the head of the coffin and then, with a hard glance at Julie Ladossa, suddenly grabbed the shroud and disclosed the body.

There was something vengeful in the quick movement as if to say 'See, this is your doing! This is what became of the son you abandoned!'

Julie Ladossa did not move. She looked for a long time at the prematurely aged man with the thin wasted face and parchment-like skin and grey hair at his temples. It was the face of an Egyptian mummy, but who was he? Could it be the same being she had remembered through so many long self-accusing nights, only as a baby, as a three-year-old, a growing boy who still kept the round rosy features of babyhood? She had had to imagine him as a youth, counting the years so as to guess what the growing man had looked like ... but this, this skeletal corpse, with a razor-sharp aquiline nose and long moustaches, dressed in a morning coat and starched collar and patent-leather shoes? There were

313

no memories which tied him to her. In his petrified calm he was as strange to her as some unknown inanimate object.

She tried to force herself to kiss his face, but she couldn't do it: so she made the sign of the cross with her finger on the dead man's forehead and then stepped back beside Balint who had previously placed his wreath at the foot of the bier.

From outside came the sound of a powerful car. It was Dodo Gyalakuthy. She was followed by Mrs Bogdan Lazar from Dezsmer. Both of them brought wreaths which they placed beside Balint's, and both of them said a short prayer beside the coffin. And to them too the dead man was a stranger, seeming to bear no resemblance to the Laszlo with whom they had both been in love. Then they took their seats beside Julie Ladossa and waited.

Someone came forward and covered up the body with the shroud which was made of silk with a wide border of lace.

The provost of the county arrived, with two deacons, an altar boy and six singers. The officiating priest wore a black and silver cope, and the others similar funeral vestments. The service began.

*Dies irae, dies illa.* The traditional requiem hymn sounded as beautiful as ever. Then the provost circled the coffin twice, sprinkling it with holy water, followed by the incense, wafted from a thurible of massive gilt metal.

'How thoughtful of you to have arranged such a worthy service!' whispered Julie Ladossa to Balint.

'It wasn't me,' he replied. 'Perhaps it was our good Aunt Szent-Gyorgyi. I really don't know who did it. Geza Simay took care of everything. He had his orders but he wouldn't say who from.'

Hearing this Julie Ladossa sat up even straighter, and it seemed to Balint that something of a secret joy flashed briefly in her eyes ... why, he wondered?

The wreaths were taken up and the coffin placed on a wooden stretcher which was lifted onto the shoulders of eight men who then carried it outside, where the priest and the deacons were waiting, crosses held high, to lead the procession to the Gyeroffy vault.

Balint offered his arm to Laszlo's mother, but she shrank back.

'Up there? To the vault? No! No! I won't go there ...!' she whispered. Balint could hardly catch what she said, but her face was set and there was terror in her eyes. Balint answered, also in a whisper, 'Wait for me in Laszlo's house then. I'll be back soon.'

The procession formed up and started on its way, the people from the village crowding around behind. Julie Ladossa waited until they had all gone, and then turned and walked away.

At Laszlo's little house the door at the left of the porch was half open, so she went straight in. In the corner by the stove, hunched up like some wounded animal and crouching on the floor, a young girl was sobbing. It was Regina.

She had collapsed there in the morning when they had carried out the coffin. Until then she had been sad but had remained calm. She had busied herself by seeing that everything was in its proper place, by seeing that Laszlo's bedding in the coffin was neatly folded as it should be, by putting a cushion beneath his head so that he should lie as comfortably as possible, and then she had smoothed his clothes and adjusted his tie. All this time she felt he still belonged to her. Through the night she had watched by the coffin, sitting next to him on the floor and he was still hers, just as he had been when wasting away before her eyes. For her he remained forever her fairy prince, that noble, resplendent prince of her dreams in whom she had always believed and whom she worshipped. Until that morning.

But when the funeral director's men had come in and started to carry out the coffin she realized for the first time that they were going to take him away from her, take away for ever the man she loved, whom she had loved ever since her childhood, whom she had served and nursed and worshipped with every fibre in her being, heedless of misery and humiliation, heedless of all the obstacles put in her way, for he had always been hers, only hers. Until this last awful moment. It was terrible for her that now these strangers should come in and tear from her every joy and dream for which Laszlo had stood, even deprive her of that pain she had always felt in loving him. She grasped the coffin firmly, defying them to take it from her, fighting so that they shouldn't rob her of what was rightfully hers, only hers. The men pushed her roughly away and she fell in the corner by the stove. It was as if she had been broken in two. Her head was between her knees and her arms folded tightly above it. All that could be seen of her was her thin body in its torn cotton dress and the flaming red hair that tumbled over her shoulders.

Julie Ladossa was taken by surprise to find this adolescent girl crouched there alone in the almost empty room.

She went over to her, lifted her carefully up and sat her on the bed beside her despite the girl's resistance. Now this resistance stopped and Regina collapsed into Julie's lap, once again overcome by a frenzied weeping. Soon the hot rebellious sobbing faded into a more peaceful released sorrow.

Then Laszlo's mother's tears also began to flow.

They sat there together for a long time, the older woman rigidly upright, the young girl lying softly in her lap. Julie Ladossa's hand gently stroked Regina's hair, smoothly, gently, continuously stroking, stroking … eternally stroking …

At last the woman spoke, just one phrase, in a low voice: 'Did you love him?'

'Desperately,' whispered the girl. 'Desperately, desperately!' Then she got up and put her arms around the sad unknown lady who sat beside her, and kissed her. And so they remained, kissing each other's cheeks with their arms enlaced, the lady in the silken dress and the forlorn girl in her rags.

Together they mourned Laszlo, the mother who had forsaken him and the little girl who had remained faithful unto death.

The bells had just chimed midday when Balint came to find Julie Ladossa and take her back to Kolozsvar.

Her eyes were opened wide as if she were seeing visions. The wrinkles around her mouth seemed even deeper than before.

They had barely passed the Hubertus clubhouse when Julie Ladossa was already asking, 'What times do the trains leave?'

'There are three. One leaves soon, at half-past one; the next at six o'clock, and at eleven there is the night express. You can get a sleeper on that.'

'I'd like to catch the first if it's possible.'

They got to the station in time.

'Thank you … for everything! Thank you very much …!' she said as she stopped at a second-class carriage. Then she shook hands quickly and got in hurriedly as if pursued.

*

Balint was walking up and down in his room, thinking about Laszlo and of all those past memories that his death had brought back and which had now been buried with him, when his valet came in. It was about five o'clock.

'Someone has come from the Central Hotel with something for your lordship. Shall I ask him to come in?'

'Of course.'

A messenger entered with a long package wrapped in tissue paper.

'This was brought from one of the flower shops for Countess Ladossa, my lord; but she left no address and so the manager told me to bring it round here to your lordship.'

'Thank you,' said Balint. 'Put it down over there, will you?' and handed the man a tip.

Flowers? Someone had sent flowers to Julie Ladossa?

He opened the parcel to see if there was any card enclosed so that he could return the gift to the sender.

There was nothing; only five beautiful old-fashioned roses, pale golden-yellow Maréchal Niel. There was no name, no card. Balint had no idea what to do with them. It would have been useless to send them on to Budapest for they would be dead long before they arrived, indeed they were already fully open and starting to wilt.

He carried them over to a table in the corner, meaning to find a vase for them. As he did so a few petals fell to the ground.

It was hardly worthwhile putting them in water.

*PART SIX*

PART SIX

# Chapter One

*Gornergrat, 3,300 metres above sea level.*

On a narrow ridge of granite there stood a small hotel built of wood on stone foundations. A broad terrace stretched across the front of the building, looking over a deep abyss. All around there was perpetual snow and, directly beneath, glaciers. Beyond these was a further immense valley shaped like a giant cauldron, so deep that from above it seemed almost unreal and the occasional houses as small as grains of rice. Beyond the cauldron was a wall of mountains over which towered the Matterhorn, a solitary peak which shot high in the air with an almost perpendicular rock-face culminating in a narrow granite spike so sharp that it was like some giant claw reaching out to the sky above.

The hotel could only be reached by cable car. Balint had arrived at midday, called there by Adrienne who had chosen this place because, in the middle of July, there would be few other guests, for in those days tourists only came to such high altitudes in August. And also because it was little more than an hour's drive from Montana where was the sanatorium to which her daughter had been taken when she became ill at school. Adrienne had been there since February.

Balint spent his time wondering why she had sent for him and what it was she wanted to tell him. Her telegram had included the words *'there are decisive matters we must discuss ...'*

His heart had constricted. What did she mean by the cold formal phrase 'decisive matters'? What could there be that she was not able to write in a letter, that she had to tell him herself? What sort of danger could be threatening them now? In her last letter Adrienne had written that her daughter had suffered a lung haemorrhage. It had been a short letter, and then there had been nothing for two weeks, though before that she had written nearly every day.

Then, five days ago before had come this telegram with every detail of their meeting carefully planned.

For what seemed an eternity Balint waited alone for Adrienne to arrive, alone with dismal thoughts and nagging distress and foreboding.

He must have walked up and down the terrace at least fifty times before he was able to pull himself together and force himself to think about other things. Otherwise I shall go crazy, he said to himself.

There were plenty of other matters to worry about.

At the end of June the Heir had been assassinated at Sarajevo, in a double tragedy which had taken the life not only of Franz-Ferdinand but also of his wife, the only being he had ever loved and probably the only person who had ever loved him. At the news of his death the Hungarian people had breathed more easily, for they all knew he was no lover of their country and no-one, as yet, had imagined that his murder might lead to war. In this their feeling was reinforced by the general indifference with which the Heir's death had been greeted in Vienna itself. He had even been buried with far less ceremony than his rank would normally have demanded and Balint had been one of the few politicians in Budapest who judged that this was a grave error, for if Austria-Hungary was to maintain her position as a great power it should at once have realized that the assassination had been the direct result of a Serbian conspiracy hatched in Belgrade and should have been treated as such. To those farsighted few the future seemed full of foreboding.

The prospects were indeed dark. Any military retaliation would inevitably explode into war, that war that had already twice seemed inevitable; once in 1908 after the annexation of Bosnia-Herzegovina and then again, in the previous year, when the Balkan conflict had started.

There seemed to be only one hope. A royal prince had been brutally murdered and it was unlikely that any European monarch would wish to side with those who had killed the heir to a brother kingdom.

If the Ballplatz were to be sufficiently adroit to exploit this aspect of the crisis and demand satisfaction without raising the spectre of official Serbian complicity, if it were possible to do this without giving rise to the assumption that Austria was seeking an excuse to invade and annex Serbia, then perhaps war might be avoided.

This was not impossible. With skilful diplomacy it might just be achieved, but the crucial question still remained – was this what Berchtold really wanted and was he sufficiently able to bring it off? So far his handling of the Balkan problem did not give rise to hope. Maybe he could do it … maybe …?

It had never seemed that he wanted war, and indeed until now he had managed to avoid it, even if only by dint of shameful concessions. Would it be the same now?

But if he failed, what then? What would be the fate of Hungary, unprepared as she was, with an antiquated army and a leadership composed only of those who had always been bitterly opposed even to discussing anything that concerned the defence of the nation?

Balint tried to force himself to think only about such matters, to drown his personal worries in analysing the world's problems: but he failed. Subconsciously he could not shake off a sense of some deep personal tragedy and his heart seemed to beat at the back of his throat.

Adrienne did not arrive until after four o'clock.

'Forgive me,' she said. 'I couldn't start when I wanted to. Clemmie was so restless that I had to wait until she calmed down.'

She was very pale. There were dark shadows under her eyes, and she was worn out after a succession of sleepless nights. She had lost weight and the skin was stretched tight over her cheekbones. Her chin seemed sharper, perhaps because she was so much thinner, perhaps because of what she had decided she must tell him. She seemed unusually solemn, and her manner was distant.

They sat down facing each other at one of the tables on the terrace.

'What is it … what is it you have to tell me?' asked Balint hesitantly. He felt so self-conscious that he could hardly get out the words.

Adrienne's eyes opened wide and her golden irises gazed straight at Balint. After a few moments' silence she started to speak, very slowly: 'We can never get married! I have to take back my promise.'

'But that is ridiculous!' he cried, almost jumping out of his seat.

'Wait a minute! You must let me explain.'

'Explain? How can you explain such a thing?'

'Be patient with me, Balint … and please don't interrupt, it's difficult enough without that!' Clemmie, she said, had been brought up to the sanatorium at Montana after her first haemorrhage. She had needed careful round-the-clock nursing and had to be watched every minute of the day and kept to a strict regime of meals and rest times and lying in the sun. It had not been easy for the little girl was wilful and rebellious and would not listen to anyone except her mother. The doctors and nurses alone could do nothing with her if her mother was not there beside them. It seemed that the girl had confidence only in her. At first she had even been suspicious of Adrienne, but as her condition had improved so had her trust in her mother.

After a while it had seemed that the child was getting better. She had put on weight and her recurrent fevers had diminished and they had even said that maybe soon she would be able to come down to a milder climate. Then came a second haemorrhage. A new lesion had opened on the other side of the lung. This was usually fatal and Adrienne had been told that if she left the sanatorium the child would be dead in a few weeks. It would be by staying where she was and strictly obeying the doctors' orders that her life could be prolonged. If she did that then she might live for a few years – perhaps five or six, perhaps ten or even twelve – but no more. That was the verdict of the specialist, and everything that Adrienne had read told her the same thing. And even this would only be if she stayed in the high mountains with the most expert nursing.

'So you see what the situation is. I have to make a choice and it is only natural that I should choose to stay with my child.'

'But there's no reason why we shouldn't marry? Why should all this stand in our way? I'd stay up here with you if I had to.'

Adrienne interrupted him.

'You know that is absurd!' she said. 'For you to give up everything, all your work, your home, everything that you have created and live for … just to live up here moving from one sanatorium to another. It's impossible! I wouldn't accept it! I couldn't!'

'Why not, if I wanted it?'

'No! Never! Not that!'

Adrienne now started speaking more softly, and as she did so she reached across the table and took Balint's hand in hers.

'Look,' she said. 'There are other things too, things we have to think about if we marry and live together here. We'd still have the same awful worry, always fearing what we both crave for, what our bodies crave for! I could never go on like that! Could I give birth to your child here? Here, surrounded by all these consumptives?'

Balint bowed his head without saying anything. For a while he gazed out over the valley. Then he turned to her and said, very slowly: 'How can this sacrifice make any sense? You say she only has a few years; so what does it matter if it is five or six, or ten, or twelve? If there is no hope of her ever getting better, if sooner or later – it may sound heartless but I have to say it – if there is no chance of recovery why do we have to destroy ourselves when there is no hope? It would all be in vain. If that is to be her fate, does it matter if it's sooner or later?'

'Don't think I haven't thought about it, though it's a dreadful thing for a mother to do. Oh, yes! The thought came, though I wish it hadn't … but it's impossible! How could I leave her here knowing that I'd be responsible for her death? For she will die soon if I go away, if I abandon her … and just think, think! If we were to have children of our own we'd never be free of the memory of what we'd done. Every time we looked at our children, every time we kissed and caressed them, I'd remember that it had been for them that I'd forsaken this fatherless child and left her here to die alone. No! No! No! The horror of it!'

For some time they sat there without speaking, both with their own sombre thoughts. Finally Balint broke the silence between them.

'You would throw away your happiness for someone who doesn't love you and never has loved you?'

'It's true,' she replied softly, almost as if she were ashamed of admitting it. 'It's true enough, but I have to do it, it is my duty. You see, I know that she's clinging to me now because she believes that only I can help her.' Now Adrienne raised her voice until she was almost shouting at him. 'What else can I do? Every night she clutches at me and cries, "You won't let me die, will you? You won't let me die?" I have to stay with her. What else can I do?'

Balint stood up and walked over to the balustrade of the terrace and leaned on it looking into the distance. After a moment Adrienne joined him there. For a long time they just stood side by side without speaking. The daylight faded into evening and soon the valley below was in complete darkness. Only the mountaintops were still lit by the dying sun. Now and again one of them would say something, a few disjointed words that were little more than punctuation to what they left unsaid.

Then Balint said: 'Why should we separate now? Why do we have to decide? Why now? Something will come up … we can wait.'

Much later Adrienne murmured: 'I will always fight for what we want, in every way I'll do everything I can,' and fell silent again. After a long time she said: 'It may be a very long time. With proper care she may live for ten years.' Several minutes later she murmured: 'To wait so long? We've waited so many years already; and I am so tired.'

'I'll wait for ever! Until the time ...'

For a long time they did not speak. It was now quite dark and a few stars appeared in the sky.

'I'll have to go back soon. I'm afraid she'll be waiting for me, that she won't sleep until I come. And she has to sleep a lot. It's important for her ... I have to go!'

But she did not move and Balint realized that she still had something to tell him, something that was even more painful for her than what had already been said. She was a long, long time making up her mind to speak and, when she did, it was very softly as if she were talking to herself, though none the less determined:

'We are no longer young enough to make plans for the future. You are thirty-six, I will soon be thirty-four. Time passes; and you cannot wait for a long, long time,' she said with renewed emphasis. Then she paused again before saying: 'It would add to my grief if I knew I had forced this waiting on you ... made you so ... so ... lonely. That is why I have to know you are free and ... and not thinking anymore about me.'

Balint did not answer but hid his face in his hands. The night grew colder as they stood there silently together.

All around them the snow-clad peaks glimmered softly in the light of a crescent moon. Below them, as far as they could see, stretched the frozen clefts of a great glacier. There was nothing to see but ice and snow, only ice and snow, a petrified world where there could be no life. Ice everywhere, like the frozen inferno of Dante's seventh hell. Even the sky seemed carved from ice, clean, majestic ... and implacable ... and even the stars held no mercy.

In front rose the ink-black outline of the Matterhorn, seeming more than ever like a claw, Satan's claw, reaching for the Heavens. The great peak was no longer a natural pyramid of rock but rather some fatal razor-sharp milestone threatening death to the sky above – a milestone that pointed to the end of the world.

The next evening Balint left the express at Salzburg. Later he had no memory of the journey. He had bought a ticket for Budapest, but on impulse got out at Salzburg instead.

He felt he could not possibly go home to Hungary. In Budapest he would meet so many people he knew; and it would be the same in Transylvania. And if he went to Denestornya he would everywhere be reminded of so many fruitless plans and of all those hopes and dreams which had come to nothing. People would greet him and talk to him, and he would be forced to reply hiding his hurt behind a face of stone and pretending that he was still interested by the farce of everyday life. He decided he wanted to see no-one and speak to no-one; for all he now desired was to hide, to creep into some concealed corner and die.

He left the train and had himself driven to some small anonymous hotel near the station where he could be alone without the risk of seeing anyone he knew.

He did not count the days but passed his time sitting aimlessly at his hotel window hardly hearing the trains that rumbled past, neither the goods trains that shunted to and fro, nor the slow-moving passenger trains that sometimes stayed half an hour or so at the station before moving leisurely on, nor even the fast expresses that hurtled into the nearby station, brakes screaming with senseless haste, and then almost at once clattering over the points as they hastened away. At dusk the lamps started to glow, little points of white or red light, some of which moved and vanished and then returned and some which remained constantly in place. Whistles shrilled and shrieked, some short and some long drawn-out, until it seemed as if the very engines were crying out in pain.

At night Balint would go for long walks partly so as to escape from the four walls of his dismal little room and partly to tire himself out so that perhaps when he returned he would be able to sleep, to sleep as if he were already dead.

One afternoon, as he was sitting at his window staring at nothing, he gradually became aware of some unusual activity below; newsboys were rushing down the street excitedly calling out:

'Extraausgabe – Ultimatum zurückgewiesen! – Extra! Extra! Ultimatum rejected!' Passers-by were stopping and buying and then gathering in groups to discuss what they read. Balint could not imagine what had happened and so hurried down and bought a paper himself. He read the news quickly. Serbia had rejected an ultimatum from Vienna and the Austrian ambassador, Giessl, had already left Belgrade.

War! This could only mean war!

He could not stay a moment longer; so he packed hurriedly and took the first train out.

Home! He had to get home!

# Chapter Two

The rail traffic was so dense that it took two days for Balint to get to Budapest. He arrived at three in the afternoon.

The capital was in a fever of excitement. As yet there had been only partial mobilization, just enough to overrun Serbia.

'At last!' people said. 'Now we'll teach that rabble a lesson!' Everyone was saying the same thing; the porters in the hotels, the shopkeepers, and even the newspapers. It seemed as if all the world had awoken from some enchanted sleep and in consequence was in high good humour. At the Casino Club it was the same, and some of the younger members were already strutting about in the gold braid of the Hussar uniform or the red and blue of the Lancers. 'We'll teach 'em!' they cried.

All at once the air was filled with heroism and glory, and politics were forgotten. All those petty issues, which formerly had aroused such bitter hatreds, had been blown away by the winds of war.

Balint took refuge in the library. There he read all the papers of the last few days, both the national and international news, so as to learn what had happened between the sending of the ultimatum and its rejection. Then he went to the party headquarters which overlooked the boulevard at the corner of Dohany Street and the Karoly Ring, where he would learn the most recent news. Above all he wanted to see Tisza himself and ask how it was that they had got to that point, what preparations had been made and what he believed would be the result. Above all he wanted to know whether, if war did come, it could be limited to Serbia, or whether Russia was expected to intervene thereby starting a general European conflagration.

There was an immense crowd at the party headquarters, more than Balint had ever seen there before, filling all the rooms and as animated and merry as if drunk on champagne.

Most were discussing the fact that a big pro-war demonstration was shortly due to arrive before the building to cheer the party leader Tisza. Any minute now they should be there, enthusiastically shouting for war. This was wonderful, for all at once the government party had become popular again after always previously having been scornfully labelled the 'lackeys of Turkey', or 'foreign slaves', or 'Vienna's paid gaolers', which for years had been the epithets lavished on them by the Coalition press. Now, at last, they were allowed to be full-blooded patriotic Hungarians!

The doors onto the balcony were open and many people stood there watching for the march down the Karoly Ring of all those who were on their way to acclaim the government, while those inside kept on asking if the demonstration was yet in sight.

Suddenly the cry arose: 'Here they come! They're turning the corner of the boulevard. Where is Tisza? They'll be here any minute! Tisza! Where is Tisza?'

The Minister-President was sitting on a low chair in the hall, smoking a cigar and looking as remote and introspective as ever. He barely said a word to all those close associates who swarmed around him.

'They're coming now, they're coming!' And indeed down the boulevard there poured a huge concourse of people who filled the street and the pavements in line after line that stretched right across between the houses on each side. They came with military precision, carrying banners and singing the national anthem, thousands of voices raised high as they marched steadily forward.

In front of the party headquarters they stopped; and, from above, it was a most impressive sight. The great wide boulevard from Deak Square to Emperor Wilhelm Street was black with people. They were so many that no-one could count them, but there must have been twenty or thirty thousand, perhaps more. All that could be seen of the dense crowd was a sea of hats and waving banners. Somewhere below the balcony someone started calling out, but there was so much noise that the words could not be heard. Then came a mighty roar: 'Tisza! Hurrah for Tisza! Tisza and the War!'

The cry rang out from as far away as Deak Square and minutes passed as 'Tisza and the War!' reverberated from tens of thousands of throats.

Then someone started to make a speech from the balcony and, though he was cheered while speaking, and after he had finished, it was soon obvious that this was not enough. The people wanted Tisza, the Minister-President himself; and no-one else would satisfy them.

'Tisza! Tisza! We want Tisza!' the crowd chanted from below.

Some men rushed in from the balcony. 'They want you. They want you to speak to them,' they cried. 'What a day! They're calling for you! They want you to speak to them. At last! At last!'

But Tisza made no move. He sent someone else in his stead.

Another speech was made; and another; and then several others and even one from a side balcony to show all those who could not find a place in front of the main balcony that their war fever too was appreciated. This went on for some time, but though the people listened they were not satisfied. They had come for Tisza and they meant to hear him, only him, no-one else would satisfy them. Again came the roar: 'Tisza! Tisza!' they shouted insistently, angrily.

Gabor Daniel, Pekar and several others ran back to Tisza.

'You have to speak to them! They only want to hear you!' they cried. For a long time they argued and insisted, distressed and upset by their leader's stubborn refusal to move.

Further away some of his followers did not hide their resentment, muttering to each other that his stubbornness was impossible to understand. How could he, who for years had been the most hated man in Hungary, refuse to appear when everything had been changed and the mob was calling hysterically for him? Now they wanted to cheer him – and he wanted none of it! Now of all times, when it was so important. And they whispered to each other: 'This is sheer masochism! He's happy only when they hate him!' The whole party was indignant.

They could not have known that Tisza was opposed to the war. No-one knew, except only those who had attended the King's Council meetings. On the day that the ultimatum had been decided, Tisza had at once resigned. He had remained in office only because ordered to by the monarch himself. He had resigned because he had thought that by doing so he would be able to modify the harsh terms of the ultimatum; but when he had found that his struggle would be in vain and that he would never be able to bring Berchtold and Conrad to his way of thinking, he had decided to stay as he knew that he alone was strong enough to hold the country together at such a critical time. At the express wish of the King he had agreed to keep his opposition secret, principally because he knew that Hungary's new-found unity would be shattered if it was known what he really felt. So he accepted responsibility for a war he had fought hard to prevent. Out of a sense of duty he had accepted a task he loathed, the task of organizing a war knowing well what it would mean. He accepted it in silence, a silence that lasted until his death. And he never changed his opinion, even though it was hidden from the world. In his public speeches he spoke only of effort, duty and self-sacrifice; but he never tried to justify the conflict.

Tisza's real views only became known years after his death when the secret files in Vienna were made public. At the time therefore the resentment of the party's rank and file at their leader's refusal to speak was only to be expected.

There was nothing to be done. They had to let the crowd go, explaining, with a lie, that the Minister-President wasn't there, that he had had to be absent on some urgent business.

Morose and disappointed the great crowd melted away. Many of the party members also went home. Darkness fell and few people were left in the party headquarters.

Balint, who had been every bit as irritated by Tisza's intransigence as the others, saw that the number of those surrounding him had diminished and decided he would try to speak to him. He started to move across the hall, but halfway across he caught sight of Tisza's face and stopped in his tracks.

There the man sat, in a deep armchair, not speaking to anyone, with a dark expression on his face and teeth clenched. What a tragic face the man had! Abady was startled and he sensed at once that there must have been some deep compulsion to explain why he had refused to speak, why he had rejected all appeals from his followers, why he could not allow himself to go out and make a speech and allow himself to be cheered – at least not that, never that!

Balint knew he could not intrude, so he turned away and went home. But he never forgot the moment when he had seen him there, sitting in silence in the deep armchair with his legs crossed, his thick-lensed glasses making his eyes seem so much larger, a bitter crease on his forehead and even more bitter lines reaching down each side of his face. He had sat there motionless, staring ahead of him as if all he could see was the fate of his country. Silent. Chewing a cigar.

Balint stayed only a day or two in Budapest, just long enough to buy a uniform and some other equipment he would need, and clear up some unfinished business in the head office of the Co-operative Movement before enlisting in the army. Then he left for Kolozsvar.

In Transylvania too everyone was happy and full of confidence, even though by then it had become clear that their real enemy was Russia, while France and England had both declared war on Austria's ally Germany. It was also fairly sure that their other ally, Italy, could not be relied upon and that Romania would remain neutral. Nevertheless euphoria was in the air and among the gayest were the young men, all reserve officers, who were eagerly preparing to rejoin their regiments. Only the women were anxious, the mothers and sisters.

Balint found a number of his old friends who were making the most of their last days carousing with gypsy music and revelling in the joys of saying farewell. At that moment life was suddenly freer – and the girls more complaisant. Some of the men were still dressed in everyday clothes, but most were already sporting their uniforms.

He saw the Laczok boys and young Zoltan Miloth, Adrienne's brother. There also were Pityu Kendy, Joska Kendy, Aron Kozma with three of his cousins, Isti Kamuthy, Adam Alvinczy and his young brother, and even the eldest Alvinczy, Farkas, who had abandoned his vicarious travels and, though it was now rather tight for him, had donned his old sky-blue Hussar's tunic.

In Monostor Street Balint met the kind Ida Kendy, Countess Laczok, who had come in from Var-Siklod to see that her sons were well provided with a host of things they would not need, scarves to keep out the cold and other oddments so that they would not get wet at the front. She was out shopping when Balint met her and though filled with anxiety she did her best to hide it and smiled gaily when Balint greeted her.

The smile faded as soon as she looked closely at him. 'Have you been ill?' she asked. 'You look so pale!'

Balint parried the question and they walked on together. This was when he encountered the three Alvinczys. Those tall, fair, good-looking and broad-shouldered young men were walking along arm-in-arm and keeping step, their heels tapping in true military fashion and spurs clinking as they went. They kissed Aunt Ida's hand and shook Abady's and talked loudly in high good humour.

Farkas gave Abady several hearty claps on the shoulder, as befitted a military man, for there was now no trace of the world-weary melancholic that Balint had last seen at Magyarokerek. Now he was all merry and extrovert. The Alvinczy brothers were as happy and confident of success as if they were just setting off for a ball. 'We'll be back by Christmas!' they cried, for had not the German emperor said the same and he, of all people, should know. 'It's carnival time!' they shouted. 'Hurrah! Hurrah! The Hussars are coming!'

'Seeing you three,' smiled Aunt Ida, 'anyone'd believe we'll beat the Russians in no time!'

'We three?' replied Farkas. 'We won't only be three. We've just had news from Fiume that Akos has escaped from the Foreign Legion. He ran off the moment he heard about the war and gets here the day after tomorrow. Then there'll be four of us!'

Balint and Countess Laczok were fascinated by the news and at once asked how it had happened and how they had heard. The brothers did not know very much. It seemed that Akos had arrived at Fiume on one of the Austria-Lloyd steamers. At Casablanca he had swum halfway across the harbour, discreetly boarded a ship and stowed away until after she had sailed. Then he had worked his passage as a stoker. At Fiume he had been arrested as he had no papers, but the governor of Fiume, who had known Farkas Alvinczy when he had been in Parliament, had believed Akos's story and wired to Farkas for confirmation. So all was well.

Standing at strict attention the brothers said their goodbyes and clattered off as if they had been soldiers all their lives.

Abady said goodbye to Aunt Ida when they reached a shop she wanted to visit.

He had just turned homewards when Aurel Timisan spoke to him: 'Well, well, my lord! And what do you think of this turn of events?' There was a mocking tone in his voice and a smile lurked behind his thick white moustache.

Balint did not care for the undoubted irony in the question and so answered only with some mild generality. Then he asked: 'Tell me, why did the Romanian minority, through your new parliamentary lobby, refuse Tisza's overtures? As a first step to national co-operation it seemed to me a most remarkable move for the government to have made.'

'A first step? We're a long way from that now! We, my dear count, are realists. Before the Balkan war, even before the peace, we might have considered it. But now? That is all history now, and all around us the old Monarchy is breaking up!' He waved two fingers lightly in the air, and went on: 'Today the Heir to the throne, the only man who might have brought us together, is dead. Perhaps he ...?'

'I'll never believe that. His ideas were crazy. A Triple Monarchy? Habsburg imperialism taking in all the southern Slavs as far as Salonika? Why, Franz-Ferdinand's programme was sheer fantasy!'

'Perhaps. I don't deny it; but there was an idea there,' replied old Timisan pensively. Then, with a flash of sincerity, he said: 'Fate has a macabre sense of humour, has she not? Our poor archduke was murdered by the Slavs whom he loved and wanted to make great; and now the Hungarians, whom he hated, are making war to avenge him. It is amusing, is it not? Really very funny indeed!'

Balint found the old revolutionary's mocking smile insupportable. They parted, and Balint went home.

## Chapter Three

Balint arrived at Denestornya in the afternoon. Two of the stable lads had already received their army papers, as had eight farm workers, a '*darabont*' – man of all work – the blacksmith and three of the under-gardeners and, most serious of all, Miklos Ganyi, his right-hand man. There was a great deal to do for all these had somehow to be replaced, and all arrangements must be made before Balint himself left to rejoin his regiment at Varad on the following day.

On his desk was a registered letter from Vienna. The envelope bore the elegant gold circle emblem of the Foreign Ministry. It was from Slawata, now head of his department. It was dated August 4th and informed Abady that Slawata had arranged for him to be seconded to the General Staff as liaison officer for the Ministry of Foreign Affairs. He was asked to go at once to Vienna where his duties would be explained to him.

Balint was sure that Slawata had done this out of goodwill for an old friend thinking that he could thereby save him from service in the front line. It also showed that Slawata at least was happy about the way things were going, because he went on to take Balint into his confidence, telling him 'Berchtold hat die Sache brilliant gemacht – Berchtold has managed everything brilliantly', and he went on to explain exactly where this brilliance lay. He had purposely, wrote Slawata, not shown the text of the ultimatum to Austria's allies; neither to Berlin lest they should pass it on to Rome, nor to Rome since they would have shown it at once to London and Paris! Even if it had got no further than Vienna there would have been cabinet meetings and discussions and the wording would have been changed and toned down. They would have ruled out the demand for compensation which would ensure 'Die endgültige Abrechnung – the final reckoning'. In this way Berchtold had so arranged it all that no-one could stop him.

Italy, of course, went on Slawata, had already abandoned her former friends, but then Austria had not taken her into account for several years past; but the German Foreign Minister, Bethman-Hollweg, good fellow that he was, had swallowed it all without a word! 'Wir haben den Kerl überrumpelt! – we caught the fellow unawares!'

Balint was horrified by the casual tone of everything Slawata wrote. He supposed that it was possible that this was not exactly what he thought but that, as a career diplomat, he was merely applauding the adroitness with which Berchtold had out-manoeuvred his allies.

Later on another sentence struck him, 'Conrad war auch famos! – Conrad, too, was splendid!' for it was he who had broken down the opposition of the emperor himself. What had happened was that Conrad, as chief of the Austrian general staff, had told Franz-Josef that the Serbs had already forced the crossing of the Sava river. It had not been true, but it had been the only way to get the monarch's signature.

Balint read this letter sitting at his grandfather's desk in Count Peter's old manor.

He was overcome with anger and the deepest sorrow. So between them Berchtold and Conrad had forced the country into war! And they had chosen this moment to do so! Balint could not conceive how they could have shouldered such an awful responsibility, even if one admitted that sooner or later war would have been inevitable.

As for Russia, she had been preparing for war for a long time and so, even if hostilities did not start at once, they were inevitable in the next year or so. The great showdown could not be postponed more than three years at most; but to provoke it now, when the Dual Monarchy was at a severe disadvantage, seemed to Balint to be sheer folly. Surely it would have been better to wait, for the situation was so fluid that things might well have improved. It was always possible that Russian and English interests in Asia might conflict; while, in Africa, English, French and Italian aims could well be so opposed that any alliance between those nations would be gravely threatened. There were sinister stirrings in Ireland that might preoccupy the British. Given time anything could occur to diminish the encircling threat to Germany and Austria.

But they had chosen this moment when everyone was their enemy!

Balint sat for a long time before the window. Then he sat up and shook himself. He had not come there to waste time in gloomy thoughts but to put his affairs in order before he had to leave.

He picked up a telegram form, addressed it to Slawata, and wrote:

DANK. KANN UNMOGLICH KOMMEN. HABE MICH BEI REGIMENT
GEMELDET – THANK YOU. UNABLE TO COME NOW. AM RECALLED TO
MY REGIMENT.

He had joined the Vilos Hussars and was expected at regimental head-quarters for posting to the front. Of course he could save his skin by accepting some important job on the general staff, but why should he worry about his own life? After all it wasn't worth anything anymore – a bullet would be better …

This thought was uppermost in his mind as he started to work with Ganyi. Together they went over all the files and arranged matters so that the Co-operatives could carry on despite their absence. He decided to burn all his private papers, and sent word up to the castle to light a fire in the tower room for this purpose.

Ganyi took his leave, and Balint was about to follow him out when he again started thinking about what the war might bring. Unlike everyone else he was convinced that it would last for a long time and that it was bound to be lost. He had not said this to anyone because he did not want to undermine their warlike enthusiasm, but he had thought this from the very beginning. It was possible that the Russians might well get as far as Denestornya, and, if they did, then everything would be destroyed and he would be far away if he were not already dead.

His eyes now fell on his grandfather's desk, and he thought that he really should open it and know what was in it before an invading enemy hacked it to pieces. What sacrilege, thought Balint, that this simple old piece of furniture which held so many memories of his childhood might be thoughtlessly destroyed. He felt for the key and fitted it into the lock. Then the unexpected happened. The key turned easily and the lock clicked. This had never happened when he had tried it before, but perhaps now he had unknowingly been more adroit. He pulled the drawer out and looked inside. A strange old scent assailed him, a scent made up of tobacco in an old wooden box, and sealing wax long turned to resin.

Then he took up the other keys and opened the side drawers. There he found all sorts of little mementos – a golden amber mouthpiece for a pipe, a fine whetstone that Peter Abady must have brought from England, a green leather case with six handsome razors, one for each day of the week; and a little wreath carved from lime wood which Balint remembered his father showing him and explaining that it was the work of Ferenc Deak himself who had given it to him many years before. Its history was engraved on the base.

There were so many things, now of no possible use.

In the left-hand drawer he found the pair of satin slippers that he also recalled having seen when he was a boy. They were heel-less and the soles were paper-thin. Narrow ribbons were attached to them and they were so small that their owner must have had feet as delicate as wafers. Now, as Balint picked them up, he fancied he saw his grandfather turning them over, showing him the wear on the soles, smiling, and saying 'Look! See how much that little charmer danced!'

Under the shoes was a thick envelope, quite small, only about three inches wide, wrapped in yellowing paper, tied with string and sealed at every flap with black wax. On it was written *'To be burned after my death.'* Above the words was a cross and the date: 1837. The writing was Count Peter's.

They must be letters, a woman's letters, for their edges could be felt through the paper covering. Inside could be felt something else, which seemed to be a little oval frame with a glass front. Balint felt sure it must be the miniature of the letter-writer. Now he recalled what his grandfather's old school friend, the actor Minya Gal, had told him. Though it had been ten years before, he remembered it well. In guarded terms the

337

old man had told the story of Peter Abady's first love, of a tragic passion that had been shattered by an enforced parting, and how after it his grandfather went off on his travels and no-one had heard from him for nearly three years.

It had been an ancient romance whose relics were imprisoned in that carefully fastened envelope, and one that had no doubt ended in a death, which was perhaps what the cross had signified.

It was lucky that he had managed at last to open the drawer for now Balint would be able to ensure that the old count's long-kept secret could be kept from the prying eyes of strangers. He would see to it that his grandfather's wish was respected. Putting the slippers in his pocket he gathered up the packet of letters and the few documents of his own that he wanted to destroy and made his way up to the castle.

He decided to wait until the evening when the fire would be burning well.

The windows were open and outside it was dark. Balint's lamp was set down far from the draught and where he sat all light seemed to come from the fire.

First Balint threw all his own writings into the flames and, when these were blazing up, he threw on top the slippers and his grandfather's envelope, which did not seem to want to catch fire but only just smouldered at the edges. Taking up the poker he tried to push a hole in the envelope so that air would get in. The flames caught, ran along the string and the envelope opened of itself. A tiny coloured miniature slipped out and fell into the embers below. The glass shattered, the metal frame curled up in the heat and in the few seconds before it was consumed by fire he could see the face of a charming young woman who seemed to be smiling up at him.

Balint sat by the fireplace for a long time. He waited until everything had been reduced to ashes, until there was no trace left of the throbbing of two young hearts almost a century before nor of their secret love and hidden tragedy. The likeness of his grandfather still hung on the wall of the small sitting room – an early Barabas in an Empire frame – but that of the other had just been burned and it had smiled at him before crumbling to ashes.

The next morning he woke early; it was the last morning he would spend in his ancestral home for a long time, perhaps for ever.

He went to say goodbye to his favourite animals, firstly to the horses out at grass in the hillside pastures, then to the young stallions and then to the mares in their separate paddocks in the park. To each he gave some sugar as a token of his farewell and became very moved by the affection of his old hunters, and especially when Honeydew, Gazsi Kadacsay's thoroughbred, came up and rubbed his face with her soft velvety muzzle.

He made the round of the gardens and then walked up to the summerhouse on the hill above the castle. From there he toured the kitchen gardens and the orchards.

Finally he returned to the house and went into almost every room in that vast building, including his mother's apartments, which had been left unchanged since her death. Everywhere he went, he stopped in front of all of the treasures of art and ancient pieces of furniture, and, above all, stared hard at the many family portraits. In the billiard room were hung great-grandfathers and great-great-grandfathers in their wigs and powdered hair, great-grandmothers holding tiny bunches of flowers or a little mirror in their delicate tapering fingers. There were also many of more distant relations, young and old, and some of children, boys little more than toddlers, clad in silken skirts but already sporting Hungarian fur hats.

He went the round of the mirror-fronted bookcases in the library and locked up two of them that had been left open so that the magic circle of looking glass in that round tower room should remain unbroken.

From the billiard room he passed into the great first-floor dining hall. Through five of the tall windows the sun shone blindingly bright on the polished wooden floor and glinted on the gilded surface of the showcases and the ormolu feet of the Chinese lacquer cabinets that stood by the walls. The contrasting shadows in the ceiling threw the baroque carved plaster into high relief. Balint stopped in front of one of the pair of copper samovars that stood on the wide serving tables and caressed it lovingly. Then he gently stroked the little white porcelain figure of one of his great-great-uncles in Hungarian gala dress. He looked into the showcases with their heterogeneous collection of many little objects, greeted the china pug and the dancing girl, and then went on through the blue salon to the yellow drawing room; and everywhere he went he murmured a soft farewell, to the four *famille verte* K'ang Hsi plates that had been set in gilded bronze in the seventeenth century, to the clusters of glass grapes in the early Murano chandeliers, to the sets of Delft vases and above all to the full-size portrait of Denes Abady, painted by Mytens in the green and gold uniform of the King's Master of Horse; and then to those of his immediate forebears, his father and mother and grandmother, that gazed at him from every wall.

And all the time he said goodbye to many childhood memories. It was on the sharp corner of this table that he had banged his head when only five years old and he had stood just there when his mother had swiftly pressed a silver coin to his forehead. It was on the corner of that carpet that he had tripped, upset the lamp and nearly caused a fire. Here, in this armchair, his grandfather had always sat, with crossed legs, when he came to lunch at the castle every Wednesday. Balint had sat on the floor at his feet and played with his tin soldiers, and from there he had first noticed that Count Peter wore soft half-boots under his trousers and how amazed he had been by the sight, not then knowing that it had been the fashion until the first half of the nineteenth century.

He opened a door at the far end of the room. It led to a small staircase and, beyond this, to the wing that he had started to modernize in the spring. The work had been well under way until he had had it stopped by telegram from Salzburg. He stopped there, feeling he could not bear ever again to see those rooms where he would have lived with Adrienne, to gaze upon anything associated with those dreams of happiness, the spacious bedroom, the day and night nurseries for those heirs of his body that would now never be born.

Resolutely, but with a sombre air, he turned and walked quickly away, back through the drawing rooms and the dining hall. Then he descended the wide stone stairs, with their rococo stucco ceiling and ancient faded Gobelin tapestries. It was a stairway fit for kings.

He went down very slowly, keeping very carefully to the very centre of the carpet; step after step, solemnly and slowly until he arrived in the dark gloom of the entrance hall, stone-faced, like a man entering his own tomb.

Early in the afternoon Balint's car drove the full circle of the horseshoe-shaped entrance court with its enclosing walls topped by baroque stone statues, and rumbled swiftly through the arched gateway.

He was driven so fast that in ten minutes they had reached the main road, but there they had to slow down, for the highway was crowded with people from Torda and wagons loaded with bales of hay. They too were on their way to the railway station at Aranyos-Gyeres. From time to time the throng was so thick that the car had to be stopped. Everyone on the road was a reservist who had been called to the colours. They were mostly in groups of between fifty and sixty men, but sometimes they were much larger, perhaps of more than a hundred. They marched in military fashion, four to a row, and on each side of the road stood women and girls crying as they waited to see their menfolk, husbands, sons and lovers, on their way to the station. Among them were some old men looking for the last time at their grandsons. Some of the young men carried bundles or trunks, others had piled their luggage on little one-horse carts.

At the head of each group there marched gypsy bands and men carrying banners. Some of the newly mobilized soldiers carried flasks of country brandy, others danced gaily in front of the bands singing as they went. But no-one had drunk too much, and indeed most of the men had a dignified, serious mien, soberly doing with good-natured calm what they knew to be expected of them.

Balint had put on his uniform, and every time he passed one of these groups they would break out into enthusiastic cheering.

'Hurrah for the war!' they cried. 'Hurrah for the war!'

Some of them recognized him, and then they called out: 'Hurrah for Abady!' and again 'Hurrah for the war!' They all felt full of courage, and were gay and confident: only the women sobbed quietly and dabbed at their eyes.

Balint saluted every band, his heart constricting with pain each time he did so; but he could only acknowledge their greetings and be touched by their simple confidence. He could not echo their cheers, but sat upright with his hand to his cap as he drove past group after group.

It was difficult to get through Torda, for there was an immense crowd in the marketplace selecting mountain ponies – pretty little animals, mostly dapple-greys with tiny hard hooves, hardy and willing, crossed with Arab blood. They were needed to draw the machine guns and man the mountain batteries on the Bosnian front. What marvellous animals, thought Balint, and not one will return. They'll all perish, every one.

When he finally got through the town the sun was already low in the sky.

The car raced up to the Dobodo Pass. Here they had to stop again for at the junction with the main road there came all the people from Torda-Turia and Szentmarton, with banners and music like the others. Now there were many more women as well as old people and children, who Balint thought had probably come because they knew they could have a rest at Torda before finally saying goodbye to their men.

Balint got out and sat at the edge of the road looking down the valley of the Aranyos river. It was bathed in sunshine and when he took up his binoculars he found he could even see the bend of the Maros far away. There he could just glimpse a small stand of pine trees, dark indigo-blue in the pale-blue distance.

It was the garden at Maros-Szilvas, which had once been the property of Dinora Malhuysen. As a very young man he had often ridden over to visit her, usually at night. What a long time ago it had been – almost twenty years! He wondered what had become of her, what Fate had held in store for poor little Dinora?

To his right, beyond the shining ribbon of the Aranyos, on the edge of the Keresztes-Mezo lowlands, lay Denestornya.

The hill on which the castle stood was covered with trees and shrubs. Here and there could be seen parts of the long walls and something seemed to be glistening in the reflected sunshine. Balint wondered if it was part of the western façade, perhaps the glazing on the upper veranda, but he could not be sure and even thought that it might be only his imagination. The green patina of the conical copper roofs of the corner towers was plain to see, and these, no matter from what distance they could be glimpsed, gave a clear impression of the size of the vast building. It was like a great stone peninsula jutting out from the wave crests of the surrounding trees. The long walls spread out in beauty, and the thin white strip to the right formed by the enclosure of the horseshoe court, and the little rectangle of the church half hidden among the con-fused roofs of the village seemed strangely small between the massive proportions of the castle and of his grandfather's manor house nearby.

Balint again bade farewell to all that lay before him, to the beauty by which he had been surrounded since his childhood, and to all those dreams which had come to such a sad end.

By now those merry bands of eager young men had passed on their way. Gone were the farm carts and baggage. Balint was alone. He returned to the car and drove on.

The road descended steeply into the valley, which was now in deep shadow. He crossed a bridge and then there came a sharp bend.

Here too he was assailed by memories, for it was just there that two years before, on returning to Denestornya, full of happiness after the evening when he had seen Adrienne again at the performance of *Madam Butterfly* at Kolozsvar, he had met Gazsi Kadacsay. Once again he fancied he could see Gazsi as he cantered towards him on his well-fed little pony. Poor Gazsi! His house was not visible from there, that house where his unhappy friend had killed himself from despair at his wasted life and because the culture for which he had yearned had seemed forever beyond his reach.

Banishing such thoughts, he drove on, determined not to waste time regretting the past.

When he reached the foothills of the Felek the car was again delayed because the road was everywhere encumbered by droves of white oxen and bullocks on their way to the slaughterhouse where they would be killed to feed the army.

He drove on slowly, for he often had to stop because the road was so crowded. About a hundred yards from the next pass the engine boiled – white steam spurting out of the radiator. As there was no water to be had nearby the chauffeur went back down the road to find a well. Balint walked on up to the summit to wait there until rejoined by the car.

In front of him lay a wonderful landscape in the centre of which was Kolozsvar. To the right the Szamos curved away until, at Apahida, it disappeared to the north. On his left lay the valley of Gyalu and beyond it a range of snow-capped mountains.

Behind him the sun went down below the horizon. But there was still light enough to see what lay before him.

He leaned against the stone wall by the road, still consciously bidding farewell to all he saw.

Not far away below there was a butter-yellow building beside the Monostor road. It was the Uzdy villa, and beside it Balint could make out the break in the palings of the garden, just where lay the little gate to the bridge through which, in happier times, he had so often passed on his way to visit Adrienne.

Not far away was the green-tiled roof of the asylum where Pal Uzdy had died and, a little to the right, was the theatre from which he had fled so precipitously on finding Adrienne in the next box on the night of the opera. There too was the hill of the Harzongard where he had walked with Adrienne in the first spring of their ten years of love for each other.

All his life lay before him, his whole past, everything. Even Kozard, where Laszlo lay buried. He wanted to say farewell to him too, and he searched the distance through his binoculars for a sight of the manor house at Kozard and the Gyeroffy family vault just above it. It lay at the most northerly point of the Szamos valley; and there it was, a tiny patch of white, a little triangle on the left bank.

A deep bitterness came over him as he stood there alone, high above the world he had known and which was now doomed to perish.

In his mind's eye he saw too the whole generation to which he belonged, that generation, still young, which had grown up in that long period of peace that had followed the troubled years before 1867. It was the men of his generation that had come after those years of reform and who were the successors of such men as Deak, Eotvos, Miko and Andrassy, who had lived through the nightmare of the revolution and the repression which followed, who had learned from their tribulations and who had known how to meet troubles with calm and moderation.

But this generation, Balint's own, had drifted further and further away from the practical wisdom of their forebears. Reality had been gradually replaced by self-deception, conceit and sheer wrong-headed obstinacy.

Everyone was guilty, all the upper strata of Hungarian society.

He saw before him the entire class of great landowners, spoiled by an arrogance that had led them to neglect the good management of their estates, preferring to vie for pompous offices of state and political advantage. He saw the professors of history, who thought only of the revolutionary struggle against the Habsburg domination and who denigrated those who would have encouraged the Hungarian people to self-knowledge and hard work, with the result that the minds of the young had been filled only with illusory ideals and chauvinistic slogans. From the turn of the century his generation had been fed with self-congratulatory theories which had so misled it that any criticism was at once dismissed as unpatriotic.

He saw before him the magnates and noble families who thought only of social prominence, who forgot their European affiliations and threw the weight of their great fortunes and moral influence behind all that nationalistic nonsense of which they did not believe a word and which, in consequence, had poisoned the nation's politics.

All this he saw before him, just as if he were looking back from beyond the grave. Now this beloved country would perish, and with it most of his generation. It would perish with this meaningless war; for until now those rousing battle cries had only meant a call to wars of words and speechifying and argument; and the repeated exhortations to hold out to the last man had only meant not to speak until the end of a debate, and were far from the true murderous reality.

Now this land would perish, and with it that deluded generation that had given importance only to theories, phrases and formulae, that had ignored all reality, that had chased like children after the *fata morgana* of mirage and illusion, that had turned away from everything on which their strength was based, that denied the vital importance of power and self-criticism and national unity.

One virtue alone remained: the will to fight.

And that too would prove in vain.

The town below was now in darkness. Night had fallen.

Only the sky in the west flamed with life.

Long shreds of cloud floated high; ash-coloured strips with shining tassels touched the far horizon. Around and beneath them fire, everywhere fire. The whole world beyond the horizon seemed to be in flames. On the line of the horizon itself the colour was blood-red, rising in the blinding heat of tongues of fire, fiery tears along its whole length as if the whole universe wept burning ash into an ocean of blood. Below the red inferno of the sky were etched heavy, dark lilac-coloured mountain peaks, their hard-edged contours merging into some endless monolith; they were the mountains of Gyalu and the Magura and, behind them, the mighty Vlegyassa itself.

Vast stony ridges that slanted upwards to the sky.

Giant coffins, a people's tombstones.

In motionless majesty they stood there beneath a world in flames.

The car arrived.

Balint started the descent from the summit.

THE END

*Bonczhida, May 20th, 1940*